PRAIS

LOST STARS
by Claudia Gray

"Writing new characters into such a beloved universe is no small feat, but Gray does it with ease—and I loved every moment of this novel." —*Kirkus Reviews*

"Put simply, if you like *Star Wars* . . . then you can't go wrong with *Lost Stars*. . . . Is it the best novel in the *Star Wars* universe? Maybe so." —SF Signal

"One of the solidest entries into the *Star Wars* canon and a book that can and should be read by *Star Wars* fans of any age."

—*Staten Island Advance*

"The best novel in the new *Star Wars* canon. . . . Claudia Gray not only does great character work, but she knows her way around a swashbuckling action scene."

—Uproxx

"In a lot of ways, *Lost Stars* is perhaps the perfect *Star Wars* book. . . . *Lost Stars* is everything I ever wanted from a *Star Wars* book and perhaps more."

—Nerdophiles

"I strongly recommend this book to *Star Wars* fans as it provides a great overview of the original trilogy and shows us a side of the Empire we have never seen."
—Star Wars News Net

"Claudia Gray's *Lost Stars* fits into *Star Wars* like a perfect puzzle piece, because it is in its very soul a story about star-crossed lovers who sit on the knife-edge of tragedy and chaos. . . . Above all, *Lost Stars* tackles the complex struggles of morality, answering the question of how good people end up doing great evils under the Empire's orders."
—Making Star Wars

LOST STARS

WRITTEN BY
CLAUDIA GRAY

PRESS

LOS ANGELES • NEW YORK

*This book is dedicated to
the memory of Karen Jones,
friend and fangirl extraordinaire.*

We were lucky to know you.

A long time ago in a galaxy far, far away. . . .

Eight years after the fall of the Old Republic,
the Galactic Empire now reigns over the
known galaxy. Resistance to the Empire has
been all but silenced. Only a few courageous
leaders such as Bail Organa of Alderaan still
dare to openly oppose Emperor Palpatine.

After years of defiance, the many worlds at
the edge of the Outer Rim have surrendered.
With each planet's conquest, the Empire's
might grows even stronger.

The latest to fall under the Emperor's control
is the isolated mountain planet Jelucan, whose
citizens hope for a more prosperous future even
as the Imperial Starfleet gathers overhead. . . .

A SHIP SLICED THROUGH the shale-gray sky overhead, so quickly it was no more than a line of light and a distant screech almost lost in the wind.

"That's a *Lambda*-class shuttle!" Thane Kyrell pointed upward, jumping with excitement. "Did you hear it? Did you, Dalven?"

His older brother cuffed him and sneered. "You don't know what the ships look like. You're too little to know."

"Am not. It *was* a *Lambda*-class shuttle. You can tell by the sound of the engines—"

"Children, hush." Thane's mother never glanced back at them. She concentrated on holding up the hem of her saffron-colored robe so it wouldn't trail in the dust. "I told you we ought to have brought the hovercraft. Instead we're wandering down to Valentia on foot like valley trash."

"The hangars will be a madhouse," insisted Thane's father, Oris Kyrell, with a contemptuous sniff. "Thousands of people trying to land whether or not they've got a reservation. Do you want to spend our whole day fighting over docking rights? Better to do it this way. The boys can keep up well enough."

Dalven could; he was twelve years old, long-limbed and proud to tower over his younger brother. For Thane, the downhill trek through the uneven mountain paths was harder going. So far he was shorter than most boys his age; the large feet and hands that hinted at his future height were, for now, merely awkward. His reddish-blond hair stuck to his sweaty forehead, and he wished his parents had let him wear his favorite boots instead of these shiny new ones, which pinched his toes at every step. But he would have made a more difficult trip than that to finally see TIE fighters and shuttles—*real* spacecraft, not like some clunky old V-171.

"It *was* a *Lambda*-class shuttle," he muttered, hoping Dalven wouldn't overhear.

But he did. His older brother stiffened, and Thane prepared himself. Dalven never hit him very hard when their parents were nearby, but those lesser shoves or punches were often a warning of worse to come later.

This time, however, Dalven did nothing. Maybe he was distracted by the promise of the spectacle they would see that day—the display of flying power and fighting techniques by vessels of the Imperial fleet.

Or maybe Dalven was embarrassed because he'd realized Thane had identified the ship when he couldn't.

He says he's going to the Imperial Academy, Thane thought, *but that's just because he thinks it will make him important. Dalven doesn't know every single ship like I do. He doesn't study the manuals or practice with a glider. Dalven will never be a real pilot.*

But I will.

"We should've left Thane at home with the house-keeper droid." Dalven's voice had become sulky. "He's too little for any of this. In another hour he'll be whining to go home."

"I won't," Thane insisted. "I'm old enough. Aren't I, Mama?"

Ganaire Kyrell nodded absently. "Of course you're old enough. You were born in the same year as the Empire itself, Thane. Never forget that."

How could he forget when she'd reminded him at least five times already that day? He wanted to say so, but that would only earn him another cuff from Dalven—or, worse, a new barrage of insults from his father, whose words could cut deeper than any blade.

Already he could sense them staring at him, waiting for any show of defiance or weakness. Thane turned as if he were looking down toward their destination, the city of Valentia, so neither his father nor Dalven would see his expression. It was always better when they didn't know what Thane was thinking.

He wasn't worried about his mother. She rarely noticed him at all.

The wind tugged at his blue-and-gold-embroidered cloak, and Thane shivered. Other worlds had to be warmer. Brighter, busier, more fun in every way. He believed this despite never having visited another planet in his life; it was impossible to think that the vastness of the galaxy didn't contain someplace better to be than here.

Jelucan had been settled late in galactic history, probably because nobody else had been desperate enough to want a nearly uninhabitable rock at the very edge of the Outer Rim. Nearly five hundred years before, an initial group of settlers had been exiled here from another world, equally obscure. They'd fought on the wrong side of some civil war or other. Thane didn't know the details. His parents had told him only that those first settlers had gotten themselves mired in the valleys, in nearly total poverty, and had barely been able to keep themselves alive.

True civilization had only come later, a hundred and fifty years ago, with the second wave of settlers, who had come here voluntarily in hopes of building their fortunes. They'd managed to establish mining, engage with galactic commerce, and lead modern lives—unlike the people from the valleys, who behaved more like pre-technological nomads than modern people. Of course they were Jelucani, too, but they were unfriendly, isolated, and proud.

Or maybe it was only that the valley kindred were still mad about being dumped on this icy rugged rock of a world. If so, Thane didn't blame them.

"A pity the Emperor himself won't be able to attend," his mother said. "Wouldn't it have been something to see him for ourselves?"

Like the Emperor would ever come here. Thane knew better than to say that out loud.

Everyone was supposed to love Emperor Palpatine. Everyone said he was the bravest, most intelligent person in the galaxy, that he was the one who had brought order after the chaos of the Clone Wars. Thane wondered if that was all true. Certainly Palpatine had made the Empire strong, and made himself the most powerful man within it.

Thane didn't really care if the Emperor was nice or not. The Empire's coming was a good thing, because it brought its ships with it. All he wanted was to see those ships. Then, later, to learn to fly them.

And, finally, to fly far away from here, never to return.

"Ciena! Your eyes on the path or you'll fall."

Ciena Ree couldn't stop staring into the gray sky. She could've sworn she'd heard a *Lambda*-class shuttle, and she wanted more than anything to see one, too. "But, Mumma—I know I heard a ship."

"It's always ships and flying, with you." Her mother, Verine, chuckled softly and picked up her daughter, then placed her on the wide furry back of the muunyak they were leading uphill toward Valentia. "There. Save your strength for the big parade."

Ciena buried her hands in the muunyak's shaggy hair. It smelled agreeably of musk and hay. Of home.

As she peered upward, she saw a thin line in the clouds—already disappearing but evidence that the shuttle had been there. She shivered with excitement, then remembered to take hold of the braided leather bracelet around her wrist. Pressing the leather between her fingers, Ciena whispered, "Look through my eyes."

Now her sister, Wynnet, could see it, too. Ciena lived her life for them both and never forgot that.

Her father must have heard her, because he wore the sad smile that meant he was thinking of Wynnet, too. But he only patted his daughter's head and tucked one wayward black curl behind her ear.

Finally, after two hours' trek upward, they reached Valentia. Ciena had never seen a real city before, except in holos; her parents rarely left their home valley and certainly had never taken her with them when they did, until today. Her eyes widened as she took in the buildings carved into the pale white stone of the cliffs—some of them ten or fifteen stories high. They stretched along the side of the mountain as far as Ciena could see. All around the carved dwellings stood tents and awnings, dyed in a dozen brilliant colors and draped with fringe or beads. Imperial flags fluttered from poles newly jabbed into the ground or mounted in stone.

Thronging the streets were more people than she'd ever seen together in her eight years. Some were hawking food or souvenirs for the great occasion—Imperial banners or small holos of the Emperor smiling benevolently, translucently, above a small iridescent disc. Most, however, walked along the same crowded roads as she and her family, all headed toward the ceremony. Even a few droids rolled, hovered, or shuffled through the crowd, each of them shinier and obviously far more modern than the one battered cutter droid in her village.

Those people and droids would have been far more fascinating if they hadn't all been *in her way*.

"Are we going to be late?" Ciena said. "I don't want to miss the ships."

"We won't be late." Her mother sighed. She'd said so many times that day, and Ciena knew she needed to be quiet. But then Verine Ree put her hands on her young daughter's shoulders; as soft as the gesture was, the muunyak knew to stop walking forward. Mumma's faded black cloak blew around her too-thin body as she said, "I know you're excited, my heart. This is the biggest day of your life so far. Why shouldn't you be thrilled? But have faith. The Empire will be waiting for us when we finish traveling up the mountain, whenever that may be. All right?"

Mumma's smile could make Ciena feel like she'd stepped into a patch of sunshine. "All right."

It didn't matter when they finished climbing. The Empire would always, always be waiting for her.

As Mumma had promised, they reached the paddock in plenty of time. But as her parents were paying for a day's corralling and feed, Ciena heard the laughter.

"They rode that filthy muunyak to the Imperial

ceremony!" yelled a teenage second-wave boy. The livid red of his cloak reminded Ciena of an open sore. "They're going to stink up the entire place."

Ciena felt her cheeks flush warm, but she refused to look at the kids taunting her any longer. Instead she patted the muunyak's side; it blinked at her, patient as ever. "We'll come back for you later," she promised. "Don't be lonely." No taunts from some stupid big kids could make her ashamed of the beast. She loved it *and* its smell. Stupid second-wavers didn't understand what it meant to be close to your animals, or to the land.

Yet now that she saw hundreds of second-wave folk in their long silken cloaks and richly quilted clothing, Ciena looked down at her light brown dress and felt shabby. Always, before, she had liked this dress, because the fabric was only slightly paler than her skin, and she liked that they matched. Now she noticed the ragged hem and the loose threads at the sleeves.

"Don't let them affect you." Her father's face had become tense, pinched. "Their day is over, and they know it."

"*Paron*," whispered Ciena's mother as she clutched her husband's arm. "Keep your voice down."

He continued with more discretion but even greater pride. "The Empire respects hard work. Absolute loyalty. Their values are like ours. Those second-wave folk—they don't think about anything but lining their own pockets."

That meant making money. Ciena knew this because her father said it often, always about the second-wavers who lived in the highest mountains. She didn't see what was so bad about making money, really. But other things were more important . . . especially honor.

Ciena and every other resident of the Jelucan valleys were descended from loyalists cast out of their homeworld after the overthrow of their king. One and all, their people had chosen exile rather than betray their allegiance to their leader. Hard as life on Jelucan was, unceasing as their labor and poverty had been ever since, the people of the valleys still took pride in their ancestors' choice. Like every other child in her village, Ciena had been raised knowing that her word was her bond and her honor the only possession that could ever truly matter.

Let the second-wavers strut around in their new coats and shiny jewelry. Ciena's plain cloak had been woven by her mother, the wool spun from their muunyak's fur; her leather bracelet was rebraided and expanded as she grew so it would remain on her wrist her entire life. She owned little, but everything she had—everything she did—contained meaning and value. People from the mountains couldn't understand that.

As if he could read his daughter's thoughts, Paron Ree continued, "We'll have different opportunities now. Better ones. We've already seen that, haven't we?"

Ciena's mother smiled as she wrapped her pale gray scarf more tightly around her hair. Just three days before, she'd been offered a supervisory position at the nearby mine—the kind of authority the second-wavers tended to save for their own. But the Empire was in charge now. Everything would change.

"You'll have more choices, Ciena. You have the chance to do more. To be more." Paron Ree smiled down at his daughter with stern but unmistakable pride. "The Force is guiding this."

So far as Ciena could tell from the few holos she'd ever been able to watch, most people in the galaxy no longer believed in the Force, the energy that allowed people to become one with the universe. Even she sometimes wondered whether there could ever have been such a thing as a Jedi Knight. The amazing tales the elders told of valiant heroes with lightsabers, who could bend minds, levitate objects—surely those were only stories.

But the Force had to be real, because it had brought the Empire to Jelucan to change all their futures, forever.

"People of Jelucan, today represents both an ending and a beginning," said the senior Imperial official at the celebration, a man called Grand Moff Tarkin.

(Ciena knew that was his title and his name, but she wasn't sure whether his title was Grand Moff and his name Tarkin—or whether his name was Moff Tarkin and he was very grand indeed. She'd ask later, when no second-wavers were around to mock her for not knowing.)

Tarkin continued: "On this day ends your isolation from the greater galaxy. Instead, Jelucan begins a new and glorious future by assuming its rightful place within the Empire!"

Applause and cheers filled the air, and Ciena clapped along with all the rest. But her sharp eyes picked out a few people who remained silent—elders, mostly, who would have been alive since before the Clone Wars. They stood there, still and grave, more like mourners at a funeral or witnesses to public dishonor. One silver-haired, pale-skinned woman bowed her head, and a tear ran down her cheek. Ciena wondered if perhaps she'd had a son or daughter who died in the wars and seeing all these soldiers had reminded her of the loss and made her sad on such a happy day.

Because there were *so many* soldiers—officers in crisp black or gray uniforms and stormtroopers in gleaming white armor. And there seemed to be nearly as many ships as troops: hard-cornered TIE fighters black as obsidian, assault cruisers the same gray as mountain granite, and high above in orbit, twinkling like the south star at morning, a few specks that she knew were actually Star Destroyers. Each and every Star Destroyer was bigger than the entire city of Valentia, they said, two or three times over.

Just the thought of it made Ciena's heart swell with pride. Now she had become part of the Empire—not only her planet but she herself, too. The Empire governed the whole galaxy. The Imperial fleet's power exceeded that of any other fighting force in all of history. Seeing the ships fly overhead in precise formation, never deviating from their prescribed paths, thrilled her to the bone.

This was strength, grandeur, majesty. This was the kind of honor and discipline she'd been raised to value, but taken to heights of which she'd never dreamed. Nothing could be more beautiful than this, she thought.

Unless someday she could actually fly one of those ships herself.

Grand Moff Tarkin kept speaking, saying something about Separatist worlds that made everybody seem uncomfortable for a moment, but then he went back to how great the Empire was and how proud everyone had to be. Ciena cheered when the others did, but by then she was wholly focused on the nearest ship, a shuttle just like the one she thought she'd seen in the sky. If only she could get a closer look . . .

Maybe after the ceremony she could.

When the speeches and music ended, the Kyrells had a private reception to attend with Very Important Officials, and they told Dalven to keep an eye on Thane. As they said the words, Thane silently estimated how long it would be before Dalven ditched him to go hang out with friends. *Five minutes,* he thought. *Five or six.*

For once, he'd overestimated Dalven, who'd abandoned his little brother after only three minutes.

But Thane could take care of himself. More important, he could get a lot closer to the Imperial hangar on his own.

Although most of the Imperial ships had already zoomed back to their Star Destroyers, or to one of the new facilities being built on the southern plateaus, a few remained in the Imperial hangar. The nearest was a *Lambda*-class shuttle, just like the one Thane was certain he'd seen in the sky earlier.

Sure, the signs said to stay back. But sometimes people assumed little kids couldn't read signs. Thane figured he was still young enough to get away with that excuse if anybody caught him.

All he wanted to do was look at the ship up close—maybe touch it, just once.

So he crept around to the back of the raised stage erected for the day's speeches, then ducked under it. Although Thane had to keep his head low, he could run beneath it all the way to the hangar itself. When he emerged, he smiled with pride, then saw to his disappointment that he wasn't the only one who'd had that idea. Several other kids he knew from his school had gathered nearby, too—slightly older boys, ones he'd never liked—and one other, a skinny girl dressed in shabby clothes that marked her as someone from the valleys. Next to the brilliant crimson and gold of the boys' robes, her brown dress reminded Thane of an autumn leaf about to fall.

"What are you doing here, valley scum?" said Mothar Drik, the grin on his broad face nastier than usual.

The awestruck smile faded from the girl's face as she looked from the shuttlecraft toward her new tormentors.

"I just wanted to see the ship. Same as you."

Mothar made an obscene gesture. "Go back to your sty and slop out the dung. That's where you belong."

The girl didn't budge. Instead she balled her hands into fists. "If I were slopping out dung, I'd have to start with you."

Thane laughed out loud. A few of the other boys saw him, then. One of them said, "Hey, Thane. Going to help take out the trash?"

They meant that they were going to beat up the girl from the valleys. Six of them, one of her: Those were the kind of odds that only appealed to a bully.

Growing up with Oris Kyrell as a father had taught Thane many things. It had taught him how strictly and harshly rules could be enforced. Taught him that his brother responded to their father's cruelty by being equally cruel to Thane, if not worse. Taught him that it didn't matter who was really right or wrong—because the rules were set by whoever held the cane.

Above all, it had taught him to *hate* bullies.

"Yeah," Thane said. "I'll take out the trash." With that, he charged straight at Mothar.

The idiot never saw it coming; his breath went out in a *whuff* of surprise as he landed on his back, hard. Thane got in a couple of punches before someone towed him off Mothar, and when he saw another of the boys reaching for his collar, he prepared for the inevitable fist to the face—but the skinny girl flung herself onto his attacker, pulling the boy's arm back. "You let him go!" she yelled.

Two against six still wasn't great odds, but the girl fought hard. Thane knew he did, too, mostly because, thanks to Dalven, he'd already learned how to take a hit and keep going. Still, the two of them were getting herded toward a corner, Thane already had a bloody lip, and this wasn't going to end well—

"What's going on here?"

Everyone froze. Only five meters away stood Grand Moff Tarkin, surrounded by Imperial officers and white-armored stormtroopers. At the sight of them, Mothar fled, his toadies at his heels. That left Thane and the girl standing there alone.

"Well?" Tarkin said, strolling closer. His face could have been etched in a quartz crystal, with its hard, pale lines.

The girl stepped forward. "It's my fault," she said. "The other boys were going to beat me up, and he tried to stop them."

"Very silly of you," Tarkin said to Thane. He seemed amused. "To fling yourself into a fight you would have lost? Never go up against superior forces, lad. It doesn't end well."

Thane thought fast. "It did today, because of you."

Tarkin chuckled. "You realized an even stronger force would be along shortly, then? Excellent strategic thinking. Well done, my boy."

They were off the hook now, but the girl from the valleys didn't seem to know it. "I wasn't supposed to be in the hangar," she said, head bowed. "I broke a rule. But I didn't mean to do anything dishonorable. I only wanted to see the ships."

"Of course you did," Tarkin said, leaning down a bit closer to them. "That tells me you're curious about the galaxy beyond Jelucan. And you two stayed when the other children ran. That tells me you're brave. Now I want to see if you're intelligent. What kind of ship do we have here?"

"A *Lambda*-class shuttle!" they said in unison, then looked at each other. Slowly the girl began to smile, and Thane did, too.

"Very good." Tarkin held out one hand toward the ship. "Would you like to look inside?"

Did he mean it? He did. Thane could hardly believe his luck as one of the stormtroopers opened the hatch for them. He and the girl ran inside, where everything was black and shiny and lit up with a hundred small lights. They were shown into the cockpit and even got to sit in the pilots' seats. Grand Moff Tarkin stood just behind, rigid as a flagpole, his boots gleaming as brightly as the polished metal surrounding them.

"Show me the altitude control," he said. They both pointed to it instantly. "Excellent. And the docking guide? You know that one as well. Yes, you're both very bright. What are your names?"

"I'm Thane Kyrell." He wondered if Grand Moff Tarkin would recognize his last name; his parents insisted that the Imperial authorities would know them well. But Tarkin's face remained only vaguely curious.

The little girl said, "I'm Ciena Ree, sir."

Sir. He should've thought to call Tarkin sir, too. At least Tarkin didn't seem to mind. "Wouldn't you like to serve the Emperor someday, and fly ships like these? Then you might become Captain Kyrell and Captain Ree. What would you think of that?"

Thane's chest swelled with pride. "That would be the best thing ever. Sir."

Tarkin laughed softly as he turned to one of the junior officers standing just behind him. "You see, Piett? We should never hesitate to use the lash, when necessary—but there are moments when the lure is even more effective."

Thane had no idea what that meant, and he didn't care, either. All he knew was that he could no longer imagine any fate more glorious than becoming an officer in the Imperial fleet. From the grin on Ciena's face, he could tell she felt the same way.

She whispered, "We'll have to study hard."

"And practice flying."

His answer made her face fall. "I don't have any ships to practice with, and our only simulator is old."

Of course they didn't have good simulators in the valleys, and probably only one person in fifty of the valley kindred owned their own craft. Thane felt bad for a moment, until inspiration struck. "You can come practice with me, then."

Ciena's face lit up. "Really?"

"Sure." Lots of maneuvers could only be performed with a copilot. He would need a partner if he wanted to learn to fly well enough to get into the Imperial Starfleet someday.

Besides, Thane could already tell—in spite of all their differences, he and Ciena Ree were going to be friends.

CHAPTER ONE

Five Years Later

THIRTY MINUTES remained until flying practice—hardly even enough time to get to the hangar, by now. And Ciena still had to sit here on this stupid bench. . . .

No, she thought. *It's not stupid. The Nierre family's honor has been questioned. They need their friends to stand with them in their hour of trial. Even if it means missing flying practice.*

But I would so much rather be flying.

The rough-hewn granite bench stood in front of the small domed house of the Nierre family, other kin of the valleys whose lands had bordered the Ree family's for generations. In front of the bench lay a long trench filled with sand, which now had several flagpoles stuck in it, each flag representing a family that had declared its loyalty to the Nierres during this dark time. The tradition was an ancient one, going back to the first days of settlement on Jelucan, but it still had meaning. One member of every loyal family would remain with the Nierres, constantly, until the cloud of suspicion over their honor had been cleared.

Most of the valley kindred had brought a flag, but not all. Some few thought the father of the household was abusing his power as an Imperial communications monitor—reporting meetings and messages that were private. However, Ciena's parents had declared that no one should even want to hide important information from the Empire and those who accused the Nierres were the ones without honor. Still, it was the Nierres who had been accused, and they had to bear the weight.

The family's genes passed down blond hair and milk-white skin. Even so, their faces had gone paler, to the point where they all looked sick. If the formal complaint to the Imperial governor was upheld and a new monitor was named, the Nierres would share in that disgrace forever—a difficult threat to endure. So friends needed to stay close to them to provide what comfort they could.

I'd want someone to do that for me, if I were falsely accused, Ciena thought. *But the Nierres would be even more comforted if my parents were here, like they said they would be a whole hour ago.*

Her eyes searched the skies, as if she would already see the old V-171 soaring overhead. From the bench,

Ciena could see farther down into the valley, all the way to the distant silvery gleam of water several thousand meters below. Surrounding her were countless snowy peaks, like white claws scratching at a stone-colored sky. Her dark blue cloak was heavy enough not to be disturbed by the winds, and it also disguised the fact that—instead of a traditional dress—she wore the oversize flight suit she'd managed to buy at a surplus store earlier that year.

Then she heard the distant whir of a ridgeclimber—the mountain-ready hovercraft Empire-backed merchants had introduced to the world five years before. Already Ciena could hardly remember how they'd managed without them; she still loved the old muunyak, but he was even slower these days. When the ridgecrawler rounded the bend, she wanted to leap up in delight. *Finally!*

But she remained on the bench, face solemn, until her father had stepped out and walked over to her. He was alone.

"Where's Mumma?" Ciena said as she rose to her feet.

"Another late night at the mine." Her father shook his head. "We knew her role as supervisor would require hard work, and I'm proud of her—but I miss her sometimes."

"Me too." And Ciena absolutely meant that, yet she couldn't keep her eyes off the ridgecrawler. If Pappa would let her borrow it, she could still get to the hangar in time.

Her father saw her haste and pressed his lips together in a thin line that threatened to become a frown. "Flying again today?"

"Pappa, please. How else am I supposed to get into one of the Imperial academies?"

"You should practice, and often. Nothing would make your mother and me prouder than to see you become an Imperial officer." Paron Ree paused. A few birds flew overhead, screeching their usual calls; Ciena watched them fly, because whenever her father brought up this next subject, she found it hard even to look at him. Sure enough, he continued, "We only wish you would practice more at the new simulators in Valentia, instead of spending all your time with that boy."

"Thane's my *friend*." She stressed the last word.

"We shouldn't take anything from second-wavers. We should rise by our own power, not because of their gifts."

Sometimes Ciena flew into a rage at this point in the fight—but if she did that today, she definitely wouldn't get to fly. So she took a deep breath before she continued: "I help Thane as much as he helps me. We work *together*. Neither of us owes the other anything, and he remembers that as well as I do."

Her father sighed. "His kind have short memories. But go. Take the ridgecrawler; I'll ride the muunyak home. Your mother and I will be back later, and you will have finished your lessons and cleaned the kitchen top to bottom."

"Yes, sir." Her spirits lifted. She'd fly today after all.

"Become a better pilot than this Kyrell boy," said her father, as he straightened his robe and began to walk inside the Nierre home. "If there's only one slot for a Jelucani cadet, I want it to be yours."

Ciena laughed. "We're *both* going. The Imperial Starfleet won't be able to do without us!"

Even Pappa had to smile.

Thane wondered if he could manage to jar loose the restraining bolt on the CZ-1 tutor droid. If so, then the droid would let him go even if he hadn't completed his stupid mathematics test.

"Your concentration is faltering," said CZ-1. "This is not conducive to optimal performance."

Thane pointed to the nearest chrono. "I'm late for flying practice."

"You must complete your lessons in order to master the subject. How else will you gain admission to an Imperial academy? Your parents' fondest hope is that you will follow in Dalven's footsteps."

Sometimes Thane believed CZ-1 was slier than a droid ought to be. Nothing made Thane fume like the knowledge that Dalven had, somehow, managed to get into one of the academies—one of the lesser ones, but still. Thane suspected his father might have bribed the local recruiter to admit his elder son to bolster the family pride. But Oris Kyrell wouldn't exert himself like that for Thane, who would have to get into the academy on his own.

So he thought fast. "I won't gain admission to an Imperial academy if I can't fly well," Thane pointed out. "And how can I fly well if I don't practice?"

"Your family has its own hangar and aircraft. Therefore you can practice at any time."

With his best smile, Thane said, "But we also have you, CZ-1. That means I can take math lessons at any time, too. I can only fly with a partner when Ciena's free, and she's coming today, so doesn't it make sense for me to prioritize flight time?"

CZ-1 cocked his head, and Thane heard the faint whirring that meant the droid was thinking hard.

Very casually, Thane said, "You know, when I get

back, I really ought to give you a lubrication bath. A nice long soak. It's been a while, hasn't it?"

A few more moments of silence followed before CZ-1 said, "Now that you mention it, my couplings *have* been stiff lately."

With a grin, Thane snapped off the mathematics holo and grabbed his flight jacket. "I'll be home before my parents get back from that stupid banquet. Okay?"

"And mathematics tomorrow morning!" CZ-1 called as Thane dashed out the door.

His family had a private hangar, but—as with most people on Jelucan—their territory ran more vertically than horizontally. Their gold-tiled home stretched almost the entire width of their property, mostly because his parents had insisted that people of their stature needed a home grander than the neighbors'. The snobbery annoyed Thane less than the fact that this meant his hangar was three hundred meters away—downhill.

At least he'd figured out a solution. With a grin, Thane slid on his flight goggles and ran for the far ridge. The handlebars were in position and ready, so all he had to do was grab them tightly, release the brake, and jump.

Immediately, he was zooming along the cable that led from his home to his hangar, dangling from the handlebars as he sped down the long ridge of stone. Cold mountain air whipped around him as he looked down into the valley far below. It wasn't as good as flying, but it came close.

He reactivated the brake as he slid toward the end post, but only gradually, because he liked to have some velocity left at the end. Just before he would've crashed into the post, Thane let go and leaped to the ground, laughing out loud.

Then he heard, "You know, someday you're going to break your face on that thing."

Thane turned to see Ciena standing there next to her family's clunky old ridgecrawler. She looked even shorter and skinnier than she was in that oversize flight suit, and her face still appeared younger than her age, with its rounded cheeks and snub nose. Her arms were folded across her chest and she was trying to look stern, but he could see the smile hiding in her dark brown eyes.

He righted himself and clapped his hands together to clean his gloves. "You're just jealous because I never let you do it."

Ciena stuck her tongue out at him. "I *could* do it, you know."

Of course she could; Thane never doubted that. But the line started at his house, and his parents hated her even more than her parents hated him. The few times they'd met, his family had treated Ciena so rudely that it made Thane almost sick with shame. Ciena was no more eager to encounter the Kyrells again than they were to see her.

However, the two of them always pretended there was no reason they shouldn't spend time together. It was easier than talking about how their families wanted them apart.

"Here I was worried about running late," Ciena continued, "and I beat you here."

"Trigonometry." Thane grimaced, an expression Ciena matched. "Come on, let's get started. Lizard-toad-snake for pilot?" They each silently counted to three and held out their hands. Thane had gone for the snake, but Ciena chose lizard, and lizard ate snake. She beamed, and he gestured toward the V-171's hatch. "Pilots first."

He didn't actually mind being copilot/gunner; cadets had to be expert at flying in both positions if they wanted to get into the academy. But sitting backward in the cockpit was never quite as much fun.

Technically, the V-171 was Dalven's. When he'd left for the academy, he'd given strict instructions that nobody was to fly it while he was gone.

Yeah, right.

Thane never passed up an opportunity to fly—or to get a little revenge on his older brother.

(Dalven was always ruder about Ciena than anyone else in the Kyrell family. Not long before Dalven had left for the academy, he'd sneered and said that there was only one reason to pick up some girl from the valleys—and if that was what Thane was after, he ought to get one who had breasts already. Thane had split Dalven's lip before their parents pulled them apart.)

"Hey," Ciena said. Thane realized he was just standing on the ladder instead of climbing inside the cockpit. "Still with me?"

"Yeah." Thane slid into the ship while determinedly not looking at the front of Ciena's flight suit. "Sorry. Let's go."

They slid on their helmets, buckled their harnesses, and lowered the hatch to seal themselves in. By now the procedure was second nature, something Thane could do without conscious thought. He knew the moment Ciena would start flipping the switches to activate the motor, and even the rhythm of her fingertips as she did it. His own console lit up in response. "All systems check out."

"Confirmed we are ready for takeoff," she said. "Full thrusters. Let's grab some sky."

The old V-171 rose from the ground with a shudder,

engines glowing blue on either side of them. Then they turned, banked, and soared away.

Ciena took them up higher, toward the peaks too cold and hostile for anyone to settle. A handful of mining droids dotted the landscape, gleaming darkly against snow and pale stone, but otherwise the area remained untouched. Thane felt as though he and Ciena had the world to themselves.

When they flew near one of the eastern ridge arches, Ciena's voice crackled through his helmet's speakers. "I see some icicles that need to be taught a lesson."

"Got it."

The arch came into focus on his viewscreen grid. Three icicles hung from the rock like stalactites, most of them about as thick as his arm. Big for an icicle—small for a target.

Thane took aim, fired, and sent shattered ice spraying into the air. He grinned as he heard Ciena's victory whoop.

"Think you can find me a couple more targets?" he said. They never blasted indiscriminately, because a few falling rocks or icicles at this altitude could turn into an avalanche down at habitation levels. But he and Ciena had learned everyplace safe to shoot where ice could possibly hide.

"Oh, yeah," she replied. "Hang on."

Thane knew exactly how she'd loop the ship downward. Even without guessing their exact destination, he could sense just from the slightest shift of their wings which way she would move next. He and Ciena had flown as a team every chance they'd had for the past five years. By now they worked together like two hands of the same pilot.

The V-171 dived into Stepson's Gorge, a narrow, craggy pass that challenged ships at every turn. Ciena steered them down deep, no doubt intending to give Thane some practice targeting overhead. As they descended, they swooped past one of the many small waterfalls within the gorge. Despite the freezing chill, the falls still flowed, though more in a trickle than a gush. At that hour of the afternoon, the light caught the water at the perfect angle for a rainbow, and an icy outcropping nearby caught the prismatic light, reflecting it in a dozen directions at once. Every rock and line of snow seemed to glitter. It was one of those perfect moments all the more spectacular because in an instant it would be gone, never to be seen again.

Thane heard Ciena whisper, "Look through my eyes."

He'd known she would say that.

Maybe it was finally time to find out why.

———

After flying practice, Ciena and Thane went to the Fortress.

So they'd named it when they were eight years old and inclined to be dramatic. Really the space was nothing but a cave, albeit a cave they'd spent several years fixing up to their satisfaction. Every few weeks, one of them would show up with something else to add to their collection. Most of the nicer stuff (the proton-fuel heater, the holo-games) had been brought by Thane—castoffs from his family, luxuries they had tired of or would never miss. Ciena's offerings were humbler, but she consoled herself by thinking they were more important. The Fortress would have been incredibly uncomfortable without the thick blankets and hide rugs she'd brought. Those, too, were castoffs, passed on by valley kindred trying to modernize their dwellings to Imperial standards. But they were warm and soft, the ideal lining for their nest hidden away from the world.

Really the cave was located fewer than fifty meters from the Kyrell family's hangar, but the mouth was tucked above one outcropping and overshadowed by another, making it so secret that Ciena sometimes thought she and Thane might be the first people in the history of Jelucan to walk inside. In short, it was the perfect hangout.

Occasionally, each of them went there alone, but

mostly they visited the Fortress together, talking about everything in the world and dreaming about their future among the stars.

"My father said it was three dozen senators who walked out," Ciena said.

Thane shrugged. He was less interested in politics than Ciena was and continued lounging on the red rug, staring out at the sunset. "What difference does it make whether it was twenty or thirty-six? Out of hundreds of senators, that's not that many either way."

"They refused to cast votes. They're going to be replaced by Imperial appointment. That's a big deal, Thane."

"It's just some rich old politicians being self-important. That's their idea of fun."

"How could they betray their oaths? Their *honor*?" Ciena still couldn't fully believe it. "Everybody knows it was the Senate that steered the galaxy into civil war before the Emperor established order again. Why would anyone take the peace we have now for granted?"

Thane shrugged. "Probably they're really fighting about something else entirely and just saying it's all about these high ideals. When they realize they don't have any power anymore, they'll come crawling back to the Emperor and forget all about the stuff they were arguing over before."

"You're really cynical sometimes."

"I'm right, though. You'll see."

Ciena sighed as she lay back on the black gundark hide, its thick fur as cozy as any bed. From this angle, the sunset blazed magnificently just beyond the far ridge of mountains. The light glowing into the cave turned Thane's hair to true red and added warmth to his pale skin, and something about the way it fell made his face look startlingly older.

He'll be handsome, she thought. Strange though it was to realize that, Ciena felt she was only being objective. It wasn't as if she and Thane were—as if they would ever—well, they wouldn't. If her parents loathed her having a second-wave boy for a friend, how would they react if she ever fell in love with one? And while Thane had never explicitly told her about the way his father treated him, she'd seen the bruises and sensed in his silences the things he hadn't said. Thane's father would do worse than that if he ever thought the two of them were together.

Besides, she and Thane . . . maybe they were *too close* to each other to fall in love. Sometimes she felt that they were two parts of the same person.

"Hey," Thane said quietly, carefully. "Can I ask you something that might be, uh, personal?"

Had he guessed what she was thinking about?

Ciena sat up and hugged her knees to her chest. "You can ask. I don't promise to answer."

"Fair enough." He paused again before continuing. "Every once in a while, when we see something really amazing, you whisper, 'Look through my eyes.' Is that a valley thing? What does it mean?"

It *was* personal, but Ciena found she didn't mind Thane's knowing. "Yes, it's one of our customs. A rarer one, though. See—when I was born—I was a twin."

"A twin?" Thane sat up straight. Even a second-waver would be intrigued; most planets had myths and legends about twins. "For real? But I thought you were an only child."

"I am now. My sister, Wynnet, died only a few hours after we were born."

"Oh. Sorry."

"No, it's all right. It's not as if I remember her or anything. But I live my life for both of us." Ciena held up her arm to show off her leather bracelet. "Didn't you ever notice that I never take this off?"

"Well, yeah, but I thought you just *liked* it."

Ciena ran her fingertip along the braid. "I wear it as a symbol that I'm still tied to Wynnet. All my life, everything I do, everything I see—it's as much of the world as she'll ever have, because I share it with her. So when I see something especially beautiful—anything amazing, or sometimes even things that are especially bad—I say those words. My sister looks through my eyes, and I show her the most important moments of my life."

Thane leaned back on the rug. "That's . . . really great. I mean it."

Ciena nodded. "Sometimes it feels like this huge responsibility, living for Wynnet, too, but mostly it reminds me to look for what's truly special. Maybe I wouldn't see so much of that if I weren't looking for her."

The sun had finally dipped below the horizon. Although light still suffused the lower part of the sky, higher up the blue had become dark enough to reveal small twinkling points of light.

Ciena whispered, "Someday, once we've made it to the academy—I'm going to show her the stars."

CHAPTER TWO

WHEN THEY WERE fourteen—

"Come on," Thane said. He sat opposite her, cross-legged, deep within the Fortress. "You know this."

"Do I?"

"This guy started a *war*."

Ciena's head swam. They'd been reviewing galactic history for three hours now. "Okay. The criminal gang that interfered with a legal execution on Geonosis and sparked the Clone Wars was led by . . . by . . ." She shut her eyes, winced, and said, "Mace Windu?"

Then she opened her eyes again to see Thane grinning at her. "See? You knew it all along."

Next to them, the CZ-1 droid clucked approvingly. "Your grasp of history is excellent, Miss Ree. In my opinion, you should be much more worried about calculus."

Her face fell. Thane glared at CZ-1. "I knew we should've installed the tact upgrade."

"What use is tact if it keeps you from learning?" CZ-1 shuffled closer, his ancient joints no longer easy to move. "When you first smuggled me into the ridge-climber to bring me here for study sessions, you said I was to ensure that *both* of you passed the exams. I can't do that by pretending you understand certain subjects when you don't."

Ciena could've groaned in despair. These weren't even the entrance exams for the academy. These would only allow her to qualify for the academy's preparatory courses. "If *these* tests are kicking my butt, how can I ever pass the real ones?" She tried to make it a joke, but her voice cracked.

Thane heard her. "Hey," he said, leaning closer. "You're smart enough. You're strong enough. You can fly any single-pilot ship in the Imperial Starfleet, and I bet you could even handle a Star Destroyer on your own, if they gave you the chance."

She had to laugh. "I doubt it."

"I don't doubt it." His words became firmer, more forceful. "I don't doubt *you*. So stop doubting yourself, okay? We can do this."

Ciena repeated the words to make herself believe them. "We can."

When they were fifteen—

"Kyrell!" The E&A—Endurance and Agility—coach stood over Thane, who lay panting on the ground. "Get it in gear or get out for good!"

Every month, in the preparatory track, they had to run a different obstacle course. Gradually, the courses became more difficult, even dangerous. If would-be cadets broke a limb or gained a scar, it was just proof that they weren't fit to be there in the first place.

Not finishing the course—it didn't get you automatically expelled, but it put you really high on the list of kids who would be first to go.

But his back and shoulders hurt *so much*. . . .

"Hey." Ciena kneeled beside him. "Come on. Get up."

Thane shook his head. His muscles quivered with exhaustion. Beneath his loose black E&A gear, bruises and cuts burned with each movement he made. He'd had less than two hours' sleep. Every muscle ached; his bones felt heavier than carbonite. "I can't."

"Like hell you can't."

He lifted his head from the rubbery red surface of the E&A room to see her kneeling over him. The first moment their eyes met, Thane realized he wouldn't be able to hide the truth from her. "Last night—my dad—"

Normally Oris Kyrell lectured his sons. Often he caned them, but only for a few strokes. However, the night before, his wrath had exploded as never before. Thane had not realized he needed to fight back until he was too injured to do so. His father's punches and kicks had not stopped until Thane was on the floor bleeding. Neither of his parents had helped him up afterward, nor had they acknowledged his injuries in the morning. Apparently they were determined to pretend the incident had never happened.

Bruised and aching, Thane had to bear the truth alone—at least until Ciena's eyes widened in understanding. "You can still do it," she whispered. "You got this far, right?"

"I'll try," he said, between deep gulping breaths. "But you have to get back on the course. You're losing time."

"I'm ranked number one in E&A, remember? I can afford to lose a few minutes. And I swear to you right now, Thane Kyrell, if I have to pick you up and carry you to the end of the course, I will."

"I appreciate the offer, but I don't think that counts."

More students ran past them, vaulting over the next high barrier, with only a few grunts and groans from those who had touched the sharp edges. These were the slowest kids, or close to it. Ciena would finish last, and Thane didn't expect to finish at all.

He rolled over to look her in the face so maybe she'd see how deeply he meant it. *"Go."*

Ciena only leaned closer. "Thane—don't let your father win."

Hatred of his father did what hope couldn't. Fueled by pure spite, Thane struggled to his knees, then to his feet. Though he staggered at first, he managed to catch himself.

"Ready to run?" Ciena began bouncing on her heels, eager to get moving.

"Yeah." Thane took a deep breath. "I'm ready."

Somehow he hurled himself over the barrier. Although Thane made it to the end in last place—he made it.

Afterward, in the privacy of the gear room, he sat on the bench, carefully stripped off his shirt, and let Ciena see the worst of it. The shame made his face burn. Even though he knew he wasn't the one who ought to be ashamed . . . here he was, showing Ciena how he let himself get beaten until the skin of his back split open.

If she pitied him or said she felt sorry for him, Thane thought he might have to walk out.

But Ciena said nothing. Silently, she opened the first-aid kit and set to work applying curative skin sealant, closing each cut one at a time until Thane felt whole again.

When they were sixteen—

Only a handful of kids from the entire planet of Jelucan would make it into one of the Imperial academies. While Inner Rim worlds often fielded thousands of candidates, slots were still strictly limited for citizens of former Separatist worlds. The academy instructors themselves sorted students. At the same moment applicants found out whether they'd gotten in, they learned which school they'd been slotted into, which planet they'd be living on within two weeks' time.

Ciena didn't care which academy it was. Any planet would do. Just as long as she got to be an Imperial cadet.

On the morning results were to be announced, their entire class congregated in the school's courtyard. Parents weren't allowed on school grounds—only students and Imperial officials—but families lingered outside. Afterward there would be celebrations or consolations. For now, Ciena, Thane, and the other applicants only had each other.

"I couldn't sleep," she confessed to Thane as they stood together near the far left of the courtyard, staring at the door where the proctor would appear with the announcements. "At all."

"Me either." Thane gave her a crooked smile. "That gave me time to think of a few backup plans for us."

Ciena held up her hands in protest. She'd refused even to consider alternate career paths because it felt like bad luck.

Thane scoffed. "Come on, Ciena. We took the tests. The decision's already been made! So we can't jinx ourselves at this point."

It was true. More than that, from the tone of Thane's voice, Ciena had figured out that these "plans" weren't for real. "Okay, fine. Let me hear it."

"One. We become famous acrobats."

". . . acrobats?"

"*Famous* acrobats. There's no glory in being mediocre, unknown acrobats. If we're going to do this, we have to do it right."

The proctor would walk out any moment. The crowd's buzzing grew louder, more tense. Ciena's heart raced, but she tried to match Thane's playful tone. "I'll pass. Any other bright ideas for our future? You said that was only number one."

"Two. We travel the galaxy as drummer and exotic dancer."

She raised her eyebrows. "Excuse me, but I'm not becoming an exotic dancer."

"Who said you were? I'll do the dancing. You get the drum."

This time her laughter was genuine. "Only if I get to design your costume."

"Hmmm. Maybe I should move on to plan three—"

Then Thane straightened, eyes widening, as the door opened and the proctor walked out. His black uniform seemed to steal the sunlight from the day. Ciena's gut clenched, but like all the other students, she immediately stood at attention and remained perfectly silent.

Amplifier droids hovered nearby, catching the proctor's voice as he said, "The following is a list of all the school's successful applicants to the various Imperial academies. For the Imperial Academy on Arkanis . . ."

Ciena could've groaned. They were going in alphabetical order by school? They might not know until the very end whether they'd made it in or not. She could imagine standing there at attention, minutes draining away, as the terrible realization of her failure sank in.

Then she would have to slink out, humiliated. Failure wasn't the same as dishonor, but it felt like it at the moment.

A few minutes into the ceremony—which already felt as though it had lasted forever—the proctor stood up straighter. "For the Royal Imperial Academy on Coruscant . . ."

No school in the entire galaxy was more prestigious. No other training came closer to ensuring a high-level career in the Imperial Starfleet.

Ciena had dreamed of going there, which was surely why she imagined the proctor's speaking her name.

But no. He'd really said—"Thane Kyrell and Ciena Ree." Both of them, together!

She remained at attention, but she glanced sideways at Thane. If he'd heard it, too, it was definitely for real. Sure enough, he was smiling—but a weary smile, like when he'd cleared the final barrier on an E&A course. Thane closed his eyes and whispered, seemingly to himself, "I'm out of here. I'm gone."

Ciena knew why her friend wanted to leave this planet so badly. Those were reasons she didn't share. She loved Jelucan's stark beauty, the fellowship among the valley kindred—all of it was beautiful to her. Yet she could leave her homeworld without regret.

She wasn't escaping from anything. She was chasing

her dream of becoming an Imperial officer, flinging herself joyfully into space.

The day Thane left Jelucan felt . . . perfect. Like he could do no wrong, like all the constellations had finally aligned to guide him out. His parents said their good-byes at the house and didn't bother taking him to the spaceport. It was a relief.

Boarding the vessel to Coruscant was even more satisfying because Ciena was there, too, though she remained on the boarding ramp hugging her parents so long that the captain threatened to leave her behind. Thane and she had become a team to get into the academy; it was only right that they should arrive there together. Best of all was the moment when the transport shuddered into hyperspace—their first experience of lightspeed—and the two of them grinned at each other in total delight.

Then they arrived on Coruscant, and it was like getting punched in the face.

Thane had always known Jelucan was a backwater world. Holos had told him the galaxy was far bigger and more sophisticated than anything he'd ever had the chance to see before. So he'd thought he was prepared. But when he stepped off the ship and saw Coruscant for the first time—

The buildings stood as high as Jelucan's mountains. Although sunlight slipped through various glass structures, the overall effect was one of profound claustrophobia. The ground was impossibly far below, and the sky was cut into thin slivers. Hundreds of smaller aircraft zoomed or hovered between skyscrapers in a nonstop buzz of negotiation and commerce. Every single person seemed to have direction and purpose, to be perfectly at home in this huge metal cage, this city that had swallowed a world. Thane, however, tried not to look out the windows any longer because the view made him feel so small.

At first he thought Ciena would be even more overcome. Her childhood had been spent in the open valleys, in houses only slightly more sophisticated than tents. Surely this would be too much for her.

Instead, she was elated. "This is where everything happens," she gushed as the two of them walked through the corridors of the spaceport, buoy droids floating ahead as beacons to guide them toward the academy shuttle. "It's like—electricity, this incredible energy all around. Don't you feel it?"

"Definitely," Thane said. "Totally electric."

Ciena gave him a look. "Hey. Are you all right?" But then they'd reached the shuttle, along with a handful of other new cadets, and they got caught up in the whirl of activity that was the first day of attendance: collecting data chips with the information they'd need, learning about tonight's reception for all cadets, and introducing themselves to cadets from other worlds. Imperial officers, stiff and correct in dress uniforms, moved among them as the shuttle pulled away and joined the dizzyingly swift Coruscant air traffic. Thane had to keep himself from flinching every time another craft came within two wingtips—but in a planet-sized metropolis, apparently pilots were used to small margins of error.

The intensity only sharpened when they reached the academy itself. As the new cadets walked out of the shuttle, Thane realized hundreds of students were already there. Hundreds more seemed likely to pour out of the other shuttles coming up behind them. The entire time he was checking in, he couldn't help feeling lost. When he glanced toward Ciena, she was smiling even more brightly. Before long they were separated from each other in the crush of people trying to figure out where they should be.

Thane's data chip gave him the location of his dorm room and the information that he'd have two roommates. *They couldn't be worse than Dalven,* he thought, determined to make the best of it.

Still, as he raised his hand to hit the door chime, Thane felt unbelievably small.

The door swooshed open to reveal a slim, black-haired guy with a narrow face and rigid bearing—so correct that it took Thane a moment to realize this was no administrator but one of his roommates.

"So you're the one from, what's it called, Jelucan?" When Thane nodded, the guy scoffed. "Why did you bother ringing the chime of your own room? It's ridiculous."

"Charming, isn't he?" said another guy—the tallest of the three, stick thin and long faced, with long brown hair he'd knotted at the back of his head. His accent was aristocratic but his smile infectious. "Mr. Personality here is Ved Foslo, native to Coruscant—"

"Of course," Ved cut in, lifting his chin. "My father, General Foslo, works in central intelligence."

"—and, as you can see, he manages to work in a reference to his father within the first minute of meeting anybody." As Ved scowled, the tall guy stepped closer to shake Thane's hand. "Me, I'm Nash Windrider from Alderaan. And my father makes carpets. Impressed yet?"

"Very." Thane realized he'd started to smile. "Mine does slightly dishonest accounting."

"Always handy," Nash said. "You never know when you're going to need to cook the books. Come in and get comfortable—as comfortable as you can be on the lower bunk, that is. We grabbed the two best bunks already."

Nash turned out to have traveled to more than a dozen worlds already and had visited Coruscant several times. He didn't even ask Thane whether he'd been intimidated at first; he assumed as much and swore everybody felt that way the first time they landed on the planet.

"They should pass out inhalers at the spaceports," Nash said as they hung out, sprawled on their beds to await the welcoming ceremony and dinner that night. "Or tranquilizers. Something to help people deal."

"I don't see what's so strange about Coruscant." Ved remained completely stiff but overall didn't seem so bad. "Have you really never been to a real city before? Or any other Core World at all?"

Already Thane knew honesty would serve him best. "Nope." He stretched out on the bunk beneath Ved's, trying to get used to the hard mattress. "Never even been to a city bigger than Valentia back home, and I'm guessing the entire population of Valentia would fill about—seven levels of this one building."

Nash rested his hands beneath his head. "You'll get used to it, Thane. Soon we'll all be Imperial officers and you'll have traveled to a hundred worlds, and when you go home you'll be as jaded as Mr. General's Son here."

Ved gave Nash a dirty look, but Thane couldn't help laughing.

Ciena had trusted she'd like her new roommates and enjoy the reception, but so far the afternoon was exceeding even her best expectations. She stood in front of the mirror, astonished to see herself in the cadet's uniform. Black boots, dark trousers, dark jacket—it was like a vision out of a dream.

"I hate these boots," said her roommate Kendy Idele, who scowled down at hers from where she stood nearby. "Then again, I hate shoes, period. When you grow up on a tropical world, you love barefoot best."

"You'll soon be accustomed to them," promised their third roomie, Jude Edivon. She was as tall as Kendy was short, as pale as Kendy and Ciena were dark. "Bare feet might be great on Iloh, but on Coruscant? Your feet would quickly become dirty. Plus the likelihood of scrapes, small cuts, and potential infection would be high—not that hygiene levels aren't good here, but the sheer size of the populace suggests—"

"Are you going to start quoting statistics again?" Kendy groaned.

"It's okay to be a science geek," Ciena said. "Quote as many statistics as you like, Jude. Kendy and I will get used to it eventually."

Jude's lightly freckled face lit up with a smile. "Our personalities seem to be compatible. I think you and I will get along very well."

"We will, too," Kendy promised. "Ignore my being grumpy. I'm just space-lagged and tired, and trying to get the hang of these damned braids."

Ciena had been wearing her hair pinned back in tight braids for years, ever since she'd learned that this was mandatory for all long-haired cadets. "Here, let me." Kendy's dark green hair was straight and silky—totally unlike Ciena's tight curls—but she figured a braid was a braid. "Did you really never practice fixing it?"

"Not even once. I thought it would be easy!" Kendy sighed. "Thanks for this, by the way."

"No problem."

Jude leaned closer. "You could simply cut your hair short, as I have. That provides optimal efficiency."

Kendy made a face. "On Iloh, only little children wear their hair short. Growing it long means you're really an adult. No way am I sawing it off now."

"You'll get the hang of the braids soon," Ciena

promised. "You'll have to, because I'm not doing your hair every morning."

"Even if I promised to make your bed before inspections?"

"*No.*"

Somehow they made it to the ceremony on time, with their uniforms perfect. More than eight thousand students were in Ciena's class—a stunning number, to her—but a charge went through her at the sight of them all dressed in Imperial regalia, brought together by a common purpose, a common dream. Every single one of those cadets had traveled there, from hundreds of worlds, to make themselves the best officers they could possibly be. They'd come to serve the Empire, to make the entire galaxy better through their service. Her heart felt so full that Ciena put one hand to her chest.

Was Thane doing better by now? He had to be. Her eyes searched the crowd for him, but that was one of the disadvantages of wearing uniforms; it was harder to tell people apart.

She intended to locate him as soon as she could—then was taken aback by the academy president's speech.

"You are not here merely to learn military tactics or to practice flying starfighters," Commandant Deenlark said, every word crisp. "Those are important skills, to be sure. But we ask more of you. Our students are meant to become citizens of the Empire. To think of themselves as patriots and soldiers first. Can you stop thinking of yourself as a native of your home planet and begin thinking of yourself as an Imperial first? An Imperial only? Can you accept that protecting and serving the world you came from is best accomplished by strengthening the Empire to which it belongs?"

Ciena had never thought of belonging to the Empire as giving up Jelucan. To her, the two identities coexisted comfortably. But maybe some students here came from worlds with rebellious senators—places disloyal to the Emperor. They might need reassuring that they still could belong here at the academy.

Deenlark continued: "Some few of you have come here alongside friends from home, or have older siblings already in Imperial service. Your natural tendency will be to seek these people out at every opportunity and to rely on relationships you already have. But if that was all you meant to do—you might have well stayed at home, don't you think?"

A few people laughed, obediently. Ciena felt stung. She and Thane weren't supposed to spend time together? At all?

Well. "At all" was putting it too strongly, she

decided. The instructors simply didn't want them to rely on each other completely.

Yet that was what she and Thane had been doing for the past eight years of their lives.

After the ceremony and dinner ended, students milled around, introducing themselves to each other and—sometimes—not so subtly sizing up the competition. Ciena wanted to find Thane, though she told herself she shouldn't.

Luckily, he found her.

"We both plan to serve the Empire for the rest of our lives," Thane said as they sat down in chairs facing the glittering cityscape beyond. "We're never going back to Jelucan—not to live, anyway. So we don't have to worry about 'living in the past' or however Deenlark put it."

Sometimes Thane could be very glib about authority figures—uninterested in rules—but Ciena thought he was more or less right about this. "It looks like we'll share some classes and take some separately. So we can each make our own way here."

"This place scared the hell out of me at first," Thane confessed. "You lived farther out in the countryside than I did, but it didn't faze you for a second. How did that happen?"

He was only joking, but Ciena answered him seriously. "I was ready for Coruscant because I've always dreamed of being here. You weren't ready because— because I think mostly you dreamed of getting *away* from Jelucan."

Thane remained silent for a moment, and Ciena wished she could snatch the words back. But then, finally, he nodded. "You're right."

"We shared the most important part of the dream, though," Ciena said.

"More than that. We got each other here. It's not coincidence that we both were admitted to the Royal Academy, you know? Flying together, studying together—we made each other so much better than we ever would've been on our own."

Her throat tightened. "Yeah. We did."

Thane smiled as he shook his head, perhaps in disbelief at how far they'd already come, or how far they still had to go. "Now it's the academy's turn to make us better."

"To make us officers. It's going to happen."

"You'd better believe it."

The window looking out on the Coruscant night reflected them slightly, superimposing their images over the buildings and hovercraft beyond. Ciena saw herself sitting next to Thane, both of them in the stiff, unfamiliar jackets and boots they'd been assigned today. Always they'd looked so different: Thane tall and pale, forever wearing the bright elegant clothing of a second-waver; Ciena dark and slim, in the simple homespun garments of the valleys. Now they wore the same uniform, and anyone could see that she and Thane were alike in the ways that mattered most.

They sat there side by side for a moment longer before getting to their feet. Thane smiled down and whispered, "You can do this, you know."

"So can you," Ciena said. They didn't have to lean on each other. They were more than ready to fly.

Then they turned away from each other to walk into the crowd, meet new people, and become the citizens of the Empire they were always meant to be.

CHAPTER THREE

IF THE PREPARATORY track for the Imperial academies had been hard, the course load at the Royal Academy of Coruscant was *brutal.*

The first day's easygoing friendliness had lasted exactly that long—one day, no more. Science, mathematics, piloting, physical training: every possible test challenged the students' limits, every single time. Classes shrunk to about half their original size each year of the three-year program. Few would graduate, and the competition to be among those few remained fierce. Forget sleeping in, cutting class, or even whispering to other students during a lecture; if you wanted to stay in the academy, to become an officer someday, you could never, ever slack off. You had to push yourself to the limit every single day.

Two months into his first year, Thane decided he'd never had so much fun in his life.

"You must—be—kidding me," Nash panted as the two of them ran their ninth lap around the Sky Loop, a track on the academy's roof, high above most of the bustle of Coruscant. A cool cloud had settled around the building, enveloping them in pale fog. "Getting up at dawn—doing homework until midnight—exercising until you vomit? *Fun?*"

Thane grinned as he wiped sweat from his forehead. "Hell, yeah."

"If this is how they have fun on Jelucan—I think I'll vacation somewhere else." They crossed the finish line and slowed down, loping to a stop. After Nash had leaned over with his hands on his knees and taken a few deep breaths, he continued, "Someday you've got to come with me to Alderaan. Trust me, we can show you a better time than this."

Nash didn't get it. He couldn't. As the two of them walked toward the locker room, Thane tried to find the words. "Most of my life, my parents fought me on everything I wanted to do—even getting ready for this place. I had to sneak around to practice flying with Ciena. Can you believe that?"

"Seriously?" Nash shook his head in disbelief. His gray T-shirt had gone dark with sweat. "But Ciena

Ree's one of the best pilots here. You could've gone to twenty different worlds and never found anyone better to fly with."

Was it worth explaining the divide between the Jelucani valley kindred and second-wave settlers? Thane decided to skip it. That was the kind of home-world thinking the academy instructors frowned upon. "The point is this is the first time in my life when I've been able to go after something I want without anybody getting in my way."

Nash sighed. "Sounds rough. On Alderaan, people are encouraged to learn and grow. All education is free, and people volunteer to teach various skills or crafts just for fun. Of course, someday the entire Empire will be like that." Thane laughed, which made Nash frown. "What's so funny?"

"You, thinking the whole galaxy can turn into starshine and flowers, all because of the Empire."

"That's what the Empire is for, isn't it?" Nash tried to wipe sweat from his face with his shirt but, finding it even sweatier, grimaced and let it fall. "To take the best of every world, every culture, and spread it throughout every system?"

Thane shrugged. "That was what the Galactic Republic was about, too. At least, they probably thought so at the beginning. But things fall apart."

"Don't let too many people hear you say that, all right?" Nash glanced around them, but nobody was walking especially close. "They might think you're disloyal. Whereas I, your friend, know that you're merely a cynic."

"Guilty as charged." He'd learned his lesson the first time his parents sucked up in public to the same people they'd mocked in private: appearances were deceiving.

"Well, someday you'll come to Alderaan with me and see for yourself how wonderful it is. Not even you could be cynical about my world."

Thane could tell Nash was homesick, so he decided to take his roommate's boasting about Alderaan at face value . . . for now. "It sounds like a good place. I'd like to go sometime."

"Just wait, my friend. You're going to love it."

So Thane had a voyage to Alderaan to look forward to. By then every world he learned about had become a possible destination; what began as hunger simply to leave Jelucan had ripened into genuine wanderlust. A career in the Imperial Starfleet would allow him to stand in the deep snows of ice planets, to dive into the depthless oceans of a waterworld, to bask in the searing heat of a beach beneath a binary star system.

And he got to fly every day, sometimes all day. Sure, at that point the cadets mostly used simulators—but the academy's simulators operated at a level of sophistication Thane had never seen before. (Plus, anything beat a crappy old V-171.) From the outside, the simulators were stark globes of dull metal; on the inside cadets found completely accurate cockpits, glowing control boards, and viewscreens that showed three-dimensional images of whatever starscape or planetary atmosphere they'd be training in that day.

The flying felt absolutely genuine, and the challenges presented were more immediate, terrifying, and plentiful than they were likely to encounter in real life—at least so far. One day Thane would try to bring a TIE fighter from deep space into atmosphere on a planet with gravity strong enough to crush a human. The next, he might maneuver a snowspeeder through a blizzard with winds that threatened to tear the metal plating from the hull. Some students tensed, panicking about their training scores or what it would be like when they had to do it in real life.

Thane actually felt more relaxed when he was piloting. He couldn't *wait* to do it for real. Being at the controls of a vessel remained the purest kind of joy he knew.

His combination of enthusiasm and steadiness showed in his scores, too. The class rankings always had Thane in one of the very top slots for piloting—

—and one of the few names that ever came in above his was Ciena Ree's.

They laughed about it together, congratulated each other for winning, and proudly declared they'd take back their title on the very next flight. Ciena had become his rival, but a friendly one. They saw each other more days than not, either in class or the main academy mess. Although the balance between maintaining their friendship and becoming "citizens of the Empire" was a delicate one, he felt they'd found it. While their meetings were often brief, they still got to hang out a couple of times a week—hours when they let the competition drop. Thane knew they'd always made each other better by striving to match the other's skills; even at the academy, he and Ciena kept each other at the very top of their game.

"It's ludicrous," Ved Foslo said sniffily one night after Ciena had reclaimed the top spot. "She took your rank away from you. Why are you so thrilled the competition is making her a better pilot? You should be trying to knock her down, not pick her up."

"There's room for more than one of us in the graduating class," Thane shot back as he sat at the edge of his bunk, polishing his uniform boots. "Besides, isn't the goal to create the best Imperial officers possible? This way the Empire gets two great pilots, not just one."

Ved shook his head. "Someday you'll understand."

From his place beneath the thin gray blanket of his bunk, Nash laughed. "Admit it, Ved. You're only angry because Thane and Ciena always score higher than you! Despite your father being—what's his rank again?"

"You know perfectly well," Ved said. Written on his face was his displeasure at being regularly bested by not one but two kids from a hunk of rock in the Outer Rim. Without another word, he buttoned his pajamas to the neck, like he did every night. The guy *never* relaxed.

Otherwise, though, Ved wasn't a terrible roommate. He was clean, he didn't snore, and he didn't mind explaining the finer points of military culture on Coruscant. Meanwhile, between room inspections, Nash threw his stuff everywhere in a truly spectacular display of messiness, but aside from a few arguments about why it was gross for Nash's dirty socks to wind up on someone's toothbrush, he and Thane were unshakable friends.

But the single best thing about Thane's first months at the academy was seeing Dalven again.

For most of Thane's life, he had been of an average height among his peers. Sometimes he'd looked at his statuesque mother, towering father, and lanky older brother in despair. There, too, he thought he'd be shortchanged. A few months before he entered the academy, however, his body started making up for lost time. His leg bones ached at night, and he didn't seem able to eat enough to stop feeling hungry—and he needed new uniforms within three months of arriving.

As he stood in the sector dispensary, waiting for his turn to get larger boots, he heard a droid's toneless voice: "Ensign Kyrell, H-J-two-nine-zero, packet ready."

Thane frowned. He was still only a cadet, and his call number was AV547. Yet he was sure he'd heard the name Kyrell—

Then Dalven stepped out of the milling crowd of waiting officers, hastily retrieving a uniform packet. He seemed to be in a hurry to go, but when he turned and saw his younger brother standing there, he froze in place as if aghast.

"Dalven?" Thane didn't know what to say. "Good to see you" would be a lie, for either of them.

"Well. So. You haven't washed out yet. How astonishing." With that, Dalven raised his chin, clearly ready to walk out—but Thane stood between him and the door, and he didn't move.

"Ensign? You told us you'd made lieutenant."

Dalven's cheeks darkened. "I—well—the promotion is due to come through at any moment."

Thane nodded. "Right. Sure. Which is why you're picking up a new uniform, I guess. . . ."

His voice trailed off as he saw the printed label on the bundle in Dalven's arms: CLERICAL STAFF/THIRD CLASS.

"Good-bye." Dalven hurried out, obviously determined to pretend Thane hadn't seen anything.

Maybe it was cheap—even petty—but learning his overbearing older brother had been deemed better suited for desk chairs than Star Destroyers? It made Thane's day.

That afternoon, as he headed up to the Sky Loop for an extra run, he imagined telling Ciena about the encounter. She loathed Dalven almost as much as he did; it almost seemed to Thane that he could already hear her laughter, see her dark eyes shining with satisfaction on his behalf.

Then he walked out onto the track to see several other cadets also working in additional exercise, Ciena among them.

She wore the same stuff as every other cadet: gray shirt, black shorts, and regulation shoes. Ciena was only one of a few dozen people out there, at the

farthest edge of the track. Yet he knew her instantly—
even across the length of the Sky Loop, even with the
sun blazing down so brilliantly. Thane recognized the
way she ran, the shape of her black curls braided at
the nape of her neck. . . .

She's beautiful, he thought, a realization that startled
him, then made him feel stupid. How could he not
have noticed that about a girl he'd seen more days than
not for the past eight years? But that was precisely it.
Thane knew Ciena too well to see her with any objec-
tivity. Her face was as familiar to him as his own in the
mirror—or it had been, until now.

The evidence of his blindness disturbed him. It
was as if Ciena had transformed somehow and ought
to have told him first. Possibilities he'd refused to consider in the past now pushed their way into his mind,
possibilities that were both exhilarating and frighten-
ing. He felt a shiver along his skin that he had always
associated with flight, that exact moment when he left
the earth and grabbed the sky—

Thane decided not to think about it any longer.
Instead he would run, fast as he could, until he was
worn-out and half-dazed. When he saw Ciena again,
he would be able to talk to her just like he always had.
Nothing had to change.

CHAPTER FOUR

FIRING HAND WEAPONS had never been something Ciena dreamed about, or practiced, and her initial marksmanship scores, while adequate, dragged down her overall ranking. So she spent a lot of free time on the practice range with the mock laser rifle, concentrating hard on improving her aim.

Or, as was the case today, *trying* to concentrate, with no help from her roommates.

"It was just an observation," Kendy said, attempting to look innocent and doing a terrible job. She stood in the next booth over, her white practice coveralls contrasting with the metallic black surfaces of the training range. "You won't even admit Thane's looking good these days?"

Ciena focused on the holographic target coming toward her and fired three blasts at its head. Only when the target shattered into a thousand tiny lines of light did she reply, "He's, um—filling out."

"This is a normal stage of physiological development." Jude sat on a bench behind the shooting booths, disassembling the laser rifle to see how quickly she could put it together again. "Although I must say that in Thane's case development is proceeding *very* well."

"You guys, come on. I can't aim when I'm laughing."

But Kendy wouldn't let the subject drop. "Are you honestly not at all interested in him?"

"Romantic or sexual relationships between cadets are forbidden." Jude could look very prim. "Besides, Ciena has known Thane since they were children. It would be rational to conclude that at this point their relationship is like that of brother and sister, and therefore no sexual feeling could be generated between them."

Thane's not my brother. It's nothing like that. Ciena opened her mouth to say so, then closed it. Better for her friends to assume that was how she felt so they would stop asking her questions about Thane Kyrell.

The thing was she wasn't exactly sure how to feel about him any longer. Before, they'd been together constantly, and she'd never had a moment to step back and wonder whether things could change between them—and, if so, how. Their lives were both more parallel and more separate than ever before.

When Thane edged her out in the rankings—or vice versa—they'd stare at each other in pretend anger that wasn't wholly pretend. At times Ciena felt as if she could stand to be beaten by absolutely anyone else before she could endure it from Thane. Yet the next day, when she saw how well he had done, her face would light up with a smile. She'd seen him cheering for her in races and cheered for him in turn. Their rivalry generated electricity that could turn ugly or could become—

Concentrate, Ciena reminded herself. *You're here to hit your targets.*

After the holograms came the droids, a dozen tiny spheres that darted through the range, daring her to hit them all. Ciena fired, red bolts blasting from her rifle, and refused to pause until she'd taken down every one.

"That's much better," Jude said, unnecessarily, as Ciena's score blinked on the screen above. "Your accuracy scores are already above average for our class. Soon you'll reach the top quartile."

"Then you can stand alongside the sharpshooters, like me." Like some pirate out of a spice-runner holo, Kendy twirled her blaster before holstering it, which made Ciena laugh.

She had no doubts that she would master shooting.

It wasn't arrogance—the demands of the Imperial Academy made her aware of her limitations every day. Instead, Ciena's faith came from her sheer joy in the academy, and in Coruscant itself. Although she loved and missed her life in the Jelucani valleys, her universe had expanded a hundredfold, and every new part of it seemed wonderful to her. To walk along corridors with members of a dozen different races; to hear their various languages with their unfamiliar syllables, whistles, and clicks; to look into the sky and spot a dozen different types of spacecraft every single day—it enthralled her.

Sometimes Ciena felt as though she was whispering to her lost sister constantly. *Look through my eyes.* There were infinite wonders to behold, and finally she had a chance to see them all.

She experienced guiltier moments, though. Ciena found herself sometimes thinking of her former life as . . . backward. Her life in the valleys had always been a happy one. No, she didn't possess any second-waver luxuries, but she didn't particularly want them. Besides, Thane's difficult family life had disabused her of any idea that wealthier people were automatically happier. Material things never had, and never would, mean much to her.

So it wasn't the relative grandeur of Coruscant that tempted her. It was the richness of life here, the energy in the air, the lack of any need for ritual. Every forward step she took made her wonder if she was leaving her traditional values behind.

Not entirely. *Never* entirely. She would never abandon the concept of honor, of the absolute need to keep her word, no matter what. That was as much a part of Ciena as her bones. She would also always carry her sister forward with her, allowing Wynnet to look through her eyes.

Yet now Ciena's perspective had been widened forever.

No longer did she look through the narrow prism of second wave versus valley. The huge difference she'd once perceived between her and Thane—it was nothing, really. It didn't exist.

Ciena had believed in that divide for so long that she wasn't quite sure what to think once it was gone.

Finally, they got to fly for real.

"About time," Ciena said to Thane, who had walked into the low-altitude craft bay early, just like she had. She couldn't help noticing how he came closer to her than any other cadet would—into her personal space.

"For what?" he said quickly, swerving away from her as though he feared an electrical shock. "It's not time for anything."

". . . about time *for us to fly*." Ciena gave him a look.

Thane smiled unevenly. "Oh, right. Of course. Definitely past time for that. I mean—never mind."

Why is he acting so awkward? Then again, Ciena realized she was hugging herself as though it were a cold Jelucani morning. She and Thane still got along well, but they were starting to have these moments of self-conscious weirdness.

Maybe one of her friends had told someone that they were gossiping about how hot he was during target practice. Neither Jude nor Kendy would talk behind her back, but Jude might be socially clueless enough to say the wrong thing in front of Nash or Ved. That would be the worst—especially since it seemed to make Thane want to pull back from her.

I said there wasn't anything between us. So he shouldn't be behaving this way. Unless he wants there to be something between us. But he doesn't, does he?

Do I?

Ciena snapped herself out of it. Mumma always told her not to make something out of nothing. She didn't need to jump to conclusions. She needed to get in the air.

"You've practiced on the speeder bike simulator multiple times," said the commander who taught Small Craft Flight. The several dozen pilots in Ciena's section—including her roommates, as well as Thane and his—stood in the craft bay within the enormous structure of the academy. Outside, dusk had fallen and the city lights of Coruscant glittered. "It is the most basic form of low-altitude craft, and therefore the first you should master. Handling the bike should be well within the capacity of every cadet in this class."

Ciena tried to disguise her excitement. She'd been in simulators too long; she was ready to go. And the speeder bikes seemed *so easy*—

As if he'd heard her, the commander continued, "In order to ensure that your first flight is both memorable and challenging, we've made it a competition. A race."

"Is there a prize?" called Nash Windrider, which made people laugh. Unlike most instructors, the flight commander allowed some levity from time to time. He said it bolstered "martial spirit," which they were supposed to cultivate.

The flight commander even smiled slightly as he replied, "Indeed, Cadet Windrider, but you should learn the task before you presume to perform it." A hologram rose from the center of the bay, showing a three-dimensional map of the area surrounding the academy. Small, brightly colored points blinked in ten different places, from all the way down at ground level up to the Sky Loop. "What you see signposted here are Reitgen Hoops, each big enough for a single speeder bike to easily pass through. We've cleared the surrounding airspace, so you may choose your individual course and need only account for your classmates' vehicles."

Farthest first, Ciena immediately decided. *Most people will get too caught up in trying to reach the nearest hoop, so you'll have a clear course. Then you slip through the others on your way back here.*

The commander concluded, "The first to fly through all ten hoops will be given fifty points in the rankings."

A shiver of disbelief and anticipation swept through the cadets. Fifty points! That was better than acing two or even three exams. Cadets in ranking trouble knew this could pull them back from the brink. Meanwhile, Ciena could only think, *This would do it. This would make me number one, far ahead of anybody else.*

"Eager, are you?" the commander said. "Then get to your craft and await the signal!"

Ciena dashed for her speeder bike and powered up. As the engines hummed to life, she checked the chinstrap of her dark gray helmet and the armor strapped around her forearms, calves, and thighs. Most important was the repulsor belt, which would activate if she fell from the bike. But she didn't intend to fall.

This is going to be mine, she told herself as she took hold of the handlebars and felt the controls through her textured gloves. The engine beneath her vibrated with what she imagined was excitement, as if it were a spirited beast instead of a mere machine.

The lights overhead shifted, turning slowly brighter. She held her breath. Then came the brilliant flash that meant *go.*

Ciena gunned it as they all flew out in a rush, like a swarm of Dardanellian locusts—but as soon as she was free from the building, she pulled back, tempering her speed so as few people as possible would see her flight path and realize her plan. While most of the other speeder bikes rushed toward the nearest hoop, Ciena turned and spun away, heading toward the farthest target at top speed.

She wasn't completely alone, though. Maybe a half dozen other cadets had adopted this strategy—and of course one of them was Thane. As he leaned down over his handlebars, he caught her looking at him and grinned before swerving away.

Ciena laughed out loud. They were back to normal, and this was going to be *fun.*

The tricky thing about the course wasn't handling

the speeder bike, a light craft that responded well to its pilot's movements. Instead the challenge came from choosing the best flight path. For adequate balance, speeder bikes needed to be within twenty meters of the ground, or at least a flat surface such as a larger craft, a machine—or a building. She slid over to the nearest mammoth structure and balanced her bike against its shiny surface, flying perpendicular to the ground at such speed that gravity no longer seemed to apply. Glowing windows rushed by "beneath" her with a ripple like sunlight on water.

Shift! Ciena put the speeder bike in a spiral, zooming upward and over the tunnel-laced chasm below—until she was within a few meters of another, taller building, which she used as her new balance. That let her fly higher, faster, the wind stinging her face. *Thank goodness for the goggles,* she thought—

—then cursed mentally as she saw another bike beside her, which of course was Thane's.

He shouted at her, voice only barely audible over the rushing air and humming engines: "This is going to be tight!"

"Too tight for you!" she shouted, then laughed as she took the top edge of the building at a sharp angle. The first hoop glowed in front of her, brilliant yellow, levitating slightly above the roof. Ciena accelerated, aimed straight for the center of the hoop—and then gasped as her bike and Thane's bumped.

He wouldn't have meant to do that. Neither had she. They had each been so intensely focused on the goal that they'd forgotten to watch each other. The bump alone wasn't a big deal—speeder bikes were built to take that kind of punishment and worse—but to her horror, Ciena realized the front directional vanes of their bikes were locked together.

"Pull!" Thane shouted, desperately jerking his bike to the right. She tried to yank left, but all they managed to do was wobble. Their speeder bikes couldn't be separated in flight. They'd have to stop, land, and forfeit.

Ciena gasped as she realized how close they were to the Reitgen Hoop. Too close to swerve away—they were on the verge of a crash even the repulsor field couldn't save them from.

Instinctively, she aimed for the very center of the hoop; next to her, Thane did the exact same thing, at the exact same moment. They whooshed through the hoop with less than half a meter on either side of them.

Her first thought was that they were lucky to be alive. But then she realized that, while locked directional vanes made steering difficult, balance and speed were unaffected.

If she'd gotten into this situation with any other cadet, Ciena would have powered down and forced the forfeit. With Thane, though—she knew what a good pilot he was, understood how he flew. Did they dare try it?

She shouted, "Let's do this thing!"

"What, like *this*?" Thane put one hand near the power controls, but then paused as the idea sank in. Once again she saw him grin. "All right, here we go!"

Ciena plunged toward the next hoop, just as Thane did. They accelerated at the same time, simultaneously shifted direction and pitch. If they'd practiced this together, they couldn't have done it any more efficiently. The two speeder bikes seemed to have become one.

The second hoop demanded that they slide through narrow passages between buildings that would've been a tight fit for one speeder bike, much less two. Together they tilted so that their bikes balanced against the left building (how had they both known it should be the left?), swooshing past one fellow cadet who had temporarily pulled ahead, and then dived toward the glowing yellow circle that marked their goal.

Together Ciena and Thane took the third hoop, down almost on the ground, wove through a web of walkway arches to the fourth hoop, dashed through the trenches of a spiral skyscraper to reach the fifth. Each goal seemed more impossible than the last, and yet the flying only became easier, because she and Thane *had this.*

She realized only two people who had spent years learning to fly together could ever coordinate so smoothly. The way she responded to Thane's piloting—the way he responded to hers—it didn't require thought. It was instinct, a part of them both. Those countless days soaring through the valleys of Jelucan had taught them to understand each other without words.

The bonds they'd formed during those years weren't the kind that faded away.

When they dipped through the tenth hoop at the top of the academy itself, she and Thane immediately banked and accelerated straight down the wall of the building. Ciena glanced over her shoulder and saw the blinking lights of other cadets' bikes swirling toward the bay like clouds of fireflies. They were close—but not close enough. Thane and Ciena plunged back into the docking bay first, a full forty seconds ahead of their closest competitor.

Landing the conjoined bikes turned out to be the toughest part. As they wobbled to the ground, other speeder bikes starting to swoosh in behind and beside them, they heard Ved Foslo shout, "That's a disqualification!"

"It is not!" Ciena shot back, removing her helmet and pushing her goggles up on her forehead. "There weren't any rules about what would happen if two bikes locked together!"

"Flying in that condition would have been more difficult, rather than easier," pointed out Jude, still in her full flight gear. She had been even closer behind them than Ved. "Therefore it seems unfair to penalize them."

Ved's deep golden complexion was now flushed with anger. "We're supposed to be learning how to properly fly a speeder bike. That's not exactly correct procedure, is it?"

"Situations like that can happen in battle. Shouldn't we know how to deal with them?" Ciena felt almost sick. She hadn't broken a rule—or hadn't meant to, at any rate—and here was Ved Foslo questioning her honor. Was he accusing her of doing this on purpose? Of cheating?

A small crowd had gathered by then, and the cadets parted to allow the instructor to walk closer. He said only, "That was—novel."

Thane leaned against his bike as if he were completely at ease. "I just want to point out, you never said only one person could win. You said the fifty points went to 'the first' to finish. We finished first together."

"Finding loopholes in instructions from superior officers? That's a bad habit, Kyrell." Slowly, the commander shook his head as if in exasperation. "But far be it from me to penalize flying of that quality. You shared the challenge, so you'll split the prize. Twenty-five points each to Ree and Kyrell."

Ved Foslo threw his helmet down in disgust, but most of the cadets cheered. Thane took Ciena's hand and held it high. She laughed from pure exhilaration.

First in the class. I made it all the way to the Royal Academy of Coruscant and I'm actually first in my class! Twenty-five points was enough for that. But Ciena caught herself then, realizing she was probably tied with Thane for the honor.

She found she didn't mind sharing. Not with him.

Thane let their hands fall—but he didn't let go right away.

Ciena didn't let go, either.

CHAPTER FIVE

NOTHING CHANGED UNTIL the laser cannon project a few months later.

Even the best battle plans put soldiers at risk, and at any time you could find yourself separated and in danger, your squadron pinned down or otherwise unable to help you. Your blaster could be damaged and, at any rate, couldn't defend you from an enemy ship on its own. If you quickly constructed a larger weapon, however, you could continue the fight alone—perhaps long enough to be rescued but certainly long enough to make your enemy pay. A laser cannon could be built out of standard Imperial-issue parts, if you knew how.

Thane disliked mechanical work; flying and shooting were more his speed. But he was determined to ace this project. He and Ciena had held on to their top rankings so far; the only question remaining was which of them would finish the term at number one. If Ciena beat him, he'd be the first to congratulate her . . . but hopefully she'd be the first to congratulate *him*.

"Look at that grin," said Nash, who lay under his own laser cannon in progress, a couple of meters over in the enormous repair bay. "Thinking about our off day? Ready to explore the Coruscant nightlife?"

From his place at the bench, Thane shrugged without looking away from the stormtrooper helmet he was currently cannibalizing for its power cell. "I'm working on my cannon, like you ought to be. Come on, Nash, focus."

"How can I focus when we have a chance to go to clubs, cantinas, and a hundred other places where we'll finally have a chance to meet girls?" Nash protested. "Girls who aren't forbidden like our fellow cadets. Touchable girls. Kissable girls."

"I understand, okay? But I'm trying to concentrate here so I can keep my ranking. Plenty of people have put in extra time on this." Thane gestured to the rest of the repair bay for emphasis.

A couple dozen other laser cannons sat all around them, protected by the small sparkling hemispheres of low-charge force fields. Every single one of those machines might have been repaired more ingeniously than his own, with more inspired use of random spare parts that might be found in alien spaceports. Every single one of them counted as competition.

Nash slid away from his own repair table, the better to give Thane a withering look. "We've been working for a couple of hours now. We can't talk about the one day of real fun we'll get before the next term starts?"

"I guess."

"You sounded excited enough the other day when Ved told us the best clubs to visit."

"I was. I mean, I am. I'm excited, definitely."

At this, Nash stood up and faced Thane across the array of spare parts spread across the worktable. "And yet you don't *seem* excited—not about meeting girls, at least. That means one of two things. Either you're interested in men instead—which I doubt, given your reaction to that risqué holo of Ved's—"

The curse of fair skin was that even the faintest blush stood out. Thane tried to pretend he was still looking at the stormtrooper helmet.

"—or there's a girl you're already interested in. A girl you already know." Nash leaned on the table, resting his chin on his hands, eyes wide open in mock innocence. "Could this girl's name possibly rhyme with the syllables *lie-henna see*?"

"It's not like that between us," Thane insisted. "It never has been."

Nash's grin had turned wicked. "But I suspect it will be."

The subject irritated Thane more than it should have. He still wasn't sure what to make of the way his relationship with Ciena was changing, and he didn't want Nash sticking his long nose into it. Besides, even if Nash meant well, his insinuating tone reminded Thane too much of the way Dalven had teased him about there being only one thing he could want from a girl of the valleys.

Talking about Ciena that way disrespected her. And made Thane think too much about things he couldn't even begin to change until graduation.

"We take these matters more seriously on Jelucan than most people do," he said, truthfully enough. "Speculating is . . . improper."

"This, from the man who watched that holo five times!" Nash laughed out loud. "Besides, you're supposed to stop being Jelucani and start being a citizen of the Empire, remember? And speculating is *fun*."

"I need you to listen to me." Thane put down his tools and looked Nash squarely in the face. "This subject is permanently closed. There's nothing going on between me and Ciena. We're just—"

"—good friends," Ciena said as she walked away from the martial arts room, every muscle aching. "Always have been, always will be. That's all there is to it."

Jude nodded her approval, then winced; probably her head was still hurting from the last time Kendy had slammed her into the mat. "Very wise of you. Given the prohibition on dating fellow cadets, neither you nor Thane would want to compromise your careers by violating such an important rule."

Kendy—beaming, sweaty, and triumphant—just laughed at them both. "I'd break the rules for a guy who looks that good."

For a moment, Ciena felt a twinge of jealousy. That was not at all how she wanted to feel when it came to Thane—and yet it burned within her, an ember that refused to go dark.

But Kendy was already moving on. "So, what are we going to do with our free day?"

"Personally, I don't care," Ciena said, "as long as it involves eating *real food*."

On Imperial ships, officers were encouraged to drink nutritive beverages instead of consuming food; it was more efficient in terms of both ship resources and officer time, and the medics insisted the nutritives were healthier, too. They didn't taste bad—but they definitely didn't taste *good*. The academy mess served the nutritives, and like most students, Ciena had dutifully started getting used to them. But as long as she could enjoy some real, true, delicious food without guilt, she intended to indulge.

"I believe we will be able to find acceptable meals at virtually any potential destination," Jude said, then hesitated before making her suggestion. "Would anyone else be interested in visiting the Museum of Multispecies Sciences?"

Kendy groaned, but Ciena shot her a look. Their third roommate was soft-spoken, patient, and accommodating; she deserved to get her way once in a while. "Maybe we could go to the museum first thing in the morning. But in the afternoon, I'd rather do something less"—*completely boring?*—"cerebral. We study so hard here already, you know? I'd like to try something like, maybe, sea diving."

"Diving. *Yes.*" Immediately, Kendy became excited. As a native of the tropical world of Iloh, she'd begun swimming even before she could walk. "I can't believe it's been six months since I've been in the water! And no, Jude, swimming laps in the wave pool doesn't count."

Jude didn't respond to that as they stepped into the lift. Already she was deep in thought. "Diving would be a fascinating challenge. Bespin is a gas giant, which means we have no oceans or lakes. Swimming pools are rare luxuries. Therefore my experience in the water is limited. The chance to expand my skills and observe marine life would be extremely pleasant."

As the lift settled onto their floor, Ciena had to shake her head and smile. "Everything's a science project to you, Jude."

"Science is the study of the entire material universe. Therefore everything *is* science—whether you see it or not." Only the faintest smile on Jude's thin lips revealed that she was teasing them back.

Ciena didn't mention what they might do that night. Inside she hoped they'd be celebrating her finishing the term as number one in the class, but even saying that out loud sounded prideful. The only other possible candidate for number one was of course Thane—and if he won, she thought she could be happy for him.

Maybe celebrate with him, toasting his success. She'd rather he toasted hers instead, but . . .

"Ciena?" Kendy shot her a look as they walked toward their room. "Your brain was in orbit for a second there."

"Sorry. I think my head's still scrambled from that time you flipped me." Ciena began untying the belt of her martial arts gear as the door swished open for them. "Think you could show me how that's done?"

"No way," Kendy said with a laugh. "It's one of the only things I'm better at than you."

Next morning came the inspection of the laser cannons.

Ciena stood at attention before her cannon, which she'd assembled to perfection. She'd made a point of using the most ungainly salvage parts possible so the instructors would see that she could build one under even the most unfavorable conditions. Her gut told her Thane might not push as hard to make his own task more difficult. If she could gain an edge anywhere, that was it.

Commander Harn walked along the rows of laser cannons, each one matched with a cadet at full attention. Although the repair bay was by its nature a place to work hard and get dirty, the gray rubberized floor and walls remained unstained by grease or scorch marks. Imperial discipline demanded perfect cleanliness, the erasure of every task as soon as it was done. Only Cadet Windrider's cannon displayed any smudges whatsoever—as usual.

Harn nodded approval as Kendy's cannon powered up. He opened her control panel, then nodded in satisfaction at her choices of new parts. He didn't smile, though, not then or during the next several inspections—though he did murmur, "Innovative," when he looked over Ved's work. That made Ved smile so smugly that Ciena wanted to groan.

She awaited her turn, started her engine, and watched as Harn checked the efficiency ratings and overall power. Although he did not speak, his eyes met hers as if he were assessing her anew—and well. She'd impressed him. Somehow she managed to keep a straight face, even when Kendy mouthed, *Way to go,* over the commander's shoulder.

When Harn looked over Thane's cannon and reached for the starter, Ciena held her breath—

—but the laser cannon didn't power up.

At all.

The color drained from Thane's face. Ciena didn't feel so good herself. She'd wanted to beat him but not to see him fail completely.

How is that even possible? she thought, gripping her hands together more tightly behind her back. *Thane's not an instinctive mechanic, but he works hard and he's thorough, and he would have checked his cannon dozens of times. This can't be happening.*

"This is unlike you, Kyrell," said Harn as he made

a notation on the tablet he carried in one hand. "Let's see where you went wrong."

Harn flipped open the control panel of Thane's laser cannon, then froze, his sharp features hardening into a look of displeasure, even anger.

Whatever it was, Thane saw it, too, and it made him swear out loud—right there, standing at attention, a commander right in front of him. A few people gasped.

But Harn didn't reprimand Thane. Instead, with a gesture, Harn released everyone from attention. Cadets crowded close, blocking Ciena's view at first, but she pushed through until she could see inside the open panel of Thane's cannon and realized just why everyone had begun muttering and looking around suspiciously.

The wires inside had been cut. Straight, clean—the marks made it clear that this wasn't bad wiring or an accident. Someone had done it on purpose.

Sabotage. Academy competition could be cutthroat, but up until then everyone had apparently played fair. A chill ran along Ciena's spine at the thought of it. How could anyone, much less an Imperial cadet, be so devoid of honor? She was nearly as offended at the thought as she was sorry for Thane.

"We'll solve this quickly enough," Harn promised,

his voice sharp and cold as an ice pick. "Whoever thought to improve class rankings through such a stunt will have cause for regret." He strode toward the main door panel, pressed his hand to it, and said, "How many cadets had access to this room, alone, between Cadet Kyrell's last visit and this inspection?"

The flat monotone of a synthesized voice replied, "One."

"And who was that?" Harn barked.

"L-P-eight-eight-eight."

Ciena had misheard the computer. She had to have.

But then the computer continued, finishing its answer: "Cadet Ciena Ree."

"I would never do such a thing," Ciena swore in Commandant Deenlark's office, as she stood at attention before his long obsidian desk. "Not to anyone, but especially not to Thane."

"And why not? He was your only competition for the top rank in the class, yes?"

"But—he's my friend."

"Friendship rarely endures ambition."

Ciena's stomach churned so violently she had to fight not to be sick on the floor. This nightmare had swallowed her whole. Not only had she seen Thane's shocked look of dismay, not only had the entire class glared at her as she was hastily marched out of the repair bay, but also—and worst of all—her honor was in tatters, and she didn't know whether she could salvage it.

What happens if I'm thrown out of the academy? Her thoughts raced wildly while she maintained her rigid posture and best attempt at outward composure. *I'll never become an Imperial officer. Maybe I could still get work as a pilot, but I couldn't return home to Jelucan, not ever. My parents couldn't even allow me in the house without the rest of the kindred shunning us.*

No. She couldn't put her mother and father through that. If she were expelled, Ciena would have to travel to some completely unknown planet and start over, completely alone.

The doors of Deenlark's office slid open, and the commandant barked, "We're still dealing with this situation."

"Sir. Yes, sir." Harn quickly stood at attention. "But another cadet has stepped forward with critical information."

The mixture of terror and hope flooding through her made Ciena unable to speak, even when Jude walked through the door, a tablet in her hands. Once Commandant Deenlark motioned impatiently for Jude to begin, she spoke as calmly and evenly as if she were reading a list of machine parts. "Sir. Cadet Jude Edivon of Bespin, T-I-eight-zero-three, reporting in. A thorough review of the data reveals that at the time Cadet Ree supposedly entered the repair bay to tamper with Cadet Kyrell's ship, she was in fact with me and her other roommate, Cadet Idele, in our bunk. I've pulled up data logs that show her leaving the martial arts arena, entering the lift, and coming into our room, and there is no correlating record of her departure."

Ciena felt almost faint with relief, but Deenlark continued to frown. "Data logs can themselves be tampered with, Cadet Edivon."

Jude nodded. "It is my belief that someone not only sabotaged Cadet Kyrell's ship but also the repair bay computer, in order to make it look as though Cadet Ree was the one responsible. In short, sir, I believe she was framed."

"Your beliefs are meaningless without evidence, Cadet Edivon," said the commandant. Ciena didn't dare hope that Jude and Kendy's testimony on its own could clear her. If so, wouldn't he have said so already?

"Sir—I hesitate to name the person who seems to be responsible for this sabotage, because while the data is clear, it is not absolute proof." Jude's fingers tightened around the tablet, as if she were afraid the information would be snatched from her.

Why are you holding back? Ciena wanted to shout. *Who did this to me?*

Commandant Deenlark stood up, and he was tall enough to tower over even the willowy Jude. "Report your findings."

Jude gave Ciena an apologetic glance. "Sir, it appears that the person responsible for framing Cadet Ree was . . . Cadet Thane Kyrell himself."

No. Ciena refused to believe that. There had to be another answer; Jude must have misunderstood the data.

But nobody was better at getting into the inner workings of computers than Jude. Thane was the only other competitor for the top slot, and mechanical repair was one of his main weaknesses. If he hadn't done well on the project and had feared he would fail—he could have cut the wires of his own machine to disguise his inability to repair it. By framing Ciena for the sabotage, he would not only avoid being marked down for failing the project but also drag her down so far she'd never be number one in the class.

This isn't as simple as class rank, though. This could get me expelled! Thane wouldn't do that to me, not ever.

And yet Jude stood there with the proof glowing on the datapad in her hands.

CHAPTER SIX

"WHAT DID THE commandant say?" Nash asked Thane.

"Just to come to the office." Thane resealed his uniform jacket, making himself ready for the meeting.

"Do you think he'll offer you another chance at the laser cannon?" Ved lay back on his bunk, hardly even pretending to be concerned about what happened to Thane's class rank.

At the moment, Thane cared about his rank even less than Ved did. "I think he's going to tell me what really happened."

Nash raised an eyebrow. "You still think Ciena didn't screw with your engine? Even though there's proof?"

"It's not like her," Thane said shortly as he walked toward the door.

He wasn't 100 percent sure Ciena was innocent—the data had pointed to her, and Thane had to admit data within the academy computers was difficult to falsify. However, he felt at least 95 percent sure. Not only did Thane trust her, he understood what kind of person she was and where she came from. Sure, plenty of academy cadets would cheat to get ahead. But Ciena, a girl of the Jelucani valleys—she would die before doing anything dishonorable. Surely she would never betray anyone, much less him. They meant too much to each other for that.

Still, he felt that five percent uncertainty, and he'd never doubted Ciena before, even for a second.

When Thane walked into Commandant Deenlark's office, he was surprised to see Ciena standing there at full attention. At first he was glad—*good, we can smooth this over and move on*—and then he realized that she refused to meet his eyes. Was that out of discipline or guilt?

"Cadet Kyrell. Cadet Ree. We have a conundrum on our hands." The commandant never rose from his chair as he studied them standing side by side, rigid and correct. "The first layer of data says that Cadet Ree is the only possible culprit for the tampering discovered today. However, the second layer of data suggests that Cadet Kyrell tampered with his laser cannon himself and framed Cadet Ree for the deed."

Thane had not known you could feel the blood drain from your face. It was like going numb from cold. "Sir! I absolutely did not—I would never—"

"Spare me your protestations, Cadet Kyrell." By then Deenlark seemed more bored than anything else. "I have consulted with our specialists, who inform me that either layer of data could be the falsified one. One of you attempted to sabotage the other, and covered your tracks—not well enough to hide completely but enough that we can never be certain which of you is responsible and which is innocent. Therefore we have no other recourse but to punish you both."

Good pilot though he was, Thane had occasionally "crashed" a flight simulator. As the screens had showed him the images of flames and a planetary surface rushing up to smash him to atoms, he'd wondered what it would feel like to crash and burn for real.

Probably it was something like this.

Commandant Deenlark smiled thinly. "You have both failed the laser cannon assignment. Your course rankings will reflect this."

Their ranks were high enough that even a failure of that scale wouldn't take them down further than the second quartile. Still, it stung.

"Normally," the commandant continued, "a violation of the honor code would call for disciplinary hearings and potential expulsion. As we cannot get any closer to the truth, however, this would prove useless. Although I have punished you both, I am not willing to expel two gifted pilots based on such murky information. You will both continue on as cadets. Rest assured, however—if any similar incident arises during your time at the academy, for either or both of you, expulsion will be immediate and permanent. Do you understand?"

"Yes, sir," Thane and Ciena said in unison. Her voice sounded as hollow as his.

They walked out of Deenlark's office suite in silence. From there—one of the top floors of the academy building—the view through the green-tinted windows showed what seemed to be half of Coruscant. A few benches and chairs were located there for junior officers, students, and visitors, so that when they saw the city spread before them, they would recognize the commandant's power. No one was visiting this evening, however; Thane and Ciena were alone.

As if they had rehearsed in advance, they both walked to the windows before they turned to each other. When their eyes met, she exhaled in the deepest relief. "You didn't do it."

"Neither did you." He ought to have known that all along. They smiled at each other, faith restored—but the problem wasn't solved. Thane sagged back against one of the metal columns between the windows. "So who the hell did?"

Ciena scowled. "Somebody who wanted top marks on the project. Probably that snake Ved Foslo."

"I'm not as sure about that. Ved's good with mechanical stuff; he would have placed in the top echelon even without cheating. So why bother? Besides, he's a stickler for rules, even when they work against him."

"So who would frame us both, and try to make us hate each other?" Her face looked stricken. "Sabotaging the cannon and the data wasn't just scheming to get ahead. Someone wanted to hurt us."

Who in their class had a grudge against them both? Nobody personally hated them—as far as Thane knew, which maybe wasn't far enough. "It has to be because we're both at the top of the class."

Ciena groaned. "You mean we *were*. This knocks us so far down—"

"Only for now." He realized he'd balled his hands into fists. "We have to figure out who really did this. Once we turn that person in, we'll get our rankings back and get the jerk thrown out."

"Nobody who would do something like this deserves to be an Imperial officer," she said, lifting her chin. "You're right. We get to the truth, and then we make the guilty party pay."

Thane nodded. Outside, ships and hoverbikes darted through the misty sunset of the city. "Okay, how do we begin?"

Jude agreed to help them, though as they sat at one of the spare data stations later that night, she warned, "My earlier analysis wrongly implicated Thane. Therefore my skills must be called into question."

"Don't say that." Ciena put one hand on her friend's shoulder. "You found the wrong solution because someone set you up to find it. Now that you know you need to dig deeper, I bet you'll get the answer in no time. Right, Thane?" She shot him a look and he nodded, as if he hadn't argued the exact same thing about Jude's abilities outside the commandant's office when Ciena first suggested they try this.

But she believed in her friend. If they were going to find the truth, Jude would be their best guide.

Jude worked at her terminal for several minutes while no one spoke, or hardly even moved. The only sound in the enormous data analysis room was the soft tapping of Jude's fingers on the controls; the only light came from the dozens of terminals vacant at that late hour, all of them glowing faintly blue. Ciena glanced over at Thane once to find him already looking at her. Once their eyes met, he turned his head, abashed.

For some reason, that made her cheeks grow hot.

With determination, she focused her attention on figuring out who the most likely culprits could be. Anyone might have wanted to knock them lower in the rankings. But attempting to pit them against each other—that was someone aiming to inflict pain.

We outsmarted them, though. Her heart swelled with pride, and other emotions harder to name, as she glanced sideways at Thane again. *It takes more than that to break us apart.*

"Hmmm." Jude frowned, wrinkling her long freckled nose. "The paths taken by the saboteur are quite circuitous. I traced the information about Thane and—it's as if they wanted to make it look like a higher official here at the academy was responsible."

Ciena had to shake her head. "Lie after lie after lie. When I find out who did this, I'm going to ask them why they ever thought they'd be able to frame *an instructor* and get away with it."

"Not an instructor. Someone in the Office of Student Outcomes," Jude clarified.

So what? An instructor, an administration official,

whoever—it was still a stupid move. But Thane straightened in his chair, realization dawning on his face. "Do you guys know what the Office of Student Outcomes does?"

Ciena had never even heard of it. Jude replied, "They oversee student performance and suggest methods for instructors to use in order to provide maximum improvement." Then she added, with a shrug, "But I have no idea precisely how they accomplish that."

"Apparently they do it by screwing with our minds!" Thane pushed himself back from the data terminal, as angry as Ciena had ever seen him.

Someone needed to remain rational. "Thane," she said, "think about what you're saying. Why would anyone on the academy staff want to set us up?"

"Because they don't want two cadets from a backwater world to beat all the military brats. Because General Foslo or Admiral Jasten or someone like that told them to knock us down so their kid could be number one." Thane got to his feet, expression dark.

Even though she understood why Thane would be on edge, Ciena felt annoyed. "Why are you turning this into some big conspiracy theory?"

Jude, who had been sitting silently at her terminal, chimed in: "It *is* a conspiracy of some sort. The only question is who should be held responsible."

"Nobody would be stupid enough to set up an official at the academy," Thane ranted. "Nobody smart enough to set this up in the first place, anyway. So that means the Student Outcomes people have to have done it."

"You can't be serious." Cold fear began to pool inside her; Thane was edging past understandable anger into dangerous territory. You did *not* question the methods of the academy.

"Yeah, I'm serious. They took a bribe or something. How many credits do you think it costs to buy your kid the top rank in the class? However much that is, it's as much as the academy thinks we're worth."

"You realize you're making a criminal allegation, don't you?" Ciena retorted.

He shot back, "What, are you going to report me?"

Jude sat very still at her terminal, her eyes moving back and forth between them as they argued. Ciena knew they ought to tone it down at least until they were alone, but she was too angry to do that, and so was Thane. "I'm not going to report you. But you need to remember why we're here, and who we serve."

"You think everything the academy and the Empire do is perfect!"

"And you think every authority figure is evil like your father!"

Thane's eyes went wide, and she knew she'd wounded him. He stepped toward her. "Don't *ever* bring my father up to me again. It's none of your business. Got that?"

He'd never told her anything in his life was none of her business. They knew everything about each other; they kept no secrets. Now Thane had put up a barrier where there had never been one before, a wall of stone, and Ciena felt like she'd just slammed into it at top speed.

"You realize we have to confront them about this," he continued, because apparently he was so angry he'd lost his mind.

"You want us to accuse academy officials of dishonesty?"

"Yes! I want them to admit what they've done and take it back! That's our only chance at getting our ranks reinstated—"

"They're not going to reinstate us after something like that! They'd expel us so fast we wouldn't even have time to pack our bags."

"You won't even *try*? You'd rather lie down in the dirt than admit your precious teachers could do something wrong?"

Ciena wanted to shake him. "We would only make things worse, Thane."

"So you want me to just take it. Just accept that my whole first term here at the academy was a waste."

As if everything they'd learned, done, and seen was wasted just because of their stupid course rankings. Infuriated, she shot back, "Yes, I do! You need to let go, learn to deal, and *grow up*."

He stared at her, openmouthed, with nothing but scorn in his eyes, then said, "I never thought you were a coward."

That stung. "I never thought you were unfit for Imperial service. Now, though? I have to wonder."

"Spare me your analysis, okay? We're done here."

With that he turned to walk out. Ciena both wanted to be rid of him and didn't want to leave things like this. So she called, "Don't you want to see what else Jude digs up?"

"She's not going to dig up anything else. We have our answer. You're just too naive to believe it." Thane's voice dripped with contempt. It scoured her raw. She said nothing more as he stalked out.

It felt as if a bomb had gone off. Ciena sensed this incident had only been the trigger—that some drastic change had been waiting to happen between them for a long time. But she'd never dreamed it would lead to a confrontation so ugly. A crevasse had opened in their friendship, and Thane stood on the other side.

No longer could she believe he loved the Empire as she did; no longer could she trust in his understanding and support. Somehow Ciena already knew things between them would never be the same.

"Well." Jude sounded awkward. "So. I did keep looking, and it seems like the trail ends at Student Outcomes. That doesn't mean they're guilty—the office may only have been a convenient rerouting for the original sabotage of the data records. And of course the rest of the repair-bay info has been erased. I'm afraid my search ends here."

Ciena nodded. The data terminals before her blurred and she wiped away hot tears with the heel of her hand.

Jude continued, "We should focus our efforts on improving your class rank in future, so you can make up for this loss—" Suddenly, she stood up, less prim than she'd ever been before, and hugged Ciena tightly. Then it was finally all right for Ciena to cry.

CHAPTER SEVEN

FOR THE ACADEMY cadets, the next two and a half years seemed both to last forever and to rush by in a blur. As the exams grew more demanding, the flying more difficult, and the discipline more exacting, the bunks began to empty out. The lineups tightened formation again and again. The corridors seemed less crowded as more and more students flunked out or simply gave up.

Both Thane Kyrell and Ciena Ree were too tough for that. They still both aimed for the top slot in the class, every term—which meant they clashed with each other time and time again.

In Core Worlds Classical Culture: "Who here can tell me which opera the composer Igern is best known for?"

Ciena's hand shot up, and when the professor nodded at her, she answered, "*Chalice and Altar.*"

"Very good, Cadet Ree. And can you tell me the themes for which this opera is famed?"

Uh-oh. She could hum several melodies from *Chalice and Altar,* but she didn't enjoy opera music. That made it difficult for her to connect music to plot.

After only a moment's pause, the professor turned away. "Memorizing by rote, Cadet Ree? Unfortunate. Does anyone else know?"

The sound of Thane's voice from behind her pierced her like a knife between the shoulder blades. He said, "The opera deals with the morality of self-sacrifice and the repression of desire."

"Excellent, Cadet Kyrell."

It was like Ciena could feel Thane's smug smile burning through her back. She gritted her teeth and resolved to listen to opera every single night until the next Culture exam. Kendy and Jude could just deal with it.

In Destroyer-Level Craft Operations: "All other efforts have failed," intoned the professor from the mock captain's chair of the Star Destroyer simulator. "Our vessel has been boarded, battles rage on every level, and we cannot let our enemies take the ship.

Therefore we must self-destruct. Which of the three methods of self-destruct should we choose?"

Thane swiveled around in his console chair. "We should set the automatic self-destruct, using the codes given to the three top officers. The automatic gives us the longest time to detonation, which means more of our troops will be able to make it to escape pods."

The professor steepled his hands in front of him. "An interesting choice. Does anyone see any problems with Cadet Kyrell's scenario?"

Ciena lifted her head from her viewscreen. "Yes, sir. If the ship has been so thoroughly infiltrated by the enemy, there is no guarantee that the three top officers will all be on the bridge, or even alive. Also, the extra time to detonation will only give our enemies a greater chance to escape, as well."

"Very good, Cadet Ree. What would you suggest instead?"

"Not the core engine method, which would require us to have easy access to the engine room—again, not guaranteed during intraship combat. Instead we should go for the captain's-word method. The captain signals for all to abandon ship, seals herself on the bridge with a specific password or phrase known only to her, and remains within to fire weapons at enemy vessels and provide cover for escape pods. She then pilots the ship into the nearest planetary object, star, or singularity." Ciena lifted her chin in thinly concealed pride.

"That means the captain must die with her ship," the instructor said.

"Yes, sir," Ciena replied. "But all Imperial officers should be prepared to sacrifice their lives to do their duty."

"Excellent, Cadet Ree." The instructor smiled at her. That old creep never smiled at anybody. "Your answer is the one I find ideal in a tactical sense—and a moral sense, as well."

Thane clenched his hands around the edges of the control panel to keep himself from making a gesture recognized on most worlds as extremely rude.

Moral. What was moral about blowing yourself up, when you could just as easily escape with your life and come back to fight another day? Thane fumed over that the rest of the afternoon, including in Hand-to-Hand Combat, where his temper fueled his punches until he hit Ved too hard. That meant he not only got a demerit but also had to promise Ved all his dessert credits for a week to make amends.

Screwing up in Hand-to-Hand was his own fault, and Thane knew it. But he couldn't help feeling like it was yet another mess he'd gotten into because of Ciena.

Maybe she still bought in to the idea of the Empire as the perfect state, every single planet's population singing its praises nonstop. Thane had learned better. Although the official information channels spoke of building projects, successful trade negotiations, and endless economic prosperity, he knew that shine was mostly gloss. The Empire built new bases to solidify its control. Its "trade negotiations" always seemed to result in the Empire's getting everything it wanted on terms that couldn't possibly have benefited the planet in question. And as for the mood of the populace, even the official information channels had begun spitting venom about a small group of terrorists who plotted evil and called themselves rebels.

Thane had nothing but contempt for terrorists, but he also understood that such dissident factions rarely came out of nowhere. They were a reaction to the Empire's increasing control—an overreaction, definitely, but proof that not everybody accepted the Emperor's rule.

Despite his disenchantment, Thane had no plans to leave Imperial service. How else would he get to fly the greatest ships in the galaxy? Smaller employers could also be corrupt, and the work would be less certain. With the Imperial fleet, Thane was guaranteed decent pay, access to top-of-the-line ships, and regular promotions. Best of all, he'd never have to live on Jelucan again.

So it was without envy that he saw Ciena Ree assigned to command track. His own track—elite flight—suited him far better. He even welcomed the fact that he and Ciena shared fewer classes after they divided into tracks. Thane felt relieved that he didn't have to see her every day any longer. Sometimes even looking at her hurt—

No. It irritated him. Angered him. It didn't *hurt*.

Or so he told himself. All Thane knew was that since their rift over the fake sabotage incident more than two years prior, he and Ciena had never been able to patch things up completely. The humiliation he'd felt when she brought up his father—that she would suggest *anything* he did came from his father—it still stung every time he saw Jude Edivon. (Jude had always been extra nice to him since that day, which only made things worse.) Ciena had stopped confiding in him, which felt cold and strange; he wondered if she'd become so fanatical about her Imperial duty that she took his distrust of the academy's methods as a personal insult. How stupid would that be? Nor could he forget that she'd refused to challenge their superior officers, leaving his class rank severely damaged.

It wasn't as if he hated Ciena or anything, and he didn't think she hated him, either. But neither of them cheered for the other in races any longer, or offered congratulations after a tournament win. They didn't hang out during the scant free time academy rigor allowed.

But occasionally—at the least convenient moments— the enduring connection between them would make itself known. Ashes would become embers.

One day, only a few months before graduation, Thane headed back to the uniform dispensary, a trip he'd made at least once each term. He'd finally stopped growing, which was a relief, because he topped out as the third-tallest member of their class, only a hair beneath Nash. But his body was now adding muscle to bone, broadening his chest and shoulders, which meant new uniform jackets. He was only thinking how tight and uncomfortable his current jacket was when he turned the corner and saw Ciena standing farther down the corridor, still in her loose black shorts and gray tank from E&A class. Instead of her usual proud bearing, she leaned against the wall and held one hand to her face. Even without glimpsing her expression, Thane knew she was upset.

In that instant, he suddenly remembered something

he hadn't thought of in years—the day he'd met Ciena so long before. When the other boys had mocked her as she stood in the hangar in her plain brown dress, Thane had thought of her as an autumn leaf, fallen and fragile.

He'd learned Ciena Ree was anything but fragile. Yet he thought of the autumn leaf now.

"Hey," he said. After a moment's hesitation, he stepped toward her. "Are you all right?"

Ciena startled, straightening up as she tried to compose herself. She hadn't been weeping, but Thane could see the glimmer of unshed tears in her eyes. "I'm fine," she said hoarsely. "Thanks."

You checked on her. She's good. Duty done. Get out of here. Thane hesitated, on the verge of turning to go, but then he couldn't. "You don't look fine."

She made a strange sound—half laugh, half sob. "It's stupid."

"What?"

". . . I got a holo from my parents. The muunyak died."

"The one you used to ride up to the Fortress sometimes, when we were little?" Thane had not spoken of the Fortress in years.

Ciena nodded. "Yeah. Him. He was pretty old, and I knew when I came here I'd probably never see him again—but still." She rolled her eyes, mocking her own emotions. "Stupid to get upset, huh?"

"It's not stupid. That muunyak was *great*." Thane had ridden him a couple of times, too. He remembered being a child and sitting on the beast's broad furry back, his arms looped around Ciena's waist, both of them laughing in mingled delight and terror as the muunyak nimbly walked a narrow ridge alongside the mountain.

She smiled. It had been a long time since Thane had seen her smile at him and mean it. "He was, wasn't he?"

"Yeah."

Their eyes met, and for a moment, it was as if the past couple of years had fallen away—

But then Ciena's expression dimmed. Her posture became more rigid, and she said, formally, "Thank you for your concern. If you'll excuse me, I need to change for my Amphibious Battle Tactics study group."

Thane held his hands in front of him, a push-back motion. "You're excused."

She always did that—went cold and shut him out again. He told himself he was used to it, that he'd long since stopped caring. Still, the entire way to the dispensary, Thane couldn't stop thinking of the Fortress they'd

created together and how he used to sit up there, waiting for his one true friend.

He always did that—acted nice just long enough for
Ciena to forget how he'd lashed out at her. She'd start
confiding in him the way she used to, then catch herself as she remembered how thoroughly Thane had
shut her out.

As she sat in her study group, watching holos of real
amphibious invasions from history, Ciena brooded on
that odd, fractured encounter with Thane. She wished
she hadn't gone so cold—but it seemed like every time
she tried to be herself with him, he turned away.

What had she done that was so wrong? He was the
one who had gone crazy after the stupid cannon project
two and a half years before, assuming there was some
mass conspiracy at work. He was the one who would
have dragged them into an administrative hearing
based on no evidence, which would have resulted in
their immediate expulsion. And sometimes he seemed
so offended when she beat him on tests or challenges
that Ciena felt like he couldn't believe that someone
so inferior had bested him. Did he still consider her
nothing but a little valley waif?

Maybe he'd always seen their friendship as an act
of charity. All those practice flights, all those study

sessions with CZ-1—maybe they hadn't shared those experiences as friends; maybe instead they'd been gifts from the rich boy to the little girl he expected to worship him in return.

That was too much, and Ciena knew it. She and Thane had truly been friends and on some level still were—but it was a level she could no longer reach.

Her study group leader kept talking. Ciena sat there, hearing but not listening, remembering the way she and Thane had sat in the Fortress for hours, sharing their secrets and dreaming about the stars.

A few weeks before graduation, the commandant announced that a handful of top cadets would attend a reception and ball at the Imperial Palace. The thought of it took Ciena's breath away. Of course there was little chance the Emperor himself would preside over the gathering. Yet the Imperial Palace was one of the grandest and most elegant structures on the entire planet; apparently it had once been a temple of some kind. Hundreds of senior military officers would be there, not to mention many members of the Imperial Senate. Any cadets invited to a gathering such as that were being noted for more than mere good grades; it was a sign of favor, an investment in those future officers. Their introductions to powerful people in the military and in politics could change the course of their careers.

So when Ciena saw her own name on the list, she felt like cheering out loud. Only much later did she realize who else would be in attendance.

"Thane Kyrell and Ved Foslo," she said, flopping back on her bunk. "Of all the guys in our class, those two had to be invited?"

"Any logical analysis of class performance would suggest them as likely candidates." Jude never looked up from her computer console, her fingers dancing on the screen as she finished her latest Longform Computer Operations project. "Their invitations, like ours, were all but inevitable."

"You're just rubbing it in," Kendy said from her bunk, good-naturedly. This close to graduation—with their future assignments all but guaranteed—a sense of calm had settled over the academy. With the ruthless competition at an end, people could . . . not relax, precisely, but stop worrying about the here and now and start looking avidly toward the future. "Just tell me you're not going to wear your uniforms."

Ciena hesitated. "I—well—dress uniforms are appropriate for all formal occasions."

"However, they are not required at nonmilitary functions such as the ball," Jude said briskly.

"Undoubtedly you wish to wear a dress uniform because you do not have adequate credits for appropriate civilian attire."

Thank goodness her skin tone was dark enough that nobody could see her blush. Ciena tried to sound firm. "The uniform's fine."

Jude sighed as she finally looked up at Ciena. "Your pride is usually a strong motivator, but there are times when it only gets in the way. Please allow me to purchase your attire for the event."

"I couldn't," Ciena protested, hackles rising. Her valley upbringing had taught her to be prouder of her rags than the second-wavers were of their silks—even when she had thought the silks were pretty.

More softly, Jude said, "We're friends. You've helped me tremendously during our time here. My mother holds patents on numerous devices used in Bespin's cloud-mining technology. As such, our personal wealth is more than adequate to our needs. Why shouldn't I get you a dress?"

"My culture doesn't—"

Uncharacteristically, Jude interrupted. "I have a culture, too. We value generosity and the graceful acceptance of gifts."

Ciena searched for the words to object, but—if it was part of Jude's *culture*. "Well . . ."

Jude looked hopeful.

"I don't need to own a dress, but—maybe you could help me rent one?"

So she found herself arriving at the grand ball in the only formal dress she'd ever worn. Surely vanity fueled the happiness bubbling within her, but she couldn't help it. The soft violet-blue fabric sparkled subtly, and both the short cape and the long skirt flowed around her as if in an unseen breeze.

Many of the women in attendance—and not a few of the men—wore finery much grander, such as thickly jeweled bracelets or headbands, or outfits made of embroidered silk and velvet. Yet Ciena knew she looked as elegant as anyone else there. Instead of resorting to tight braids as usual, she'd freed her curls, softening them slightly with light fragrant oil. Kendy had loaned her iridescent combs made of shells from Iloh, to hold her hair back at the temples, and simple pearl earrings. Ciena looked right for the occasion, and yet she also felt like herself—not like an impostor, the way she would have in one of the grand, wide-skirted, elaborate dresses and robes she saw.

"There you are," Jude said. Ciena turned to greet her—then stared.

Since Jude hadn't said a word about her own dress,

Ciena had assumed her friend's practicality would govern her choice of gown: something gray or ivory, perhaps, simply tailored, appropriate for all occasions. Instead, Jude stood there in tight-fitting orange fabric—at least, apart from a few strategic cutouts that showed her flat belly and willowy back. Her military-short hair had been gelled into spikes, and her gold earrings dangled all the way down her long neck to brush her shoulders in a way that was, frankly, sexy.

As Ciena gaped, Jude frowned in what looked like genuine confusion. "What is it?"

"I—you look great."

Jude beamed. "As do you, Ciena."

They flowed with the elegant crowd into an interior hall, surely one of the grandest public spaces within the entire Imperial Palace. The vast corridor stretched seemingly into infinity, with massive columns lining either side. Brilliant red banners hung from the ceiling, their hems weighted so they would remain motionless, never fluttering in any slight breeze. Shiny, well-polished droids rolled along with trays of drinks and hors d'oeuvres; they swerved easily through the throng. The air itself had been perfumed, though the heavy scent made Ciena cough a little at first. Brilliant crystalline sculptures stood on pedestals, shifting shape fluidly from abstract forms into perfect Imperial symbols. Lights had been trained on the sculptures so they would sparkle brightest at the exact moment of the transformation.

"This is astonishing," Jude said. "Think of the trouble this must have taken."

"And the money," Ciena replied. What had been spent on this evening alone probably could have rebuilt an ore refinery on Jelucan. . . .

But there she went thinking like a provincial again. Each world had to rebuild itself. Yes, the Empire was there to help and to govern, but in the end, Jelucan and worlds like it needed to become strong on their own.

Ciena meant to say as much to Jude, but that was when she caught sight of Ved and Thane.

Ved had taken advantage of the occasion to wear Coruscant fashion—a long cape, silky shirt wide cut at the chest, and so on. Yet Ciena thought it was impossible for anyone to look at Ved while Thane stood nearby. He wore his dress uniform, like at least another two hundred men in attendance, yet the rest seemed to . . . fade, next to him. And even though she'd spent the past two years watching Thane grow older and taller, only then did she see him as a man.

Her reaction confused her, but not nearly as much as the moment when Thane recognized her and she realized the sight of her had hit him with equal power. The way his eyes seemed to drink her in—

"Look," Jude whispered, pulling Ciena aside at what was either the best or worst possible time. "It's the junior senator from Alderaan—Leia Organa, the princess!"

Ciena stood on tiptoe, eager to see someone so famous. She got a single glimpse of the princess, who was wearing a slim white gown, her long hair intricately braided. Then the crowds closed around Senator Organa again, hiding her from their sight.

"Can you believe it?" Jude said as they joined the procession into the ballroom.

"It makes sense that she'd be here." Yet Ciena found it intimidating that a girl almost exactly her age could already hold a place in the Imperial Senate, could be so poised, sophisticated, *important*.

"I meant it's surprising that she came to any official function, given her speech in the Senate yesterday."

Ciena remembered then: Princess Leia had announced, on her father's behalf, impending "mercy missions" to planets the Organas claimed to be negatively affected by Imperial policies. "That was ridiculous," she muttered. "Pure grandstanding. Missions like that can't be necessary; the Empire would help the people on its own. That's what the Empire is for!"

Jude nodded in agreement but said, "We should be generous. Even if the Organas are misguided, they're probably acting out of a spirit of kindness."

Maybe so, but Ciena couldn't resist shaking her head at the arrogance of anyone who thought she knew better than the *whole Empire*.

Dancing with partners was one of those habits Ciena had thought of as second-waver decadence before she came to Coruscant. Oh, they danced in the valleys, but dances were for the entire group as part of certain key rituals. Yet Core Worlds Culture had taught her to think of the practice as civilized—even between couples, for no purpose other than pleasure. She was grateful for that now, even more grateful that the class had also taught her the steps of the most commonly performed formal dances. The glittering assembly in that huge, ornately tiled and mirrored hall did not intimidate her; she walked confidently across the floor to her position and awaited whichever partner the computers would assign to her first.

Of course, it would *have* to be Thane.

He stood in front of her, amid the shifting and settling couples all around, not quite meeting her eyes.

"I guess they wanted the cadets to begin together," he said shortly.

"Guess so." Ciena turned her head, trying to look anywhere else—but what she glimpsed made her smile. "Believe it or not, we're the lucky ones."

Next to them, Ved scowled up at Jude, who stood more than a head taller than him. Jude attempted to look dignified, but Ciena knew her well enough to tell that she was stifling a laugh.

Thane must have seen what she'd seen, because she heard him laugh slightly. "You have a point."

Then the orchestra played the opening measures—*a calenada,* Ciena thought, recognizing the dance. She knew the correct position to begin and even held her hands up, but that didn't prepare her for the moment when Thane's broad hand curved around her waist.

Their eyes met, and the dance began.

The thousand people in the hall all knew the correct steps; they moved in unison, brilliant spinning colors, ever changing but always in set patterns, like the bits of glass in a kaleidoscope. Nobody set one toe out of place. Ciena imagined them as jewels gleaming in their settings, clasped tightly in metal that was all but invisible behind the shine.

Thane said, "I thought you considered dancing—what was it—licentious? Risqué? A prelude to sin?"

She had once, before Core Worlds Culture had taught her to be less small-minded. Now it only annoyed Ciena that he would remind her of her provincial ways. "In your dreams."

That made him laugh—but from contempt or surprise? "You seem sure of yourself."

"I am."

It had been banter, not quite an argument. But something shifted in that moment. Ciena had not realized until she spoke that she was in effect declaring her own beauty and attractiveness. That gave Thane an opening to be not merely irritating but cruel.

Instead he said, quietly, "You should be."

Their eyes met again, and Ciena became newly, vividly aware of the warmth of Thane's hand clasping hers, the feel of his fingers braced against her back. They hadn't been this close to each other in a very long time. Every move in the calenada required him to lead, her to follow, which added another layer to the intimacy of the moment. The gaudy swirl of the dancers around them faded until it felt as if the two of them were alone.

Ciena parted her lips to speak, though she still didn't know what to say—but then, with a flourish, the song ended. She and Thane stopped on the beat, but they remained standing there, hands clasped, for a few moments after everyone else had begun to applaud. Then it was time to switch partners, and Thane stepped away without another word.

For the next hour, Ciena continued to play her role in the dance, to laugh and smile along with the rest of the crowd, but she couldn't have repeated anything anyone said to her. She couldn't have said which dances she performed, to which songs, or who her partners were. Her thoughts raced as she went over and over the rift between her and Thane, trying to somehow make sense of it.

Finally, during a break in the dancing, Ciena hurried toward a server droid. She reached past the many glasses of wine to grab a tumbler of cool water. As she gulped it down, she heard, "There you are."

Ciena didn't turn to face Thane. She could tell he stood very close. "Here I am."

"Listen, we should've talked about this a long time ago, and maybe this isn't the time or place—"

She wheeled around then. "Are you going to apologize?"

"Apologize?" Thane's eyes could burn gas-flame blue. "For what? Standing up for myself?"

"For shutting me out!"

"You're the one who—"

Then someone stumbled between them: Ved Foslo,

already sloppy drunk. He laughed out loud. "You guys are so stupid."

"Excuse me?" Ciena wrinkled her nose as she stepped back. Ved stank of Corellian brandy, which wasn't even being served at this party; he must have hidden a flask within the pocket of his cape.

"Stupid. You. Thane. Both of you. So stupid." Ved shook his finger at them, as if they were wayward children. "You keep arguing about that laser cannon thing. Who cares about the laser cannon thing? And you both got it upside down anyway."

At first the words didn't make sense. Then realization flooded over Ciena in an almost dizzying rush of shock and anger. "It was you?"

That only widened Ved's grin. "No! Me? Why would it be me? You still don't get it, do you? Bumpkins from a rock on the edge of the galaxy—of course you don't know how the academy and the Imperial fleet *really* work—"

Thane put one broad hand against Ved's chest. Although it could look like a sober man helping his drunk friend to remain upright, Ciena sensed the veiled threat. Judging by the way Ved's smile faded, he got it, too. In a low voice, Thane said, "Why don't you explain it to us?"

Ved took a couple of steps back, out of Thane's

reach, before he replied. "We attend the academy to become citizens of the Empire. The instructors don't like it when cadets from the same homeworld stay close to each other—it strengthens your ties to your own world. It weakens your commitment to the Empire."

"No, it doesn't!" Ciena protested, but he wasn't going to listen.

"They set you up." Ved laughed again. "They set you up so you'd hate each other, and you swallowed the bait."

Thane's eyes narrowed. "When we both were marked down on that assignment—you moved up to number one. At least, until Jude Edivon overtook you two weeks later."

"You still think I did it? No way. I can't hack like that. Even Jude can't. Only the instructors have that kind of power. And if I were going to frame somebody for anything, the last people I'd go after would be the Office of Student Outcomes. My father told me all about them." Ved's smile was both sloppy and smug. "The fact that they were able to boost the rank of a general's son? I'm sure that was an extra incentive. But they did it mostly to make sure the two of you would stop clinging to each other. And you Jelucani idiots reacted exactly the way they thought you would—except you made it worse. They probably only meant for you two to bicker about it. Not get all—" Ved's hand made a wavy motion in the air. "You didn't just get angry. You practically started *hating* each other. So I guess that makes you two the perfect academy cadets. Again."

He seemed to lose interest then, lurching off toward the server droid to grab his next drink. Ciena felt as if all the shame Ved should have felt saying such things had settled on her instead.

But she deserved to feel ashamed. She had lashed out at Thane for thinking the academy was responsible—and he'd been right all along. The academy's motives had differed, but, still, he'd understood the basics. And she had let that drive her away from the last person she ever should've let go.

Thane didn't know where to begin. "Ciena—"

She shook her head, though he didn't know what she was saying no to: Ved's story, the academy's guilt, Thane being the first to speak, anything. He put one hand on her shoulder, but she winced as if his touch hurt. What could he say or do?

So then of course the damned orchestra started tuning up again, and Ciena swiftly walked away to her next place in the dance. She never once looked back at Thane.

He had little choice but to join in, but throughout the rest of the ball, Thane could think of nothing else. Sometimes he wanted to go back to the academy, go through every single corridor on every single floor until he found that Office of Student Outcomes, then look whoever worked there in the eyes and punch them in their faces, hard. Other times he felt more like locating a time machine so he could go back and tell his younger self not to be such a total idiot. He even considered what such a ploy on the academy's part said about the Empire and the way it treated its officers.

More than anything, though, he wanted to talk with Ciena alone.

When the ball finally ended, Thane pushed through the crowds, looking for Ciena's dark cloud of hair or the unique blue-violet shade of her dress. It was hard to see through all the fawning diplomats, laughing courtiers, and black-garbed military officers—and why was it so strange to remember that he was one of them?

He saw Jude first. She was a head taller than most people in the room, and her vibrant orange gown stood out. As Thane walked closer, he could hear Jude saying, "As we have no curfew tonight or assigned duty tomorrow, this is an ideal occasion to explore the famous nightlife in this area of Coruscant. I've always been quite interested in the clubs here, especially the Crescent Star. . . ."

Only Jude Edivon could make a night of partying sound like a science experiment. Thane had to smile at the thought—but then he saw Ciena and everything else in his mind faded. "Actually, Jude," he said, seizing his chance, "I was hoping Ciena and I might, ah, spend some time catching up."

Jude looked back and forth between the two of them, one eyebrow raised.

Ciena took a deep breath. "Thane and I should talk. If you don't mind, Jude."

"Not at all. I'll be with the others." Jude gestured toward a group of younger officers, several guys and a few girls, who seemed to be waiting on her.

After Jude was out of earshot, Thane said, "Which one of them is she leaving with?"

"Possibly all of them." Ciena turned to face him, her hands clasped in front of her in a gesture Thane recognized from the valleys; he wasn't sure of its significance, but he knew it was formal, and important. "Thane, I didn't believe the academy to be responsible and argued with you about it and in effect challenged your honor. Such a transgression—"

"No. You don't get to do that. This isn't on you,

Ciena, at least not any more than it's on me. I guess we were both idiots together. But the real blame belongs to whatever monster at Student Outcomes did this to us."

She blinked, as if in shock. "They didn't intend for it to get this bad between us. We did that to ourselves."

Galling as it was to admit, Ciena was right.

"Besides, think about it, Thane," she continued. "General Foslo probably bribed someone to do it and Ved's lying to cover for his father."

That . . . seemed possible, though Thane wasn't convinced. At the moment it was irrelevant. "Either way, you were right about confronting the academy instructors." It stung to confess how wrong he'd been, but this knowledge had crept up on Thane over the past few years, and it was past time for him to admit it both to Ciena and to himself. "We would've been expelled for sure. I shouldn't have lashed out at you about it."

"I should have understood you were upset."

Ciena was so determined to apologize. Thane didn't want to hear it. "My point is, neither of us did anything wrong. I'm so tired of being angry with you. Can't we finally let it go?"

She stood up, straight and formal again. "I'm willing to restore our friendship."

That statement sounded like it should be followed

by some elaborate valley ritual of reconciliation, but Thane neither knew nor cared what that might be. "Can't we just—talk? Come on, Ciena. I don't care who should've known better or why the academy did it or any of that. I just want my friend back. The rest doesn't matter."

It wasn't as easy for her to let it go, he knew, but he also saw the shadow of her smile when he talked about having her back. "Where do we start?"

"We start with tonight."

Going out to nightclubs would mean shouting over dance music, not to mention shaking off the countless guys who seemed likely to approach Ciena while she was in that dress. Returning to the academy was no way to spend a free night. Neither Thane nor Ciena had any other ideas about what was available in the area, and rather than search, they wound up sitting on the terrace nearest the ballroom, on a low stone bench by the fountain, talking for hours as the cleaning droids whirred and buzzed around them.

They did in fact start by talking about the ball itself, who and what they'd seen. Thane got to brag, "I even danced with the princess from Alderaan. Nash is going to *choke* when he hears that. He's had a crush on her since he was nine."

"Princess Leia? What was she like?"

"Even shorter than you," Thane replied, which got him a not-very-hard kick to the shin. He mimed pain even as he continued, more seriously: "I don't know. It was only a dance, and she wasn't even paying that much attention. She wasn't being rude; it was more like she was distracted. I guess someone like her must have a lot on her mind."

Ciena opened up more when they talked about their future assignments. "Command track is an honor. Sometimes I think about having a ship of my own someday, and I just—" She shivered, and not only for show; Thane noticed the goose pimples on her arms. "But that means I'm not going to spend much time in single-pilot fighters, not after the first few years, anyway."

"Which is criminal," Thane said. Nearby, a golden server droid used its five arms to vacuum the broken shards of a dropped glass. "You're a phenomenal pilot, Ciena. You should always be in the sky."

He'd forgotten how sly her smile could be. "I will be. Only in a bigger ship."

By the time it was nearly dawn, they were confiding in each other completely again. Ciena showed him how she kept, in a small pouch, the leather bracelet that still bound her to her sister. "I always wondered," he said quietly, looking at the soft worn braid. "It wasn't regulation, and you'd never break regulation—but I knew you'd never get rid of it, either."

"No." Ciena's fingers closed softly around the small pouch; its rough-woven fabric made Thane believe she might have fashioned it from a scrap of cloth taken from home. "Never."

By then the sky had begun to turn pink. The rush of sky traffic had never ceased throughout the night, but the ships came thicker and faster. Ciena's bare feet rested on the stone bench; her sparkly shoes lay empty on the terrace tiles. The server droids had given them final glasses of wine before settling into their night recharging stations, and as Thane drank the last swallow of his, he watched Ciena yawn. As late as it was—as exhausted as they both were—she still looked beautiful.

He wasn't going to act on that now. Maybe he wasn't going to act on it ever, given that they might be assigned to opposite sides of the galaxy within a couple of months. Besides, their reunion was too new to ask for anything more. Later, Thane decided. Later he'd think about Ciena and their futures. That night was enough on its own.

"We should go to the transport," he said, getting to his feet. "Come on."

Once Ciena had stepped back into her shoes, Thane offered her his arm. She took it as she rose to her feet. Weary as they were, he expected nothing but small talk about how much sleep they would, or wouldn't, be able to get. Instead, Ciena said, very softly, "I'm so glad to have you back."

Later, he reminded himself, more forcefully. "Me too."

CHAPTER EIGHT

"TODAY MARKS NOT an ending but a beginning. Everything you have done during your three years at the academy—and in some ways, everything you have done throughout your life until this moment—was all for one single purpose: preparing you to become the best Imperial officers you can be. You have always been citizens of the Empire, but today you become a *part* of the Empire in ways no civilians can ever fully understand. The uniforms you now wear serve as a symbol of the Empire's power, and your service makes that power ever greater."

Ciena's heart sang with pride as she stood there amid the ranks of cadets—no, new officers. She wore a command-track lieutenant's uniform in gray and black, new insignia gleaming in bright squares just below her collarbone. Her new assignment had been given to her that morning, only moments before the ceremony began. The sun shone bright in the pale Coruscant sky, enormous red banners waved gently in the breeze, and she felt as if the future had been laid out before her like a velvet carpet, soft and plush, defining her path.

Several rows back, the elite flight graduates wore black TIE fighter pilot gear. Thane found that kind of ridiculous. The armor was heavy and hot, too; it was designed to be worn in the upper atmosphere or outer space, not on the surface on a sunny day. And the same helmet that felt so necessary—and so badass—while he was flying? On the ground, it looked ridiculous. Still, his irritation with the armor didn't come close to his annoyance with the speaker's address. *He talks like the Empire just swallowed us whole. Plus, he keeps talking. Could he please shut up so I can go change into something else?*

The best part of the ceremony, in his opinion, was the end, when he was able to find Ciena in the crowd. Once he'd pulled off his helmet, she threw her arms around him in a hug; Thane could hardly feel it, thanks to the chest plate, but he grinned anyway. "So where are you posted?"

"A Star Destroyer. The *Devastator*."

"Whoa. That's one of the top ships in the fleet."

Thane was pleased for her but not surprised. He'd never doubted that she'd go far.

Ciena's eyes shone with delight—and hope. "And you? What's your posting?"

"I'm assigned to the defense fleet for a space station."

"Which one?"

"That's the weird part—I don't know. Apparently, this station is brand-new and still 'classified.'"

"Exciting," she said. "And I bet there's a good chance the *Devastator* will visit this new station."

"Yeah. Sounds like it." Thane couldn't help hoping. If they'd each been assigned to opposite sides of the Outer Rim, he would've had to accept that his path might not ever cross hers, at least in the line of duty. But she'd be on one of the most important ships in the fleet—and he'd already gathered that this new station was top-of-the-line, the kind of place important ships would be docked—which meant he might see her again before long. And when they were together again, not as playmates or cadets but as fellow officers and adults—then what?

Thane wasn't sure, but he thought he'd like to find out. "Keep me posted, all right?"

"You'd better send messages and holos. All the time." Ciena tried to make it sound as if she were teasing, but he could hear the real hope in her voice. "And maybe I'll even get to see you back home."

"Definitely." Then, quickly, he bent and kissed her on the cheek. Ciena's full lips parted slightly in surprise—and pleasure. Thane realized he should've done that a long time before. He wanted to say something to her, but the right words wouldn't come. So he stuck to the basics: "Congratulations, Lieutenant Ree."

"Congratulations to you, too, Lieutenant Kyrell." She held up one hand as she turned to go but gave him a lingering look over her shoulder before she walked into the crowd.

Thane watched her go. Even amid a throng of hundreds of students wearing variations on the same uniform, Ciena remained separate and unmistakable to him. Only when she'd passed out of sight did he turn away.

Back home, he thought. Although he hoped to see Ciena before their next furlough, he liked the idea of being with her back on Jelucan. He'd planned to put off any postgraduate visit to his family as long as possible and hopefully forever; now, however, he found himself willing to return at least once. It would be different if he and Ciena took the journey together. Maybe they could even see the Fortress. Dust would have blown into their cave hideaway, but it wouldn't take much effort to make it nice again. Or they could travel down to Valentia together, as they'd always promised to do but never had. . . .

Three weeks into her service aboard the *Devastator*, Ciena finally stopped feeling like a cadet impostor and started feeling like a true Imperial officer. The change came the first day she was finally thrown into action against the rebels.

They're firing back? She could hardly believe it. A tiny blockade runner trying to take on a Star Destroyer. It was beyond impossible—it was *insane.*

Then again, weren't all the rebels insane?

"Close in," the bridge commander said. "Their power reserves must be nearly depleted by now. Let's pull them into the docking bay and end this."

Ciena activated the tractor beam, then looked up from the gleaming black console to witness the scene for herself. The small white form of the ship ahead was hardly more than a speck in the starscape, dwarfed by the desert planet beneath. Viewscreens provided far more detail, but there was something fulfilling about watching the rebel ship's defeat with her own eyes.

Once she would've taken that defeat for granted. The rebels were a ragtag bunch of malcontents reduced to terrorist acts because they lacked either popular support or military might—or so they had all believed until recently, when the rebels had struck at them from a hidden base. To the undying shame of whatever complacent Imperial officials were responsible, the rebels had actually won the engagement. Not only did the Empire have to bear that incomprehensible defeat, but it also had lost vital intelligence information. Although the specifics were not widely discussed, Ciena had gathered that the intel had to do with the plans for a new, secret Imperial space station.

That had to be the base Thane was assigned to. If these rebels had gotten away, would they have attacked that station, putting Thane's life at risk?

Ciena's eyes narrowed as she stared at the rebel ship and thought, *You actually believed you could attack us and get away with it. You know better now, don't you?*

The blockade runner continued to broadcast its protests about being on a "diplomatic mission," but Ciena ignored that, as did everyone else on the bridge. With satisfaction she saw the ship disappear from the windows, becoming only a green blip on her readouts.

An officer nearby said, "Lord Vader has given the order to board the *Tantive IV*, sir."

The captain nodded. "Excellent. They'll take the princess into custody in no time. Stand down on main laser cannons."

Ciena nodded, swiftly inputting the commander's

orders. She had to disguise her shock at the thought of Princess Leia of Alderaan as a rebel, a terrorist and a traitor. But her father had long been a troublemaker in the Imperial Senate, mistaking his planet's importance for his own. Too bad his daughter had inherited his arrogance.

Today, they'd shown her and every other rebel that they couldn't go up against the Empire without paying the price.

One of the *Tantive IV* escape pods launched; readouts showed four life forms attempting to escape to the desert planet below. The pod was shot down easily.

What could they have been thinking? Ciena wondered as she quickly routed the reports from the boarding parties. *How could they ever expect to get away from a Star Destroyer when they were already trapped inside the docking bay?*

I guess they were too scared to think straight. They deserve everything that's coming to them, but I can't blame them for being scared. . . .

Another escape pod launched, rousing her from her thoughts. The officer next to Ciena muttered, "There goes another one."

The captain seemed bored. "Hold your fire. There's no life forms. They must've short-circuited." Within moments, the escape pod was invisible against the yellow sands of the planet below.

Shortly afterward, Ciena manually delivered copies

of the auxiliary bridge's hard data files to the ISB internal affairs officer on board; the Imperial Security Bureau liked to monitor all interactions with suspected rebel targets to ensure no one betrayed any lack of loyalty to the Empire through word or deed. On her way, she ran into Nash Windrider at the doorway to the main bridge lift. He was one of the few alumni of her class assigned to the *Devastator*—and while they hadn't been close there, due to that stupid rift between her and Thane, they knew each other well enough to count as friends now. Nash still wore his hair long, though tightly braided in the back per regulations. "Don't tell me," he stage-whispered to her as the lift doors slid open and they walked inside. "You're running an errand to make sure you don't get sent to that broiling lump of sand down there."

"*Tatooine*," she pretended to correct him. The lift began its swift ascent, the glass panels in its doors showing them layer after flickering layer of the vast Star Destroyer. "I take it that's where you're headed?"

"No, and thank goodness. Going down there in stormtrooper armor's as good as being baked alive."

The lift would reach the main bridge within a few moments, so Ciena took that chance to say something that needed to be said to Nash in private. Gently, she began, "I wanted to say, I'm sorry about your princess. You must feel so . . . betrayed."

Nash's grin faded. He drew himself up to his full lanky height and clasped his hands behind his back. "Princess Leia can only have been misled by her courtiers. I feel sure that a thorough investigation will clear her of any real wrongdoing."

"Of course. I should have thought of that." Ciena didn't know if she believed such an easy explanation was plausible, but Nash knew more about the princess than she did. Maybe he was right.

The lift doors slid open, and Nash stepped out. "Until later," he said, turning away from her to return to his duty station. Ciena wished she hadn't said anything about the princess. It wasn't Nash's fault if one of his planet's senators had turned out to be a traitor. She hoped the internal affairs officer would feel the same way.

Ciena had only been to the main bridge once before, on a brief orientation tour of the ship the day she'd arrived. So the sight still awed her: the impossibly long corridor, the enormous viewscreen, the countless monitors all whirring and blinking on the lower level as senior staffers worked furiously in the data pits. It was the heart of the *Devastator*, the soul of the machine.

Quickly, she turned her attention to Captain Ronnadam, who was sitting at his station in the unique white-jacketed uniform of the ISB. "Sir. The data packets, as requested."

Ronnadam took the packets without even glancing back at her; his focus was only for whatever long lines of text were scrolling down his monitor. Ciena could not leave the main bridge without being dismissed, so she stood at attention, waiting.

"You're being lax in your protocols, Ronnadam," said a dry, crisp voice behind her. "Fortunately, the young lieutenant here follows procedure—and has better manners."

Ciena lit up as she turned and recognized Grand Moff Tarkin himself—in the form of a hologram, flickering in gray-green light. He looked at Ciena with some interest. "You seem to know me, Lieutenant. But I doubt we've served together before. Who are you?"

"Lieutenant Ciena Ree, L-P-eight-eight-eight, graduate of the most recent class of the Royal Academy and native of Jelucan, sir." *Wait until I tell Thane I saw Tarkin again!*

The Grand Moff nodded politely. "Jelucan. On the Outer Rim, yes? I was there for its annexation into the Empire."

A response was not required—but it wasn't forbidden, either, and Ciena couldn't resist. "You were, sir. I met you that day, right after the ceremony, when I was just a little girl."

Tarkin's angular face studied her for a long moment, and then, to her astonishment, he said, "The two children sneaking around the shuttle grounds. Were you one of those?"

She had heard tales of Tarkin's sharp memory—that he never forgot a favor or a slight—but the proof made her smile. "Yes, sir. You asked me that day if I'd like to serve the Empire when I grew up, and here I am."

"Well, well." Tarkin put his hands behind his back, clearly pleased with himself and with her. "The power of diplomacy in action."

"The boy with me that day just graduated from the academy, too, at the top of the elite flight track. Now he's Lieutenant Thane Kyrell."

Tarkin's smile was thin but unmistakable. "Apparently I should recruit on Jelucan more often. I shall make a point of keeping up with you both."

Ciena struggled to maintain correct military composure, but she felt sure her delight showed on her face. Grand Moff Tarkin didn't seem to mind, however. As the hologram faded out, he nodded at her—as close to friendliness as any superior officer would ever show toward a mere lieutenant. If he'd remembered that incident with the *Lambda*-class shuttle all those years later, he'd definitely remember to look up her records, and Thane's. Maybe Tarkin would be more than their inspiration for joining the Imperial Starfleet; maybe he'd even turn into a mentor.

Capturing a rebel ship and winning praise from a Grand Moff before lunchtime? Ciena grinned. This day was turning out to be spectacular.

Thane hadn't realized exactly how enormous the Death Star was until the first time he had flown his TIE fighter on patrol. Immediately, he had had to adjust the thrusters for the kind of takeoff more common within a planetary atmosphere than on a space station—because the Death Star's enormity gave it heavy gravitational pull.

Just the thought of that made Thane grin. He'd never imagined building something that colossal was even possible. Now the space station had become his home, and already he dreaded the day he'd be assigned somewhere else. The Death Star was meant to function as a world of its own, which meant it had creature comforts most other military postings didn't: decent food, rec areas, cantinas with latest-model bartender droids, commissaries with selections of treats and luxuries, albeit at a stiff price. Although Thane lived in a communal barracks, apparently there were enough private bunks that most people could expect to receive one within three to six months. Usually you had to make lieutenant commander to live in that kind of luxury. To be able to enjoy such a comfortable posting and have the thrill of deep-space flight every day—that went beyond Thane's wildest dreams.

So did the message he received that morning.

"You're coming here *today*," he repeated as he looked down at Ciena's face on the small screen. "As in, now."

"See how we're communicating without a delay? The *Devastator* should dock within the hour." Her eagerness shone through the screen; Thane imagined his did, too. "Will you have any free time?"

"Yeah. Definitely. I already finished my patrol for the day." As for the next day—well, trading duty shifts wasn't against rules if you got approval first. He'd fly any shift for anyone if it meant he could spend the whole day with Ciena. "We could go to one of the cantinas. Catch up."

"Nash can't wait to see you, either," Ciena said.

"Right. Definitely. Of course." Nash might have been one of his best friends, but Thane had never been less interested in hanging out with him. Fortunately,

Nash was savvy enough to know when to excuse himself—Thane hoped.

"And I want to see Jude," Ciena continued. "She's on board, isn't she?"

"Yeah, Jude Edivon's assigned to the Death Star, but I haven't run into her once. This place is the size of a moon—it's like she's halfway across the planet from me." When Ciena's face fell, Thane hastily added, "But when you tell her you're coming, she'll find her way to you. Count on it."

"You will, too, right?"

"You'd better believe it," he said, smiling like an idiot.

Maybe I didn't look like a total *idiot,* Thane thought several hours later, as he went through his secondary duty shift as a maintenance mechanic. Every pilot had to be able to maintain and repair all single- and dual-pilot craft, and by then twin ion engines were as familiar to Thane as his own hands. So he was able to go through his checklist, hitting every point, while still allowing his mind to race. *She was smiling, too. So that's a good sign, right?*

He didn't ask himself what it was a good sign of. The excitement he felt at the thought of seeing Ciena again remained something he preferred not to examine or name. All he knew was that he hadn't dreamed of seeing her again so soon, and yet now even another day seemed like too long to wait.

The Devastator's *already here. Ciena's on the Death Star right now. Why did I have to pull this stupid shift? I traded so I'd have tomorrow free, but what if Ciena can't get time off then?*

Thane told himself to stop worrying about it. He took a deep breath and got back to work on the TIE fighter in front of him. The control panel actually needed some new wiring, a task detailed enough to keep him occupied for a while. Just as he put the panel plate back in place, however, he heard the announcement: "All hands in sector four-seventeen to the auxiliary docking doors."

That was his sector. Luckily, Thane already stood nearby, so he was able to get into formation first, right in the front line. His mechanic's jumpsuit bore a few grease stains, but that wasn't inappropriate for the middle of a work shift. Nonetheless, he felt shabby compared with the many officers around him in either officer's uniforms or gleaming stormtrooper armor.

Probably the commander wouldn't notice, though. He strutted in front of them as he announced, "As of today, the Death Star is fully operational—and it is the will of the Emperor that we demonstrate its power to the entire galaxy!"

A few cheers went up from the group. Thane clapped a couple of times. He guessed they were going to bring the station close enough to planetary orbit for the populace to see it; that would wow anyone. He'd felt the main engines at work, so obviously the station had traveled somewhere important, maybe Coruscant. . . .

The docking bay doors slid open. Although Thane fully understood the force fields that kept atmosphere in and the hostile chill of space out, he still felt a moment's awe when he looked out on the vast darkness beyond. Slowly, as the door opened, a world appeared. The soft blue sphere seemed to shine with its own light, and as always Thane thought about how beautiful and yet fragile planets looked from that distance.

"Behold the planet Alderaan," the commander said.

Nash's home! Thane couldn't help grinning. What luck to be near that world while the *Devastator* was visiting the station. How many times had Nash promised to show Thane all the sights? It had seemed like no more than a dream, but now Thane might actually get to take a look at Alderaan for himself if he could wrangle the free time. He found himself remembering every story Nash had told him about the best places to go, the incredible natural beauty his world was said to contain. *Where should we go first? Cloudshape Falls? The Isatabith rain forest?*

"As some of you will know," the commander said, "Alderaan is represented in the Imperial Senate by a member of the Organa ruling family. However, it has been discovered that the senator, her father—and, we believe, the entirety of the upper echelons of Alderaanian government—have been secretly financing and supporting the Rebel Alliance."

It took a moment for the words to sink in. Thane couldn't be sure he'd heard correctly. How could the royal family of Alderaan be mixed up in terrorism? His cynical nature told him nobody was too pure or noble to be corrupted—but it also told him people who benefited from the status quo rarely tried to change it.

The commander went on: "This station has been chosen to send a message to the entire galaxy. We shall demonstrate, now and for all time, that the Empire's strength is supreme. Long may the Emperor rule!"

"Long may the Emperor rule!" shouted all the officers standing at attention, Thane included. He hardly paid attention to the words, which by now were so familiar as to be rote. His mind was still trying to make sense of what he'd just heard.

Then a deep vibration in the core of the station rippled through the decks, different and more powerful than any Thane had sensed in it before. His hair stood on end, though he didn't know whether that was from fear or the ionization of the atmosphere.

What's happening? he wondered—

—and then the Death Star blasted Alderaan, and an entire world exploded before him.

CHAPTER NINE

I N SHOCK, ALMOST NUMB, Ciena thought, *Look through my eyes.*

She was supposed to let Wynnet see the terrible as well as the beautiful. That meant Ciena had to show her this.

On the viewscreen, fragments of the planet Alderaan scattered in a thousand directions, all the pieces glowing with the heat of their world's death. Ciena thought of the billions of people who had just died before her eyes and thought she might begin to cry—but then she saw the officer next to her on the auxiliary assignment station.

Nash Windrider had gone so pale she thought he might faint. He was a native of Alderaan. His entire family—every place he'd ever been—his *home* had just been obliterated before his eyes, for disloyalty.

Instantly, Ciena realized that if Nash *did* faint or cry or show any visible sign of emotion, it would be seen as a protest. He would be thought guilty of the same treason as the Organas and could be thrown in the brig, if not stripped of his commission on the spot.

She couldn't help anyone else, so she would help Nash. Reaching out with one hand, Ciena touched Nash's arm to steady him. He responded by clutching her fingers and squeezing so tightly it hurt, but she did not pull away. Instead she watched as Nash forced himself to breathe deep, even breaths, holding on to her hand as if it were a towline to bring him to shore.

To home, Ciena nearly thought. But she caught herself in time.

In the aftermath of the blast, Ciena walked Nash toward the lift that would take him back to the *Devastator*'s docking bay, so he could board the ship, go to his barracks, and perhaps be alone. Nash said nothing the entire time. He didn't even make eye contact with Ciena before walking through the lift doors. In the last second before they shut again, she saw him lean heavily against the wall of the lift, as if otherwise he might fall.

At least she had a few hours free to collect her thoughts and an old friend to talk things through with. No, it wasn't the old friend she'd most hoped to see—but still, a welcome face.

"Naturally, I understood the cannon's full potential," Jude said as she and Ciena sat on one of the small observation decks, before a long line of windows. "The superlaser is fueled by an array of giant kyber crystals, which gives it nearly unlimited power. But I had thought it would be used to break up asteroids for mining purposes. Or uninhabited worlds. Not this."

Ciena glanced around to see if they were being overheard. "Jude, do you think—what we saw today, what the Death Star did—is there any justification for that? *Can* there be?"

Instead of answering right away, Jude sat very still, considering. Ciena had always liked that about her friend—the calm, reasoned way Jude worked things through. When they were young cadets, sometimes her gravity had led her roommates to tease her, but now Ciena was grateful for it.

"Even though I've only been in active service for a few weeks," Jude finally said, "it has already become evident to me that the Rebel Alliance is a far larger and more dangerous group than official broadcasts have ever acknowledged. We do not operate as a peacetime military. Our preparations are more appropriate for a time of war."

Ciena had already sensed some of that for herself, but when Jude put it in those words, everything crystallized. The threat posed by the Rebel Alliance had become very real.

Jude continued, "The Organas are guilty of treason, but most of the citizens were not."

At least it was quick, Ciena thought, but the rationalization sounded hollow even inside her head. She imagined herself as a child, looking upward, seeing the slate-colored sky turn red and knowing for one sickening moment that it could only be the end. The fear the children of Alderaan would have known—the *horror*—

"But it is incorrect to think of what happened to Alderaan as punishing the populace," Jude said, becoming more brisk. "The only justification for such an extreme act is that this alone is capable of putting down an even more severe threat. The rebels must be reckless—even foolish—to attempt to conquer the entire Imperial fleet. So how can they be made to see reason? To understand the limitations of their power and the inevitability of the Empire's victory? Nothing but a demonstration on this scale could ever accomplish that. Surely, now, the rebels see that their goals are hopeless and their tactics unwise. We'll be safe from war now. The billions of people who died today may have saved countless lives through their sacrifice."

That had to be true. No terrorist cell in the galaxy,

no matter how zealous or bloodthirsty, could believe it had the power to defeat the Empire now. But that sacrifice was one the inhabitants of Alderaan had never chosen to make.

Jude sighed and stared down at her drink for a long moment. For some reason—the way the light fell or the lost expression on Jude's face—she looked younger to Ciena, like the girl she'd been when they'd met more than three years earlier. Her immaculately pressed and tailored uniform seemed like a costume for a child playing dress-up. Maybe Ciena also felt too young, too new, to go to war.

No doubt everyone felt that way at first.

Ciena said, "So what happened today—as many people as were lost—even more would die in a massive galactic war."

"Exactly." Jude nodded. "Think of the billions who perished in the Clone Wars."

"But by ending the war now, before it truly begins, the Death Star will save more lives than it took." That was a hard thing to think about, the kind of dark calculus Ciena had hoped would never be required of her outside Command Ethics class. Yet now she had to face it and do her duty.

If only the Empire had not been forced to take such dramatic action. If only the Rebel Alliance had never arisen from whatever mixture of discontent and arrogance fueled its leaders. These terrorists had gambled on the proposition that the Empire would never strike back. Now at last they had been proved wrong—but Ciena wondered whether their leaders would ever take responsibility for the horrible measures necessary to stop this rebellion—this war—before the entire galaxy had been plunged into chaos. Probably not.

The Rebellion had started this. Even provoked it.

Ciena felt better now that she understood whom to blame.

An announcement sounded, echoing from the speakers as officers looked up. *"Attention: The* Devastator *will depart from the station at the beginning of the next duty shift. All personnel should be on board and prepared for new orders."*

"Oh, no." Ciena didn't want to leave Jude just when her friend was helping the world make sense again. The last thing Nash needed was a new and more demanding duty shift instead of some time to collect himself. And she hadn't even laid eyes on Thane, much less—

"I doubt the *Devastator* will be gone for long," Jude said. "Word has it Lord Vader intends to remain until the current crisis has been resolved. The *Devastator* is his flagship, so you would undertake only a limited number of missions without him."

Of course. Ciena's spirits brightened. Whatever

mission awaited the *Devastator* couldn't last more than a couple of weeks, not without Darth Vader on board. "Then I'll see you again soon."

They hugged good-bye quickly before Ciena hurried out into the corridor. She hardly took in the activity around her; the station's enormity failed to awe. Already her mind was on the future: helping Nash through the next few days, returning for Lord Vader—and it seemed likely the *Devastator* would visit this station often, so she'd have plenty of chances to visit Jude. She'd be back to see Thane so quickly it would be as if she'd never gone.

Thane stared at the screen of the communications monitor, willing it to light up with a response from Ciena. Only blackness stared back.

He knew she was probably on the *Devastator*, maybe on duty. How could anyone keep going after witnessing the murder of an entire planet? But Thane had continued standing at attention along with the rest, a fact that amazed him more with every passing moment.

We killed billions of people. We slaughtered billions, and afterward we were expected to applaud.

Alderaan had been Nash's homeworld. If Thane was sickened by what he'd just seen, how must Nash be feeling? The guy had to be at the point of collapse.

Thane didn't send a message to him, however. He knew the communications record might be looked over by the internal affairs officer, and any call to or from an Alderaanian would automatically be suspect. For his own sake, Thane didn't care. He knew how to choose his words carefully so the listener would hear what had to remain unspoken; it was a skill most people culti- vated at the academy. But Nash had to be furious—and in his grief and rage, he might say something that would incriminate him.

No, Thane would have to reach out to Nash later, when it was safer. Anyway, it was Ciena he needed to talk to. She'd always been his touchstone. If he were with her, he thought, he wouldn't feel so nauseated and angry. He'd feel as if he could breathe again—

The communications monitor lit up, and Thane's spirits rose for the split second it took him to real- ize the message wasn't from Ciena. Instead, it was his company commander, ordering them to report for duty, immediately.

"Dantooine?" he repeated to one of his fellow offi- cers as they boarded the troop transport. "That's in the middle of nowhere." The place was nearly as obscure as Jelucan.

"That's the whole point," said the other officer as

she climbed the entry ramp. "Where else could the rebels hide?"

They'd better hide, he thought. Now that the galaxy had learned what this space station could do, surely nobody would rise up against the Empire again.

At least Thane had a couple of moments before boarding was complete to record a message, one Ciena could listen to whenever she got off shift: "Bad news— some of us are being shipped out on a last-minute patrol. That's only going to take a day or two, but I don't know how much longer the *Devastator*'s going to be docked on the—station."

The words *Death Star* were harder for him to say now that the death was real.

"I really hope I get to see you," he said, willing her to hear how deeply he meant it. "If not—next time on Jelucan. I promise. So you have to promise, too. All right? Kyrell out."

Probably he should have sent Nash a message, as well, but he still had no idea what to say. During the troop lander's voyage to Dantooine, Thane kept wondering what to do for Nash, but he could think of nothing more useful than sitting his friend down with a bottle of Corellian brandy.

Once they reached the planet, scans picked up

evidence of a rebel base fairly quickly. Before Thane could get into battle armor, however, word came that the base was deserted. They'd do a sweep for intel but no more than that. Sounded like they'd come a long way for nothing.

But then the troop lander arrived at the abandoned base in the heart of Dantooine's gloomy badlands, and Thane saw not some ramshackle hangar or scrubby smuggler's den but the remnants of a real military organization.

They could've had dozens of small starfighters in this area alone, he thought as he scanned the vast enclosure. Data scrolling past on his screen told him the installation had also held dozens of droid-charging ports, sophisticated communications technology that would allow for near-instantaneous cross-galactic information transfer, and bunks for several hundred rebels. And there seemed to be at least a dozen structures similar to that one. Plus they found evidence of extensive digging underground, so apparently the rebels had at one point planned to expand the base.

This was no small band of malcontents. The Rebel Alliance was an army.

No, their fighting force was nowhere near the scale of the Empire's might. But Thane had taken enough tactics classes at the academy to know that an enemy didn't have to be your equal; as long as its forces reached a certain critical mass, they had the power to cause real damage. It looked to him like the Rebellion was nearly there.

His usual train of thought about the rebels began: *They're terrorists, they're thugs. The Empire has its flaws, but so did the Republic these guys worship. You can't trust power no matter what. It doesn't really matter who's in charge.*

He'd thought he was being so worldly and wise. Now—with the blaze of Alderaan's destruction still glowing in his mind—Thane knew how hollow his rationalizations had been. Terrorism could never be the answer, but as of that day, the Empire was as guilty of acts of terror as the Rebel Alliance was, if not more.

His tour of duty, postgraduation, was five years. After that, technically, Thane could resign his commission and take whatever work he chose—but the vast majority of Imperial officers remained in service until they hit mandatory retirement age or died, whichever came first. He'd always figured he would be a lifer. Now it felt like he couldn't wear that uniform another five minutes.

How many times had he said he'd stay in the Imperial Starfleet just so he'd get to fly the greatest ships in the galaxy? The words sounded so callow now. Juvenile, even.

You don't really want to walk out, Thane told himself as he continued taking readings, his expression carefully impassive. *What you've seen today proves we're on the brink of galactic war. They need you.*

But when he thought of *they*, he wasn't imagining the Emperor and his admirals needing him. He imagined protecting his fellow troops, the people around him he'd already begun to think of as friends. And Nash.

And Ciena.

Although the *Devastator* had left the Death Star behind, the Star Destroyer's crew had been instructed to remain linked to the station's data feeds. The designated viewscreens were slightly to the left of Ciena's station, so from the corner of her eye she could see the febrile surface of Yavin, an immense red gas giant. Other screens showed one of the world's moons, Yavin 4, apparently the real location of the rebel base.

So they sent Thane away to Dantooine based on bad intel. For nothing. She longed to talk with him about the terrible events of the past couple of days. Talking with Jude had helped steady Ciena, but she still couldn't sleep. Over and over again, in her mind's eye, she saw Alderaan exploding.

Now she might be about to watch the death of a second world.

But this is a military target, she assured herself. *No civilians will be hurt.*

That explanation would make sense to her eventually. At the moment, her gut ached at the thought of seeing another planet's destruction. It was too soon after Alderaan; her nerves were raw.

The rebels realized their doom, and they fought back—but in the most absurd way possible.

"Unbelievable," muttered a commander standing near her duty station. "The rebels sent a handful of starfighters to target the Death Star? That little uprising must be on its last legs, if that's all the power they can muster."

It's uninhabited, she reminded herself. *The only people there are members of the Rebellion, the ones who are trying to start a war. They chose their path willingly. This is what war means.*

Yet she thought of the animals that lived there, small innocent creatures, and even the trees—

One monitor showed X-wing fighters racing through a trench, with TIE fighters in pursuit. She wondered why they had even sent the TIEs out against such a pitiful attack. Then again, even minor damage to the station would have to be repaired. The ships zoomed past at such speed that the firefight was out of sight again in moments. Maybe another camera would pick it up.

Instead, a short time later, she saw an X-wing and a clunky old freighter headed back toward Yavin 4 at top sublight speed. Ciena reported, "Sir, the rebel ships are flying away from the Death Star."

"Track them," her commander said. "We will want to provide the most complete report possible for Grand Moff Tarkin."

She continued logging every data packet that arrived from the Death Star, important or incidental. The auxiliary bridge continued its buzz of activity, but voices dropped and tasks slowed. Ciena knew everyone was waiting for the moment Yavin 4 would explode. Nausea welling inside, she attempted to brace herself for the sudden blazing light—when instead every screen connected to the Death Star went black.

Instantly. Simultaneously. Ciena realized the stream of data flowing from the station had stopped, too.

"Did the circuits fail?" someone said, checking out those monitors. He thought the screens themselves were at fault. She knew better.

"The Death Star has gone silent, sir," she reported. "No incoming data."

Her commander's face took on a strange expression, both confused and angry. "That's impossible, Lieutenant. The rebels have created some form of interference, or those fighters were sent to knock out the station's communications."

X-wing fighters couldn't do that to a space station the size of the Death Star. Could they?

But the only alternative was—unthinkable.

CHAPTER TEN

"THAT'S IT? They don't know anything else?"

"Try again to get through to Coruscant."

"Every communication network is completely jammed—"

Voices echoed throughout the abandoned rebel base on Dantooine, which had become for the time being a makeshift Imperial station. Groups of officers huddled around—some still in full landing armor but most by then wearing only pieces of the plating. Although their troop commander remained in charge, for hours no orders had been given to anyone but communications officers. There was nothing for them to do but wait and be afraid.

Thane paced the length of the hall, which seemed to have been blasted from solid rock, making it feel a bit as if they were huddling in a cave. The pieces of information they'd been able to gather so far were contradictory, confusing, and ominous. Some said the Death Star had been destroyed; others claimed it was damaged and unable to communicate; still others said the news had to be false—a ploy meant to coax the rebels out of hiding so they could be more efficiently slaughtered.

Most of the soldiers in the room seemed to believe the last scenario, which had led to a lot of cursing and big talk about how when *they* were in charge, they'd never initiate an action like that without properly informing and preparing everyone down the chain of command. A few others protested, saying that spies could be anywhere. If even a member of the Imperial Senate as illustrious as Princess Leia Organa could turn traitor, anyone could. So this big diversion had to be kept secret until the last possible moment.

Not everyone was convinced, though. Thane had exchanged glances with a handful of others who remained tense and silent.

The Death Star can't have been lost. It would take a dozen Star Destroyers and attack cruisers to make any impact on a station that size. The Rebel Alliance is clearly more powerful than our superior officers let us know, but if they had a fleet that large, they would've provoked direct action before now. That part of his analysis felt rock solid to Thane; however, the rest was less certain. *If the Death*

Star has been damaged, how badly? It's the size of an entire moon, so how can all *the communications systems be down? And why wouldn't the ships docked there be able to respond, either?*

If the rebels had attacked the Death Star with a fleet capable of causing real damage, the big Imperial ships would have been launched. They would have gone into battle.

Thane leaned against the rough-hewn stone wall of the rebel base, canteen of nutritive milk in one hand. He thought of the *Devastator* in all its majesty and power, and he imagined its laser cannons blasting the rebel fleet to shreds. He pictured it over and over—the shards of metal, the spinning debris, the brief pulses of flame before they were snuffed out by the vacuum of space.

If he imagined the *Devastator* winning, he didn't have to imagine what else might have happened during the battle he envisioned—to the ship, to Nash Windrider, or to Ciena.

After a few hours at her post, Ciena's ears rang with the squeals of badly filtered transmissions. Her head swam with the endless amounts of data she had to process, fast. For now she had to give her ship and her Empire everything she had.

The *Devastator*'s senior officers were in conference, as they had been for what seemed like hours. If any of them knew the reason behind the Death Star's sudden, terrifying silence, they had not yet shared it with the crew.

For the time being Ciena could do no more than continue to sort through the endless data packets sent from the Death Star before it went quiet. Many of these contained no useful information whatsoever, but until they had a full explanation, she could afford to ignore nothing.

When she recognized Jude's number on one packet, she opened it immediately. She didn't care whether this one was important or not; Ciena needed to know what Jude had been doing before the Death Star—became damaged, or infiltrated, or whatever had gone so horribly wrong.

But Jude's data *was* important. Ciena read a report from Jude Edivon to her superior officer and all local commanders in which Jude explained that her analysis had shown the rebel attack with small starfighters did in fact pose a threat to the Death Star. She'd found a flaw nobody else had suspected—something to do with an exhaust port—and had sensed a weakness where everyone else saw invulnerability.

Although the likelihood of a direct hit is remote, Jude had written, *the consequences could be highly destructive to the station, even fatal.*

If anyone had sent a response to Jude's warning, Ciena had not yet found it.

Fatal to the station? To the Death Star? No. Jude must have meant only that officers would be killed in some resulting small explosion. That made far more sense than the idea that an X-wing fighter could destroy something the size of a moon.

Yet the darkness and silence remained.

Shortly after Ciena had sent this information to command, she received a message to report to docking bay forty-seven. Nash shot her a look as she walked out, clearly as curious as she was about what could possibly be going on. She hoped to be able to fill him in soon.

Instead, she found she had a new assignment.

A stone-faced commander told her and the other pilot, "Lieutenant Ree, Lieutenant Sai, you're to take a *Gozanti*-class freighter to the Yavin system to rendezvous with Lord Vader and bring him back to the *Devastator*."

It was as though steel bands had been tightening around her, then were suddenly loosed. Ciena managed not to sigh out loud. *Darth Vader is alive. He was able to contact our ship. So whatever happened on the Death Star wasn't the worst-case scenario.* She still hadn't allowed herself to fully contemplate what the "worst-case scenario" might be.

The commander continued: "You are to disclose your mission to no one—not during your journey or at any time afterward. You will maintain communications silence unless otherwise ordered by Lord Vader, or if . . . the rendezvous does not take place as planned."

What was that supposed to mean? Ciena glanced sideways at her fellow pilot, whose expression might as well have been carved in stone.

Once they were alone in the freighter's cockpit, however, Lieutenant Sai proved to be anything but stoic. "What are we supposed to do?" she said just after their ship had gone into hyperspace. "Fly up to the totally silent Death Star without asking them any questions? Or even getting permission to dock?"

"It's going to make more sense when we get there," Ciena said.

"Why are you so sure?"

"Because it can't make any less sense than it does now."

That earned her a laugh. "True. By the way, I'm called Berisse."

"Ciena."

Berisse turned out to have graduated from the academy on Lothal the year before. Her brilliant smile shone brightly against her tan skin. She was as stout as regulations allowed, with dark, shining hair she kept even more tightly braided than Ciena's. When she learned that Ciena had been on the *Devastator* only a few short weeks, she promised to show her around, and even offered some sympathy for Nash. "That's rough," she said. "Imagine finding out your entire planet turned traitor."

Even that can't be as bad as seeing it completely destroyed, Ciena nearly said—but that was when the sensors began to chime. "Yavin," she said, swinging back into position at the controls. "Dropping out of hyperspace."

"Dropping out of hyperspace," Berisse confirmed. She, too, was back in official mode.

The dread Ciena had kept at bay by chatting with Berisse returned, stronger than before. She told herself that at least now she would know how bad the situation was. She wouldn't have to worry about Jude any longer. Nothing could be worse than not knowing.

The freighter dropped out of hyperdrive and into hell.

Berisse gasped out loud. Ciena couldn't even catch her breath. They were on the outskirts of a vast debris field, twisted metal floating in every direction. Some pieces were enormous—the size of a light cruiser—but others were fragments even smaller than a human head. Splinters connected with the freighter's windows and stuck to the transparency in patterns like frost or cracks.

"I can't believe it," Berisse said, voice shaking. "It's gone. It's completely gone."

The Death Star had been destroyed.

Jude's warning echoed louder in Ciena's head. *Fatal.* Now she knew Jude was dead.

A few other classmates had been stationed aboard the Death Star; at least a dozen people Ciena knew had been murdered that day. Thousands upon thousands of soldiers, most of them not even roused to battle stations—they would have been sleeping, eating, getting a drink in one of the cantinas, with no idea that moment was one of their last. But Jude had known the danger. Was she frightened? In her last terrible moments, had Jude known it was the end? The idea made Ciena's throat tighten and her eyes fill with tears.

"Lord Vader's signal." Berisse snapped out of her shock to get back to work. "Let's go."

Numbly, Ciena steered the freighter around the edge of the debris field. She wanted to cry; she wanted to scream. The command officers had to have known what happened. Why hadn't they told the fleet? The entire galaxy? But maybe they had believed this as impossible as she had. Ciena finally recognized that her mission was not only to retrieve Darth Vader but also to confirm that the worst had happened. They had sent her to bear witness to another massacre.

Her sorrow for Jude flooded her mind until she couldn't feel anything. Ciena went through the motions as they approached Lord Vader's damaged TIE fighter, grateful for the training that had taught her how to respond even when she was falling apart.

Vader's ship slowly took form in the darkness. She first saw the strange rotation of several pieces of debris, as if they were being shoved back by repulsor beams. Then she saw the form of a TIE fighter with angled wings. Vader was flying just beyond the ever-expanding debris field.

"Initiating airlock sequence," Ciena said. She was grateful Berisse didn't know her very well yet, so she wouldn't hear how strained and unnatural her voice had become. "Three—two—one."

Berisse hit the controls that would release one of a quartet of docking umbilicals from the ship's belly. Carefully, they extended the tube to the top of the TIE fighter's spherical cockpit.

"Met Lord Vader yet?" Berisse said lightly.

"I—uh, no." Ciena could hardly focus enough to speak.

"I'm going to let you go back there and greet him."

Normally, Imperial officers strove to be the first to

talk to anyone of higher rank. Those were opportunities to stand out from the pack. Ciena had never cared less about advancement. And yet she had the impression Berisse wasn't doing her a favor.

They say he is a great man, she reminded herself as she stood at the airlock, waiting for the all clear to enter the bay. *That he has the Emperor's favor. And they say he can bend the Force itself to his will.* Though Ciena believed in the Force, she was doubtful that anyone could control it so completely. She wondered if she would be proven wrong.

Ciena needed a superior officer she could respect. Someone who would take charge, someone in whom she could put her trust. She walked into the airlock corridor just as the pressure door hissed open. Reassured, she stepped forward—

—then stopped as she saw Vader for the first time.

Black armor sheathed him entirely. This was no TIE pilot's gear, however; instead Ciena recognized a life-support suit, one more comprehensive than she'd ever seen or imagined before. Nothing of Vader's human skin or face remained visible beneath his gleaming carapace, and a black cape shrouded him from shoulder to floor. As he stepped forward, she realized how tall he was—taller than any other human she had ever encountered. In the cramped corridor, his stature was even more intimidating. But worst of all was the sound of his breath. The harsh rasp of his respirator system echoed until it seemed to fill the space.

What is *he?* Ciena wondered. Her splintered mind refused to accept Lord Vader as human. He seemed more like a nightmare vision, or a creature from the scary stories Mumma used to tell around the kindred gathering fires. Evil seemed to ooze from him, to pool within the space until there was no more air. Ciena's uniform collar felt too tight.

Only a few moments before, she'd been determined to greet her superior officer with dignity. Now she only hoped not to faint.

As Darth Vader stepped away from the airlock door, she heard his deep metallic voice for the first time. "Are you here by the Emperor's command?"

"We received our orders from the command staff of the *Devastator*, sir," Ciena managed to respond. She had to fight the instinctive need to draw away from Vader. "I have no information regarding their contact with the Emperor."

Vader took this in for what seemed to be a very long time. Ciena's nervousness continued to grow until he ordered, "You and your fellow pilot will remain in the hold for the remainder of the voyage. I will take command of this freighter until we have returned to the *Devastator*."

"Yes, sir."

She didn't care about being hauled back to her Star Destroyer like so much cargo. Ciena was grateful to sink down to the floor, put her head on her knees, and take deep breaths. At least now she didn't have to act. Even to think. She tried to forget she'd ever seen Darth Vader, and almost succeeded. Her battered mind could hold on to nothing but the scene of devastation she'd witnessed, and her grief for Jude.

A thousand memories of her friend shone in Ciena's memory like candles: the times they'd laughed and talked in their bunks late at night, how Jude had rushed to defend Ciena when she'd been accused of sabotaging Thane's laser cannon and then comforted her after the argument that followed, even how unexpectedly glamorous Jude had looked at the reception. One of the best friends she'd ever had, or would have, had been annihilated. Blasted to atoms.

Berisse was apologetic when she joined Ciena. "Lord Vader can be a little—overpowering when you first see him."

"Yeah," Ciena said faintly.

"I didn't feel like I could take it. Doesn't mean it was any easier for you. Sorry." Berisse leaned back against the wall like a puppet freed from its strings. "I know he's just wearing a life-support suit, and it's stupid to be frightened of someone who has different needs, right? But that respirator—"

"He could be monitoring us right now," Ciena pointed out. Berisse fell silent.

When they returned to the *Devastator*, Ciena was grateful to finally be off duty. She went to the deck where her crew quarters were located. She freshened up. She spent a few minutes crying into a towel for Jude. Then she pulled herself together and walked back toward her bunk—only to pause as she saw another junior officer in the corridor heading to the auxiliary bridge. "Nash?"

Nash Windrider nodded. He still moved slowly, a bit like a man sleepwalking, but his uniform was regulation neat and his voice calm. "All hands are needed."

"You're sure you're ready?"

"I have to be," he said simply.

She put one hand on his arm. "Are you positive? You've been through a lot." How inadequate. His entire planet had been destroyed in the hopes that it would end a war, and those hopes had proved futile. Nash had to be profoundly devastated.

His voice low, he said, "The Empire is all I have left. I need to be of use. I want to serve."

Ciena still wondered whether Nash could handle it,

but she decided to stop fighting him. He deserved the chance to try. "Okay. I'll walk you up there."

Nash nodded, his silence perhaps a tacit acknowledgment that he remained on the emotional brink.

She noticed then that he'd cut his hair; the long braids he'd worn tied at the nape of his neck throughout his academy years had been shorn completely. Maybe the braids had carried meaning on Alderaan, or maybe the change was symbolic for Nash—something he'd done as a kind of farewell. Regardless, Ciena knew better than to ask.

The corridors of the *Devastator* were eerily silent; only a few courier droids and a handful of guards walked along the metal-mesh floors. Without the usual bustle of activity, the few sounds remaining were amplified to strange effect: the echoing of their footsteps, even the faint hiss of the ship's ventilation system. Despite her misery and fury, she realized that deep within her was a small sense of—reassurance.

The Death Star will never destroy another world.

She would always mourn Jude and the others who had died aboard the Death Star, would always recognize its explosion as the act of terrorism it was. Yet Ciena took some comfort from the fact that no other planet would suffer Alderaan's fate. Its destruction had been the Emperor's last-ditch effort to end a bloody war before it began; that effort had failed. War had come. The devastation to follow would no doubt be terrible; Ciena expected to see constant combat and war readiness for a long time to come. She would have to kill and risk being killed.

But that was war. The combatants would be soldiers prepared for battle. That Ciena could accept.

Shortly before they reached the auxiliary bridge, Nash said, "Ciena?"

"Do you need out of this duty shift?" Exhausted though Ciena was, she would volunteer to work the next few hours in Nash's stead if it would help.

"No. It's just—before I left my cabin, I was thinking of Thane. I wanted to talk with him. So I searched for information about the Dantooine transport." Nash hesitated before finishing. "They'd received orders to return to the Death Star."

The blood in her veins froze. Ciena stood stockstill in the corridor, unable to take another step. She swallowed hard. "And Thane?"

"He would've been aboard. Do you know if the transport docked before the explosion?"

"No."

All that time, Ciena had kept going by promising

herself that she'd be able to talk about everything with Thane soon—by reminding herself that at least her best friend in the world had escaped.

But what if he hadn't? What if Thane had been killed, too?

It took almost a week—the longest and most agonizing of his life—for Thane's ship to receive new, definite orders. His vessel, a short-haul transport, hadn't been stocked with nearly enough provisions, so they'd had to commandeer foodstuffs from the nearest town. Although the ship had bunks, they were intended more for emergency use by the injured than for actual sleep. Rather than lie on those, Thane and several others had moved into the bunks the rebels left behind.

How strange it felt to lie on the enemy's bed, to see where someone had drawn a crude figure of an X-wing fighter on the wall, and to know an X-wing like that had been the weapon that destroyed the Death Star—and maybe Ciena with it.

So Thane should have been relieved to be back aboard his own ship, fully armored and with his blaster at his side. Nothing was worse than not knowing, he'd told himself. Once they'd rendezvoused with the Imperial fleet, he would finally find out for certain what had happened to all his friends.

But when he tried to imagine what he'd do if they told him Ciena was dead, his mind went blank. It was as if his brain refused to show him anything beyond that point.

"Kyrell," his commander said as they prepared for lightspeed. "Did you not send family messages confirming your survival? I show you as a yes, but we've got no responses."

"You wouldn't," Thane said, without much emotion. He didn't think his family actually wanted him dead—though maybe Dalven wouldn't have minded—but writing back was apparently beyond their interests.

What did I ever do to them, besides being born? he thought for the thousandth time.

Yet thinking of that made him want to talk to Ciena, the only person who'd ever really understood how screwed up his family was. The pit of fear in his belly grew heavier, and he spoke hardly one word on their way to rendezvous with the fleet.

When the transport came out of lightspeed, a few people muttered and one person emitted a low whistle of surprise. Outside hovered more ships than Thane had ever seen in one place, even over Coruscant. TIE fighters swarmed like gnats scurrying over the surface of every larger vessel. Countless transports and smaller ships had been pulled into rough formation around the dozen or so Star Destroyers that obviously formed the new core of the Imperial Starfleet.

Was one of those Star Destroyers the *Devastator*? From the outside the ships were as identical as slices of the same pie.

Even as their transport rose into the main docking bay, their commander was shouting their new orders. "N-O-Seven-One-Eight, you're to report to the Star Destroyer *Eliminator* immediately, to Lieutenant Commander Cherik. N-Y-One-One-Two, same orders. A-V-Five-Four-Seven—"

Thane lifted his head.

"You transfer to the troop ship *Watchtower* for transport and deployment to Kerev Doi."

He was being sent to a spice-mining world? The order sounded absurd to Thane for the instant it took him to put the pieces together. Wherever spice was a commodity, finances became shady. If you wanted to hide money—vast sums of it, the kind of funds that could support an entire rebel army—Kerev Doi was one of the very few places in the galaxy to which you could turn. They were being sent to shake the place down, maybe to cut the Rebellion off at the source. That made sense. Yet he found himself thinking of Kerev Doi in a very different light. Spice worlds were heavily trafficked by ships both legitimate and criminal.

Even many of the legitimate vessels didn't keep careful records about their trips there. Every storybook or holo about running away from home featured one of the spice worlds and colorful images of the exotic ships and traders who might whisk anyone away from the life they had known before.

Kerev Doi was a place where he could get lost.

Thane caught himself. It wasn't like he was actually planning on leaving the Imperial fleet, at least not yet. Not until he'd learned what had become of Ciena, Nash, and the rest, and maybe not ever. But he was perhaps . . . testing the idea. Getting used to it.

If Ciena had died, what was left for him there? Nothing.

"Sir?" he said to his commanding officer, who looked annoyed at the interruption. "Which Star Destroyer is this?"

"Does it *matter*, Lieutenant Kyrell?"

"It does to me, sir."

His commanding officer wasn't impressed by any show of independence. "You're on the *Devastator*. But if you're not on the *Watchtower* within the hour, you're out of the fleet."

The Devastator. Thane breathed out. *Okay, Ciena's probably fine. She was safe and sound on her ship the entire time.*

Unless maybe she stayed behind on the Death Star for a duty assignment—or she was visiting Jude and the Devastator *pulled out too quickly for her to rejoin it—*

He disembarked with only a wrist communicator to tell him where to find the *Watchtower*'s docking berth. From the looks of things, he didn't have much time, but maybe enough to stop at a communications panel. Even if the system informed him she was on duty, it would be proof she was alive. How was he supposed to get on another ship and fly away from the *Devastator* without even knowing?

"Thane!"

He turned and saw Ciena, halfway across the crowded bay, and it was like the hard shell around him cracked and crumbled away. He forgot about Kerev Doi, about escape. It was impossible to think about anything but the sight of her there, then, *alive*. "Ciena!"

Then all that mattered was pushing through the crowd, shouldering aside stormtrooper grunts and senior officers alike, so he could get to her.

Ciena flung her arms around Thane's neck, and he embraced her back so tightly that she could barely breathe. She didn't care, not now.

"You're alive," she said, her voice breaking. "You're alive. We didn't know whether your transport had returned to the Death Star—"

"I didn't know if the *Devastator* made it, and nobody knows what the hell is going on—"

"It's so terrible—"

"Did you—?"

They stopped trying to talk over each other and just laughed for a moment, out of pure joy. Ciena looked up at Thane, and she saw the man he had become, the one she was in some ways only beginning to know—and yet who was already as much a part of her as her bone or blood.

"I'm supposed to report to the *Watchtower* within the hour," Thane said. "Are you free?"

She could've groaned. Already she was late to report for her next shift—but then, to the side, she saw Berisse gesturing at her, clearly saying, *Go on! I've got it!* Ciena turned back to Thane. "I have a few minutes."

They worked their way through the busy docking bay to a side corridor; it led to a recreation area and, as such, was currently deserted. Though the roar of activity continued only a few meters away, there the two of them could be nearly alone.

"Are you all right?" Thane brushed a loose curl back from her cheek as he framed her face with his hands.

Ciena knew he wasn't talking about battle injuries. "Nash Windrider is safe. He's torn up about

Alderaan—" It was hard even to say the planet's name. Thane winced when he heard it. "Still, he's on duty. But Jude died on the Death Star."

"I'm sorry." He pulled her back into his arms, and she leaned her head against his chest.

They'd never touched each other like that; no doubt Thane was as vividly aware of that as she was. And yet embracing him, being held by him, felt natural. Right.

"I really thought I'd lost you," she whispered. "Everything else I could handle, because I had to, but when I realized you might have been killed—I knew I couldn't get through that. Not ever."

Ciena expected him to say something like, "Of course you could; you're strong" or "Don't worry about me." Instead, Thane folded her deeper in his embrace. "This whole week, I didn't know if you were dead or alive. The Empire has been turned upside down, and we're going to war, and not one damn bit of it mattered. You were the only one I could think about."

Ciena stood on tiptoe to hug him tighter. Thane's fingers traced along her jawline as he brushed his lips against her forehead, then tilted her face up toward his. But it was Ciena who brought their mouths together for their first kiss.

Oh, she thought as their lips opened against each

other. *It's not whether he's my friend or someone I love. He's* both. *Thane's always been both, since the beginning.*

This wasn't the start of something; it was their discovery, their admission, of what had been between them for a very long while.

When they pulled apart, Thane took a deep breath. "That was—very—"

"Yeah." Then they both laughed, more gently this time, and he kissed her forehead again.

She slid her arms down his shoulders to take his hands in hers. Thane's crooked smile made Ciena feel as if she were melting inside. Why couldn't this have happened at a moment when they could really be alone?

But a few stolen minutes in a noisy docking bay were all they had, and she didn't intend to waste them. "Listen to me," Ciena said. "As crazy as things are, we'll be together again. I don't know where or when, but it's going to happen."

"It will," he answered, brightening. "No matter what, I'm going to find you."

That was a strange way to put it. Once they worked past this initial confusion, Imperial records would be able to connect the two of them at any time. But Ciena didn't care. She was too overcome, already yearning for the next time they'd be together before they'd even said good-bye. "How can I miss you when you're still here?"

"Because I already miss you, too. But it's not forever. Not even for long."

Thane kissed her again, and after days of holding strong against loss, grief, and terror, Ciena let herself surrender to a moment of happiness.

Then she walked him to his transport, kissed him once more at the ramp as a few officers inside whistled, and, finally, ran like hell for her duty station.

When she got to her console, Berisse stepped aside with a motion like a waiter presenting the dessert. "I owe you one," Ciena breathed as she tried to steady herself.

"You owe me *way* more than one," Berisse answered.

Ciena glanced sideways at Berisse; the two of them started to smile at the craziness of it all. Amazing how, in situations like that, you could become good friends in only a couple of days. She got back to work, but on one viewscreen she brought up the docking bay feed so she could see the *Watchtower* disengage and set off for the infinity of space, taking Thane with it.

CHAPTER ELEVEN

IN THE ADVENTURE stories and swashbuckling holo-series Thane had watched as a child, spice worlds were exotic lands peopled with beautiful dancers, wisecracking gangsters, and daring pilots who flew souped-up starships as they outran those no-good Old Republic enforcers.

The stories all suggested that spice smugglers longed for a day when they could trade their goods fairly—and that the Empire had delivered the spice worlds from their more dangerous, yet colorful past. Thane no longer believed in the Empire as anyone's salvation, and he knew he'd learned all that from tales told to children; yet the romance of spice worlds lingered until the moment he set foot on Kerev Doi.

He didn't know what he'd expected, but it wasn't *this*.

Kerev Doi's pink skies no longer spread over vast open land; instead they had turned darker and hung over a grim, disheartened populace. People didn't wear fancy outfits or trade quips; they hid within heavy cloaks and said as little as possible. Spice farms dominated the landscape. Everything about the planet that wasn't ordinary was profoundly depressing.

Okay, so your childhood stories didn't pan out, Thane told himself roughly. *Get over it. This is reality.*

His duty would have been easier if he'd had more to do on Kerev Doi, but the *Watchtower's* role was primarily to ferry the officials in charge of shaking down the planet's notoriously corrupt banking system and to provide a show of strength. So Thane's tasks were limited to taking out his TIE fighter every day and flying low over areas that needed a reminder of the Empire's power and reach.

Once, Thane might at least have found it funny, the way people cowered and scattered as he flew overhead. After Alderaan, seeing people scared of the Empire— well, he no longer felt like laughing.

On a free night, he went out to the Blue Convor, a local nightclub famous from many of the holos. That was where heroes and heroines met each other, exchanged soulful glances over drinks that glowed in the radiant light, and made plans that would earn them money beyond imagining. Thane held out little hope for the place; at worst it would be as seedy and run-down as most of what he'd seen of Kerev Doi so far. At best it would be a tourist trap.

But somehow the Blue Convor turned out to be relatively close to what Thane had pictured. The ambiance was low-key (helped along by the new rule that only Imperial officers could bring their blasters inside). Low couches were cushioned in deep orange and rich pink, and hanging plants dangled their lush blooms overhead. Levitating candle droids illuminated only their immediate surroundings, leaving plenty of inviting shadows. The music was excellent, low sultry rhythms played by a long-snouted guy at a circular keyboard. Thane's drink came in a tall glass and was just strong enough to soften the edges.

I'll tell Ciena about this in my next message, he thought. *She used to like those holos, too, when she got to see them. It would make her happy to know at least one thing about Kerev Doi is just as good as we imagined it.*

Thane felt himself grinning and tried to stop, but he couldn't. Even the thought of Ciena blew his mind these days.

Ever since that day on the Sky Loop when Thane had first realized the new potential in his relationship with Ciena, he'd resisted it. Even when he hadn't been angry with her about that dumb-ass incident with the laser cannon, he'd been afraid of what would happen if the bond between them changed.

But it *hadn't* changed. That was the amazing thing. They'd always belonged to each other in ways that were difficult to define; Thane felt as though they'd simply acknowledged what had been true from the start.

And she, too, was considering leaving the Imperial Starfleet.

That made sense, of course. Ciena defined herself by her honor, and there could be no honor in what the Empire had done to Alderaan. Obviously, the Rebel Alliance was no better; it had blown up the Death Star with nearly two million people on board. But one wrong didn't excuse another. She had probably thought about abandoning her post even before he had.

Once again, Thane replayed those few incredible minutes in his mind—the one and only time he'd been able to hold Ciena in his arms and kiss her. She had said, *We'll be together again. I don't know where or when.*

She wouldn't have said that if she thought they'd both remain in the Imperial Navy, where they could find each other through any database. Surely she, too, wanted out.

But wanting out and getting out were two different things. What exactly was he supposed to do if he abandoned his post? He would immediately become a wanted criminal. A low-priority criminal, maybe—especially with the rebels out there as a more dangerous threat—but he'd still be at risk of being thrown in the brig the first time an Imperial officer performed a scan and realized he was a deserter. Plus Ciena would find it incredibly hard to break her promise to serve the Empire. She believed in both oaths and honor as sacred. What happened when those oaths and her honor were at odds?

I guess we have to wait, he thought tiredly. *Do our five years. Try to get assigned to the same station or ship for a while. Maybe put down this damned rebellion and avenge Jude, before our tours of duty are up. Then we can resign and walk away.*

And after that . . . Thane didn't know. They wouldn't return to Jelucan; that much was certain. But it was a big galaxy. The possibilities were endless. All they had to do was search for their future together.

He sipped his drink and daydreamed about this night as a scene from one of the holos. Now he was a swaggering spice pirate, all ego and charm. Ciena could slink in dressed like one of those classic femme fatales—in a deep-red robe that clung to her body—and whisper to him that she needed help from a man who was afraid of nothing.

"That's me," he whispered to the Ciena in his

mind. He imagined kissing her again, and the next daydreams lasted him until he had paid for his drink, left the club, and returned to his bunk.

Thane's five-year plan fell apart eight days later, when he flew over the Lower-Sea Province.

He did a few dramatic swoops and dives for the best effect. The distinctive scream of a TIE fighter's engines would echo in the canyons. No one who heard it could doubt that the Empire remained strong and omnipresent throughout the galaxy. By the time he landed to meet with the local garrison and grab his midday meal, Thane was feeling fairly pleased with himself.

But as he walked toward the local HQ, his smile faded.

A line of workers trudged along the trail leading up from the mine crevasse. In most of the spice mines Thane had seen up until then, droids and lesser automatons served as the main labor force. There, however, the miners were all sentient beings. He even recognized their species: a pale reptilian people called the Bodach'i. Their planet had continually resisted Imperial regulations—everyone knew that, as the Bodach'i had been open in their defiance—but some months before, it had been announced that order was restored and new sanctions levied.

Thane had imagined that "sanctions" meant fines or trading penalties. He had not realized it meant slavery.

The Bodach'i wore restraint collars and wristlets. On their own, the restraints were no more than heavy and cumbersome; however, any deviation from the programmed tasks or paths would result in electric shocks or even metal spurs jabbing into the wearer's flesh.

I thought those restraints were for violent criminals, not for . . . regular people, Thane said to himself, dazed, as he walked slowly along the border of the Imperial outpost. Beyond, the Bodach'i staggered under their burdens, unable to stop and rest. They were monitored by Imperial stormtroopers who stood many meters apart along the line that seemed to stretch into infinity. A few townspeople watched, either in silent fear or complete apathy. Thane couldn't tell the difference.

Nausea tightened his throat and belly as he saw the Bodach'i struggling. Most of them weren't even fit laborers. There were youngling Bodach'i there, hardly big enough to carry the burdens they'd been given. Elders, too, their scales gone dusty with age.

This was wrong. Worse than wrong—*evil*. If the Bodach'i had defied the Emperor, sanctions might be appropriate, but not this. Nothing could justify punishing an entire race this way.

Enslaving them.

Why doesn't someone help these people? Thane wondered as he scanned the blank expressions of the locals. Their collars could be unfastened during the night, their escapes covered up. . . .

Then it hit him.

Nobody helped the Bodach'i because these people all feared the Empire. And when Thane had flown overhead, showing off his TIE fighter and letting the populace hear its engines scream, he had made them even more afraid.

The crushing weight of that truth settled on him, and for a moment Thane felt as if he could hardly breathe.

One of the local children had begun jeering at the Bodach'i. "That's what you get! You think you can push the Emperor around? Showed you!" One of the stormtroopers nodded in approval, then patted the child's head.

That boy could be no more than seven or eight years old—the age Thane was when he'd decided to join the Imperial fleet. That was how evil magnified itself: it took root in the young and grew along with them. Each generation provided the next level of abuse.

We're teaching children to approve of slavery. We're teaching them cruelty is a virtue.

But the worst part was—Thane had been that kid. He'd sat in the pilot's seat of a shuttle and felt proud. Felt big. All because he might be part of the Empire someday. He'd followed the path that led from there, and where had it taken him? Now he flew ships only to frighten people, in the name of an Empire that slaughtered entire worlds. If he could go back, would he have the strength to choose a different path?

Do I have the strength to do that now?

Another stormtrooper cuffed one of the Bodach'i, who staggered to the side. She had lost many scales and her tail dragged along the sand, even though the rough terrain had to have nicked and bruised it countless times by then. The creature's weakness lanced Thane through, especially because there was nothing he could do. Absolutely nothing. Not against an entire garrison of stormtroopers. He had to just stand there and watch, and know his part in the evil he beheld.

That night he paid the exorbitant amount of credits it took to buy a holonet message. If Ciena didn't get the signal in time, or wasn't free to respond, he'd just have to try again the next day—but to Thane's relief, she signed in almost immediately. He took his seat in the dark holo-booth, felt the warm beams of light scanning his face and body—

—and Ciena materialized before him.

Her hologram was nearly life-size. The soft blue light caught every facet of her—the curls half-loosed and falling down her back, her full lips, the way she smiled to see him. "I wasn't expecting this," she said, her voice only slightly blurred by the transmission. She wore uniform trousers but had stripped down to her singlet, exposing her arms and shoulders. "I can't believe you sprang for the holonet—but I'm so glad you did! It's so good to see you."

"Even better to see you." The sight of her now had lost none of the power of that first moment he'd glimpsed her on the *Devastator*. Thane still felt just as grateful and humbled at the mere fact she was alive. "I needed to talk. I didn't wake you up, did I?"

"No. My shift just ended, and my roommate's out."

One word of that struck him as odd. "Roommate, singular?"

Ciena's grin beamed at him through the darkened holo-recording booth. "You're talking to Lieutenant Commander Ree, as of yesterday."

"That's amazing." As little as either of them cared about advancement at a time like this, Thane could still appreciate what the promotion meant to Ciena. It was proof she'd done her duty, and brilliantly. "It's not surprising, though. Not for someone as good as you are."

Yet that made Ciena's face fall. "It's not only about my performance. Not even mostly about that. I got promoted because the Empire lost so many people on the Death Star."

Of course. The station had been hosting many of the top officials of the fleet and their staffs. Now there was a power vacuum at the top. "Everything has changed," he said, carefully.

Ciena nodded. One strap of her singlet slipped off her shoulder, and the illusion of the hologram was so strong that Thane wanted to lean forward and nudge it back into place—or maybe nudge the other one off, too. But he had to stay focused. He had to think. Holonet messages like these wouldn't be directly monitored, but there were programs to scour what they said and look for suspicious words or phrases.

So Thane couldn't come out and say exactly what he was thinking. Neither could she. But maybe they could make each other understand.

Ciena sat on the edge of her bunk, drinking in the sight of Thane's hologram in front of her. In the darkness she could almost pretend he was really there.

"Are you all right?" she asked, speaking as softly as she could, right into the holo-receiver. "As happy as I am to talk with you, I know you wouldn't have surprised me like this for no reason."

Thane's face was etched in golden light, only a shade lighter than his red-tinged hair. In it she could read the deepest concern and sorrow. "It's hard to know how to go on after a tragedy like this," he said.

Again Ciena thought of Jude, and she had to blink back tears. "I can't get it out of my head, either. It's like the explosion plays over and over in my mind, and I want to save them but I can't. I just . . . can't."

"Do you feel like we have to wait and see what happens with this war?" Thane said, his eyes searching hers so intensely that it was like he truly was there with her. "Or does this change how we go from here?"

Her heart ached to think of him systems away, trying in vain to imagine the right strategy that would give them a quick victory and prevent further bloodshed. Those daydreams were only natural, but that was all they could ever be: dreams.

"We can't just stand aside and let such things happen," Ciena reminded him. "Not when we have the power to make a difference. Whatever we have to do—however much we have to sacrifice—then we'll face that as it comes. Together."

"Together," Thane repeated, and his smile then was so sad that she could feel his vulnerability, and hers, as surely and painfully as any wound.

Ciena reached out to touch the hand of the hologram; Thane responded, and the flickering light of his fingers passed slightly through her real hand. "I miss you," she said once more. The words were so inadequate; nothing she could possibly say would communicate what she felt.

"It won't be long before we're together again," Thane promised, so confidently that she had to believe him. In fact, he seemed so sure that Ciena wondered if he'd already received his next orders—whether he knew something she didn't.

Thane looked down at her hand, carved of flickering blue light, reaching toward and through him.

"I hope you're right," Ciena said, her voice echoing slightly within the booth. "I wish it would only be a few days. No—as long as I'm wishing, I wish you were with me right now."

"Me too." The meter began to blink, signaling that their time was almost up. Thane wanted to stuff more credits into it and buy another few minutes—but they'd said all they could, and now more than ever, he needed to save his money for more important things.

"Gotta go. I'm sorry the call's so short, Ciena—"

"It's all right! I'm so glad I got to see you." Ciena kissed her own fingertips, then held them out until they seemed to brush his lips; Thane imagined he could feel the energy of the beams, electric and warm. "Good-bye."

"Good-bye," he said in the last instant before her image blinked out.

As he walked from the holo-booth back to his barracks, Thane kept replaying their conversation in his head, marveling at how they'd managed to say everything and nothing. Ciena had agreed with him about the tragedy of Alderaan and felt the same desperate, futile longing to save the lost. More than that, she'd agreed they couldn't just hang around in Imperial service, doing what they were told. They had to take action immediately.

Thane had already known what his path must be, but now that he knew Ciena was with him, nothing could hold him back.

The next day, he completed his morning flight pattern as usual, then managed to switch to a night flight instead of his usual afternoon run. He used those afternoon hours to withdraw as many credits as possible from his account, trade them in for spice, and then trade the spice in for unmarked credits. Thane used the money to buy civilian clothes—a dark blue jacket, black pants and boots, and a gray shirt that would look at home on any world in the galaxy.

Then and only then did he go to the spaceport and find an independent freighter.

"I want to get to the nearest Hub world," Thane said, trying to sound as confident and cocksure as the characters in those holos from long ago. "That's all you need to know. Ask no questions and you get two-thirds of the fee up front, one-third at landing."

The reptilian Falleen pilot laughed. "Silly human. I don't ask questions anyway. You ready to go? We blast off within the hour."

For one moment Thane hesitated, thinking of Ciena. Would she know where to find him?

Of course she will. She might even have left the Empire before I did, and got there before me. We're both heading in the same direction. Nothing in the galaxy can stop us.

"Yeah," Thane said. "I'm ready."

As Ciena lay in her bunk a few nights later, she whispered, "Do you think we should do something for Nash?"

"Ughhhh." Berisse's voice was hoarse from sleep. "You do realize this is the middle of my down shift, right?"

"Sorry. I'm just worried about him, that's all. It's like Nash is sleepwalking through his duties. Only half alive."

"Sounds about right, after what happened." Berisse leaned over the edge of her top bunk; her long black hair streamed around her upside-down face. "You're thinking about Nash mostly because it's the only thing that keeps you from thinking about Thane, aren't you?"

"It isn't!" Ciena rolled over on one side, flipping back her gray blanket so she could gesture for emphasis. "I've hardly been daydreaming on my shifts—they even let me handle auxiliary navigation yesterday."

"I didn't mean on the job. Put you at your duty station and you're flawless. It's only *every other* waking moment that you're dedicated to Thane."

"You're just teasing me because I wouldn't stop talking about his holo the other night."

"Exactly. So shut up and let me sleep." Berisse's face vanished, and above Ciena heard the rustle of blankets and mattress.

Still, Berisse wouldn't be asleep again yet. "We really do have to do something for Nash. I meant that. He's hurting terribly and won't admit it."

"He's doing about as well as can be expected. Nash

is picking up extra shifts—keeping busy. Best thing for him."

Probably that was true. "Still, we could figure out other ways to fill his time. Maybe invite him to work out in the gym someday, play grav-ball, that kind of thing."

"Sure. Give it a try," Berisse mumbled. By then she was deeply drowsy, barely conscious. No doubt she had no idea what Ciena had even said.

Grav-ball. The suggestion was so trivial it embarrassed Ciena; that was no consolation for the loss of a world. Then again, what was? Nash would have to rebuild his life day by day, even hour by hour. For now, as a friend, all Ciena could do was help fill some of those hours.

She rolled over and clutched her pillow as she tried to settle down. But she remained worried about Nash, miffed that Berisse had accused her of thinking about nothing but Thane—

—and happy to keep thinking about Thane.

That was the time to think of him, though. No duty, no distractions, only the memory of the extraordinary holo-message from a few days before. Ciena smiled to herself as she thought of the way they'd said so much in so few words. Thane had agreed with her about sticking to their duty, concentrating on fighting the war to the best of their ability, and finding ways to be together again as often as their service would allow.

She fell asleep amid a vision that was half hope, half dream—Thane transferred to the *Devastator* as a TIE pilot, flying alongside Lord Vader himself, coming back to her at the end of every shift. That dream suffused her entire night, which was one reason why the news the next morning came as such a wretched shock.

"There has to be a mistake," Ciena said, staring at Nash. "You got the names wrong."

"I was his roommate for three years. Trust me, I know his name." Nash even turned the tablet around so she could see for herself. They stood outside the commissary; nobody was around to overhear except a few groggy pilots staggering in to get their breakfast and caf. "Lieutenant Thane Kyrell, designation A-V-five-four-seven, deserted duty as of three Kerev Doi days ago."

She clutched at the sleeve of Nash's uniform. "He wouldn't desert. His ship crashed—or he's been taken prisoner by some local roughs, something like that."

"You'd think his superiors would have checked that out. But perhaps you're right. It's not like Thane to run." Nash stepped closer to her, lowered his voice. "I didn't tell you this to frighten you. One of the ISB officers questioned me this morning about Thane's loyalties, political beliefs, all the rest. I was able to assure them that Thane is no rebel, but I can tell they're not satisfied."

Ciena understood now. They would question her next.

So she walked straight to the office of the senior ISB officer aboard, Captain Ronnadam, and had herself announced. She stood in front of him at attention as she said, "I've come to volunteer what information I have about Lieutenant Kyrell, sir."

"Our vagabond on Kerev Doi. Or once on Kerev Doi." Ronnadam squinted at her. "Do you think he's a traitor or merely a deserter?"

"He is no traitor," she answered with as much force as she dared. It was important that the general understand they were on the same side—all three of them. "Thane—Lieutenant Kyrell has repeatedly described the rebels as terrorists, sir. In our last communication, he expressed his deep sorrow and anguish about the destruction of the Death Star."

"Then why, Lieutenant Commander Ree, has he abandoned his post?"

"I can only think that he is—in despair, sir. Overcome by the loss of so many friends." Ciena hesitated before continuing. This came close to betraying Thane's secrets, and she had almost done that once before, when she'd mentioned his problems with his father in front of Jude. But she needed to save Thane and his commission now, any way she could. "Lieutenant Kyrell grew up in extremely difficult circumstances. His family provides no support whatsoever. So his fellow officers—*we're* his family. All he has. That loss has affected him profoundly."

"He's not the only one who lost people," Ronnadam snapped, but then his expression grew more thoughtful. "And he's not the only officer we've seen falter. The same offenses that would have gotten a man cashiered two years ago are now handled on a case-by-case basis . . . for now. There will of course be a penalty to be paid, but if Lieutenant Kyrell returns to duty in short order, he can continue his career without undue difficulty."

Ciena breathed out in relief. At least there was still time to save Thane from a terrible mistake.

"Do you know where he is, Lieutenant Commander Ree? If so, you realize you must report that information."

"No, sir. I don't have Lieutenant Kyrell's current location. But I know where to begin looking for information: our homeworld, Jelucan."

"Very well, Lieutenant Commander. I'll put through orders for you to travel to Jelucan on the next transport."

Her eyes widened. "Me, sir?"

Ronnadam snapped, "Do you think such duty is beneath you?"

"No, sir! I simply thought—an ISB officer—"

"Our agents are busier now than at any other time in our history. You're already familiar with the area, so sending you instead is a better use of resources." His voice had acquired a dangerous edge. "Unless, of course, you have superior ideas?"

Ciena was almost glad for the misunderstanding; better if Ronnadam didn't realize how badly she wanted to be the one to find Thane. "No, sir. I'll leave for Jelucan immediately."

"Search for him high and low. Use whatever resources you must." Ronnadam's eyes narrowed. "And if you hear so much as one whisper of Kyrell's involvement with the Rebellion—you will follow that whisper wherever it leads and report every word. Do you understand?"

Ciena had a chance to rescue Thane because the Empire wanted to use her as a spy. She'd never wanted to inform on anyone, for any reason. Duty demanded loyalty, but loyalty was owed to friends as well as superiors. For the first time she realized how dark the tasks that fell to her in this war might be.

But that was the price of finding Thane again.

"Yes, sir," she said, thinking, *Whatever it takes.*

CHAPTER TWELVE

IT WAS THE FOURTH and final freighter haul that got to Thane.

He'd kept his head down, remained quiet, and made it off Kerev Doi easily enough. The ships he had boarded for the next few trips gave him no trouble, either. On a passenger ship, he would've had little privacy and an overly interested crew to deal with. On a freighter, however, the few extra berths were sold to workers who wanted cheap transport and no frills. Thane didn't have to worry about being noticed there.

But when the last freighter came out of hyperspace near Jelucan, Thane grabbed his bag and headed for the disembarkation area. Long metal benches bolted to the walls had a few harnesses for those worried about a bumpy ride down; he strapped himself in and waited.

Another passenger did the same—then another—and a fourth.

None of these people behaved markedly different than Thane himself. They wore the sort of nondescript clothing that could be purchased on almost any world. They showed no undue interest in the people around them.

And yet any one of them could be an Imperial spy.

The idea latched on to Thane so hard he could scarcely breathe. The woman with the long salt-and-pepper braid—had she just glanced at his face? The Ottegan, with his wide-set eyes—who knew what he might be observing? Or the Volpai there, with all the fingers on all four of his hands tapping at his data feed—was he reporting Thane to the authorities even now?

Everywhere else, Thane had known he possessed the advantage of surprise. There was no way for the Empire to predict his earlier moves, but they might have guessed he'd return to Jelucan. So someone could have traced him to that freighter. Or an entire platoon of stormtroopers might be waiting for him in the landing bay—

Instead, the freighter landed without incident. The other four passengers dispersed without even looking at Thane. He laughed at his paranoia as he shouldered his bag. *You're on familiar ground now. Soon you'll feel like yourself again.*

Yet he didn't.

At first Thane believed he was only suffering from reverse culture shock, the strangeness of home after a long time away. Valentia, the grand city he'd admired as a boy—of course it would look small and provincial after he'd spent three years on Coruscant. If people seemed guarded and less friendly, probably that was because he was contrasting their reactions to the small boy he'd been with the more reserved reception they'd give an adult. And he was still on edge. His unease deepened the shadows.

But the longer he looked around, the more certain he was. His world had changed. The Empire had changed it.

The senatorial building everyone had been so proud of on the day Jelucan joined the Empire—that had been taken over by the military to sequester troops. Thane kept his distance, but he could tell that it was no short-term emergency measure. Already engineers were constructing a high surrounding wall, and the perimeter force field overhead glinted when sunlight broke through the gray sky.

Valentia might never have approached Coruscant's polish and sophistication, but it had been a vibrant, bustling city. Now the entire place seemed more crowded and emptier at the same time. Ramshackle, makeshift shanties had been built next to the older, stone-carved buildings; these clearly served as housing for itinerant workers, who had come out of the mountains looking for new opportunities that never materialized.

Or had these people been forced out? Thane wasn't sure. He could tell from the clothes they wore that both valley kindred and second-wavers were among the new vagabond population. Yet the two groups were harder to tell apart than they'd been before. Both the brilliant silks and plain homespun cloth had begun to be replaced by cheap mass-produced garments. A dense, stultifying sameness had settled over the land.

Even the entertainment was affected. Thane's rented room stood on the higher floor of a building that also housed a cantina at ground level. When he was a boy, his father had sometimes taken him into such establishments, promising to have "just one drink." So Thane had spent many long hours sitting in a far corner watching podraces or the spice-world holos he enjoyed so much.

The cantinas were rougher now—less neighborhood pub, more seedy bar. Most of the patrons were not local characters; outworlders seemed to have crowded them out. As Thane nursed his ale, he stared at the screens in disbelief. Every single program was Imperial propaganda of some kind or another: a documentary ostensibly about the Empire's successful "building programs" on Thurhanna Minor (really enormous power facilities that squatted over once-pretty countryside) was broken up by recruiting calls for stormtroopers ("Discover adventure and serve your Empire!") or news items about Emperor Palpatine receiving guests as he smiled and nodded. Worst of all was an ad for a special report scheduled to air soon, in which the "full extent of the treasonous acts of sedition on the planet Alderaan will finally be exposed!"

Thane had thought everyone would be talking about Alderaan. No one did. The silence about an entire Core World planet's destruction told Thane more than any gossip would have. *Everyone is thinking about it. Everyone is afraid.* If the Empire would destroy a world as important and prosperous as Alderaan . . . no place in the galaxy was safe.

(The Imperial broadcasts were vague about the Death Star's destruction, speaking only of an "unprecedented attack by the Rebel Alliance." Thane had first thought the Empire would play it up as a rebel atrocity, but then he realized that it was more important for the populace to believe that the Empire could destroy another world at any moment.)

When he walked outside, he was disturbed even by the color of the sky. Jelucan's atmosphere usually showed itself as more gray than blue, but the air had always been clear and sparkling, and the gray overhead had the sheen of a fine mineral. Now the skies were darker even when they were cloudless, as if expecting a storm that never came. Had the mining begun to affect the atmosphere?

Thane had argued with himself about whether or not to contact his family when he arrived. Little as his father cared for him and as much as his mother wanted to curry favor with the Empire, he couldn't believe they'd actually turn him in. Even if they wouldn't have protected him, they wouldn't have wanted to endure the shame. At home he could have saved his credits, taken his time, and waited for Ciena.

He could even have ridden his old line down to the Fortress, tidied it up, made it nice. It seemed so right to meet her there again—

In the end, though, Thane had decided against contacting his parents. He had no need for his father's drunken contempt or his mother's outrage; least of all did he want to hear them talking about how Dalven was doing.

(Given the severe shortage of Imperial troops, even an oaf like Dalven had probably received a promotion. He'd be fool enough to take pride in it, too.)

But as the days went on, his spirits sunk lower. Ciena still hadn't appeared. What if she'd tried to desert but been captured? The thought of her in jail, feeling shamed and hopeless, sickened him. (He didn't give in to despair; Ciena was too smart, too capable to be easily caught. She'd wait until the moment was right, but that moment might not come for a while.) The scant funds Thane had managed to escape with had mostly gone to pay for his freighter trips. His rent on the tiny room already seemed like too much, and he was living on nothing but street food—thin slices of suspiciously sourced meat cooked on small makeshift grillers outside the shanties, or thin "stews" thickened with ground grain.

Like most cadets, Thane had dreamed of having a few days to sleep late, ignore military discipline, and do whatever he wanted. Yet without the strict framework he'd lived within for the past few years, he found himself rudderless—bewildered and irritated by more freedom than he knew what to do with. Instead of fulfilling his assigned tasks at a preset schedule, he did . . . nothing. Stubble appeared on his face as the beard suppressant wore off, and buying more didn't seem worth the credits it would cost. Every night he had nightmares—about Alderaan, the Death Star, his father, or Ciena in danger. The only thing that separated him from the down-and-outers around him was that Thane didn't spend all his money on ale, though by now he understood why some people did. With each day he sunk deeper into melancholy.

At first he'd thought it would be easy to find some kind of employment; there was always work for pilots, even unlicensed ones. But now he realized he couldn't do that on Jelucan. The Empire's presence there was too strong for a deserter to wander through the ports asking for a job. No doubt he could indenture himself to one of the less savory freighters that passed through— they never looked into people's backgrounds—but that was only one step removed from selling himself into slavery.

Very few things seemed worth trying any longer. It felt as if his entire life were frozen in time, waiting for Ciena to arrive. And if she never came, he didn't know what would become of him and didn't much care.

Thane hit his limit one night about two weeks in,

as he sprawled on his bed in his sleep tunic and pants. The pale plaster walls of his room were blank, his coverlet a light beige without any pattern. Given its price, the space was surprisingly comfortable—but Thane felt as if it were taunting him with its emptiness.

In the academy's Security Protocols and Interrogation Techniques class, they'd taught that one of the most effective methods for breaking a person down was simply to make that person stare at a plain wall without ever sleeping. The sleep deprivation and boredom did what pain and threats could not. A prisoner's mind would split itself open, spilling every word hidden inside, just to end the exhausting monotony. Thane had never understood how that worked until now.

A commotion outside made him sit upright. It sounded like some of the street merchants were folding up their not-quite-legal wares in a hurry. Thane went to the one small window in his room and pulled back the screen. On the ground a few floors down, he saw an Imperial patrol cruiser that had obviously just pulled up.

Then, on the stairs outside, he heard the thump of boots as someone headed his way.

All right, think fast. That's a single-person cruiser. They only sent one guy. You can take one guy out. Not without a weapon, though. Was there anything he could use? But the few items in the room were all either too big to be lifted or too small to do any meaningful damage.

Maybe he isn't coming for you. There are dealers in the neighborhood. Prostitutes. Smugglers. Plenty of people to arrest. But then they'd send one of the local paramilitaries, not an Imperial officer.

Thane took a deep breath as he ran his hands through his short hair. He'd have to bluff his way through it as best he could. If he denied being Thane Kyrell and acted completely confused, he might throw the guy off for a minute—long enough to grab the officer's blaster.

But could he shoot a guy who was just doing his job? Someone who had been his fellow officer just a few days ago?

A fist thumped on Thane's door. He mussed his covers as if he'd been asleep, went to the door, and said—as if groggy—"Mmhmmn. Yeah? Who is it?"

The reply: "I'm here on official business."

He knew that voice.

Instantly, Thane opened the door and saw Ciena standing there in uniform. The sight of her felt like the first breath he'd taken in years.

"You made it." He pulled her inside his room, locked the door behind them, and hugged her tightly.

As he breathed in the scent of her skin, he had to marvel at Ciena's brilliance. She hadn't deserted; she'd come here on official business, making sure the Empire would pay her way and delaying any other pursuit. "You're a genius, you know that? I kept waiting, and I thought they might have stopped you, but here you are. Here you are."

Thane kissed her then, long and deeply. That damned gray uniform was too stiff against his hands, but they could worry about that later. Ciena kissed him back just as passionately—but when their lips parted she looked so troubled that he wondered if he'd done something wrong.

Or maybe she was worried about their safety. "Did the Empire send anyone else?"

"No. They were sure you'd go somewhere besides Jelucan. I knew you'd guess that, so of course you'd come here—"

Thane grinned. She understood him so well.

But Ciena looked even more distressed than before. "Thane, *what have you done?*"

And then he finally began to realize how far apart they still were.

An hour later, Ciena sat with Thane in the cantina below. She'd been afraid they would be overheard, witnessed, maybe even turned in, but Thane had shaken his head. "Trust me," he'd told her. "The kind of people who come here? They give Imperial officers a wide berth. Nobody we know is likely to show up."

"It's not worth the risk," she'd said.

But Thane's square jaw had set in the way that she knew meant complete determination or just plain stubbornness. "If I don't get out of this room, I am going to lose it. Trust me. We'll be safe."

Sure enough, they had the entire corner of the place to themselves. Most of the patrons were newcomers to the planet, not natives, and they crowded at the front near the viewscreens. She and Thane sat at their small table alone. Merely being in a run-down cantina like that would have unnerved her a few years ago or even now, if she weren't so wrapped up in trying to stop Thane from making the worst mistake of his life.

"You can come back," she repeated. "I know you think they'll arrest you, and at any other time they would have, but they badly need qualified officers after what happened."

"I don't want to come back," he said, not for the first time.

Ciena still refused to believe it. "Three years in the academy—all that work, all that effort, for nothing?"

"You think I'm happy about this? I'm not. But

after what I've seen, what the Empire is doing to the Bodach'i—after Alderaan—I can't wear that uniform any longer." Thane leaned over his glass of ale, head in one hand, like a man with a headache. "I thought we agreed about this."

"I thought we agreed that after what happened to so many of our friends aboard the Death Star, we needed to stand together. The rebels killed thousands of our fellow officers. They killed Grand Moff Tarkin—"

"Tarkin was nice to us," Thane admitted. "Meeting him changed our lives."

"—and they killed Jude," Ciena continued. "Do you condone that?"

"I'm not joining the damned Rebellion, Ciena. I'm not condoning what happened to the Death Star *or* what happened to Alderaan. Are you? That's impossible. You'd never think destroying an entire world was the right thing to do."

Miserably, she shook her head. "No. I understand the thinking that led to the attack on Alderaan—but I don't condone it. The thing is, I *don't have to.*" Ciena leaned closer, looking into Thane's blue eyes and willing him to understand. "The Emperor and the Moffs have to see, now, that destroying Alderaan did no good. It didn't stop the Rebellion; if anything, it made the rebels more desperate."

"So two billion people died in vain," Thane said.

"And nearly a million aboard the Death Star." Ciena refused to ignore Jude's death. She still had nightmares of running through the station's corridors, screaming for Jude to get on a shuttlecraft, but never finding her friend. "Now the Death Star is gone. Even if the Emperor wanted to do something so drastic again, he couldn't. Besides—the only reason to attack Alderaan was to prevent an even more devastating war. The war has begun anyway. It's too late to save the galaxy from that. All I can do is fight on the side of law and order and stability."

Thane's laugh was harsh. "Things fall apart, Ciena. Our parents saw the Republic self-destruct. The Empire might last another year or another decade, but eventually there's going to be a brand-new order and brand-new law. Who will you serve then?"

"You don't have to be cruel just because I won't—because I can't desert my post." She couldn't even be angry with Thane; her sorrow was too great. Of course he would rage against Alderaan's destruction, but that didn't have to change everything. And of course he hated slavery—she did, too—but the Empire had scarcely invented the practice. What counted now was bigger than any individual incident. This was a matter of the deepest principle. "We *took an oath*. We swore ourselves to the Empire's service. We can't break that, not ever."

Thane shook his head. The amber lights in the cantina painted his hair a deeper red and cast shadows on his face that showed how much he was struggling. "You're still the girl from the valleys. You won't go against your word, even when you've promised yourself to a leader and a fleet that don't deserve you."

"And you're still the second-waver. You find it easier to break your promises than to keep them." But Ciena was ashamed of the words as soon as she'd spoken them. That was her father's prejudice talking, and her own misery at the thought of losing Thane.

He wasn't offended. Instead he whispered, "It's not easy for me to leave you. It's the hardest thing I've ever done."

She turned away, unable to look at him any longer.

Thane seemed to think she was reacting out of anger rather than grief, because he spoke more formally when he asked, "Will you report me?"

"I—" What could she say or do? She was trapped now between her loyalty to Thane and her loyalty to the Empire. As angry as she was with Thane for deserting his commission, she couldn't imagine sending him to jail. How could she ever do something like that to the person she loved? "I don't know."

"You don't know. Great." He ran one hand through his hair. "Do you at least know if you're going to report me *tonight*?"

Something within her broke. "Of course not."

Thane's voice had turned harsh, cutting. "That won't be breaking your oath? Destroying your precious honor?"

"Sometimes we're loyal to more than one thing. When there's a conflict, we have to choose which loyalty to honor." Ciena had begun trembling; she felt as if she were being torn in two. "I don't know what I'm going to do tomorrow. But tonight, right now, I choose my loyalty to you."

All the anger melted away from Thane then. His hand cupped the side of her face, and she couldn't hold back any longer. Ciena leaned closer, clutching at his jacket so he wouldn't get away from her. She wanted nothing but for him to stay with her now, tonight, however long they could have. She wanted to believe he wouldn't go away.

Thane kissed her again, more deeply than before. Ciena closed her eyes, wound her arms around him, and imagined that she could stop time. This moment would be crystallized and eternal—his chest pressed against hers, the soft rasp of his stubble against her cheeks, the low rough sound he made as his hand found the curve of her waist.

When they pulled apart, breathing hard, she leaned her forehead against his and whispered, "Upstairs."

It took Thane another couple of breaths to answer. "Are you sure?"

In that moment she felt as if she could be sure of nothing. Thane—one of the constants in her life, her polestar—was leaving forever. The world had turned upside down, and she suspected it could never be put fully right again.

But that was why she was determined to take everything she could have. To live completely in this moment, this night with Thane. To stop time.

"Yes," she whispered against his mouth. "Yes."

Thane couldn't sleep.

It was the dead of night and he was worn out, but it didn't matter. All he could do was look at Ciena.

She drowsed against his shoulder, not entirely asleep or awake. Her tightly curled hair, set free, spread around her head on the pillow like a dark halo. Her full lips were swollen from their kisses. And even though he'd spent the better part of the last three hours learning absolutely every detail of her body, it still exhilarated him to see her lying next to him, wearing nothing but a corner of the sheet.

As he lay beside her, Thane—for the first time—asked himself if he could do what Ciena asked. Could he return to base, admit to a moment of weakness, and go back into service? Probably Ciena was right about the current crisis absolving many sins. What would've earned him months in the brig a year ago was now likely to be no more than a smudge on his record.

If he returned right now, he could stay with Ciena—

But he couldn't go back. Not after what he'd seen. He'd spent his entire childhood suffering under the cruelty of one hypocrite; he refused to inflict suffering on behalf of another, even if that person was the Emperor.

For Ciena it was different. Her loyalty, once given, was absolute. The Empire didn't deserve her, yet it had her in its grasp forever. She didn't remain a part of the Emperor's machine because she was ambitious or corrupt. No, the Empire had found a way to use her honor against her. The strength of her character was the exact reason why she would remain in the service of evil.

It was as if she were already gone forever, even as he felt her soft breath against his shoulder. Thane hugged her tighter, burrowing his face into the curve of her neck. Ciena sighed softly as she came closer to consciousness; her hand slipped around his waist to deepen their embrace.

"You awake?" he murmured.

"Mmm-hmmm." Then she stirred again and answered more believably, "I am now."

"I love you." He couldn't believe he'd never said it before. It was like stating that the sky was overhead—so obvious, so fundamentally true, that verbalizing it ought to be unnecessary.

She lifted her face to his. "I love you, too. Always have. One way or another."

"I love you in every way."

"Yes." Ciena smiled, but the expression was so sad that it hurt Thane—a literal ache in the center of his chest. "In every way."

"If I begged you to stay with me, it wouldn't make any difference, would it?"

She shook her head. "If I begged you to get on the next transport back to Coruscant, you wouldn't, would you?"

He didn't have to say anything. They both knew the answer.

"So that's the end." The words came out more harshly than Thane had intended, but he trusted Ciena to understand his anger wasn't aimed at her. "The Empire takes us from each other forever."

"If it weren't for the Empire, we would never have come together in the first place. Think about it. Would you have ever made friends with a girl from the valleys any other way?"

Thane had been so small when Jelucan was annexed by the Empire that his earlier memories were jumbled and unsure. In some ways, it felt like his life had truly begun that day, with his dream of flying for the Empire, and with Ciena. "I guess not."

Ciena sat up, as if she was going to get out of bed, but Thane pulled her back. She wouldn't look him in the face any longer. "I should go."

"Stay."

"If I stay, leaving will only be harder."

"Would leaving now be any easier? Really?"

"No." Finally, Ciena met his eyes. "Thane, you have to get off Jelucan, within the week. Because at the end of one week, I'm going to report you."

Thane felt it like a stab wound between the ribs. "What happened to choosing which loyalty to honor?"

"I chose you tonight. I wish I could always choose you. But if I covered for you forever, my oath of loyalty to the Empire would be worthless. This is the only time, do you understand?" By now her voice had begun to shake. "This is the first time and the last."

Somehow, deep inside, Thane had still been convinced he would see Ciena again. He wanted to believe they could find each other no matter what. But now he realized that was foolish, the dream of a child.

"Do you understand?" Ciena repeated.

". . . yes." The word was bitter. "So you'd throw me in a military prison, even after this." Thane gestured at the rumpled bed, their discarded clothes on the floor. Her insignia plaque shone slightly in the dim light.

"I gave you fair warning, just now! Besides, you have to get on the move sooner or later. How much time have you wasted here?"

"Wasted? I was waiting for you." He hadn't known he could be so angry at someone and still love her. "I guess that was wasted time after all."

Ciena winced but she kept on. "You can't get a job on Jelucan. Catch the next freighter to an independent world—and don't even think about indenturing yourself, okay? Find yourself some work somewhere else in the Outer Rim, where they'll never look for you."

"I don't need your *advice*—"

"You need *someone's* advice. Otherwise you're just going to stay here in Valentia, moping and losing your way."

That stung, but Thane began to realize she wasn't completely wrong. "Okay, fine. I'll ship out of here soon."

"Within the week."

Because after one week she would report him. The woman he loved would report him to the Empire. "Yeah," he said flatly. "Within the week."

She took a deep breath. "So there's nothing more to say."

But Ciena made no move to leave. Instead she brushed her palm against his cheek; her thumb traced the line of his cheekbone.

He ought to tell her to get out. To tell her he was done sharing his bed with someone who cared more about the Empire than she did about him. Cruel words like the ones his father and Dalven used came into his mind fully formed, as if the wickedness he'd known from them had been buried deep inside, waiting to hatch: *I've already had everything I want from you. Gave it up easy, didn't you?*

But he said none of that. Instead he asked himself what he'd regret more—leaving her now or going to bed with her again. Either way was going to hurt.

Their gazes met, and when she leaned closer, he cupped his hand around the back of her head to bring her in for a kiss.

The time Thane had left with Ciena could be measured in mere hours. They wouldn't waste it.

Ronnadam scowled down at her report on his screen. "You're quite sure of this, Lieutenant Commander Ree?"

"As certain as anyone can be without finding a body—and in the crevasses, it's difficult for even scanner droids to search. The sky burial takes the dead within days, sir."

"Sky burial?"

Ciena wished she could have taken back those words; her thoughts were too much on Jelucan and all she had left behind there. "On Jelucan, sir, we put our dead in open cairns at high altitude. Birds devour the body, taking both the flesh and the soul of the deceased into the sky with them, forever."

"Barbaric," Ronnadam said with a sniff. She managed not to flinch. "But I suppose the same thing would happen with an accident—or suicide, as it seems we have here."

Ciena nodded. "Lieutenant Kyrell was overcome with grief after the loss of so many fellow officers and friends aboard the Death Star. Based on my interviews on Jelucan, I believe that he originally deserted and returned to his homeworld in an effort to restore his will to live, but it didn't work. He leaped from one of the higher cliffs in our home province, leaving his ridgeclimber behind. Still running."

She shouldn't have added that. Lies were best kept simple, or so Ciena had been given to understand. But she had lied so little in her life. The dishonesty tasted foul in her mouth.

When she'd parted from Thane, Ciena had fully intended to live up to her word and report his desertion after one week. A week was long enough for him to get his act together, escape to some obscure world, and vanish from her life forever.

That also gave her time to go home to her parents, who had been happy and surprised to see her—and no doubt even more surprised when she burst into tears at the door. Although Ciena had pulled herself together well enough, and had said not one word about Thane to her family, she knew they sensed that this was no routine visit. Mumma had sat up with her late into the night, asking no intrusive questions, simply braiding Ciena's hair the way she'd done when Ciena was a little girl. Her mother's touch had been comforting, but nothing could assuage Ciena's misery at the thought of turning Thane in.

In the end, she hadn't been able to do it. If the Empire made any effort to track him down, however minimal, it was possible they would find Thane and bring him back to stand trial.

So she chose her loyalty to him once again and protected him with the best lie she could create.

"Very well." Ronnadam signed off on her report without even fully reading it. Had Thane deserted at any less desperate time for the Imperial fleet, Ciena realized, her story would have been scrutinized much more closely. Now all Ronnadam wanted to do was cross a task off his list. "You handled this well, Lieutenant Commander Ree."

The praise felt like stones on her back, growing heavier throughout the day. Ciena burned with shame to have been commended by a superior officer for violating her oath of loyalty.

Never again, she promised herself. From that day on, her service to the Empire would be more than her duty: it would be her atonement for loving even one person in the galaxy more than her honor.

CHAPTER THIRTEEN

Seven Months After the Battle of Yavin

THANE TURNED DOWN the blue-white flame of the welding torch, lifted his goggles, and frowned at the snarl of metal he was attempting to fix. The independent freighter *Moa* had been old before he was born but kept going thanks to a series of makeshift upgrades installed over the decades. Right then he was trying to make a sixty-year-old power cell work inside a twenty-year-old processor—with limited success.

Cursing under his breath, he shut off the torch and walked through the *Moa*'s corridors until he reached the bridge. It wasn't the dark, angular kind of space Thane had learned to expect on Imperial vessels but a small, brightly lit chamber where console panels glowed in five different colors, each testifying to a completely different origin. Everything on the ship had been pieced together from parts to suit the very particular needs of the *Moa*—or, more precisely, the ship everyone on board usually called the *Moa*. That was only an acronym for its full name, *Mighty Oak Apocalypse*, a title that apparently sounded a lot more badass to Wookiees, such as their captain.

"I'm still only getting sixty percent charge," Thane reported to Lohgarra. "When we dock at Zeitooine, we've got to pick up a better power cell."

Lohgarra growled, wanting to know where, exactly, they would get the credits for a new power cell.

"I know we're broke." Technically, Thane was only a hired copilot and navigator, but Lohgarra treated her crew members with respect—like members of a team. He could bring up objections; he could say *we*. "But it doesn't have to be a *new* power cell. Just one that's not quite as old."

Lohgarra asked whether Thane thought all old things should be thrown out. That was a joke at her own expense; she was elderly even by the standards of the long-lived Wookiees, her fur by then almost entirely white.

Thane leaned against the wall and smiled. "Most things don't age as well as you do, Lohgarra."

That earned him a dismissive wave of her hand. She agreed to give him a budget to search for a newer battery for the aft sensor array but warned him with a growl that Zeitooine might not be the cheapest place to pick one up.

"I know. But we're not going to do much better in this area of space. We'd find something less expensive in the Outer Rim."

Being within the Inner Rim of the Empire made Thane uneasy. He'd signed on to the *Moa* precisely because Lohgarra and her crew mostly stuck to the Outer Rim, or the Expansion Region. Working for her had seemed like a good way to hide out for a while. Lohgarra transported only legal cargo, but she operated on the fringes, where Imperial oversight was rarely an issue. Although Thane hadn't outright told Lohgarra that he was an Imperial deserter, he could tell she'd guessed right away, and that she didn't care. Even though her dark blue eyes had gone slightly milky with age, her vision and mind were still sharp.

Lohgarra hired crew members who were not only competent but also easy to get along with—and not driven to make money by any means possible. The jobs they took were determined more by Lohgarra's character than by any quest for riches; a lucrative run of luxury goods might be followed by a zero-sum haul of emergency generators to a troubled outpost. She said she needed people around her who could be trusted; privately, Thane believed she was too trusting, but it was her ship and her business. She'd run a freighter for a couple of centuries without his help, so he figured she could size people up well enough. As he'd learned to understand Shyriiwook better, he'd realized how intelligent his captain was. And when Lohgarra really took a crew member under her wing—as she had Thane—she could be affectionate to the point of acting maternal. It was a little ridiculous, but he didn't mind. At least he worked for someone he could respect.

Always perceptive, Lohgarra had obviously picked up on his unease. She reminded him briskly that Zeitooine was a jungle planet with only a handful of large cities, and not an active trading center.

"Yeah, I know," Thane admitted. "We'll be fine." But he still felt uneasy and probably looked it, too.

The only other "crew member" on the bridge at the moment was their astromech droid, a JJH2 model in purple and black. Thane was grateful that nobody else would see his discomfort at the thought of landing on a world with an Imperial presence. Lohgarra had to remain the only one who really understood what was going on.

Concerned, she leaned forward to peer at Thane, squinting her blue eyes, then said he'd become too thin and asked if he was getting enough food.

He managed not to roll his eyes. "*Yes*, I'm eating."

But Lohgarra knew it could be difficult, finding rations that would provide adequate nutrition for all the different species aboard—

"I promise I'm fine. Don't worry, all right?" Thane turned to go.

As the bridge door slid open again, Lohgarra whined on a low, scolding note.

He laughed in exasperation as he walked out. "My coat is plenty shiny!"

As he walked down the corridor, he thought, *I just called my hair "my coat." Before too long I ought to spend some time with other humans again.*

Even then, he didn't consider returning to Jelucan. He had no reason. Every once in a while he'd watch news holos from home, but never out of a sense of nostalgia, only to make himself even happier he'd never have to go back. His family was no doubt glad to be rid of him, and Ciena—he had to close his eyes for a moment when he thought of her—she wouldn't be there, either. Not given the intensifying war between the Empire and the Rebel Alliance. He doubted Ciena had gotten more than three days' leave in a row since they'd said good-bye.

If Thane ever went back to Jelucan, he would imagine Ciena as a little girl in any of the small fliers darting through the skies. The mountain trails would remind him of how they had explored together as children and had found the cave that became the Fortress. And Valentia would never be only a city to him; it would always be the place where they'd come together for one night—and where they had parted forever.

It's been a while now, he told himself. *You ought to be over it.*

That was a lie. You didn't get over losing your first love, your best friend. But Thane had thought it wouldn't always hurt as badly as it had that last terrible morning in Valentia.

So far he had been wrong.

Zeitooine was a cold world—not one of the ones trapped in perpetual winter but chilly enough that Thane and his crewmates stepped out into a hard frost. The spaceport stood at the edge of the city, so in the distance he could see tall deciduous trees, all bare of their leaves. His breath made clouds in the air.

"Times like this, it's good to have fur," said Brill, their Tarsunt engineer, who had dyed her long-haired pelt shocking pink. "Don't know how you humans do it."

"Sometimes I wonder myself." Thane turned up the collar of his coat. "Let's just get this job done, okay?"

That was met with a thumping purr of agreement from Methwat Tann, the Ithorian maintenance officer.

His enormous curved head and neck were wrapped in a scarf specially knitted for him by Lohgarra, but he, too, was shivering.

Their job on Zeitooine was simple enough: delivery of several constructor droids. Thane helped Methwat and Brill unload, then hurried deeper into the spaceport to locate a vendor of secondhand parts. Usually you could find one or two hanging around. After a few minutes without any luck, he finally dared to ask someone, who told him the nearest place was ten minutes' walk away. He frowned, checked his chrono, and decided to go for it. Better to run a little late and get chewed out for it than to work with that damned antiquated power cell any longer.

So he cut through the town, going as quickly as he could, until he came to a crowded town square—and stopped. Nobody was walking, or even moving, and then he saw why.

"You're under arrest," a stormtrooper captain said in a bored voice as at least a dozen of his men stood around, using their blasters to keep everyone back from the scene as people were dragged out of a nearby house. *A family,* Thane realized with a jolt. The daughter couldn't have been more than thirteen, and she wept as a stormtrooper pulled her after him so fast she could barely walk; his fist was clenched in her hair.

"Please," the mother said, on her knees in front of the captain. "Please. We'll pay the fines—you can sell our house, all our possessions—"

The stormtrooper captain sounded bored. "Repeated violations of the prohibition against independent publications are punished with imprisonment without term."

Another stormtrooper brought out an even younger girl, perhaps only five, small enough to be tucked under his arm. This girl didn't cry; she was too terrified for that. Instead her wide eyes stared into the crowd, as if looking for someone to help them.

Nobody made a move. The stormtroopers' blasters saw to that.

Less than a year ago, I stood by while slaves were beaten, Thane realized. Once again he remembered prowling the sky in his TIE fighter, all so the people of Kerev Doi would be afraid.

The mother continued begging. "Not the children. My husband and I, we did this. The children are innocent. Why should they—"

Her words choked off as the captain smashed the butt of his rifle into her face. She fell to the ground, crying, as another stormtrooper bent down to cuff her.

Do something! But Thane was powerless. He couldn't act against that many armed men. He couldn't even speak up. By deserting the Imperial Starfleet, he had put himself in a position where he could never draw attention to himself or step out of line again. The invisible cage around him was of his own making.

Sickened, he turned away and headed back to the spaceport. As he walked toward the *Moa*, Brill caught sight of him. "Hey! Where's that new power cell?"

Thane snapped, "They didn't have anything in our price range. Okay?"

Behind him he could hear her mutter, "Sorry I asked."

That wasn't how you made friends with your new shipmates. But Thane didn't want to make friends. He wanted to lock himself in his bunk, turn off the lights, and try to forget everything he'd seen, or been.

Ciena stared at the scene before her on the planet Ivarujar and thought that this could only be hell.

In the distance, the volcano continued to spew ash into the air, so far up that no one on this world would be able to see the sky for years. Lava glowed orange and ominous on the horizon; already the capital city had been completely overrun. When Ciena looked through her quadnoculars, she could see yet more buildings blackening as they crumbled to ash from the heat alone.

As the closest ship in the sector, the *Devastator* had

dispatched several troop transports to evacuate the Imperial garrisons on Ivarujar. Their own ships had been badly damaged in the original eruption, so they were trapped—and, if she didn't reach them soon, doomed. Ciena had been put in charge of the transport flying closest to the volcano itself. Hazardous duty, but she found herself energized by the experience. It wasn't that she didn't like working on the bridge of a Star Destroyer . . . but she'd been overdue to get her boots on the ground.

"Lieutenant Commander Ree, we have visual," said the stormtrooper pilot. She turned back from the transport window to see the screen image of stormtroopers atop a building. They stood in formation, rigid and motionless as they awaited rescue, though by then the heat had to have been unbearable.

"Good work," she said. "Bring us in."

The pilot hesitated, then double-checked his instruments. Ciena understood why he was uncertain; the intense heat was starting fires, creating backdrafts, and whipping up winds that could destabilize a larger craft than their transport.

You got strange winds up in the mountains, sometimes.

"Here. I'll take the helm." Ciena motioned him out of the chair.

"Ma'am—I'm capable of the flight—"

"I know you are. But you have the strength to carry any injured men onto the craft and I don't." Well, not more than one or two.

Assured he wouldn't be reported for cowardice, the pilot joined the other stormtroopers in the back. Ciena took the transport in low, through urban canyons where lava ran over what had recently been streets. The hellish red light from below contrasted with the black sky. Although it was a bumpy ride, she could stabilize them well enough.

Clunky thing, she thought, wishing briefly for a ship with some agility to it. Still, the transport could endure the heat, and nothing else mattered.

She set the transport down on the roof of the garrison building, and as soon as they'd opened the doors, the troops began crowding in. Their armor had gone gray from volcanic ash, and several of them coughed and stumbled. Within another half hour or so, they would have passed out, or died. Ciena remembered them standing in formation—holding true to discipline to the last—and felt such pride her heart could have burst.

"All right," she said, and she was about to utter the words *Moving out* when she saw another building farther away. People had huddled on that roof, too—Ivarujarian

CHAPTER 13/261

citizens who must have failed to make it to the civilian transports in time. Or maybe there hadn't been enough room for everyone. . . .

"Lieutenant Commander?" The pilot had returned to the cockpit. "Are we ready for takeoff?"

"Yes," she said. "We're going to make one stop before returning to the *Devastator*."

"A . . . stop?"

No orders had told her she could rescue civilians, but no orders had told her she couldn't. "Make as much room back there as you can. We're picking up more passengers."

When Ciena took off again, she could feel the unsteadiness of the air currents around her. Biting her lower lip, she took the transport higher up so they'd have to dive into the worst of it only at the very end. The volcano rumbled again so loudly that the sound vibrated through the entire ship; they'd been given warnings about a potential secondary eruption, which seemed as if it could happen at any minute.

You don't have the right to risk the lives you're responsible for to save those you aren't, she thought, her old academy training kicking in. After a moment, though, Ciena shook it off. Lives were lives—and besides, she could do this.

Once again she alighted on the corner of a building, and then she left the cockpit to help civilians on board.

They were coughing even harder than the stormtroopers, since they hadn't been wearing helmets with ventilation masks; a few of them were only semiconscious. Ciena held her arms out for a small child, lifted him into the ship, then put her hand out to help the father in, too. Around her, the stormtroopers did the same, following their commanding officer's lead as always.

By the time the last person had been pulled on board, the ship was filled to capacity and then some. Ciena had to push her way back through to the cockpit, where the pilot was no longer even attempting to fly. He stood aside, saying, "At this weight, I don't know if we can—"

"We can and we will," Ciena said, with more confidence than she felt. The transport was capable of carrying that much weight, but its maneuverability would be compromised—a serious risk when dealing with superheated gale-force winds.

She took the engines to full power and soared into the air. At first the transport rocked beneath her, so violently that she nearly fell from her chair; she could hear the rescued Ivarujarians crying out in fear from the hold. By then buildings were flaring into flame like struck matches. In another moment, it would become a true firestorm—and her ship could be caught in the middle of it.

Ciena pointed the nose straight up. They were ascending more slowly than they should, but they were moving. . . .

On the horizon she saw flames whip up higher, then higher, then begin to swirl in a cyclonic current. If the transport got caught in one of those, they were dead.

But she remained steady, fighting the terrible winds every centimeter of the way, until at last they were out of danger. Ciena breathed out with relief, and from the back of the transport she heard cheers.

If she couldn't resist a smile—who could blame her?

The answer turned out to be "Captain Ronnadam."

"You were tasked with retrieving the soldiers in that garrison," he said, pacing the length of his office while she stood at attention, still in her soot-grimed uniform. "Not with a civilian rescue."

"My orders did not forbid me from doing so, sir."

Ronnadam's eyes narrowed. "Looking for loopholes, Ree? A dangerous trait."

"No, sir! I mean—I reacted instinctively and saw no obstacle to doing so."

"You reacted *instinctively*," he sneered. "In other words, you failed to clear your plans through your superior officers!"

We had no time, she wanted to protest, but she knew

better. "I'm sorry, sir. I should have cleared my mission before undertaking it. I won't make that mistake again."

"See that you don't." Ronnadam stared her up and down before adding stiffly, "You have no other demerits on your record, so your punishment will be lenient—only five weeks of double-duty shifts. Next time, however, we will not be so merciful."

"There won't be a next time, sir." And five weeks of extra duty was a small price for forty lives.

As she walked out of his office, Ciena breathed out in relief. At first she'd been angry that they planned to reprimand her for saving lives—but now she understood that they were displeased only because she'd subverted the chain of command. It wasn't as if she had actually done something wrong, rescuing those people. The Empire would never object to that.

Besides, that was some of the best flying she'd done in her life. If only she could talk to Thane about it. In Ciena's mind she could see his face as she told him about the cyclonic fire. He would have been *so jealous* he didn't get to fly in that himself.

Even the things she was proudest of felt hollow without Thane to tell them to.

CHAPTER FOURTEEN

Eighteen Months After the Battle of Yavin

THE *MOA'S* CARGO holds were filled with medical supplies for the far southern peninsula of Oulanne's single megacontinent. A month before, a massive earthquake had struck, devastating virtually every structure over a vast radius. However, the Empire had sent no medical aid—an economically unimportant planet didn't merit such attention. A few wealthier Oulannists who lived on other worlds had offered what they had. The medical supplies the freighter carried were only a fraction of what was needed, but they would help. Thane strongly suspected Lohgarra had agreed to do the run for free.

As they came in through the very highest levels of the atmosphere, Thane checked the climatological sensors and whistled. "Not good."

Lohgarra wanted to know what they were in for.

"We're looking at a massive storm. A megahurricane, covering a good quarter of the land area."

JJH2 confirmed this, beeping in alarm. Methwat made a vibrato sound of dismay.

"Like these people haven't got enough trouble already," Brill said, shaking her furry pink head.

Thane added, "And now we've got trouble, too." Normally storms weren't an issue for spacecraft; anything that could take the ravages of space could handle a little rain and lightning. However, a cargo ship as overladen as the *Moa* currently was could become unwieldy in the atmosphere, and winds this extreme would have the power to overwhelm their stabilizers. (Only for a few minutes—but that was more than long enough to plow a ship into the dirt.)

They could simply have headed to the nearest safe port. In this case, though, that meant being thousands of kilometers away from the disaster. The medical supplies were probably needed now more than ever.

So when Lohgarra asked Thane if he could land in those conditions, he said, "Damn right I can."

Methwat turned toward Thane with a worried look on his face; he was too polite to question anyone outright, but it was clear he didn't like the look of this.

"Trust me," Thane said. With that he strapped into his chair and took the ship in.

The blackness of space brightened into sky—still blue but not for much longer. Beneath them swirled the storm, the ominous spiral cloud sprawled out like the tentacles of some vast ocean creature. As the winds began buffeting the ship, the hull shuddered around them.

Lohgarra growled for all crew members to brace themselves. JJH2 swiftly fed Thane's station all the atmospheric data it could handle.

Brill muttered, "Hope you know what you're doing, Kyrell."

"That makes two of us."

He dived into the eye of the storm—the calm patch at the center of any cyclone. As the broad white wings of the *Moa* stretched over the churning sea, the viewscreen displayed the surreal image: sunlight on the water as they sped toward black clouds and sheets of rain so thick they blinded Thane to the world beyond.

The sensors would tell him all he needed to know. He aligned the ship, decreased speed, and took them so low they could make out the whitecaps on the restless waves—and then the debris strewn on the rocky shore below.

The entire ship tilted hard, as if it had been punched by a giant fist. *Damn!* The wind shear was even worse than Thane had thought. "Come on," he whispered as he steered them into the angle where that current could work for them instead of sinking them. "We can do this."

"Are you talking to the ship or to me?" Brill said.

Instead of answering, Thane asked, "Did you lock the system on to the hangar coordinates?"

Brill's pink hair stood on end. "You want to take this in on autonav?" From her captain's chair, Lohgarra growled her disbelief, and JJH2 whistled the high note of droid panic.

"Not just autonav!" By then the *Moa* was shuddering so strongly that Thane had to shout to be heard above the rattling and groaning of the hull. "This boat's so old we've cribbed its systems from a dozen different spacecraft. So turning on the autonav doesn't deactivate the manual navigation. We're going to use them both at the same time."

Brill's fingers tapped on the controls, doing what Thane asked. "You realize if you can't sync your movements with the autonav, you'll rip us in two."

"I've got it."

Thane felt the autonav kick in. It was a bit like having another pilot try to wrench the controls away from him.

But he'd spent most of his childhood learning how

to fly with a partner. You didn't fight for control; you built it together.

The autonav remained locked on its target, oblivious to severe wind conditions; that made it Thane's job to tilt and steer the ship in ways that would fight that wind while they stayed the course. At one point the disconnect between the two jerked the ship hard, shaking everyone violently enough that even mild-mannered Methwat yelped. But Thane got them back in sync within a few moments.

When the hangar appeared on the horizon, Thane finally felt like he could breathe again. Dampers—slow thrust, hover down—and the *Moa* settled safely onto the ground.

As Brill and Methwat began to applaud, Thane folded his arms behind his head like he hadn't been worried at all. "That's right," he said. "I'm good."

"You're lucky!" Brill insisted, but with a huge grin.

"All right, I'm lucky. Whatever works."

You wouldn't have believed it if you'd been there, he imagined saying to Ciena. *Then again, if you'd been there, you would've insisted on taking the controls instead of me—and probably would've brought us in for an even smoother landing.*

Thane kept storing up anecdotes to tell her someday, even though he knew that day would never come. He'd tried to stop, but he couldn't help it.

Lohgarra told Thane she was very, very proud of him and wrapped her huge furry arms around him in a hug. Then she showed the highest form of praise and affection, for a Wookiee: she started grooming him.

Thane sighed as she got to work on his hair in earnest. This wasn't how they did things in the Empire.

The next day, the storm had moved along far enough that they could start distributing their supplies. To Thane's surprise, another group of pilots had landed a few days before with a substantial haul of medical gear and emergency rations, so they wound up working side by side.

"You brought that ship in yesterday?" said their leader, a black-haired man a few years older than Thane. "That was a nice piece of flying."

"Thanks."

"You do a lot of hauls like this? To worlds in trouble?"

"Sometimes. Lohgarra gets the credit for that," Thane said as the two of them unloaded crates. "But I like that she does it."

"Less money in it for you."

"Never cared much about money."

"What other runs have you been on?"

Thane hesitated before answering. If he was suspected of disloyalty to the Empire, he could be reported . . . but there was no way to talk honestly about his experiences of the last several months without making his feelings clear.

He'd known the Empire was rotten, but he hadn't realized how deep the rot went. The plight of the Bodach'i had disturbed him deeply, and yet now he knew they were only one of hundreds of entire species the Empire had subjugated for labor. He'd flown the *Mighty Oak* to worlds mined so savagely that new seas had been carved into what were once cities and farmlands. He'd looked down at cities strafed to rubble and ash by Imperial laser cannons as punishment for even mild defiance.

"Zeitooine," Thane said. "And Dinwa Prime, and Arieli. More recently, Ivera X." He spoke evenly but was aware what he'd said was in effect a list of the Empire's war crimes.

The other man met his eyes evenly. "Then you've seen a lot."

"Yeah."

"When we get done here, you and I should have a chat. I've been to several of those worlds. Good to hear what other people believe should be done."

Is he thinking about reporting me? Thane knew it was possible, but his gut told him no. Slowly, he nodded. "Sure. We'll talk. I'm Thane Kyrell, by the way."

The black-haired man smiled and held out his hand to shake. "Wedge Antilles."

They wound up sharing a couple of ration trays just inside the hangar doors. The worst of the hurricane had passed through by that time. Heavy, silvery sheets of rain still fell, but the winds had died down until the palms and jungle trees merely swayed. The sound of rustling leaves and raindrops on the metal roof remained loud enough to drown out their conversation if anyone attempted to listen.

"You showed courage," Wedge said. "Leaving like that."

Thane shrugged. "I laundered my credits and sneaked away. Not the bravest thing anyone's ever done."

"You defied the Empire alone. You gave up the life and career you'd built rather than violate your principles. I'd call that brave."

"Stop trying to get on my good side and say what you're trying to say."

This was met with a sharp look—apparently Wedge Antilles wasn't used to not being taken at his word. Maybe Thane was being unfair, but so what? He had to be careful about whom he chose to trust. Lohgarra and the rest of the *Moa* crew had earned that; Ciena would always have his loyalty to some degree, even if he never saw her again.

But this guy? He needed to come out with it already.

Evenly, Wedge said, "We could use pilots like you in the Rebel Alliance."

The rebels? Here? Thane wouldn't have dreamed they'd dare show themselves only to help a planet in distress. But he knew Wedge was telling the truth. "No. Sorry."

"You hate the Empire. After what you've seen, you couldn't help it."

"True," Thane admitted. "But I don't care much for your rebellion either."

"We're fighting to free the galaxy—"

"You started a war, and a lot of people are going to die because of it."

Wedge's dark eyes blazed with intensity. "Palpatine began the war. We're going to end it."

The strength of the man's belief was slightly unnerving. "Against the Empire? I'll grant you this much—you're brave. But you're fooling yourselves if you think you can take on a force like the Imperial fleet and win."

"We destroyed the Death Star, didn't we? With a handful of single-pilot fighters! I flew on that mission, and I'm still here. A lot of Imperial officers can't say the same."

"Including some friends of mine," Thane said quietly. He hadn't been that close to Jude Edivon, but he remembered how kind she'd been, how bright. She'd deserved a longer life than that, and a better death. And the fellow officers he'd just begun to know, young guys like him who were starting their careers together— sometimes their faces flashed through Thane's head at night when he was trying to sleep. "Listen, I get why you did it. I know the Death Star had to be stopped. But don't fool yourself. That was bloody work."

"I know," Wedge said quietly. "It's like you said: the Death Star had to be stopped. Just as the Empire must be destroyed. If that's going to happen, some of us have to get blood on our hands. We have to be willing to kill, and willing to die. It's not easy and it never will be. But I can tell you this much, Kyrell. It's easier than standing by and doing nothing."

Thane remembered that day on Zeitooine and the family he'd seen dragged away to prison. He'd felt so useless, so powerless. As long as he remained a refugee from the Empire, he would never again be able to act on his beliefs. He would never be able to stand up for anyone again.

Unless he did not stand alone.

Late that night—after hours of work, hours more of talking with Wedge, and a couple of Corellian ales—Thane returned to the *Moa*. He walked toward his bunk quietly, knowing both Methwat and Brill would be asleep, but Lohgarra sat in the galley, munching on an enormous slab of cheese.

"Hey," he said. "Can't sleep?"

Lohgarra admitted she'd woken up hungry, then said Thane looked worried.

" 'Worried' isn't exactly the word." The number of people he trusted enough to share this with could have been counted on one hand, with fingers left over—but Lohgarra was among them. "Lieutenant Commander Antilles, from the, uh, unaffiliated group earlier today? He wants me to fly with them."

That earned a roar of indignation. How dare that man try to steal her best pilot? Taking advantage of a crisis like that was unthinkable. She'd see to it that Thane got a raise, if that was what it took to keep him—

"No, no, Lohgarra, you don't understand." Thane lowered his voice. "They're with the Rebellion."

She fell silent. Was that shock or disapproval?

He leaned forward, trying to put his thoughts into words not only for her sake but also for his. "I never thought about joining the Rebellion. You know, I understood the Empire was corrupt, but I thought so was the Old Republic by the end. So would be whatever other government might follow. I told myself it was all the same. But what I've seen these past several months—it goes beyond corruption. The Empire wrecks worlds and enslaves entire species and doesn't give a damn about anyone under its rule. I mean, as rich as Coruscant is, they couldn't send any humanitarian aid here?"

Lohgarra quietly said the need on Oulanne was great.

"Exactly. The Empire didn't come here, but the rebels did. These guys are fighting a war, always on the run, and they still shared their supplies." None of it made sense to Thane. Most people didn't do the right thing even when they weren't in danger—

—but he'd learned from Ciena that there were actually a few idealists out there.

He continued, "Ci—This girl I knew believed the Empire would never destroy another world once the Rebellion had been defeated, but that's because she's so good she can't even recognize evil when it's staring her in the face. I mean, why would the Empire go to the trouble of building a space station that could destroy planets if it wasn't going to use it? And if the Empire would do that, there's nothing it *wouldn't* do." Thane straightened and took a deep breath. "I don't know what comes after the Empire. I can't say that whoever gets power next will be any better—but it can't get any worse. That's not possible. If there's even a chance I can do something that helps take the Empire down, I feel like I have to do it."

After a long moment, Lohgarra quietly said that her own people had been enslaved by the Empire. Kashyyyk had been such a beautiful place when she was young. Now it had been turned into a hell. She found it difficult to speak of her homeworld's tragedy, but she never forgot it.

Thane thought about the sheer level of brutality necessary to conquer a species as powerful as the Wookiees. "Is this your way of telling me you're joining the Rebellion, too?"

She shook her head. The *Moa* was hardly in shape to haul cargo, much less go into battle—and for Brill and Methwat, it was not only a ship but also their home. A decision to join the Rebellion would have to be unanimous, and Lohgarra felt Thane knew as well as she did that they weren't there yet.

That was true. But—"We could put in somewhere, refurbish the ship. Talk to the others. Nobody here has any love for the Empire. In a month or two, I bet we could bring them around."

Probably, Lohgarra admitted. After a pause she asked if he wanted to wait to join the Rebellion, if he wasn't ready right away.

Thane flushed. "I'm not a *coward*."

Her massive hand petted his head. Lohgarra knew he was brave. Yet she also suspected Thane had other reasons to hesitate.

All those months Thane had tried so hard to keep his past, and his feelings, to himself. He should've known his captain was too perceptive not to guess at some of the truth. "It's just that I used to serve in the Imperial Starfleet. A lot of my friends and classmates are still with the Empire, including someone who I . . . who means a lot to me. On some level, attacking the Empire feels like attacking them."

Lohgarra pointed out that he had accepted the risks of combat when he joined the Imperial fleet, and so had everyone else.

"Yeah, I know." He leaned back in the creaky seat and took a deep breath. "But joining the Rebellion— leaving the Empire is one thing, but taking up arms against it is another. The friends I served with before would never forgive that. Especially the woman I was telling you about, Ciena. She'd never speak to me again if she knew. Not that she's likely to anyway, I guess."

With a soft whine, Lohgarra told him the Force had a way of bringing people together when the time was right.

Oh, great, the Force. My best bet is this crazy magic old valley kindred still believe in. But Thane said nothing, knowing Lohgarra's beliefs were important to her. Instead he asked, "Is this your way of saying it's all right for me to go? Since 'the Force' will make sure we meet again?"

His answer came in the form of a big hug that enveloped him in white fur. As he hugged Lohgarra back, she told him to promise her he would eat well.

He had to laugh. "I promise."

I'm really doing it, he thought. It still seemed unreal. *I'm going to war against the Empire. I'm joining the Rebel Alliance.*

CHAPTER FIFTEEN

"**Y**OUR SERVICE THESE past two years has been exemplary, Lieutenant Commander Ree."

Ciena stood at attention in front of Admiral Ozzel, hands held firmly at her sides. Junior officers did not make eye contact with superiors during evaluations, so she stared fixedly at the metal-tiled wall behind him.

"You frequently volunteer for extra shifts or to help train newer officers on Star Destroyer protocols. Aside from the unfortunate incident on Ivarujar, you have received no punishments or reprimands—and it does not escape my notice that your offense then has never been repeated. You've never even been admonished about your uniform."

The leather bracelet she carried for Wynnet remained in its cloth pouch in her pocket. No regulation said she couldn't keep something in her pocket.

"You were transferred to the *Executor* from the *Devastator* at the request of Lord Vader himself. A high honor indeed."

Ciena did not respond. Privately, she thought Vader's request had been more threat than reward. She had seen him adrift in space, nearly helpless. He would not want anyone to think of him as vulnerable in any way. So he had to remind Ciena that she remained forever vulnerable to *him*.

Ozzel continued: "Although you are far too senior for TIE fighter duty, you put in the simulator time to make sure your piloting instincts stay sharp."

Ciena decided she could speak. "We never know what a crisis may demand of us, sir."

She also loved flying for its own sake and sometimes dreamed all night of swooping through the canyons of Jelucan with Thane by her side. But it wasn't against regulations to love what she did—or to remember what she had lost.

"Very well said." Admiral Ozzel came as close to smiling as she'd ever seen from him. "In short, Lieutenant Commander Ree, your performance aboard the *Executor* exceeds expectations on every point. Keep this up and you'll make commander before long."

Commander. Ciena wasn't as wrapped up in the idea of advancement as she had been three years ago, but she could take satisfaction in having done her duty so well. Even with the unnaturally fast rate of promotion following the Death Star's destruction, making commander less than five years out of the academy was a major achievement. "Yes, sir. Thank you, sir."

Afterward, as she walked through the dark metal corridors of the *Executor,* she mulled over her likely promotion. It ought to have been cause for celebration; she should've messaged Nash and Berisse immediately, telling them to meet her later for a cup or two of ale. Instead, the praise from her superior officer only reminded her of how she had failed the Empire once—when she had lied to protect a friend.

Worst of all, Ciena knew if she had to make the same choice again, she would still pick Thane.

As she walked past one of the observation decks, she looked out at the stars and wondered where he might be. Surely he'd left Jelucan as she'd told him to do. Their world was dangerous for him; those snakes he called family would turn him in for a two-credit piece. Yet Ciena remained haunted by the vision of Thane trapped where she'd seen him last—broke, stuck in a tiny room above a seedy Valentia bar, with that lost look in his blue eyes.

Stop it, she told herself. *Thane's smart. He's a talented pilot. By now, surely, he's found work and a good place to live. Probably he's happy.*

You're not small enough to begrudge Thane a happy life without you. Right?

Ciena straightened up and smoothed her hands down the front of her uniform jacket. The shadowy reflection she saw silhouetted against the stars in the window was once again that of the perfect Imperial officer. The excellence of her service had long since ceased to be only a matter of honoring her oath. She also thought of it as the price she paid for giving Thane his freedom. No one would ever be able to say she hadn't paid in full.

I know; I'll tell Mumma and Pappa I might be promoted. Most Imperial officers limited their messages to and from home as a symbol of their commitment, but Ciena figured that was easier for people from Core Worlds, who could expect to see their families in person more than once every five years. She still communicated with her family at least once a tenday, telling them about everything from grav-ball tournaments to Berisse's jokes—well, the jokes that were repeatable.

The only subject her family never discussed was Thane Kyrell. Ciena didn't want to lie to her parents about him; also, she knew they'd realize she was lying right away. The fewer people who suspected the truth about Thane, the better.

Her parents always seemed happy to receive her messages, especially Mumma. But lately, Ciena had begun to notice that their replies were almost entirely about her life, not theirs. They no longer knew all the valley gossip, or no longer cared to share it. Mumma would sometimes speak about her supervisory job at the mine, but over the years, her tone had shifted from pride to a matter-of-fact weariness. Maybe that was only natural, but Ciena couldn't help noticing it—as well as the fact that her father rarely mentioned anything about his own life or the greater valley at all. . . .

"There you are," said a pleasant, cultured male voice. Ciena turned to see Lieutenant Nash Windrider walking toward her with a slight smile on his face. During the three years since Alderaan's destruction, he had gradually recovered some of his old wit and dash. No, he would never be the same again—but she no longer saw the terrible shadows under his eyes that had scared her so in the beginning. Both he and her friend Berisse Sai had been transferred from the *Devastator* to the *Executor* when Darth Vader chose it as his new flagship; they were also posted to the same quadrant within the vessel, so she saw them often. "I've been looking for you, Ciena."

"Why? Is this about Berisse's birthday?" Ciena folded her arms and glared at him. "You ruined the surprise, didn't you?"

"You don't give me nearly enough credit—either for my expertise with surprise parties, which is considerable, or for knowing what's important enough to merit pulling you back onto the bridge when you're off duty."

The hairs on the back of her neck prickled with a sense of both danger and excitement. "What?"

"One of the probe droids picked up a very interesting signal on the ice world of Hoth," Nash said with relish. "We may have finally located the rebel base."

Ciena sucked in a sharp breath. "And we're going in?"

Nash's grin widened. "With five *Imperial*-class Star Destroyers by our side."

The image of Jude's smile flashed through Ciena's mind. At last they had a chance to avenge themselves on the people who had destroyed the Death Star and murdered her best friend—and to stamp out the Rebellion once and for all.

Thane groaned as they opened the bay doors again and a blast of frigid air swept past them. "I'm going to freeze my choobies off."

The guy showing him around—Dak Ralter—laughed

as he unsaddled another of the tauntauns. "There are easier ways to switch genders, you know."

"I didn't mean I *wanted* to freeze 'em off. I just meant—it's *so cold*." After a childhood spent in the high mountains of Jelucan, Thane had thought he knew how to handle being cold—but Hoth was on another scale together.

"Don't talk about it. Don't even think about it," Dak said earnestly. "Just keep your pants on and focus on the big picture."

"I know, I know. We made our base on this frozen hunk of rock because the Empire would never think to look here. Because who in their right mind would subject themselves to this?" Thane's gesture took in the ice walls of their base, the bitter chill that pierced to the bone, and the pungent odor of the tauntauns they were currently freeing. "Nobody could ever say we joined the Rebellion for the fun of it."

"Nobody *would* say that!" Dak Ralter's face fell as if somebody really had accused them of fighting a war just for kicks. "Or they'd better not. Anybody who doesn't think we need to stand up to the Empire—"

"Take it easy. I was just joking."

Dak shot Thane a reproving look, as if to say this war was far too serious for anything as lowbrow as humor. Some of the new recruits were like that at first—so idealistic that spending time with them felt like biting into pure sugar.

Or so the long-timers said. Thane outranked Dak by a grand total of three weeks. But he felt like he was two decades older than Dak, rather than two years. Thane had never been one of the idealists; he'd accepted Wedge Antilles's invitation not because he believed the Rebellion was pure good but because he'd learned the Empire was pure evil. Even for him, though, the adjustment felt strange. Small as the *Moa* was, every crew member lived in a private cabin of his or her very own; even in Imperial service, he'd never had to bunk with more than seven other guys. In the Rebellion, Thane slept in an enormous bunker with a couple hundred other people, the majority of whom seemed to snore. Rations were scanty, the odds terrible, and the risks even greater than Thane would have imagined—and so far he'd been in none of the epic battles he'd been anticipating. Instead, he had made a few supply runs while avoiding Imperial border controls. He'd helped set up the Hoth base. And now here he was taking it down again: setting their pack creatures loose so they'd be long gone by the time the Empire arrived, because apparently a probe droid had found them already

They'd just gotten set up on Hoth, too. He half

wanted to ask Rebel Command how they were supposed to win a war when the Empire could find the rebel bases within a month.

He looked over the back of the grunting tauntaun nearest him to take in the entire base around him. Mechanics worked feverishly on fighters, their bluish-white welding torches lighting the murky repair bay. Princess Leia spoke intently to General Rieekan, her intensity obvious even at that distance, Thane thought. (They'd passed each other in corridors twice without her recognizing him from that long-ago dance.) Droids whirred through the fray as noncombat personnel ran for the first transports; boarding had begun already. Thane knew only that his group—Corona Squadron—wasn't up yet. For now, he just had to keep freeing smelly tauntauns.

Dak's chatter broke his reverie. "I still can't believe I got assigned as gunner to *Luke Skywalker*. The guy who singlehandedly destroyed the Death Star!"

"Somebody's going to be his gunner. Might as well be you." Thane was mostly glad it wasn't him. Yes, Skywalker had shown incredible courage and made a near-impossible shot—he deserved respect—but that particular act of heroism was one Thane preferred to admire from a distance.

"And they say he hopes to become a Jedi Knight,

just like in the olden days," Dak continued, talking as dreamily as a schoolkid with a crush. "Do you know he has a real, true lightsaber? He even learned how to use the Force from the great General Kenobi, the last of the Jedi!"

It was all Thane could do not to groan. *Please, not more superstitious nonsense about the "Force."* In his opinion, the rebel troops needed to be motivated by the harsh truth about the Empire, not crazy religious beliefs.

Then he remembered Ciena's voice so vividly that it was as if she'd whispered in his ear. *Believing in something greater than ourselves isn't crazy. It's proof we're sane. Look how vast the galaxy is. Don't you have to admit we can't be the greatest power within it?*

She had said that to him during one of their final days on Jelucan, before they left for the academy. He'd laughed at her for suggesting that maybe the Force had made sure they went to the same school on Coruscant, to keep them together. By now, even Ciena would have to admit they weren't lucky enough to share a destiny.

So why was the memory of her still more real to him than the person actually standing a meter away?

"Let's just get this done, all right? We don't want to run off and leave these things to starve penned up in here." Thane patted one tauntaun on the nose before slipping off its halter. The beast bounded away, eager to find a pack and burrow down for warmth. "We have to haul out of here within the day, Rieekan says. I don't want to get stranded on Hoth because we didn't finish tauntaun duty in time."

"Sorry," Dak said so earnestly that Thane felt a twinge of guilt.

So he gentled his tone. "By the way—you must have impressed somebody to get assigned to fly with Skywalker. They wouldn't pair him up with just anyone."

". . . really?"

"Definitely."

He glanced over at Dak and saw that the kid was smiling. With that, they cleared the stall of the final two tauntauns. As the beasts ran into the snow, leaving only their stink behind—

—every siren on the base went off at once.

The shrieking echoed within the cave walls; Thane jerked upright and dropped the harnesses within the first second. Dak yelled, "What does this mean?"

As green as he was, Dak knew the answer. He just didn't want to believe it. Thane shouted over the din: "The Empire got here faster than we thought. They've found us!"

After a quick briefing from Princess Leia, it only took Thane four minutes to suit up and run to his snow-speeder. Four minutes was almost too long.

"Haul your Jelucani ass up here!" shouted Yendor, Thane's Twi'lek copilot and a fellow member of Corona Squadron. He'd already donned his specially fitted helmet, which allowed his blue lekku to trail down his back. "We've got multiple Imperial walkers marching in."

"I trained on walkers at the academy." Thane swung into his seat. Even as he put on his helmet, the overhead canopy descended and locked. "I know them inside and out."

"What can you tell me about these things?" Yendor flipped the switches that would prepare them for takeoff.

"They're the most heavily armored ground vehicles in the Imperial Army."

". . . so what you're saying is that you have a thorough knowledge of just how screwed we are."

"Pretty much," Thane said. "Look at it this way. If even the Death Star could fall, there's nothing the Empire has that we can't take down."

Yendor released the clamps. "Let's test that theory."

Thane put his hands to the controls and felt the engines surge to life beneath him. "Here we go."

The snowspeeder shot out of the base and into the fray. Laser bolts striped the silver-white sky, and rebel ships scattered wide to face the intruding army . . . because that was what they had here. Not a strike team. They were up against the full ground forces of this Empire, at least. *How many snowtroopers are down there?* Thane wondered. *And they'll probably send flametroopers into the base to burn everything still inside—and everyone.* Worst of all, he could already see five AT-AT walkers on the horizon. Each one would carry dozens of soldiers and countless armaments, not to mention the deadly cannons mounted in front.

It wouldn't matter how far the walkers made it if the rebels could just get the transports away, Thane reminded himself. Actually destroying one of those monsters would be a bonus.

Yendor said, "Did your classes at the academy tell you how to deal with the walkers' heavy armor? Because our blasters aren't worth a damn against these things."

Thane took the speeder in fast and low, sending flurries of snow out in a plume beneath them. "Not every place can be fully armored. Think about it. The legs are vulnerable exactly where any creature's legs would be."

"Gotcha," Yendor replied. "Targeting the joints."

The entire snowspeeder vibrated with the power of

the fire they shot at one of the walkers, specifically its "ankles." While their blasters didn't have the strength to destroy those alloys, it might be possible to weaken the bolts and fry some of the circuitry.

We can make them unstable. Slow them down. Anything to help the transports get to safety.

Each of those transports would contain nearly a hundred rebel soldiers, the heart of their fleet. If the Empire triumphed today—it truly could be the end of the Rebellion.

But Yendor's aim was sure and steady. He kept hitting the AT-AT's lowest joints in the exact same spots, maximizing the damage. As Thane zoomed in with his sensors, he realized they even had a chance to take one of the feet off the thing, which would stop it dead.

"Keep it up!" Thane shouted to Yendor. "I'm taking us all the way in!"

"I can actually target quite well from a distance, you know," Yendor joked, even as he started firing faster.

By then the lowest section of the walker loomed large in the viewscreen. Thane looked upward to see the thing for real. At first he wished he hadn't—the monsters looked big enough when you were in them, but from below they seemed to outweigh the entire sky.

But then he told himself, *They're not as big as the mountains back home. You flew through those. You can make it through these.*

So he accelerated until the snowy landscape was no more than a blur, bringing them back in as fast as possible. Yendor kept firing with pinpoint accuracy, every hit now winning a puff of black smoke or a shower of sparks.

They were within two hundred meters—one hundred meters—

Thane made the decision in an instant. At the last second he could've swerved, he didn't.

Yendor yelped—still firing—as Thane steered their snowspeeder directly at the AT-AT's feet. In the final moments before impact, he jerked the speeder sideways until it was perpendicular to the ground, sliding between the AT-AT's legs until he spun out behind it, still in one piece.

That was more than he could say for the walker, now hobbling on burning, damaged feet. One of the legs lifted minus its foot, then froze; that AT-AT wasn't going anywhere

"So, that was *not* a suicide run?" Yendor said.

Thane laughed as he took the snowspeeder around for another pass. "I used to turn sideslips like that through mountain stalactites every day back home. You were safe as a baby the whole time."

"Remind me never to hire you as a babysitter."

As Thane zoomed back toward the conflict, he

realized that somebody else had managed to bring a walker down—as in, all the way down, flat in the snow. The head blew as he watched, a cough of black smoke against the white ground. For a moment he imagined himself inside the walker. It would've been so unbearably hot just before the explosion; the heat must've cooked those guys in their armor. . . .

That's right, he told himself savagely. *We're here to kill them, just like they're here to kill us. Better them than you.*

Yendor said, "Got word from Commander Skywalker. They looped the walker's legs with a tow cable."

"That's faster," Thane said. "And saves our energy for later."

"And doesn't make us do that damned death-somersault thing—"

"Don't knock the move that just saved our butts," Thane said as he headed straight for the next walker. "Just get the tow cable ready."

As they sped back into the thick of the battle, Thane saw a transport rocket through the atmosphere, preparing for its leap into hyperspace. Were they actually going to escape this mess after all?

Some of them would. But there were crashed snowspeeders lying on the ground, cinders blowing in the wind around them. No matter how many transports got away, the Rebellion had to leave behind a tremendous amount of ships and material. And all the work that had gone into building the base had been wasted. Now they'd have to wander through the galaxy again, looking for someplace even more obscure and unlivable than Hoth . . . if such a planet even existed. Maybe the Rebellion brass had a long-range plan that would render the day's battle meaningless, but for now, the Empire was making them pay dearly for their defiance.

Thane gritted his teeth. The larger strategy of the Rebellion wasn't up to him. He had one job only: to cover the transports.

For the next long while, he allowed himself to think of nothing but the targets, to do nothing but fly in as close as possible so Yendor could make every shot. The ground troops beneath their speeder were sometimes no more than shadows, their white snowtrooper armor rendering them almost invisible against the wintry landscape. Once the last walker went down, the other rebels cheered. Thane stared up at the bleak sky above them. *What are they going to send down next?*

Nothing came. No more Imperial ships descended. That meant they were waiting above the atmosphere to pick off the rebel fighters one by one.

The moment the final transport streaked into the sky, Thane and Yendor rushed their snowspeeder back to base. By now they had mere minutes to get their individual starfighters off the ground.

All Thane had to do was fly safely out of planetary atmosphere before going to lightspeed—but first he had to outrun the TIE fighters that had just zoomed into range.

Damn! If he'd taken off five minutes earlier, the TIEs would have missed him entirely. Now Thane would have to shoot his way to freedom.

But TIE fighters weren't as sturdy as walkers. They provided almost no protection for their pilots—which was the main reason why being a TIE pilot was so revered in the Imperial Starfleet. Flying one of those things took guts.

Knowing that didn't make it easier for Thane to shoot the TIE fighters down, but he did it anyway. As his blaster bolts raked across one of the TIEs, a shower of green sparks flumed into the air, and then the ship was spiraling down, wings clipped, falling to its doom.

Thane had experienced that in TIE fighter simulators. He knew what it looked like from the inside.

This was a war. They'd all chosen their sides. So Thane accelerated upward, not bothering to watch on sensors as the TIE fighter crashed to the ground.

As soon as the space outside his X-wing had turned black and the sensors showed all clear, he laid in a course for the rendezvous coordinates and prepared for the leap to lightspeed. Only in the last moments did he see the Imperial fleet amassed off his starboard side, so enormous that even the darkness of space did not dwarf it. There was no time to study it in detail, hardly even a flash of silver before the stars changed from points into a tunnel and his engines whined as his ship leaped into lightspeed.

Thane felt as if he couldn't breathe. He knew what he'd seen in that final split-second view of the Imperial fleet: a Super Star Destroyer.

When I left, Ciena was assigned to the Devastator. *They'd never post her to any ship smaller than a Star Destroyer again. By now she probably isn't assigned on TIE patrols very often, but she could be—and she'd volunteer just for the joy of flying.*

He was being ridiculous. Of the many Star Destroyers under the Emperor's control, what were the odds that a particular one would be assigned to that battle, on that day?

But however remote the chances were, the possibility was real. And now, sickened by fear, Thane realized the TIE pilot he'd just killed could have been Ciena. It was no less likely to be her than any other pilot in the fleet. If so, he hadn't even bothered to watch her die.

The worst part was that he would never know.

CHAPTER SIXTEEN

THE METALLIC RASP of Lord Vader's breathing echoed throughout the *Executor*'s bridge. Ciena knew better than to glance upward or give any other indication that she even realized he was there, standing on the higher level only a couple of meters above. Although she didn't believe some of the wilder rumors about Darth Vader's vindictiveness, by now she knew it was wisest not to draw his attention for any reason. His rages when he was displeased were legendary.

Right now, he had to be displeased in the extreme.

How could so many rebel transports have gotten away? Even coming out of hyperspace too early shouldn't have undermined their entire attack. The Imperial Starfleet had sent down a strike force that should have been able to paralyze the enemy's defenses. But instead of victory, they had three demolished AT-ATs, one badly damaged one, several dozen destroyed TIE fighters, and several hundred dead snowtroopers. The high number of rebel casualties they'd inflicted was small consolation.

Later, Ciena resolved, she would watch the recordings of the Battle of Hoth and study the rebels' tactics in detail. The Empire possessed every advantage in terms of manpower and firepower. Today ought to have been the day they dealt the Rebellion a final, fatal blow. Instead, their victory was incomplete. If the rebels could avoid being completely crushed by an Imperial strike force led by six Star Destroyers, then superior or at least surprising tactical moves had to be the reason. Analyzing those in greater depth might give the Imperials the information they needed to finally end this gruesome war.

For now, though, Ciena and everyone else on the *Executor* had another, far more vital priority: capture the *Millennium Falcon*.

If anyone on the bridge understood why it was so important to catch that antique piece of junk, nobody said so. Lord Vader wanted the ship towed aboard and its passengers taken alive. So instead of simply blowing up the *Millennium Falcon*—something they could have done in an instant—they had to try to pluck it from the sky.

Unfortunately, whoever was steering the *Falcon* was one hell of a pilot. He'd gone into an asteroid field, apparently choosing suicide over capture. No small ship could hope to emerge from an asteroid field intact. The rebel ship at least had shields; TIE fighters didn't even have that much protection.

Yet four of them had been sent in. While Ciena sat there trying to fathom the purpose of that suicide mission, Captain Piett said, "Ree, provide auxiliary navigational assistance."

Her heart sank even as she said, "Yes, sir."

She went to the aux-nav post in the data pit and looked down at the four screens that showed her the TIE fighters' designations and coordinates. Any assistance she could provide would be minimal—but if she could give those pilots a chance, she would. Her fingers flew as she set the triangulations between their ships and the *Millennium Falcon*, and then she yanked on the headset that would let her talk to the pilots directly. "O-L-Seven-Zero-One, adjust thirty-seven degrees starboard and down—N-A-Eight-One-One, follow but go up—"

NA811 was a guy called Penrie, whom she talked to once in a while, a graduate of the academy on Lothal. When he laughed, no one could help laughing with him, and since he seemed to find everybody's jokes hilarious, the laughter was constant. Although Penrie was a couple of years her senior, he sounded younger as he said, *"Affirmative."*

"C-R-Nine-Seven-Eight, pull up—pull up!" But Ciena's order had come too late; one of the TIE fighters vanished from the grid.

That was one dead man on her watch. *Please, no more.*

"O-L-Seven-Zero-One, new trajectory linking to your nav computer now—"

"Got it."

"J-A-One-Eight-Nine, your computer isn't linking up—"

"I can't—" Then a burst of static accompanied the wild spinning of another TIE on her screen grid. *"Clipped one of my engines! Can't steer—need a tractor—"*

Louder static was followed by silence as the image of JA189's TIE fighter faded away for good.

Sweat made Ciena's gray jumpsuit stick to her skin. She kept her eyes locked on the grid and her voice as even as she could manage. "O-L-Seven-Zero-One, N-A-Eight-One-One, you're getting in really close to one of the larger asteroids—"

"Target seems to be looking for cover. We're on him." That was OL701. Through the NA811 uplink, Ciena heard only breathing that was too shallow, too quick. Penrie had just seen two other pilots explode in front of his eyes.

To Captain Piett, she said, "Sir, if the *Millennium Falcon* lands on a larger asteroid, we could focus our laser cannons on that and blow it away. We'd take the *Falcon* out in the process. Can I order the TIE fighters back?"

Piett stood very still, obviously waiting for Lord Vader to countermand the order. Vader said nothing. He didn't even turn around. Finally, Piett said, "Very well, Ree."

Hope rushed through her. At least she could save two of the pilots. "N-A-Eight-One-One, O-L-Seven-Zero-One, abort pursuit. Chart your safest course back and—"

"He's in one of the canyons," OL701 replied. *"We've almost got him—"*

Ciena waited to hear from Penrie. Instead he screamed—a terrible short sound cut off too soon. In that instant, both of the remaining TIE fighters disappeared from her viewscreen, leaving it dark.

Four pilots dead, and it was partly her responsibility. Would Piett reprimand her? Worse, would Vader?

What if those rumors were true, about how Vader treated those who displeased him?

But nobody paid any attention to her. Piett and Vader acted as if she hadn't let anyone down, as if four loyal officers hadn't just died for no reason. There was nothing for Ciena to do but return to her usual station and go back to monitoring the situation.

To the commander who sat beside her in the data pit, she whispered, "Why aren't we at least firing on the asteroid?"

"No clear shot. The target could just as easily have changed course. We no longer have it on visuals or sensors."

A wave of nausea swept through her. Those four TIE fighter pilots had died for nothing. No one would ever hear Penrie's laugh again. In command-track courses at the academy, the teachers had counseled them that they couldn't think of their troops as individuals; to do so would lead only to hesitation and thus defeat. They protected their people by forgetting they *were* people, instead viewing them as pieces in a vast, elaborate game. It was the only element of command-track training that had ever given Ciena pause. She knew now that she would never be able to do that, not the way Piett and Vader did.

Yet Vader could not have been totally devoid of emotion, because he then—unbelievably—ordered the *Executor* into the asteroid field, too.

Impacts began to send shudders throughout the ship. Ciena winced as if the damages were actual injuries to her body. What Star Destroyers had in sheer power, they lacked in maneuverability; they would take countless hits today. What registered as minor damage on a Super Star Destroyer could mean the demolition of two entire decks down for a few thousand meters— and all the people stationed on those decks. More officers and stormtroopers would die needlessly, all because Lord Vader couldn't let one ratty old ship go—

No, Ciena reminded herself sternly. The deaths she'd seen that day, the useless risk and damage—that was all because the Rebel Alliance had started a war.

When her shift ended, Ciena stood to go and winced. Every muscle in her body had tensed so badly during the TIE fighter flights through the asteroid field that she felt as sore as if she'd run thirty kilometers. The doors slid open to let her walk out—or, as it turned out, to let Piett return. Immediately, she stood at attention, awaiting the reprimand she no doubt deserved.

Piett said only, "Well done today, Lieutenant Commander."

"But—" Was he thinking of someone else? "I lost all four pilots, sir."

"They had no chance, really. You kept them alive longer than they could have made it on their own."

He was telling her she'd done a good job. On one level she understood why he said so, but it didn't change how wretched she felt. There was nothing else for her to say, though, except—"Thank you, Captain."

"Oh. Yes. You weren't on the bridge yet for—when—" Piett drew himself up. "I have been promoted to admiral, effective immediately, assuming Admiral Ozzel's command."

What happened to Admiral Ozzel? The question died on her lips. In the Imperial Starfleet, sometimes it was better to be able to believe you didn't know the answer. "Yes, Admiral. Congratulations."

Piett's expression looked bleak. "That will be all, Ree." With that he returned to the bridge, the black doors sliding shut behind him.

Ciena felt too exhausted to move, much less put in extra hours. Yet instead of returning to her bunk, she went to a spare analysis booth and pulled up all the footage from the Battle of Hoth available to someone at her clearance level. She intended to go over every single second of it, until she figured out how a bunch of poorly armed, ragtag rebels were outwitting the greatest military force the galaxy had ever seen.

Was it arrogance to think she could come up with an answer that had eluded the admiralty's finest tactical minds? No, she realized. It was desperation. She wanted this war to end—*needed* it to end—so that the bloody, merciless methods of war would end, too.

Strong as she was, determined as she was to see this through, Ciena knew she couldn't endure years more of sending people to futile, meaningless deaths.

It's not like Penrie and I were friends, but he was more than a call number. I remember his laugh, his birthmark. So I can't forget that he was human, that somewhere out there he has a mother and father who want him home. When they hear the truth, it will destroy them, as surely as it will destroy Mumma and Pappa if I die during my service. That's just one little tragedy. Multiply that anguish and loss by the billions of people already dead in this war and it's unbearable.

Whenever Ciena spoke in her head like that, she always envisioned the same listener. If only she could talk to Thane for real—he would know how to advise her, how to comfort her. Even if he could do nothing else, he would've taken her in his arms and let her hold on tightly until the worst of the pain had ebbed away. Sometimes she couldn't fall asleep without imagining the one night she and Thane had spent together—not the sex (well, not *only* the sex) but the afterglow, the way he had tenderly kissed her hair and curled his body against hers. She couldn't remember any other time she had felt so safe and warm.

Ciena bit her lower lip; the pain brought her back to the here and now. Every few months she resolved not to think about Thane ever again. He had chosen his path. Wherever he was in the galaxy, she hoped he was well, and happy. She would never know for sure, and she needed to make her peace with that.

So concentrate on what you're doing, she told herself. Ciena began playing back the Hoth footage, taking notes on her datapad the whole time. *Abandoned snowspeeders—means they lost ships and valuable material when we ran them off—possible to simply chase them until resources run out? War of attrition?* And the next footage showed the rebel laser cannons. The armaments themselves were a match for Imperial standard, or very nearly, but—*Inadequate body armor for soldiers appears to be standard throughout the rebel forces. Look at weapons that expel shrapnel, possibly razor-edged microdroids?*

Next was footage of the destruction of the Imperial walkers. Ciena could've groaned when she saw how easily the harpoons and towlines took the first AT-AT down. Surely there had to be some kind of defense they could install for that. The second one seemed to explode from inside, so that was probably the Imperials' fault rather than the rebels'. *Mechanical malfunction? A possible saboteur?* she jotted. And then another walker fell prey to a rebel pilot who somehow knew one of the only vulnerable spots in the armor—

Her mind went blank. The beeping and buzzing of the computers around her turned into so much white noise. Astonishment and betrayal rippled through her like an earthquake and its aftershocks. But Ciena shook her head. *I imagined it. Must have. Because there's no way.*

Quickly, she put the footage back in and watched again. She hadn't imagined it. The rebel snowspeeder kept firing at the ideal targets on the lowest joints of the walker's legs as it zoomed forward at suicidal speed—then, at the very last moment, it spun sideways through the narrow gap that led to safety.

Just like flying through the stalactites back home.

Any number of pilots in the galaxy must have learned that move. Ciena knew that. But it didn't change what she was absolutely sure she'd just seen:

Thane Kyrell had joined the Rebellion.

CHAPTER SEVENTEEN

THANE WENT THROUGH the motions as blankly and automatically as his astromech droid: reach rendezvous point, input codes to receive location of the next rendezvous point, leap into hyperspace again, and finally connect with their new base ship, the Mon Calamari cruiser *Liberty*.

The *Liberty* was far larger and more sophisticated than most of the vessels in the motley rebel fleet. However, it was designed for the comfort of the Mon Calamari, not humans. Temperatures were higher, and the humidity in the air was so intense Thane's skin grew damp within minutes.

He needed some distraction from the discomfort, Thane decided. Better not to be alone with his thoughts anyway. He kept seeing that TIE fighter tumble down, kept imagining Ciena dying in the heart of it—and he had to stop that somehow.

First he sought out friends. Wedge clapped Thane on the back, and Thane managed to smile as they congratulated each other on the walkers they'd taken down. But Wedge's face fell when Thane asked about Dak Ralter. "Dak died during the battle. Their snowspeeder was hit; only Skywalker made it out."

Only half a day before, Thane had been teasing Dak about hero-worshiping Luke Skywalker. Now Dak lay dead and abandoned on Hoth, his body crushed by an AT-AT.

The kid hadn't even been nineteen years old.

"If it's any consolation," Wedge said, studying Thane's expression, "Luke said Dak died from the blast. Instantly."

"Consolation," Thane repeated. "Right."

Wedge looked like he might say more, but Thane didn't want to hear it. He turned and walked through the launching bay, watching the activity around him as if he'd never seen any of it before. Pilots laughed and joked, because that was how you dealt with unending mortal danger: you pretended it didn't exist. Only a handful of the rebels standing around showed any evidence of grief or shock.

They were probably imagining scenes as terrible as the one playing over and over in Thane's mind—Ciena and Dak, both dead, their bodies broken as they lay on the surface of Hoth. Soon they would be covered by the snow, never to be seen again.

"Hey, are you all right?" Yendor fell in step beside him, his blue lekku hanging down his back.

"I'm fine."

"If this is what 'fine' looks like for you, I *really* don't want to see your version of 'bad.'"

"Dak Ralter bought it."

"Sorry to hear that," Yendor said. "He was a good kid."

"Yeah."

"Didn't think you guys were that close, though."

"We weren't." *It's not just Dak. I might have killed Ciena today—and I realize it almost certainly wasn't her, but it* could've *been her and I'll never know—*"Skip it, all right?"

Yendor was smart enough to move on. "Consider it skipped. Come help me get the new recruits set up with some gear, why don't you? A couple dozen of them were on their way to Hoth when the alert went out."

"Sure," Thane said. It was something to do.

He even had one pleasant surprise as he handed out helmets, blasters, and communicators to the rookies—a familiar face. "Look what the gundark dragged in," said Kendy Idele, a broad smile spreading across her face. Her dark green hair hung in a long braid down the back of her white coveralls, a few damp strands clinging to her forehead. "Thane Kyrell. Never thought I'd see you here."

"Kendy. I thought you were in the Imperial Starfleet for life."

"Shows how much you know." Kendy laughed out loud. She seemed a little happier to see him than he was to see her. It *was* good to find Kendy again, in some ways; they hadn't been good friends at the academy, but he'd always admired her. In particular he remembered how deadly she'd been on the practice range, how she could take down three target fliers per second with her blaster. The Rebellion needed people who could shoot like that.

But she had been one of Ciena's bunkmates and best friends. Thane couldn't even look at Kendy without expecting to see Ciena at her side.

Nothing much would get done that day except taking names, taking stock, and sweating. Echo Base command center had been hit, which meant disorganization and uncertainty had taken over. Several vital personnel were missing, apparently. Not only had

Luke Skywalker failed to show at the rendezvous point, but the *Millennium Falcon* had gone missing also, with Princess Leia Organa aboard. General Rieekan had called an emergency conference of the senior officers attached to this portion of the fleet, which Wedge got pulled into. That left the rest of them to fix damage to their starfighters, haul equipment into something vaguely resembling regulation, and wait for new orders and their next destination.

So it wasn't that surprising when one of the transport pilots mentioned that they'd brewed a little engine-room hooch.

Making jet juice was one of those things the brass officially banned but in fact turned a blind eye to as long as neither the manufacture nor consumption interfered with duty. For the next day or two, before they migrated to their next location, they were as free from danger as it was possible for a rebel army to be: if the Imperial Starfleet had any idea where the rebels' rendezvous points were, it would have immediately followed them in force. Any good officer knew soldiers needed a chance to blow off steam, particularly after a big battle—so nobody said a word when the cups started being passed around.

Thane gulped down his first so quickly his eyes

watered. Whatever else engine-room jet juice might be, it wasn't "mellow." But as soon as he'd finished coughing, he held out his cup for a refill.

"Hitting it hard tonight," Yendor observed, one lek quirking inquisitively.

"Why not?" Thane said. He didn't meet Yendor's eyes.

It wasn't as if Thane never drank. He'd had a couple of cups of hooch on occasion, and he didn't mind an ale or two. Over time he'd even developed a taste for Andoan wine. But heavy drinking had never interested him, not even when he was a kid on Jelucan and the other boys in his school would get completely wasted on festival nights.

He had never even tried any inebriates before that evening in the Fortress, with the flask of valley wine Ciena had smuggled in her robes. They had been no more than fourteen. Both of them had hated the sticky-sweet stuff and wound up pouring most of it out. Her full lips had still been stained berry dark as she had rinsed out the flask, laughing, saying they shouldn't even have to smell it any longer—

Ciena. Always Ciena. Did Thane possess a memory worth having that she wasn't a part of? Could he drink enough to blot out even the thought of her?

Apparently not. But he didn't fail for lack of trying.

Another drink. Then another. Thane's experience of the evening became fragmented and surreal. He knew Kendy had told the story of how her entire patrol had mutinied on Miriatin, and how only one-third of them had managed to escape with their lives. He remembered a game of sabacc but none of the cards he'd held. Maybe some guys from Ord Mantell had sung an obscene song about the unique pleasures each species could provide in bed. At some point, Yendor had asked Thane whether he didn't want to lay off and go to sleep, but Thane had told his Twi'lek friend to mind his own business. When the room spun around him, Thane simply braced himself against the side of the nearest X-wing and kept going.

That was how he found himself, at some unknown hour of the night, stumbling through the unfamiliar base alone and trying hard not to fall flat on his face.

C'mon. You can figure out where the bunks are. They showed you earlier. But his drunkenness had folded the strange corridors of the Mon Calamari ship into even stranger angles. The walls kept showing up where the floor should be, and vice versa. Finally Thane decided sitting down would be a great idea.

As his back slid down the wall, he felt his stomach turn over, a threat of what was to come. He'd never drunk to the point of vomiting before. That was not an experience he'd been eager to try. *First time for every-thing,* he thought in a haze.

Then someone helped him to his feet, a woman he'd never met before—or he thought he'd never met before—but she seemed kind as she put one of his arms around her shoulders. That seemed as good a reason as any for Thane to tell her his life story.

"I mean, really I'm only—only telling you the parts about Ciena," he mumbled as the woman steered him toward the nearest head. "But that's pretty much my whole life. The good part of my life, anyway."

"Sounds like it. Here, sit down."

She poured him into a chair. Thane let his head droop backward. "I know I probably didn't shoot her down today. But I *could've* done it. Or any of the other guys—they could've done it, and they're on my side, you know? They're my friends, and we all hate the Empire, but if I ever found out one of them had killed Ciena— and it's crazy, because, you know, she turned me in to the Empire. Can you believe that? She gave me a head start, but she turned me in. Sometimes I think about that and I get so angry I could—but it still *kills* me to think about her getting hurt—"

"Shhh." The woman laid some sort of cool, damp towel across his forehead. This was the best idea anyone had ever had. Thane decided she was some kind of genius.

So maybe she could help him figure out what was going on.

"What happens if—what if someday I'm in battle against the Empire again and I freeze up? What if I can't fire because I know Ciena could be in any one of those TIE fighters? What if I do fire and she *is* in one of them?" Thane became aware that he was on the verge of tearing up and managed to stop. He might be a sloppy drunk, but he'd be damned if he'd break down. "I don't want to kill her. And I don't want other people to die because I'm afraid of hurting this one person in the entire Imperial Starfleet that I love."

"I understand," the woman said, putting a cup in his hands. "Drink some water. You'll thank me later."

After that, things became even blurrier. At some point, Thane must have found his bunk, because he dimly perceived crawling into it fully clothed, down to his boots. And that was where he woke up the next morning, hating life.

"This is where a lesser being would say, 'I told you so.'" Yendor grinned as Thane leaned over the nearest bucket.

"Please shut up."

"Not until I tell you that our squadron has a briefing with the top brass in, oh, half an hour."

Thane rolled his eyes at his own stupidity, then winced. He hadn't known rolling his eyes could *hurt*. "Can you get rid of hangovers by dunking yourself in a bacta tank?"

Yendor considered that. "Huh. You know, that's not a bad idea? We'll have to test it someday. Right now, though—you're out of time."

"Great. Just great."

Through what felt like superhuman effort, Thane managed to shower and get into uniform. The dark circles under his eyes and the faint reddish stubble on his cheeks—well, people had showed up for roll call looking rougher than he did. The surgical droid 2-1B gave him an injection that would restore his blood chemistry to bearable levels within an hour or two. All Thane had to do was make it through the briefing.

When the entire squadron stood at attention, General Rieekan entered the room—but he wasn't alone. Behind him walked a composed, majestic woman with dark red hair, dressed all in white.

"I don't believe it," Kendy whispered.

"Me either," said Yendor, who stood by Thane's side, a huge grin on his face. "We finally get to meet Mon Mothma herself!"

Mon Mothma. One of the only senators to openly defy Palpatine as he rose to power. "Most Wanted" on every list of criminals the Imperial Starfleet kept. One of the leaders of the Rebel Alliance.

And the woman who had spent the previous night listening to Thane spill his guts, literally and figuratively.

How could he have failed to recognize her? He'd been even drunker than he'd thought. Of course the news reports from the Empire only showed images of Mon Mothma from many years before; she had been underground for some time. But Thane had been too intoxicated to recognize the woman even when she held his head over a basin as he puked his guts out.

Great. Just great. If only he could have sunk into the floor and let it close back over him to hide any evidence that he'd ever existed—but Thane had to stand there and pretend everything was normal.

"Good morning," she said, her voice as calm and steady as it had been the night before. "It is an honor to meet more of the warriors who have helped the Rebel Alliance stay strong during these dark times."

Pride rippled through the squadron, even getting to Thane despite his shame. To think that the leader of the entire Rebellion would say it was an honor to meet *them.* He doubted the Emperor had ever said such a thing to any of his troops.

Mothma continued, "All of you understand that obviously we must be on the move soon." Her eyes studied each of the pilots in turn; Thane wondered how a voice that gentle could belong to the same person as that steely gaze. "However, Corona Squadron, you will not accompany the rest of the fleet to their new rendezvous point."

Everyone exchanged glances. Was it some kind of penalty for their carousing last night—or some other, more significant infraction? But they hadn't done anything worth any kind of penalty, so far as Thane knew; in fact, they were one of the top squadrons in the fleet.

Mon Mothma then said, "We have . . . important tasks for you."

No further words were necessary. She meant intelligence work. That also meant danger. But Thane hadn't joined the Rebellion to play it safe.

"You've been chosen for this work even though many of you are new to the Rebellion. However, you have the right skills for the tasks to come." Mon Mothma took a seat at the one desk in the small space. Somehow the sheer power of her presence transformed the room into a chamber of state.

She's already the Emperor's match, Thane thought, *even if Palpatine doesn't know it yet.*

General Rieekan spoke up. "For the foreseeable future, Corona Squadron will remain based on the *Liberty*. You'll get permanent bunk assignments within the next few hours."

"Aw, man," Yendor deadpanned. "I always hoped I'd get to live in a sauna someday."

Rieekan raised an eyebrow. "Excuse me, Private Yendor?"

"I meant, I always hoped I'd get to live in a sauna someday, *sir*."

That made the others laugh, and even Rieekan smiled. Mon Mothma's face remained impassive—but not disapproving. The same minor informality would've landed an Imperial officer in the brig; in the rebel fleet, discipline could coexist with humanity.

"Both group and individual assignments will be discussed as they arise," Mon Mothma continued as smoothly as though there had been no interruption. "But you all deserve to know—the risks will be considerable, even greater than those you already face. It is possible that any or all of you may be asked to go on missions with little or no chance that you will ever return. If you feel you cannot accept such missions, speak now. There is no shame in doing so."

Everyone remained silent and at attention, wordlessly accepting the danger. Thane kept his gaze straight forward, not directly looking at anyone in the room. But he could feel Mon Mothma's gaze on him.

When the quiet had gone on long enough, Rieekan nodded. "Good. For now, get your new members up to date on our protocols"—that was accompanied by a nod toward Kendy, the newest of them all—"and await further instructions."

"Thank you for your courageous service, officers," Mon Mothma said. "You are dismissed." As everyone turned to go, and just as Kendy leaned toward Thane to ask a question, Mothma added, "Lieutenant Kyrell, I'd like to have a word."

And he'd been so close to making a clean getaway.

Thane turned around, again at attention, to face Mon Mothma. From the corner of his eye he caught a glimpse of General Rieekan; the general seemed surprised. At least Mon Mothma hadn't shared the tale of Thane's drunken moping with the entire Rebel Command.

Not yet, anyway.

The doors slid shut after the last of the others left, and Thane was alone with Mon Mothma. Under most circumstances, junior officers waited for their superiors to speak first. Thane thought this might be an exception to that rule. "Ma'am. I apologize for my—impropriety last night. Obviously, I overindulged in our, uh, celebrations. It won't happen again."

Mon Mothma leaned back in her chair, mouth quirked. "Lieutenant Kyrell, if I drummed pilots out of the service every time one of them had a little too much of the engine-room hooch, there would be no Rebellion."

"Yes, ma'am." But why then had she singled him out? He remembered some of what he'd said last night about freezing up, and his horror deepened. "If you're concerned that I'll fail to do my duty on one of the special missions for Corona Squadron, you don't have to be, ma'am."

"My concerns are irrelevant," she said crisply. "The problem here is that you're questioning *yourself.* Self-doubt will cripple you more surely than fear ever could. I hear you're an outstanding pilot, Kyrell. Moment to moment, I feel certain you'll do your duty. However, if you fall apart after every major engagement, you'll self-destruct before long."

Thane could say nothing. He knew she was right.

She continued, "Many people in the Rebellion have friends or family who serve the Empire in some capacity, or on planets or ships that may fare badly in this war. You aren't the only one with conflicts."

Yendor sometimes spoke quietly of his son, Bizu, left behind on Ryloth. Kendy's entire family back on Iloh would now be at risk because of her defection. "Yes, ma'am. I realize that."

Mon Mothma rose to her feet, and as she stepped closer Thane saw in her expression the kindness he'd sensed through his haze the previous night. "It's all right if you still love someone on the other side of this war—as long as you love what you're fighting for even more."

He had never thought of himself as fighting *for* anything. Thane had joined the Rebellion to fight against the Empire, not for the restoration of the Republic or any of the other grand schemes people talked about. As long as the Empire fell, he'd figured, the rest could sort itself out. Now, however, he finally asked himself what his decision really meant.

Fighting against the Empire meant fighting for galactic authority that valued justice and valor more than raw power, that treated the governed with respect instead of endless deception and manipulation. Fighting against the slavery of the Bodach'i and the Wookiees meant fighting for individuals to have the right of self-determination. Fighting against those who had callously and brutally destroyed Alderaan meant fighting for every other inhabited world in the entire galaxy.

Thane believed in all those things, enough to die for them, and yet he knew that wasn't why he was in the fight. He'd joined the Rebellion to take down the Empire and remained unmoved by all those starry-eyed notions of the New Republic to come. Just because he thought the next galactic government would be better than the Empire didn't mean he thought it would be *good*. In the end it would be another bureaucracy, another group dominated by the Core Worlds while the Outer Rim had to handle problems on its own—superior to the Empire in every way, of course, but that wasn't exactly a high bar to clear.

So his answer was no. He didn't love the Rebellion more than he loved Ciena.

But he could be willing to die for only one of those things, and he knew which one he had to choose—no matter how much it hurt.

Mon Mothma said, "Can you do your duty, Kyrell?"

"Yes, ma'am," he said. Thane felt the full weight of his words. He had just sworn to do whatever it took, up to and including taking Ciena's life.

Yet he knew he would never hesitate to fire in battle again.

CHAPTER EIGHTEEN

JUDE HAD NEVER mentioned that Bespin was so beautiful.

Ciena stared down at the viewscreen displaying the images of round-edged, clay-colored buildings seemingly aloft in the clouds. It was so like Jude not to have mentioned the way the filtered sunlight turned the sky an eternal sunset pink, or the elegance of Cloud City's structures, which bloomed above slender unipod cables as though they were parasol sunshades dangling in midair. Instead, whenever she had talked about her homeworld, Jude had discussed the geological reasons tibanna gas mining was so difficult or the aerodynamic properties of the gliders she'd flown as a child. No matter what, Jude had always been a scientist first. She had searched for truth as avidly as those bounty hunters had searched for the *Millennium Falcon*.

(How galling to have that scum succeed where Imperial officers had failed. Yet small civilian vessels had the advantage of passing through space largely unnoticed—the one thing no Star Destroyer could do.)

Although Ciena would have liked to have gone down to Cloud City, perhaps to meet Jude's parents, she remained aboard the *Executor*. The strike team tasked with capturing the crew of the *Falcon* comprised only a few individuals—including Lord Vader, who usually preferred to oversee operations personally. Whatever else was happening, all the thousands of other people assigned to the *Executor* had little to do but wait.

Ciena would have appreciated a task at the moment—any task, no matter how difficult or time-consuming. It would have been a distraction from her fury at Thane Kyrell.

Bespin made things worse, because Bespin meant Jude. Even thinking of her lost friend reminded Ciena of the way Jude had helped figure out the truth about that stupid laser cannon project.

That incident had proved that Ciena and Thane could disagree—as did his decision to leave the Imperial Starfleet. As upset as Ciena had been when Thane deserted, she had at least understood his decision, even if she would never agree with it.

But joining the *Rebellion*?

How could Thane ever have become a terrorist? He'd always held the Rebel Alliance in as much contempt as she had—when had that changed and how? Had he forgiven the destruction of the Death Star, and of the hundreds of thousands of people aboard? Yes, Alderaan had been destroyed first as a gambit to end the war before it began, and that gambit had failed. But that was one space station, one planet, one terrible day. The rebels' attacks on Imperial ships and bases had never ceased, as if they could not spill enough blood to slake their thirst. If they fought for a principle instead of mindless hatred of the Empire, they would propose peace talks or attempt to claim an independent star system where they could live under whatever governance they chose. But no. Instead they killed again, and again, and again. For all Thane's strength, for all his skill in combat, he had never been a violent man. So how could he be a part of such horror?

Maybe his father did this to him, Ciena thought as she walked through the corridors of Cloud City. A few grunting Ugnaughts hurried past her, but she hardly even registered them. In her mind's eye, she stood behind Thane the day he'd collapsed on the E&A obstacle course, when she had bandaged him afterward. At the time she had been moved almost to tears by the evidence of the abuse, the knowledge that his father's

cruelty had become physical as well as emotional—
and by the full realization of how bravely Thane had
endured his injuries until the very moment of his fall.

Those who were brutalized sometimes became brutal in return. Was Thane now lashing out at the world
that had hurt him first?

No. He'd always sworn he would be nothing like
his father; Ciena had always believed him. But that left
her with no answers at all.

"I don't believe it," said Nash Windrider.

Startled from her reverie, Ciena saw she'd reached
the landing platform, where her friend stood in front
of the *Millennium Falcon*. Their prey had flown straight to
Bespin, as Lord Vader had predicted. *So why did we even
bother with the asteroid field chase?* she thought. *We could just have
come here and set the trap for them even earlier.*

She walked onto the platform where Nash stood,
hands on his hips as he looked at the captured ship.
"When I saw it during the initial chase, I couldn't
understand why that thing wasn't in the junkyard. Now
that I study it up close, I realize no junkyard would
accept it."

"It's a miracle the thing still runs at all." She felt a
spark of grudging admiration for the *Falcon*; as someone who'd learned to fly on a V-171, occasionally she
got sentimental about clunky old ships. "Our orders?"

"We're to disable the hyperdrive."

"Why are we disabling a ship we've already captured?"

"Lord Vader has his reasons," Nash said, raising one eyebrow. The subtext seemed to be, *Do* you *want to tell him he's wrong?*

Ciena nodded. "Got it."

She and Nash worked together for several moments in silence. Even in the tight confines of the engineering pit within the *Falcon*, it seemed to her that Nash stood closer than necessary. But maybe she was imagining things because she wanted so much to be alone while she worked out her thoughts about Thane.

Disabling the hyperdrive proved simple. Before long she and Nash were on the shuttle that would take them back to the *Executor*; they were cleared to fly openly now, because another pilot sought by Darth Vader—another target lured into this trap—had just landed. Within minutes, this entire chase would be over. Princess Leia would stand trial. Her fellow rebels would be made an example of. Perhaps the Rebellion itself would be exposed . . .

. . . and Thane with it.

She moved through the ship on autopilot, reporting to her bridge shift with gratitude that the next few hours promised to be uneventful. That promise didn't come true; Vader's suspicions did. Sure enough, the *Millennium Falcon* zoomed off its platform, nearly made its escape—then inexplicably headed back to Cloud City and dived beneath it.

"Where do they think that's going to get them?" Nash's long fingers hit the toggles that would focus all sensors on the *Falcon*.

"Who knows?" She could almost pity these people, believing in their freedom when in reality Darth Vader had been two steps ahead of them the entire time.

Although the bridge of the *Executor* now buzzed with renewed activity, Ciena could do little but monitor these final moments of the hunt. Still she felt oddly detached from everything that was happening, even when Lord Vader returned to the bridge.

Admiral Piett said, "They'll be within range of the tractor beam within moments, my lord."

Through the heavy rasp of his respirator, Vader said, "Did your men disable the hyperdrive on the *Millennium Falcon*?"

"Yes, my lord."

"Good," Darth Vader said. "Prepare the boarding party and set your weapons for stun."

Ciena would normally have felt a little thrill of pride at her service being recognized. Instead she felt detached, as if this were only a drill, or a memory—until the horrifying moment when the *Falcon* leaped into hyperspace and vanished.

How the hell did they do that?

Nash gaped at her in disbelief. Ciena might have shared his outrage if she hadn't caught a glimpse of Admiral Piett's face. He had turned ashen, and even from her place down in the data pits, she could see the knot in his throat bob as he swallowed hard.

We're about to be killed, she thought. *The admiral, Nash and I—Vader will murder us all. We completed our assignment but it doesn't matter.*

For years she'd been thankful she'd never seen one of Vader's "eliminations" in person. Now it looked as if the first one she'd ever witness would be her own.

But Vader simply stood there a few moments longer, in silence, then turned and walked off the bridge without another word. When the doors slid shut behind him, Piett sagged for a moment, like someone who had put down a heavy burden and whose body still felt the weight. Nash leaned onto his monitors, head in hand. Ciena waited to feel relief, too, but the dread only dulled and deepened until it felt as if it had sunk into her very bones.

———

That evening, as they sat in a corner of the quadrant cafeteria, empty plates in front of them, Ciena asked, "Why do you think people join the Rebellion?"

Berisse shrugged. "The same reason other people commit robbery or go into business with the Hutts. They can't fit into any normal society, so they hate those of us who do."

Thane had been at the top of the elite flight track. If he'd stayed in the service, Ciena had no doubt he'd be looking at an early promotion to commander, too. She'd have to find another answer. "What do you think, Nash?"

"Who cares how scum like that get started?" he said, too lightly. "I only want to see them finished."

"Why do you ask?" Berisse took another sip of her nutritive milk. While more "regular" meals were available upon request, only the most senior officers could indulge without being thought soft. Ciena had eaten her last piece of bread more than two years ago.

Ciena shrugged. "No reason."

"You're in an odd mood today," Nash said. His warm brown eyes studied hers. He had become so thin since they'd graduated from the academy, his frame going from wiry to gaunt—but his eyes, at least, were the same. "What's wrong?"

She didn't dare tell the whole truth, but if anyone

could help her understand Thane's choice, it would be Nash. "I've been thinking about Thane a lot lately."

Berisse slid an arm around Ciena's shoulders; Nash's smile faded into sadness. "I still can't believe it," he said softly. "Thane was the last person I ever thought would commit suicide."

"After the Death Star, none of us were ourselves," Berisse said, shaking her head.

"But he had so much to live for. His commission, top ranking as a pilot, revenge against the rebels, and— and he had you, Ciena." Nash stumbled over the last part, though he covered it well enough. "That ought to be enough for any man."

Ciena didn't meet his eyes. "I keep wondering why he felt so hopeless."

Only a man without hope would go from the Empire to the Rebellion. It was one thing for Thane to walk away from his oath because he felt he could no longer keep it. But to join a group of nihilistic guerrilla warriors? He was no idealist, so he couldn't have been converted to whatever bizarre political dogma they used to sway the gullible. Thane could only be going through the motions, no more.

"Did Thane have any other close friends aboard the Death Star? Maybe someone you didn't know about?" Berisse hesitated, tucking a loose strand of black hair back into her regulation bun. "Like—well—a girl from the academy? From before he fell for you, I mean! He could still have been upset by her death."

It was Nash who answered. "He was never with anyone while we were at school. I don't suppose there was anyone back on Jelucan?"

"No." Ciena had occasionally seen him walking out with second-wave girls, but never the same one twice.

With a shrug, Berisse said, "Maybe it was something that happened on your homeworld. He was upset after the Death Star, he left his duty but meant only to go home and collect himself—and then the visit went terribly wrong."

"I always had an inkling his relationship with his father was strained at best. Abusive at worst," Nash said. "Oh, don't give me those wide eyes, Ciena. I lived in the same room as Thane for three years. You think I never saw the scars on his back?" His expression had become set, hard. "I'll bet his father lit into Thane at the worst possible moment. Drove him over the edge."

"I wouldn't put it past Thane's dad." That much, at least, was completely true. But by then Ciena realized Nash had no answers to offer. Thane's choice to join the Rebellion would remain an infuriating mystery—an arrow lodged in her flesh, one that couldn't be pulled free and so kept the wound open forever.

She remained lost in thought until Nash had escorted her almost all the way back to her room. Her door stood at the far end of the longest corridor of the barracks section, so they were far away from anyone else when he put one hand on her arm.

"Going to bed already?" he said, his tone light. But nobody could miss his true meaning.

Ciena had suspected this might be coming, but in her preoccupation had failed to see it would be tonight. No wonder Berisse had excused herself earlier; she was going to be in serious trouble for enabling him. "Nash—it's a bad idea."

"On the contrary, it's a *wonderful* idea." His eyes danced with mischief and anticipation. "Don't you think we deserve to have a little fun?"

As gently as she could manage, Ciena answered, "I think you want more than fun. And I can't give it to you."

Nash tilted his head, not disagreeing with her but not withdrawing, either. "Could I perhaps persuade you to spend more rec time together? So we could get to know each other without Berisse or our other friends in the way? I realize the shift from friends to, well, *more*—it can be tricky. But I think it's worth trying. And for you, I'd be willing to wait."

She took a step away from him. Her back bumped against the metal mesh of the wall. How ridiculous, to be as bashful and clumsy as a schoolgirl. More firmly she said, "I can't."

His face fell, and she could see he'd gone from flirty to aghast in only seconds. "What an idiot I've been. We were talking about Thane only an hour ago. I ought to have realized this is hardly the time. Please forgive me."

"It's okay. Really."

"I miss him, too, you know." Nash looked so stricken that Ciena found herself feeling guilty. The lie she'd told about Thane's suicide had saved his life but wounded his other friends forever. "I didn't mean to make light of how you felt about him."

"I know you didn't." Ciena managed to smile. "So let's say good night."

Nash sighed. "Let's." He squeezed her hand once, just for a moment, and then walked away.

As her bunk doors slid shut and locked, Ciena sagged onto her bed, so tired she felt as if she'd pulled three shifts in a row.

She told herself that she'd turned Nash down

because she had no romantic feelings for him. So far as it went, that was true.

But she couldn't deny that a big part of the reason was what she still felt for Thane Kyrell.

I should hate him now. I have to learn to hate him. But I can't. I never could.

The small communicator unit in her corner of the bunk blinked—the blue light that meant the message was from a non-Imperial source. For Ciena, that could only mean a holo from home. Her fingers had almost hit the button before she caught herself. *Should I watch this right away?*

Should I watch it at all?

She still missed Jelucan. Even though she drank her nutritives, she longed for a piece of bread every single time she walked into the cafeteria. She spoke to her family regularly, by holo, instead of relying on the bimonthly communiqués suggested by the internal affairs officer.

From her pocket, Ciena pulled the small pouch in which she kept the leather bracelet that tied her to Wynnet. It had been a long time since she'd last asked her dead sister to look through her eyes.

Too long, she thought with a surge of feeling that made her fingers close tightly around the pouch. *I don't*

have to choose between being Jelucani and being a good Imperial officer.
I can be both.

Ciena was smiling as she started the holo and saw her pappa's face looking out at her. After only a few words of his prerecorded speech, her smile faded.

Ronnadam's gray eyebrows were arched so high they nearly reached his receding hairline. "You want to return to your home planet for an . . . undefined period of time."

"I've accrued seven weeks of leave time, sir. I strongly doubt I will use them all."

Ideal Imperial officers used no leave time whatsoever, unless they had to recover from a serious illness or injury. Ciena had never asked to take a single day until now.

Ronnadam rose from his desk and clasped his hands behind his back. His green eyes had a strangely milky quality, as if they belonged to a far older man. "Your decision to use your leave time is your own. But I am not questioning the length of your absence. I'm questioning your motivation to return to your home planet at all."

"My mother will be put on trial for embezzling funds from the local mine where she works—worked as a supervisor." The words alone sounded surreal to

Ciena. Her mother, a thief? It was impossible. She cared nothing for physical possessions beyond the few things they already owned, and her promotion at the mine had made them all so proud. "In the valleys of Jelucan, to have one's honor questioned is the most serious crisis an individual can face, sir. Those who believe in that person's honor must gather around them at that time. It is a sacred duty."

"'Sacred,' indeed." In Ronnadam's mouth, the word became a sneer. "You do realize, Lieutenant Commander Ree, that the charges against your mother would have been brought by the local Imperial authority. Are you questioning the judgment of a fellow servant of the Emperor?"

"Of course not, sir. But my mother could have been framed for the crime, or there may be some other mistake that has led to a . . . misunderstanding."

Ronnadam pursed his lips in sympathy, an expression that was meant to mock Ciena more than convince her. "Do you hear your own rationalizations, Ree?"

"I don't want to judge based on incomplete information, sir. I must investigate this for myself." She managed to look him in the eyes. "No matter what the truth may be, I will face it."

Slowly he nodded. "Yes. This could be a learning experience for you." He paced in front of her, step by measured step. "Take your leave, Lieutenant Commander. Witness your mother's trial."

Ciena tried to imagine her mother standing before a judge, hands shackled. She couldn't.

Ronnadam began to smile. "And when you return, report to me immediately. Let me know the final ruling on her guilt or innocence—and tell me whether you believe that judgment to be justified."

No matter what the judge ruled, Ciena would be expected to support it—even if he sent her mother to a prison camp. . . .

That won't happen. It can't. The judge will make the right decision in the end.

So she told herself. She wanted to believe it.

But for the first time, her oath to the Empire did not sustain Ciena. The feeling she had worked hard to keep at bay for the past three years—the one she had never allowed herself to consciously think of before—could be held back no longer:

Doubt.

CHAPTER NINETEEN

THANE ANGLED HIS X-wing low, until it nearly skimmed the thick canopy of trees covering the surface of D'Qar. In the twilight he could see leaves thrashing beneath the other ships as if caught in a windstorm. If anyone were on the ground beneath them, Corona Squadron would be detected within minutes.

We're not going to be here that long, Thane reminded himself. He opened the secure channel. "Corona Five, this is Corona Four, do you copy?"

"Copy." Kendy replied. "Negative readings here. I'm not picking up any artificial power sources."

"Same here."

Corona Squadron had been sent to check out D'Qar for any possible sign of a new Imperial outpost. Apparently, deep-cover spies on Coruscant had reported massive amounts of materiel being processed for the Imperial Starfleet; nobody knew precisely what it was being used for, but there were rumors of a new large-ship construction facility . . .

But if the Empire had begun building new Star Destroyers or some other kinds of superweapons, it wasn't doing so on D'Qar. They'd run scans on every hemisphere, searched planetary and solar orbits, and come up empty.

Thane realized he'd rather have found something. At least then they'd have learned what the Empire was planning, and they could have taken meaningful action: sabotaging the factories, placing a few surveillance droids in key locations, and so on. For now, he simply had to endure the suspense.

He said, "Corona Two, do you also read negative?"

"Confirmed. Complete negative on Imperial activity," Yendor replied. "Unless the Empire's drafting small woodland creatures all of a sudden."

"Doubt it." Thane considered for a moment. "We should list this planet as a potential base in future. The Empire's not interested, not much space lane traffic in this area, and there's plenty of water."

"Plus it beats Hoth," Yendor said.

"The belly of a sarlacc beats Hoth." Thane began

punching in the navigational codes that would take him back to the *Liberty*.

Corona Leader apparently agreed. "Let's get out of here."

Once they had returned to their ship, the rest of Corona Squadron went through maintenance on their X-wings in the muggy repair bay of the *Liberty*, trading the usual banter back and forth. "Come on," Yendor said to the squadron leader and the eldest pilot in the group, a stately woman who was addressed only as the Contessa. "You can't tell me this isn't more fun than life in a palace."

She gave him a look. "You need to spend more time in palaces."

"You know, I do," Yendor agreed. "You can fix me up with that, right?"

"Honestly," the Contessa huffed—but not without affection. "You could learn from Smikes here. He never pretends we're having a better time than we are."

"We're never having a good time," Smikes said from beneath his X-wing. He had a bandana tied around his forehead to combat the endless sweat suffered by any human who lived on a Mon Calamari ship. "We're in a war. What's fun about this?"

"So cranky," Yendor said amiably. "Someday I'm

going to hear you laugh, and I hope a protocol droid is around to record it."

"Don't be so hard on Smikes," Kendy said, tossing her dark green hair over her shoulder. "He's just grumpy."

"I'm not grumpy, I'm a realist," Smikes insisted. He was in fact *always* grumpy, but a great pilot.

Thane shook his head as he looked at all of them—as mixed up a crew as you were likely to find, people who wouldn't have spent time together outside this squadron or this war under any circumstances. But at least they had his back.

Unlike some people.

Much later, once everyone else had finished up, Kendy said, "I have to admit, intelligence work is a little less glamorous and dramatic than I always thought it would be."

Thane didn't look up from the open panel in his wing. "My guess is that the dramatic stuff is what's most likely to get you killed. We can deal with that when we come to it. I'll do whatever we have to do, but I'm not suicidal."

No reply followed for a few minutes, during which Thane remained engrossed in his work. He'd almost forgotten he and Kendy were even speaking until she said, in a low voice, "You know that's what Ciena reported."

He remained where he was, staring into the wires and chips that powered his ship. The wrench in his hand remained poised above the coupling he intended to work on. He didn't look up at Kendy. "What did Ciena report?"

"She identified you as a probable suicide on Jelucan. I heard about it through some other class-mates of ours—and I sent a holo to Ciena right away, because I couldn't believe it. She didn't really want to talk, though. At the time I thought it was because she was hurting. Then when I realized you were here with the Rebellion, I figured, hey, Thane covered his tracks pretty well. But the more I think about it . . . you could've fooled anyone else in the galaxy more easily than Ciena. The two of you know each other too well. She covered for you, didn't she?"

"Yeah." It was as if Thane were back on Jelucan, shutting the door behind Ciena as she left. He'd believed she would turn him in no matter what. "She did."

Kendy whistled. "Ciena Ree broke an oath?"

"Sometimes we're loyal to more than one thing." He spoke from memory, haltingly, but still sure. "When there's a conflict, we have to choose which loyalty to honor. I guess—I guess she chose me."

Ciena had covered for him. She'd orchestrated that elaborate lie—when she *never* lied—all for him. Knowing her as he did, knowing where she came from, Thane realized what it had cost her to do that. The hard knot of anger he'd been carrying in his chest for the past three years finally went slack.

But that made it worse, because his anger had been his only shield against losing her.

The thump of boots hitting the floor of the hangar made Thane look up from his X-wing. Kendy had hopped down from her own starfighter to stand beneath his, hands on her hips. "Then why isn't she here?"

"—Ciena?"

"She always said an oath was forever, a promise is a promise, you had to be true to your personal honor," Kendy said, and she had begun to sound angry. "I didn't even think she could lie. Now I discover that she broke her word to save you, but she still serves in the Imperial Starfleet. How can she do that? If she could defy them for your sake, why won't she do it for the sake of the *entire galaxy*?"

"Ciena was never disloyal to the Empire." Thane hated that but knew it to be true. "One time, back then, she chose her loyalty to me. That doesn't mean she set aside her oath to the Empire."

"I don't see the difference."

"That's because you're not from Jelucan." *And you don't know Ciena like I do.* The coupling could wait. Thane shut the panel, stowed his tools, and slid down to face Kendy. "Listen. You and I were in the Imperial Starfleet, too, remember? Good people can wind up in the service of evil."

Kendy shook her head as she folded her arms across her chest. The air smelled like welding tools and engine grease; her dark green hair glinted in the harsh hangar lights. "Good people can start to serve the Empire. But if they stay, they stop being good. You do one thing you thought you'd never do—follow one order that makes you feel sick inside—and you tell yourself it's the only time. This is an exception. This isn't the way it's always going to be."

Thane remembered how he'd tried willing himself not to notice the pitiful slavery of the Bodach'i. "Yeah. I know."

"But you keep going," Kendy continued. Her gaze had become distant. By now she spoke to herself more than to him. "You make one more compromise, and then another, and by the time you realize what the Empire really is, you're almost too far down that road to turn back. I managed to do it, but if the others hadn't felt the same way—if I'd had to leave on my own instead of getting away with a group—I might have stayed. And I don't like the person I would have become."

By now Thane had realized that Kendy was trying to warn him that the Ciena he had known, the one who had saved him, might not even exist any longer.

Probably that was true. By now Ciena might have participated in one of the punitive massacres the Empire inflicted on noncompliant worlds. She could have been in one of the Star Destroyers in the Battle of Hoth, coolly aiming their lasers at the many rebel starfighters that never got away. The Empire had probably corroded her honor into stiffness, snobbery, and ruthlessness.

Knowing all that didn't make it easier to accept.

Thane said only, "Guess we'll never know. Not like either of us is ever going to see her again."

In the instant before he turned to walk away from the hangar, he glimpsed the expression on Kendy's face. It was pity.

Although he continued working throughout the day, Thane brooded enough that Yendor finally asked him who died, and even Smikes told him to cheer up. After they'd finished the full briefing about D'Qar, he excused himself from the usual group meal and after-shift card games. Instead he holed up in one of the rare empty computer bays on the *Liberty*, so he could be alone.

Solitude was a rare luxury for a rebel pilot—just as it had been for an academy cadet. He rarely got to be alone with his thoughts. As a boy, if he'd wanted to be alone, he was always able to sneak out to the Fortress. Sometimes Ciena had been there, but her presence had never disturbed him. Before they were ten years old, they'd known when to let each other remain silent, how to be close to each other without intruding. How many people ever understood someone that well?

We wouldn't understand each other at all, now, he reminded himself. *She's been an Imperial officer for years. Everything good inside Ciena got poisoned a long time ago. If we met up again now, she wouldn't cover for me; count on it. I need to move on.*

Thane stretched out, wiped his brow, and pulled up the news feeds from Jelucan. Seeing his native world made him . . . whatever the opposite of "homesick" was. The planet changed month by month, always for the worse; it was impossible to read the reports without realizing that the rugged, primitive world he'd grown up on didn't really exist any longer. The girl he'd known and come to love, the Ciena who had been, was as lost as the old Jelucan.

So he let the first few gloomy images play out in

front of him, the desolation ironically easing the ache he felt inside—

—until they reported on the upcoming trial of Verine Ree.

Thane sat up so fast the holo rippled into static, unable to assess the ideal distance to project from its viewer. *That's not possible,* he told himself. *I imagined that because Kendy and I just talked about Ciena and I've got her on my mind.* But then the face of Ciena's mother again took shape. The label hovering beneath her image read THE ACCUSED.

Embezzlement? Impossible. Someone from the valleys might snap in a fit of rage and hit or kill you. Crimes of passion took place there the same way they did anywhere. Perhaps they also fell prey to other criminal impulses—stealing from shopkeepers, that kind of thing. But a crime as premeditated and corrupt as embezzlement went against everything they believed.

Surely there were hypocrites among the valley kindred, but not anyone in Ciena's family. He only had to know Ciena to be sure of that.

Thane's lips pressed together in a hard, tight line. If anything remained of the Ciena he'd known, it wouldn't survive this. Once Ciena condoned her own mother's conviction and imprisonment, she would truly be lost forever. As lost to him as if he really had killed her that day above Hoth—

Good-bye, he thought, remembering the little girl in her plain brown dress, the fallen autumn leaf. It was time to leave her behind forever.

This can't be Jelucan, Ciena wanted to say to her shuttle pilot. *You've brought me to the wrong system.*

Yet she knew too well that she was on the right planet. It was just that everything had changed.

Thick fog seemed to have settled permanently on the ground, and the air was thick with grimy soot. The mines that had carved gouges in so many of the mountains did not attempt to filter the byproducts of the work, so people simply walked through it, coughing, some with kerchiefs or light masks over their mouths and noses.

At first Ciena thought the masks were confusing her, making it harder for her to tell valley folk from second-wavers. Although she'd seen more mass-produced clothing the last time she'd been home, the two groups had still been distinct. Now it was impossible to discern any difference. She'd never thought she would miss the gaudy long coats of the second-wavers, but she searched in vain for even one flash of crimson or cobalt. No shaggy muunyaks wandered the streets any longer; people either rode ridgeclimbers or walked.

Valentia had seemed greatly changed to her three years ago, but it had at least been recognizable then. Now the migrant-worker shanties had multiplied to the point that the original buildings carved of stone were almost invisible. The senatorial building that had become an Imperial garrison was now a full military outpost, ringed by a force field that glowed a sickly green and with a constant flow of officers and storm-troopers walking through its gates.

Jelucani people walked more quickly past the out-post, Ciena noticed. They didn't want to attract notice. Nobody would meet her eyes.

"I shouldn't have asked you to come," Paron Ree repeated, just outside the door of her old bedroom. "I thought of myself, and not of you. What will your superior officers say?"

"They'll say a mistake has been made, because it has." Ciena tossed aside her uniform jacket, which landed atop her trousers and boots. Her old clothes still fit and were only slightly musty. The mauve leggings and tunic seemed so impossibly soft; had she really worn things like this every day? She opened the door and stepped into the main room, where her father stood with his hands clasped, as if preparing to give a formal report. She took hold of his shoulders and squeezed. "It's all right, Pappa. The truth will come out."

Her father's face remained tense and drawn. "The real culprit is unlikely to be identified by the authorities."

"Because they haven't found him yet? Well, we'll see about that." If only she'd already made commander! That rank might have done her some good when she went to speak with the magistrate the next day. "Forgive my saying it, Pappa, but you don't look good. Have you been eating?"

"With your mother gone, I—lose track of time."

Ciena paused. She hadn't realized until earlier that day that her mother remained jailed, and she couldn't believe her father when he said Mumma couldn't even have visitors. That was another thing to take care of with the magistrate the next day. She'd requested an audience for first thing in the morning, so surely she would hear from his staff shortly.

Surely.

Her father had some meat and root vegetables in the refrigeration unit, so she started throwing together a basic soup. She hadn't cooked in so long, but she still remembered which herbs to crush and the way the scent clung to her fingers afterward. Her stomach growled, eager for something—anything—that wasn't Imperial nutritives. (Ciena had taken a couple of bottles of nutritive drink with her, but . . . better to save those for the trip home.)

When the broth began to bubble, Ciena stepped away from the hearth and sat on the floor cushions beside the low table, across from her father. Only after she'd taken her place did she realize it didn't feel awkward at all, even after years of eating at higher tables, sitting on benches or in chairs. Home remained home.

Paron shook his head slowly. "It's good to see you again, my girl." He touched the side of her face, just for a moment.

"I should have come earlier."

"No. I know there's a war on. You do what you have to do."

The new gray hair at his temples surprised Ciena, but not as much as his demeanor. Her father had always been her rock—unyielding and often tough, but invariably fair. Forever strong. Now his spirit was weary, so much so that she could see it as clearly as she could see the new lines on his face.

"There aren't any flags out front," Ciena said. "Are the kindred refusing to acknowledge the charges?" That was an act of defiance against authority—anathema to those in the valleys—and yet truly unjust accusations sometimes earned that response.

"They acknowledge them." Her father's voice tightened. "But no one has come."

That couldn't be right. "No one?"

He nodded.

She remembered the days she'd remained at the home of the Nierre family, standing by them in their darkest hours. They had all celebrated together when the accusers had finally backed down and accepted the Imperial version of events . . . though now that made Ciena wonder. "How could anyone who knows Mumma think she would ever steal?"

"They know she didn't take the money!" her father snapped. "They all know it, but not one will say so."

"But—to refuse to stand by someone wrongly accused—"

"The Empire accuses her. We owe our allegiance to the Empire. To stand against it would be the most base dishonor!"

"You can't stand against Mumma." Ciena stared at her father in shock. ". . . can you?"

"Your mother understands the demands of honor, as do I. Have you forgotten them, Ciena?" His piercing gaze caught her short, and she dared say no more.

But what about the truth? she thought. *How could the truth not matter anymore? When did it become honorable to accept bald-faced lies?*

"Forgive my temper," he said, and he sounded even more exhausted than before. "These days have been difficult."

"I know. I'm sorry. But I'm here now."

An hour passed. They ate soup and bread in silence, and all her fear and worry could not keep Ciena from relishing the taste of real food in her mouth. Sitting near her own hearth, being with her father, even hearing the cries of salt hawks—at moments she could imagine that she had never become an officer, never even left Jelucan. That it was all a dream.

But she couldn't indulge in daydreaming for long. Reality weighed on her more heavily with every minute that passed, because the answering message from the magistrate's office never came—and neither did anyone from the valley kindred. Not one soul. The low trench of sand outside their home remained empty, advertising the depths of the Ree family's shame.

The sky had gone completely dark overhead before Ciena dared to ask, "Pappa, why are you so sure no one will find who really did this?"

"You know the answer. Don't insult us both by making me tell you."

She had already drawn the most logical conclusion:

the embezzler was an Imperial official, someone who ranked high enough to falsify the records. "The magistrate won't publicly question Imperial officials? Even then, prosecuting Mumma—"

"Ciena, listen to me. You are a member of the Imperial Starfleet, and I'm proud of that. All that is good in the Empire comes from you and those like you." He patted her hand. "But every rule, and every ruler, has its bad side as well. Here on Jelucan, we . . . have seen more of the bad. But we shall not waver in our loyalty."

She thought again of the sooty skies, the mountains scarred with deep gashes that looked like the claw marks of some monstrous beast. Her father refused to give way even when everything around him spoke of corruption and ruin.

It's only Jelucan, the result of one dishonest governor. Higher officials don't know the truth, because if they did, they'd take action.

So Ciena told herself. But even within her own mind, the rationalizations sounded so laughable that she could not believe them, much less speak them aloud. She kept thinking of Ronnadam's face as he'd granted her leave, and how he'd been so completely certain that the Imperial courts would make the right decision. He knew that because he knew the "right" decision would not be the one that arrived at the truth;

it would be the one that justified any actions taken by Imperial officials. The appearance of fairness mattered more than the reality.

And yet. "Not *one person* from the kindred, Pappa?"

He gestured toward the empty sand, the lack of flags.

After that, there seemed to be nothing more to say. Ciena moved through the house as if in a trance, putting away the extra soup and cleaning the pots. Once again half her world seemed dreamlike, but now it was her own home that had become surreal to her. How could she be in such beloved surroundings and still feel so small and sick inside? She almost longed to be back on the *Executor*, where the recirculated air smelled of ozone and nobody ever deviated from the safety of the rules.

The final transport journey to Jelucan had taken ten hours; Ciena had been too agitated even to think of sleeping during the trip. Now, another ten hours later, weariness had more than caught up with her. Her head swam and her eyes stung. But during times of trial, someone always remained awake at the house of the accused. Normally, loyal friends and family members took turns for the overnight vigils, but Ciena and her father were alone. As tired as she was, she knew Pappa was even more worn down.

"Go to bed," she said quietly. "I'll keep the vigil."

"You need your rest."

"And you don't?"

"After you made the trip all the way here . . ." But her father's voice trailed off. He lacked even the strength to fight her.

Outside she heard the humming of a ridgeclimber. She was so eager for the approach of a friend that the sound made her ears prick up, but immediately she chastised herself. *Many people travel this way farther down into the valleys. They haven't come for you.*

But then the ridgeclimber stopped. Next Ciena heard footsteps and—oh, thank the Force—the unmistakable sound of a stick being thrust into sand.

Smiling triumphantly, Ciena patted her father's shoulder and ran to the door. At least one person had been faithful. One person stood by them no matter what. Would it be one of the Nierres, pale skin blushing scarlet as they apologized for coming so late? Would it be one of the elders, saying he took the risk of defying the Imperial officials on behalf of all the kindred?

She flung open the door even before their visitor could knock—then froze in shock. It was impossible to move, or even to speak any word besides his name.

Ciena whispered, ". . . Thane?"

CHAPTER TWENTY

A S OFTEN AS Ciena had thought about Thane, even though he remained a part of her, she had genuinely believed she would never see him again. And yet there he stood in front of her, unsure of his welcome, his pale blue eyes unfathomable.

Her father spoke then. "Yes?"

"Mr. Ree. It's Thane Kyrell. I heard about Ciena's mother and—I wanted to stand vigil with you. If you'll have me." Thane gestured toward the trough of sand, where a lone flag stood. "Ciena told me once that people from outside the kindred could bring a plain red flag, since we don't have family banners. At least . . . I think that's what she told me." He hesitated for the first time, and the uncertainty she briefly glimpsed in him made Thane look more familiar, like the boy she remembered. But that moment didn't last long; that boy faded away, leaving a stranger behind. "Did I remember the ritual correctly?"

"You did." The words came out more evenly than Ciena would have thought she could manage.

Thane nodded, acknowledging her words as rigidly as he'd once acknowledged orders. "Then may I stand with you? Or should I leave?"

The obvious subtext: *Are you going to turn me in to the Empire?*

She had sworn to do it. Her oath of loyalty demanded no less, especially now that she knew Thane had joined the Rebel Alliance.

But the sanctity of standing vigil was supreme. Anyone who staked his honor on yours deserved the protection of your house. So when her father glanced at her, eyebrow raised, she nodded and took a step back from the door so Thane could walk inside.

He had been listening more carefully than she'd thought back in those days in the Fortress, when she'd tried to explain the beliefs and rituals of the kindred to him as they whiled away the hours. He addressed her father properly, bowing his head slightly in respect. "Paron Ree, I believe in the honor of your family."

"I thank you for your decision to stand vigil with us." Her father hesitated—he had met Thane on only a few occasions and had never seen him as anything but a privileged rich boy who piggybacked his way to success on Ciena's shoulders. Certainly he had never shaken Thane's hand before, but he did so now.

Ciena shut the door, her hands so numb with shock that she fumbled with the bolt. It had been three years since they'd said good-bye. She'd made it down to ground level that night before she'd begun to cry; she doubted Thane had lasted much longer.

I told him I would turn him in if I ever saw him again. I told him if he ever returned to Jelucan, he would be captured. Imprisoned. Possibly killed. Even lesser treasons had become capital crimes in the past few years.

But Thane had returned anyway.

"All right." Thane stood in the center of their main room, tall and imposing in a domed room that seemed too small for him. "What do you need me to do?"

Her father gestured to the table. "Your presence is enough. Have you eaten? We have soup, thanks to Ciena."

"I don't want to impose—"

"You're standing vigil," Ciena said. The words came out more sharply than she'd intended. "You stand with our house. That means you're entitled to our hospitality and our protection—while you're here."

"Then I'll have some soup. Thank you." Thane lowered himself to the floor, folding his long legs beneath the low table with some difficulty.

Pappa took it upon himself to get Thane's meal, both as part of the ritual welcome of their one ally and because he must have felt Ciena and Thane wanted to talk. They *should* talk; Ciena knew that much. But she had no idea where to start.

Best to begin with what mattered most. "Thank you," she said. "For standing with our family."

Thane nodded toward the trough outside. "I didn't see any other flags."

"The kindred have abandoned us." A bitter smile twisted her lips. "No one else came. Only you."

He hesitated before saying, "I know your mother is innocent. Nobody from the valleys would ever do something like that—least of all anyone connected to you."

Their eyes met for a long moment before they both turned away.

When her father set the bowl of soup in front of Thane, she saw how slowly Pappa moved. He couldn't have known one moment's peace since her mother's arrest more than a week ago. "Remember, I'm standing the vigil tonight," Ciena said to her father, putting her hand on his arm. "Go to bed."

"I can do it," Thane said. "Someone has to stay awake until dawn—that's right, isn't it? If so, it ought to be me."

Pappa, apparently assuming the matter was settled, kissed Ciena on the cheek and went to his room without another word. She hoped he would lie down and fall asleep immediately, both because he obviously needed the rest and because she didn't want him to overhear anything she and Thane were about to say.

They remained silent until her father's door had closed. Ciena's knees felt watery as she took her place on the cushion next to Thane's; being that close to him reminded her so powerfully of the one night they had spent together. He'd lost the last of his boyhood softness, and instead had become almost aggressively masculine—broad shoulders, solid muscles, and a thick shadow of reddish stubble along the strong line of his jaw. But she turned until she could not see his face and said only, "You know it's dangerous for you here."

"I've been careful," he said. "I didn't leave my transport until after dark. Rented a ridgeclimber under a fake name, came straight here. I'll leave at night, too. So I'm not going to see anyone who doesn't come into this house. I'm safe—unless you turn me in."

"By now you know I'm not going to."

"Because I'm owed the 'protection of the house'?"

Thane asked. The obvious subtext: *Or do you have another reason?*

She gave him no direct answer. Wrapping her arms around herself in a hug, she said, "I'll keep the vigil tonight."

"You're exhausted—it's obvious," he said, so harshly it seemed like a judgment. "I slept on the transport, so I've got a few hours in me."

"I can't let you do that."

"It's not a ritual thing, is it? If it were, your father would have said so. So why?"

She was tired enough to tell him the truth. "Because I don't want to owe you anything."

He laughed, not in humor but surprise. Thane hadn't expected her to be this angry; obviously he'd had no idea she knew the truth about his involvement with the Rebel Alliance, though he probably suspected it now. But he seemed to be nearly as angry with her—despite the fact that the last time they'd seen each other they'd had to tear themselves apart.

"Look at it this way." Thane spoke very quietly, and almost against her will Ciena looked up at him again. "I already owe you one, for faking my suicide instead of turning me in. So if I keep the vigil tonight, we'll be even. Nobody will owe anyone anything. Okay?"

In her childhood, Ciena had read horrible stories of the cruel, barbarous punishments used in the old times, back before her people had ever left their original planet or knew that others lived among the stars. She'd had nightmares about one in particular, where a person's four limbs would be tied to four separate beasts, which would then be driven in opposite directions until the victim's body was torn apart. That torture had haunted her, and she had given thanks that it could never happen to her.

Now it was happening, not to her body but to her soul.

She had sworn an oath of loyalty to the Empire, had made friends there who would be with her for a lifetime, and had served with distinction. Yet the shadows she had glimpsed long ago had lengthened and darkened—the useless deaths of so many pilots, the increasing pressure to put aside everything she had been, the corruption and devastation here on Jelucan. And, above all, she could not forget Alderaan, a world destroyed in an effort to prevent a war, an effort that had utterly failed.

None of that divided her heart as brutally as simply being with Thane again. Not only had he abandoned his duty—and her—but he had also joined the

Rebellion. The people responsible for Jude's death and this wretched war. It was the most complete betrayal she could imagine.

But when everyone else had failed her, Thane had risked his life to stand by her side.

Ciena rose from the table. "Good night, Thane." She didn't thank him for keeping the vigil. She simply walked to her bedroom and closed the door behind her without looking back. In her exhaustion, she thought she would fall asleep instantly, but instead she lay awake for nearly an hour, listening for the faint sounds Thane made as he moved about the house. Ciena knew he would not come to her, nor did she want him to, but she couldn't stop wanting to hear him. To know where he was, and be sure he was near.

The next morning, when Paron Ree rose, Thane excused himself for a quick nap. By that time he was tired enough to sleep despite the questions burning in his mind, the same ones that had plagued him all night long.

Such as, *Why is Ciena furious with me?* He suspected she'd learned he had joined the Rebellion, which was bad news. Did that mean the Empire had a dossier on him? They couldn't unless the Rebel Alliance had intelligence leaks of its own. Maybe Ciena had been punished for covering up his desertion; that, too, would explain why she seemed to find it difficult to look at him.

Another: *Will I be able to rejoin my squadron when I return?* Thane had reported his upcoming absence to General Rieekan but had given no details and been given none in return. Probably his relays for the *Liberty's* current coordinates would still be good when he left—but if the Rebellion got even a hint that the Empire might be coming after the ship, they would move on. Then Thane would have to go through the laborious process of reconnecting with the Rebel Alliance from scratch: sounding out pilots in various spaceports, traveling to worlds known to be sympathetic in hopes of hearing the right whispers, and so on. It could be a lengthy process and would certainly be a dangerous one.

But the question truly tearing Thane apart was, *What am I doing here?*

Thane had told himself Kendy was right—the Empire wanted not only its officers' service but also their souls. Years of thought control and moral compromise would have worn away everything he'd loved about Ciena, leaving only one of Palpatine's creations behind.

Then he'd seen the news report about Ciena's mother. Instantly, he'd known Ciena would return to

Jelucan. And just that quickly, he'd known he had to come back, too, and face her one more time.

If the Empire had hollowed her out—left nothing behind but a cold, empty shell—then Thane could finally let go. If she'd still been the exact same girl he remembered, then Thane would have turned into the most zealous recruiter the Rebellion ever had.

Neither of those extremes had come to pass. He knew that much. But he could look no further into Ciena's heart. She had become a mystery to him, one he didn't know how to solve.

He rose from his nap in what he thought must be midmorning. It was hard to tell now that the pollution in the air had become so thick. When he walked into the main room, Ciena lifted her head to look at him. She sat on one of the floor cushions, in leggings and a white tunic; she hadn't braided her hair, so the curls fluffed around her face like a cloud. That was how she'd worn her hair the night they danced together at the Imperial Palace.

He'd been so sure that years of Imperial service would've hardened her. Had tried to envision her only as a stiff, sharp-edged Imperial officer. Instead Ciena remained graceful, gentle—even delicate, though Thane knew that was appearance rather than reality. He remembered the firmness of muscle along her limbs and her back, just as he remembered what it had felt like to gaze into her dark brown eyes as she lay beneath him. . . .

Snap out of it, he told himself.

No "good morning" seemed to be forthcoming, so Thane didn't offer one, either. "Where's your father?"

"At work," she said, motioning to some bread and cheese that must have been meant for his breakfast. "Pappa's an administrator at the garrison. He doesn't get time off because his wife is in danger and his heart is broken. He can't even be late."

Was that anger with the Empire he heard? Thane wanted to feel hopeful, but Ciena remained as still and unreadable as she'd been the night before. He helped himself to some bread and managed to sit at the damnably short table. "What does the ritual require of us today?"

"Nothing much. Someone should be here constantly, watching the house—but since only one person stands with us, that rule doesn't matter." Ciena hesitated, then added, "I requested a meeting with the local magistrate yesterday, then again this morning. There's been no reply. I don't expect one."

"You're telling me we could leave, but we have no place to go."

No response. Her gaze was fixed on the one round

window in front, where his makeshift red flag flapped in the wind. The soot in the air would stain it dark, soon. He'd followed Jelucan's degeneration over the years, but that didn't make it easier to witness first-hand. If only they could travel back in time to when they were kids, when their world still felt like home and they understood each other without words . . .

Then he knew exactly what he wanted to do, exactly how he would know if she was still *his* Ciena.

He said, "Fly with me."

She turned to look at him. "You want to fly? Now? Today?"

"We can take the ridgecrawlers to my family's hangar. I bet the old V-171's still in there."

"If your parents saw you—"

"I checked before I left the spaceport. They're halfway across the planet on business. We're clear."

Ciena looked doubtful. "The V-171 might not be skyworthy any longer. It's been a few years."

"So we check her out. If she's broken down, okay, we're done. But maybe she isn't."

Thane watched her struggle to find a reason to say no. Finally, she sighed. "Okay."

He grabbed his dark blue jacket and cap with more dread than optimism. Ciena remained closed off to him, and Thane wasn't sure things weren't better that way. Yet they had rarely been closer than when they were in the air together. That was where they had taught each other, learned about each other, and explored their world as one. So that was where he'd finally see whether they could still communicate at all.

The ride to the hangar provided more suspense than Thane had expected. While the trails to that area had been obscure years ago, they'd come into common use. Each time they passed another ridgecrawler, his gut tightened. He half expected each driver to be a stormtrooper who would draw a blaster at any moment. But nobody gave them a second glance; he and Ciena were just two more figures climbing the mountain, shrouded in morning fog and gritty mining ash. Her ridgecrawler traveled in front of his. He felt like her shadow.

Whatever Dalven was up to these days, he wasn't visiting home, or at least he hadn't been by the hangar in years. The doors had almost rusted shut, and when Thane and Ciena tugged them open, clouds of dust swirled out and made them cough. Unsurprisingly, the V-171 was dusty, but when he hit the control panels, they lit up, glowing green.

He patted the side of the ship, absurdly proud. "All systems say go."

"Then we go." Ciena held out her hand for

lizard-toad-snake before she consciously recognized what she was doing—to judge by her sudden embarrassment. Thane simply held out his hand as well. One, two, three: he went for toad, but she chose snake, and snake ate toad.

"You always were luckier with this than I was," he muttered.

That won him a smile, fleeting but real. "Too bad, Kyrell." She sounded like herself again. "You're copilot today."

The familiar rhythms of preparation and takeoff came as a relief. They knew how to talk to each other again, and what to do. Within moments, the V-171 had hovered off the ground. As Ciena eased them out of the hangar, he said, "Come on. Let's grab some sky."

"You got it." And they soared up toward the sun.

They fell into sync immediately. Perfectly. Thane knew which way she'd want to turn before she did it; Ciena responded to every move he made almost before he was finished. It shocked him how much they hadn't changed in this one way, even as the rest of their lives had been turned upside down. They still knew how to fly as one.

Several thousand meters up, the pollution thinned until they were surrounded by the same brightness he remembered from when they were children. The clouds shone white; the rugged peaks of the highest mountains rose through them, looking like islands in snow. Those altitudes couldn't be mined; they remained pristine, untouched.

From here he could almost believe Jelucan was still beautiful.

Ciena wanted to linger in the sky as much as he did; Thane knew that without having to be told. Together they drew loops in the air, circled the familiar mountain ranges, caught the upwinds that still blew from Wavers' Peak. When she tilted the wings to catch that drift, Thane had already begun to lean with her, and he laughed. "You love this."

"So do you." He could hear the smile in her voice.

This isn't a truce. You're still with the Rebellion; she's still a loyal Imperial officer. We can never share anything more than a stolen hour, one flight.

So Thane told himself. Yet he couldn't make himself believe it.

Even when a storm began to blow in, they postponed coming down as long as they could. Once the winds picked up enough chop, though, they wordlessly agreed on the moment when the V-171 had to descend. In the tiny craft, they could even feel the way each other's weight shifted as they responded to the shear.

He still knew how she moved.

"Come on!" They were ten and Ciena wanted to weave through the stalactites for the first time. "We can do it!" He sent them spiraling down toward their goal, the sudden dizziness sweeping over them both at the same moment and making them laugh.

Their speeder bikes were locked together as they soared through Coruscant, each of them leaning toward the other as they aimed for the exact center of the final Reitgen Hoop, and victory.

"Like this?" He could feel the warm breath of Ciena's whisper against his bare shoulder. Too overcome to speak, Thane had only been able to nod.

They took the V-171 in before the rains began. Ciena powered down in silence; whatever rapport they'd regained in the air had disappeared. As they disembarked and left the hangar, they might have been any two coworkers in a commercial spaceport.

But Ciena didn't return to her ridgecrawler. Instead she walked to the far edge of the hangar's terrace, toward the narrow, rocky path that led away from the main road—toward the Fortress. She paused for a moment to look over her shoulder, clearly daring Thane to follow.

He never could resist a dare.

Neither of them spoke until they had climbed inside the Fortress itself. When Ciena turned on one of the old lights they'd left up there, Thane looked around, blinking in surprise. He'd expected a dusty ruin; instead, the surfaces were clean, the blankets beaten. A few of their toy spaceships still dangled from the wire mobile they'd built when they were nine. He said, "This place held up well."

"I came here yesterday," she said. "My ship landed before my father could leave work, and Valentia—I couldn't bear to stay there long. This was the only place I wanted to be. It needed some cleaning, but less than you'd think." Ciena turned to face him then, and in the approaching dark of the storm, he could not read her expression. "So much had stayed the same."

Thane took a step toward her. "Ciena—"

"You joined the *Rebellion*." The words burst out of her, like water after a dam broke. "How could you do that? They're terrorists! They killed Jude!"

"We are *not* terrorists. If anyone's a terrorist it's Palpatine himself, because he rules by fear—"

"You said you weren't going to the rebels, you told me that to my face—"

"That was before I realized just how bad the Empire really is. The rebels might not be perfect but somebody's got to do something!"

"So you decided you hate the Empire. You're willing to kill the people you went to school with—your fellow officers, your friends." Ciena took a step closer to him, her hands in fists at her sides. "You're even willing to kill me."

"Don't you think that nearly destroys me every single time I go into battle? Don't you know I'd rather die first? But I can't stand aside and do nothing, Ciena. I can't."

She shook her head. "You had to stop being a cynic *now*?"

Thane wanted to shake her. He wanted to plead with her to listen. More than anything he wanted to be back in the air, where they still understood each other. But the storm was on them now. "That's all you have to say? You dragged me up here just to yell at me?"

"No."

"Then what—"

Ciena pulled his face down to hers and kissed him, hard.

The next few moments were a feverish blur—her small hands reaching beneath his jacket to splay across his chest—the feel of her in his arms—the taste of her lips. He couldn't be close enough to her. Even now, entwined together, they were too far apart.

Thane embraced her tightly enough to lift her feet from the ground, then backed her against the wall, pinning her there with the weight of his body. He covered her open mouth with his.

When they parted long enough to gasp for breath, Ciena whispered, "Don't you *dare* stop."

He didn't.

CHAPTER TWENTY-ONE

HOURS LATER, Ciena sat at the mouth of the Fortress cave, wrapped in a blanket as she watched the last of the storm. The winds had died down a while ago, but the rain still fell across the lower ranges in silvery sheets. How had she forgotten the view could be so beautiful?

This had always been the place where she went to dream. Imperial service allowed so little time for that—no hours in which to let your mind wander, to imagine anything you liked.

Ciena rose and walked back inside the Fortress on legs that still felt pleasantly wobbly. The furs and blankets were piled in the back, near the old heater they'd dragged up there ten years before, and only the faintest light shone back that far. She paused for a moment to take in the sight of Thane sprawled facedown, more asleep than awake, almost completely uncovered.

She leaned one shoulder against the wall as she whispered, "Look through my eyes."

That made him stir. Thane rolled over and smiled drowsily. "You're showing your sister this?"

"I'm supposed to show her the most beautiful and extraordinary moments of my life. This qualifies."

He held one arm out to her, and she curled by his side, draping her blanket over them both. Despite the small heater, the air inside the Fortress remained cool—but Thane kept her warm. Ciena wished they never had to acknowledge the world beyond the Fortress—that it could always be the two of them together, inseparable.

"You probably know this," she said, "but I still love you."

"And I love you. Everything else might change, but not that."

Ciena rolled over to look at him. It was so hard to say this without anger, but she had to speak. "If you could join the Rebellion, you've changed more than I would have thought possible."

"Do you still buy the Imperial dogma that they're 'terrorists'? They're idealists, really. They believe the New Republic will be all the grand and glorious things the Old Republic never was. I'm not that kind of fool. Never will be. But the Empire must fall."

"You took an oath—"

"Enough with the oaths, Ciena!" Thane paused until he had a handle on his temper again. "I'm sorry. I know what your honor means to you. But this isn't about whether or not we've kept faith with the Empire. It's about whether the Empire has kept faith with us."

Too many of her own doubts responded to those words. In Ciena's mind she saw the officers dying in vain, heard Penrie's last scream, watched Alderaan explode again. And now, even her mother had to suffer.

She buried her face against Thane's chest. It felt safer to speak within the warmth of his arms. "I see the darkness within the Empire. How could I not?"

He wound one of her curls around his finger, his playful touches contrasting with the gravity of what he said. "If you see that, then I don't understand how you can keep serving the Empire just because of a promise you made years ago, when you didn't know the whole truth."

"Nobody ever knows the whole truth. That's why promises mean something. Otherwise they'd be too easy, don't you see? We look toward the unknown future and promise to be faithful no matter what comes." Ciena sighed. "My oath matters to me, but that's not the only reason I stay."

"Then why?"

"Because the Empire is more than—than corruption and brutality." It cost her to say those words, but Thane forced her to be honest with herself. "It's also the structure that keeps the galaxy from collapsing into chaos again, like it did during the Clone Wars. And for every petty bureaucrat making himself rich by skimming profits, there's also someone like Nash Windrider, who's genuinely trying to do the right thing. If the good people leave, doesn't that make everything worse? Don't we have a responsibility to stand our ground and change the Empire, if we can?"

"Still an optimist." Thane hesitated before he asked, "How is Nash?"

"He's doing better now. The first year after Alderaan was hard, but he came through. I think he's still lonely sometimes." Ciena remembered the night Nash had propositioned her in front of the door to her bunk—but she had said no, and it was nothing Thane needed to hear. "He talks about you from time to time. I hate that he has to keep thinking you're dead."

"Me too."

They lay together in silence for a while after that, her head pillowed against Thane's chest. Ciena thought back to those first few months at the academy, when they'd all been so trusting, so sure of their place in the galaxy. Could that have been only six years ago? It felt like another lifetime.

"Ciena?" Thane sounded wary. "I want to ask you a question that you might not like. Hear me out, okay?"

She figured that if she hadn't killed Thane for joining the Rebellion, he was safe no matter what. "Ask."

"What's happening to your mother—have you asked yourself whether this is all a test? Another of the mind games the Empire plays on its troops?"

If only she could still believe those "tests" were meant to strengthen them, that they served a greater purpose. Had she really once been angry with Thane for suggesting otherwise? The memory of her naivety embarrassed her. In the years since, Ciena had learned that the Empire administered extreme tests of loyalty sometimes. Maybe for personnel being considered for sensitive positions, those tests could be justified. But to toy with the friendship between two young cadets, only to divorce them from any ties to their homeworld . . . that had been almost childish in its cruelty.

Maybe the Empire *was* testing her by putting her mother on trial, but Ciena doubted it. What was happening to Mumma was more likely simple, stupid provincial corruption. Everyone involved knew it, and no one would say so because they were all too afraid of what the Imperial officials would do to them.

From the Emperor down to the lowliest administrator—so much had to be transformed. Where could they even begin?

"I don't think what's happening to Mumma is part of any larger plot," she said, and left it at that. "Do you trust your superiors in the Rebel Alliance?"

She expected Thane to say no immediately; he put his trust in so few people, and surely the dregs that ran the Rebellion wouldn't qualify for the honor. Ciena was shocked when he said, "Some of them. Most of them, actually. You know I didn't even have to ask permission to come here? They trusted that I'd only leave for a good reason, and believed I'd return. Sure, they dream some crazy dreams about this perfect galaxy they think they can build—but at least they respect the people who serve."

Ciena could hardly believe what she'd heard. Thane Kyrell had finally found authority figures he didn't hate and they were *rebels*? Surely he was talking like this in an effort to convince her to leave the Empire; she thought he might have said even wilder things if they would keep her with him. "How long have you been with them?"

"I joined up several months ago." His thumb brushed along her cheekbone, the tiniest possible caress. "At first I did supply runs, but as the war intensified—I'm in combat more often now."

"I recognized you at Hoth, you know."

"You *were* there?" Thane's face paled almost to white. "I told myself—the fleet is so huge—I thought the chances that I'd fight against you were—I didn't think it would happen."

"I was never in danger," she said, sitting up and tucking the blanket around herself. Seeing his fear at the thought of hurting her—she couldn't bear it. "It was that move of yours, when you spun through the AT-AT's legs. I knew that instant it could only be you."

"The one person in the entire fleet who could have identified me by how I flew—"

"Maybe the Force is guiding this. Bringing us together even though we ought to be apart."

That made him grimace. Thane hadn't changed enough to become religious, it seemed. "I seem to remember using my own fake identification to cross the galaxy and reach you. No Force involved."

She held up one hand. "All right, all right."

Thane sat up beside her and slid his arms around her waist. The sky outside the Fortress had nearly turned dark. "Listen," he said. "I know you're not ready to come with me today. And maybe you won't consider joining the Rebellion."

"Never."

"But if I thought you might leave the Empire *someday*—even if it's just to come back here, or start your life over on another world—"

Was he promising to leave the rebels and join her, if only she would desert? Ciena didn't want to know. "I'm not going to leave, at least not before my tour of duty ends. If there's any chance that the good in the Empire can outweigh the bad, then it's our duty to preserve it."

"The Empire's rotten to the core. It's our duty to destroy it."

They were still at odds, and always would be it seemed. Ciena knew that. Yet the hard facts seemed so distant as he embraced her again, and she leaned her head against him. She and Thane had never been more in love—or further apart.

The next morning, the trial of Ciena's mother began.

Trial. That word sounded far too official and grand for the hasty, sordid proceedings. Ciena sat in the semi-circular stands around the judicial chamber, wearing her uniform with its red and blue rank squares proclaiming her an Imperial lieutenant commander. Next to her, Pappa kept his head bent as if he could not bear to see Mumma standing in the dock with her wrists cuffed.

The prosecutor—a man with small hands and oiled hair—officiously read the evidence line by line, entering it all into the record. He had not one bit of proof that couldn't have been doctored by a halfway competent data engineer, a point that would no doubt have been made by the defense if her mother had been allowed a defense.

But now that was allowed only in civil cases, never in trials for crimes against the Empire.

Ciena could hear Thane's voice in her head, asking if the Empire had kept faith with her. She did not dare answer him even in her own thoughts.

He had left late the night before to catch a red-eye shuttle—to where, she would never know. Thane had bid her father a formal, correct farewell; Pappa had been wise enough to let Ciena walk Thane out to the ridgecrawler on her own. They had kissed each other so long and so fiercely that her lips remained swollen, the discomfort welcome because it was proof he'd really been with her.

"Whatever else becomes of us," she had said, *"thank you for stand-ing with my family. You took a tremendous risk to be here when I needed you the most. It was an act of . . . the truest loyalty and friendship."*

His smile had been so sad. "Actually I came here thinking I'd finally get over you. Should've known better."

Ciena tried to catch her mother's eye, hoping to give some comfort just by being there. Yet Mumma wouldn't even look at her directly. It was as if she were ashamed, even though by now everyone in this sham of a trial had to know the charges were false.

Then the realization pierced her through: her mother wouldn't look at her because she didn't want to endanger Ciena any further by making her show sympathy to someone accused by the Empire.

Imperial rule wasn't as cruel to every world as it had been to Jelucan. Ciena's travels had told her that much. But it didn't matter, because the cruelty was there, now, destroying her family and her home.

"You realize we can't ever meet again," Ciena had said as Thane held her close. *He'd already started his ridgecrawler, the motor's hum almost lost in the fierce winds.*

"We said that last time."

"It's different now. You shouldn't have come back this time, and I—I don't know if I'll ever return again."

"We keep telling each other good-bye," Thane had whispered into her ear. *"When am I finally going to believe it?"*

She didn't answer, because she couldn't. Even if she and Thane never saw each other again, she knew that in some ways their bond would endure. He was too much a part of her to be completely lost, not as long as she lived.

It was some consolation, but not much.

The magistrate didn't even look up from his screens as he pronounced judgment. "Guilty of embezzlement and fraud against representatives of the Emperor. Sentenced to six years' labor in the mines."

Ciena felt the verdict like poison injected into her veins—agonizing down to the bone. *Hard labor?* Jelucan had banned that as a punishment nearly a century ago, and even then had limited it to those accused of violent crimes. Her mother was a middle-aged woman, never particularly tall or strong; how was she supposed to endure long days of hauling heavy ore? With modern mine-droids, there was no need for anyone to do that kind of backbreaking work. The sentence was both primitive and punitive . . . and had been levied against a woman the judge *had* to know was innocent.

Verine Ree didn't even glance at her husband and daughter as she was led away; Ciena realized they wouldn't be given a chance to say good-bye.

"This is impossible," she whispered as everyone else filed out of the courtroom, leaving only Ciena and her father behind. "A mockery of justice—"

"Say nothing more."

"Of course." There were probably recording devices somewhere in the room. "We can't have more trouble."

"No, Ciena. You should not speak against your government, ever, under any circumstances."

"Pappa—how can you say that *today*?"

Paron Ree folded his hands together as solemnly as a village elder. "Because we gave our loyalty to the Empire on the day Jelucan was annexed. Because we do not betray our word, even when we are betrayed in return. Otherwise we are no better than they are." His eyes blazed, but his voice remained low and calm. "This life has never been one made for fairness or justice. We endure, and we prevail not as crude matter but in the realm of the spirit."

She had grown up believing that so devoutly, and now the words sounded hollow. Ciena could not take comfort in anger or in faith. All she could do was put her arms around her father and hope his beliefs sustained him more than they did her.

"And was justice done on Jelucan, Lieutenant Commander Ree?"

"Sir. Yes, sir."

Ciena stood at attention in ISB officer Ronnadam's office, staring past him at the small circle of starfield revealed through his one window. Her hands were clasped tightly behind her back, palms sweaty.

Captain Ronnadam studied her for what seemed to be too long a time. His thin mustache twitched once, but she could not tell whether he felt amusement or irritation. "Your mother was guilty, then."

"The evidence presented was very clear, sir."

"You surprise me, Ree." His tone made it impossible to know whether that was a good thing, and his eyes were narrow. He held her in contempt for doing the very thing he had forced her to do. Did he recognize his own hypocrisy? Probably not. "Very well. You have used two weeks' leave, but otherwise your record remains unblemished. I believe we can expect a promotion in your near future."

Ronnadam honestly thought she would betray her own mother just for the sake of advancement. Ciena dug her fingernails into her palms, using the pain to steady herself. "Thank you, sir."

Do your duty. Keep the course. There is good here in so many of the people who serve. I owe it to them to fulfill my oath and learn how I can help save the Empire from its own corruption.

They were noble sentiments, and she meant them. Yet in her mind she imagined saying all this to Thane, and he only shook his head.

CHAPTER TWENTY-TWO

THANE MADE IT back to the *Liberty* just in time. Corona Squadron was already preparing to move—not in the frenzy that followed any threat of imminent attack but quickly enough that he would have missed them if he'd returned a few hours later.

"Mr. Kyrell. How kind of you to join us," said the Contessa as she walked through the hangar, where pilots busily loaded astromech droids and checked ration packs. He nodded at her but didn't slow his steps until he'd walked straight to General Rieekan.

"Kyrell." Rieekan hardly looked away from his tablet. He stood in the center of the activity; a firework spray of blue-white sparks rose from a nearby welding torch. The air smelled of rubber and fuel. "Excellent. You've got two hours until takeoff."

Thane stood at attention with his chin slightly

lifted, the way he'd learned at the academy. The old training had kicked in the first moment he'd acknowledged he might have screwed up. "Sir. I need to report my movements during my absence."

"This is a volunteer army, remember? You're free to come and go as you please, as long as you observe all security protocols."

"I returned to my homeworld of Jelucan to—assist a friend in trouble," Thane said. Rieekan didn't glance up until Thane added, "My friend is an officer in the Imperial Starfleet."

That did it. Rieekan stared, and all around him the buzz of work began falling silent. Thane could almost feel the eyes on him, as hot as searchlights.

General Rieekan's decibel level rose markedly. "You made contact with an enemy officer."

"Yes, sir." Thane offered nothing more. He knew he had to report it, but he'd be damned if he'd apologize for seeing Ciena.

"That's highly irregular, Kyrell," Rieekan said. "But you concealed your activities with the Rebel Alliance from this officer?"

". . . Lieutenant Commander Ree was already aware I had joined the Rebellion. Sir."

Murmurs rose around him; by then, he'd drawn a crowd. From the corner of his eye, Thane could see shocked expressions on the faces of Yendor, Smikes, and Kendy. However, he never turned away from Rieekan.

"How the hell did she know that?" Rieekan's alarm was very real. "Do we have a double agent feeding them intel?"

"No, sir. Not regarding this. She—she had identified me based on Imperial battle footage." Nobody would believe it if he confessed that Ciena had known him only by the way he flew. They were the only two people who could ever understand that.

Rieekan accepted this explanation, which was a relief, but Thane wasn't out of trouble yet. "Are you absolutely sure this officer lacked any opportunity to place a tracking device on your vehicle or your person?"

"It didn't happen, sir." He wasn't going to get into the many things Ciena had had an opportunity to do to his person. "I guarantee that. At no point did I share any information about Rebellion members, bases, or activities. Nor did she ask. This was a personal matter."

"Personal." Rieekan shook his head. "We'll scan you and your ship. If those scans check out, we'll let this drop."

"Thank you, sir."

"And we can take it as a given that you're not going to make contact with any Imperial officer ever again?"

Thane remembered their final moments together in front of her house, the way her fingers had tightened around the collar of his jacket as if she could hold him there by will alone. "Yes, sir."

"Very well. Just for the record, Kyrell? The galaxy is full of women who *don't* fight for the enemy."

With that, Rieekan walked off. A couple of the droids zoomed in on Thane's X-wing to search it. That left him to finally face the rest of Corona Squadron. The other pilots had already gathered around, their expressions displaying everything from disbelief to outrage. Smikes spoke first. "You abandoned your post to *bang your ex*? The *lieutenant commander in the Imperial Starfleet* ex?"

Thane refused to be cowed. "They're about to promote her to commander."

People groaned. Obviously, he was going to be the least popular member of Corona Squadron for some time to come—a loose cannon, someone who would take risks for no reason. Fine by him. As long as they didn't doubt his allegiance, Thane didn't give a damn what they thought of his choices.

"We all have to put our pasts behind us. *All of us.* That includes even the people on our side, much less Imperial loyalists." The Contessa had never showed anger before, but she did now.

"That doesn't mean we're never supposed to acknowledge the people we love ever again," he retorted.

"Oh, great," Smikes moaned. "He's talking about *love*. This is going nowhere fast."

Yendor, more calmly than the others, leaned against the strut of the nearest starfighter and said, "You realize this Imperial woman of yours would kill us all, right?"

That did it. Thane got in Yendor's face. "You don't know Ciena. I do. I made a choice based on that knowledge. None of you were endangered, or even *affected*, so it's none of your damned business."

In the silence that followed, he backed away from Yendor, whose hands were raised in the gesture that meant, on every planet, *Hey, man, simmer down*. Thane figured the only productive thing he could do right then was report to 2-1B for the scans. But as he turned to go, Kendy spoke almost under her breath: "You're going to tear yourself apart."

She wasn't wrong.

Thane said only, "She's still Ciena," and walked off.

Kendy would understand that, probably. Nobody else would. He didn't care. It was his own business if he crossed the galaxy, or broke his heart, or steered his X-wing straight into the core of a star.

———

The rebel fleet's new base was on an uninhabited planet so small and obscure it had no name, only the numerical designation 5251977. This world's rotation moved slowly, meaning days and nights each lasted the equivalent of several weeks on most planets; for now, the Rebellion hid in the enduring darkness.

Thane's first thought as he took his X-wing in to land was that they'd built a much larger hangar than usual this time. The scale of the structure reminded him more of Imperial facilities than the hasty makeshift setups the Rebel Alliance had to rely on. When he came in through the shield doors, however, he realized why the building was so enormous—it had to be. In the previous two months, the size of the rebel armada seemed to have doubled.

"What happened?" Thane asked, flight helmet under one arm, as Corona Squadron went to report in. He wondered if the Empire had destroyed another world or committed another atrocity so horrific that a huge swath of the galaxy had finally had enough.

Most of the others ignored him, but Yendor replied, "Usually they don't bring the whole fleet together like this. A couple divisions stay separate, just in case, you know? Not anymore. Rumor has it something big is planned."

"We have new recruits, as well," the Contessa

said, pointing to several nonregulation ships that stood around them. While these kinds of ships had always been a part of the fleet, there were definitely more than usual and more people milling around who had no uniforms, only Rebellion patches hastily applied to their coveralls. Even as the war grew more pitched and more deadly, recruits continued to flock to the rebel cause. If that kept up, Thane thought, they might actually have a shot. He could see several individual starfighters, a few Dornean gunships, and one freighter that seemed to have been put together out of the parts of at least a dozen other ships—

A broad smile spread across Thane's face as he yelled, "The *Mighty Oak Apocalypse!*"

The rest of Corona Squadron turned to him with expressions suggesting that he had well and truly lost his mind. He didn't care, because now people were spilling out of the ship to run toward him—Brill grinning through her pink fur, JJH2 rolling toward him and whistling, Methwat wearing his version of a smile, and behind the rest, roaring her welcome, Lohgarra.

"About time you guys showed up!" Thane said, laughing, as he submitted to a wooly Wookiee hug. Lohgarra growled plaintively, and Thane somehow resisted rolling his eyes. "I am *not* too thin."

"We refitted the whole ship," Brill said with pride.

"New shields, new dampeners. She's toting guns from more kinds of fighters than you can count on both hands. Or claws. Tentacles. Whatever you have."

"Ready for action, huh?" Now that he'd had a moment to think about it, he wasn't surprised Lohgarra and the *Moa* had joined the Rebellion at last. Still, there was something great about knowing that so many of the people he cared about now stood by his side. It took him back to the moment he'd chosen to join the Rebellion in the first place, and reminded him why when he needed that memory the most.

Aboard the Super Star Destroyer *Executor*, all officers and stormtroopers were expected to keep their combat skills honed. But the number of certifications required lessened at higher ranks. Now that Ciena had made commander, she no longer had to spend at least one hour a week practicing hand-to-hand combat. However, that just meant she spent more time on the few skills still remaining.

"I could live without using this thing ever again," Ciena grumbled as she shouldered the practice flamethrower. "If we ever need this on the bridge, I'm guessing we're already done for."

"Ciena Ree complaining about regulations?" Berisse shook her head in amazement. "Hey, if you don't want to do this, you've got days left to fulfill your regs. We should take advantage of being out in the middle of nowhere." Technically, the ship was still in hyperspace on its way to the middle of nowhere, but Berisse's point stood. Since they were being called on to do nothing but go to an uninhabited system and sit and wait, all junior officers had more free time than usual. "We could see if Nash and some of the other guys are free, head to one of the cantinas, let our hair down—"

"I'm staying here. If you want to go party, nobody's stopping you."

"Okay, okay. You've been in a mood for almost three weeks straight. Isn't it time you snapped out of it?"

Berisse didn't know the reasons for Ciena's temper and no doubt had not guessed it was the shield behind which Ciena was hiding her wretchedness. Once Ciena had felt free to confide nearly everything in Berisse— and she longed to hear her advice now. Berisse was so practical, so matter-of-fact, that she'd listen to the whole story without blinking and probably come up with the perfect words to help Ciena cope.

But that was the rub: *probably*.

Berisse could be irreverent and wasn't above bend- ing a regulation for practicality's sake, but Ciena had never doubted her friend's fundamental loyalty to the

Empire. If Ciena spoke about the injustice of the verdict against her mother, Berisse might sympathize; on the other hand, she might well report the conversation to Ronnadam.

Of course, Ciena couldn't admit the truth about Thane to anyone. That heartbreak was one she had to carry alone. Still, carrying that weight would have felt less terrible if she could have shared the rest with someone.

Instead, she was forced to admit that she had not one friend in the entire world she could entirely trust.

"Let's just torch some junk, okay?" Ciena pulled on the flametrooper mask and readied the controls. Berisse, obviously knowing better than to interrupt, began the holographic part of the simulator. Attackers made of shadowy green light began running toward them, and Ciena pulled the trigger.

Explosive fire shot out, incinerating her enemies. Again. Then again. She had never relished combat duty—flying was her joy and her passion—but today Ciena poured all her bottled-up sorrow and fury into every blast. When the first simulation ended, she immediately signaled for Berisse to start another, then another. The featureless green holograms simply vanished when they took a fatal hit; Ciena found herself wishing the programming were more honest and graphic. She wanted to see her kills for once.

"I am really glad we don't room together anymore," Berisse muttered when the final holo faded. "Because I do *not* want to be the next person you're mad at."

"You're right. You don't." Ciena slid up her face mask and wiped her wrist across her forehead. Even though she'd remained in firing position the entire time and the flamethrower wasn't unbearably heavy, exhaustion already racked her body. Sleep had been elusive since her return to the *Executor*.

Despite her weariness, she might have gone for another round had she not felt the subtle shift in the vibration beneath their feet. "We've left hyperspace," she said to Berisse.

"Never ceases to amaze me how you can feel that." Berisse sighed. "So much for free time, huh?"

Even sitting out in the middle of nowhere—namely, the Hudalla system, notable only for its largest, massively ringed planet—required everyone back at duty stations. Ciena was relieved. Nothing helped but keeping busy.

As the two of them walked out of their simulation room, however, Ciena glanced through the triangular windows into space beyond. What she saw stopped her where she stood. Instead of the planet Hudalla or the void of space, the view showed countless Imperial ships. Star Destroyers, attack cruises, light cruisers, almost as many TIE fighters as stars—

"What the hell?" Berisse said. "Did we get called back to Coruscant instead?"

Ciena shook her head. Only captains, admirals, and Lord Vader himself knew plans very far in advance, so she couldn't say exactly why the Hudalla system had suddenly become a meeting spot for nearly the entire Imperial Starfleet.

But she only had to look at the assembled ships to know: whatever was happening was important—and would affect them all.

Corona Squadron had received their next intelligence mission only ten hours after reaching 5251977. For the first time, they had received their orders not from Rieekan but from Admiral Ackbar of the Mon Calamari.

"Remote sensors detected an unusual level of Imperial activity in the Hudalla system," he had said, pacing in front of them. *Ackbar was an imposing man—taller than any human and with protruding, wizened eyes—so the entire squadron remained far more rigid and silent than usual. "Nothing in that area should be of interest to the Empire or to anyone else. Why then is the Empire establishing a presence there?*

Corona Squadron, you will go to Hudalla. Observe the Imperial ships and obtain as much data as possible."

They were supposed to stroll into an isolated system and take readings on the Imperial Starfleet, then get out alive? Thane wasn't sure whether Ackbar was a deluded optimist or someone who didn't mind putting lives at risk for uncertain gain.

Then Ackbar had dismissed them by saying, "May the Force be with you." So. Deluded.

As Thane checked the sensors on his X-wing's panel, he gave thanks for Hudalla's enormous ring. The gas giant swirled in shades of red and violet, but the most notable aspect of this world was its planetary rings, which were some of the largest in the galaxy. Those rings comprised several million pieces of debris, most of them smaller than the average asteroid—

—and yet just large enough to hide a ship behind.

Like every other member of Corona Squadron, he'd tethered his ship to one of the larger rocks on Hudalla's outer ring. Their X-wings floated through the gradual rotation of the countless pieces of debris in the field, the soft violet glow of that system's distant star casting strange shadows. The slow orbit of the ring had allowed them to take their positions far enough away to avoid detection. Now they were within scanning distance and could take all the readings and holos they needed, and they didn't even have to worry about being scanned in return. With their ships running on minimum power and well concealed by the ring's debris, there was almost no chance of their being spotted.

Almost. Thane hated that word. He knew how thorough Imperial officers were trained to be. Still, the odds were on their side for a change. He'd take it.

"This is almost as large as the attack fleet they sent to Hoth," Yendor said, his voice crackling over the comms. "Do you think they got some bad intel telling them we put a base on one of Hudalla's moons?"

Thane answered, "If so, you'd think they would've figured out the mistake by now. But they've been here for days, with more ships coming in all the time."

What were they up to? Thane kept trying to come up with an answer and failing. If a new hyperlane had been discovered in this area of space, their sensors would have detected it by now. If the Empire were planning an attack, it wouldn't need this much time to assemble. No critical elements could be mined from any of the planets or moons in this system. The mystery seemed complete.

He'd asked for the job of tallying single starfighters—an enormously detailed and irritating task, so the squadron had been happy enough to let Thane handle it. The work kept him too occupied to think much about the odds of Ciena being part of a fleet that large or to find out which specific Star Destroyers had gathered there.

It's like they brought all these ships together just to show off, Thane thought sourly as he continued his calculations, adding in new pieces of data as his sensors provided it. Why show off in the middle of nowhere, without anybody around to see you? What could call for a display this ostentatious, a concentration of the Imperial firepower in a place where it could do no good?

Then his hands froze, allowing long scrolls of numbers to spill by. Thane cursed under his breath as he realized what this was.

The Empire displayed its power often, with a degree of theatricality he'd found absurd even when he'd been a part of it. But it never did so without reason. Most often a show of strength was meant to intimidate the people who lived under Imperial control, but sometimes officers and ships made a point of displaying their power to impress their superiors. The greater the number of men or ships put at a commander's disposal, the more important that commander was.

This fleet had been assembled to prove someone's importance. Only one person in the galaxy would merit this much attention, firepower, and awe.

He whispered, "The Emperor."

CHAPTER TWENTY-THREE

CIENA HAD NOT regularly flown TIE fighters during the past couple of years, so when she received a summons to report to the main docking bay, she was both surprised and pleased. Maybe she needed to spend some time flying through the stars; then she might feel like herself again.

When she'd suited up in the black armor, Ciena walked into the bay with her helmet under one arm to see the other three pilots she'd be flying with—two strangers and Nash Windrider. He grinned like a boy when he recognized her. "What a delight to be flying with you again, Commander Ree. I hadn't thought you would still lower yourself to serving alongside the likes of us."

"Hush." She risked a smile; Nash seemed to be teasing her as a friend, not as a would-be lover. The sooner they skated past that, the better. "You know, I've always wondered how you manage to pilot TIEs at all. How do you fit?"

"I'll have you know that I am fully one centimeter below the maximum height for TIE pilots. TIEs are more cramped than a warship, I admit, but what isn't? You, on the other hand, are far more compact and should fold up nicely."

"I'm not that short!" No matter how many times Ciena protested about this, nobody ever seemed to believe her, or their own eyes.

Nash opened his mouth for his next jab, then straightened as Admiral Piett strode toward them. They all came to attention, helmets facing out.

Piett didn't bother with preamble. "Scans have picked up some strange readings on the outer edge of Hudalla's ring, including life forms. Possibly it's no more than metal ores and mynocks. However, if we have some spies lurking out there—well. You know what to do."

"Aye, sir," they said in unison. Everyone saluted and turned on the beat, ready to board their ships. But Piett said, "Ree, I need to have a word with you."

She turned back, again at attention. Why would Piett need to speak with her specifically? Her imagination conjured visions of psychological interrogations; they whispered that the questioners could sense the moment anyone began to turn traitor. Had they picked up on her doubt?

Instead, Piett said, "You have an additional assignment on this flight."

"Yes, sir?"

"Those aren't mynocks in the planetary ring. They're almost certainly rebel spies."

Ciena nodded, hiding her consternation. It made no sense for him to give her this intel and conceal it from Nash and the other TIE pilots. "We'll take care of it, sir."

Piett held up one warning finger. "One of the rebels must escape. You're to see to it that at least one of the pilots manages to make it to hyperspace. Beyond that, it's irrelevant whether the rest live or die."

She was confused for a moment, but then she understood. Senior fleet command wanted the Rebel Alliance to know that a large portion of the Imperial Starfleet was assembling. Why, Ciena couldn't yet guess. It didn't matter. She'd been entrusted with a difficult and demanding task—and a secret one. That meant her superiors didn't doubt her; if anything, they held her in higher esteem than ever.

All she'd had to do was deny her mother's innocence.

Ciena tried to cast that thought from her head. "Consider it handled, Admiral Piett."

He nodded, dismissing her, and she headed to her ship. Climbing into the pilot's seat came as a relief. She didn't have to think about her mother any longer; she wouldn't be haunted by her growing doubts about the Empire. Sensors needed to be checked, the hatch sealed, weapons readied. Soon she could fly and forget all her troubles in doing what she did best.

Nash's voice came over the comm. "Prepared for takeoff, L-P-Eight-Eight-Eight?"

Ciena lowered the black helmet over her head. Now she had no face, no identity. Now nothing remained of her but her duty to the Empire. "Ready."

Among the many problems with flying on minimum power: heat inside the cabin dropped severely—not enough to endanger anyone's life but enough to be extremely uncomfortable. Thane's breath had begun to make small frost crystals on the edge of his helmet's visor.

As if he could read Thane's mind, Smikes said over comms, "We should've worn winter uniforms for this trip."

"Affirmative, Corona Three," Yendor replied. "I could do with my old Hoth parka right around now."

The Contessa added, "And I miss my fur coats. But hold steady. In about an hour, we'll orbit far enough from the Imperial convoy to slip out of here."

"Holding steady, Corona Leader," Thane said. He had not yet shared his theory about the Emperor with the rest of Corona Squadron; if true, it was information too sensitive for any open comm channel. And after only a few minutes' consideration, he felt positive his hunch was right. Yet knowing that these ships had been massed to form a convoy for the Emperor raised another host of questions. It had been many years since Palpatine was last seen off Coruscant. What would draw him away from the seat of galactic power— and where was he going?

And if this many ships had massed in one place, that meant elsewhere in the galaxy, the Imperial fleet might be stretched thin. Widely dispersed, at any rate. Thane's adrenaline spiked as he realized the Empire's useless show of strength here might have created weaknesses elsewhere. Weaknesses the Rebellion could turn to its advantage . . .

His sensors began to flash, and he swore. "We've got TIE fighters incoming. I count four."

"Any chance it's a random patrol?" Kendy asked.

Possible. But not probable. The TIE fighters came closer every second.

Thane said, "I've got a bad feeling about this."

"Do you see what I see?" Nash sounded delighted, as if they were headed toward a party instead of into combat.

Ciena bit her lower lip as she studied her readings. "I read five ships, probably starfighters. So far I can't ID ship models, but I'd guess we're looking at X-wings or Y-wings." While a handful of those starfighters remained in civilian hands, by now X-wings and Y-wings were used almost solely by the Rebel Alliance. Piett's intel had been correct; the TIE patrol would move into attack mode at any moment.

Out of five ships, she needed at least one survivor.

That would be most easily accomplished by having five survivors and avoiding combat altogether. Nash and the other pilots were too smart to mistake what they were seeing for something else, which meant if she wanted to avoid a dogfight, her best bet was to flush out the rebels in time for them to escape.

She said, "If I break up one of the larger asteroids in the planetary ring, we could get better readings."

One of the other pilots objected. "Then they'll know we're here!"

"Ten to one they know it by now. Their sensors are nearly as advanced as ours." Ciena put her black-gloved hands on the controls, feeling the red trigger button under her thumb.

"It's a bad idea," Nash said. "We don't need further readings, and at this distance, they'd have time to make the jump into hyperspace before we could engage them."

So much for that plan.

Now at least one of the rebel ships—and possibly four of them—would have to be destroyed, all for the sake of some tactical masquerade. They might well lose a TIE fighter in the process.

More useless death. More futility. More waste.

The TIE fighters were unquestionably zeroing in on their location. Combat seemed certain.

The Contessa ordered, "All wings, disengage tethers and return to full power."

"Don't think we can escape from this position, Corona Leader," Yendor said, even as sensors showed him complying.

"We can't. They're coming in for a fight." Thane pressed the controls that brought his ship back to full life, the cockpit lighting up in red and gold. "Weapons ready?"

Yendor reported in first. "Corona Two ready."

"Corona Three ready," Smikes confirmed.

"Corona Four ready." Thane kept his eyes on the sensors as he spoke, in case the TIEs accelerated into attack mode.

And Kendy finished, "Corona Five ready."

Thane braced himself as the Contessa said, "All we have now is the element of surprise. Let's take the fight to them."

Ciena had expected the rebel starfighters to remain hidden as long as they possibly could in hope of avoiding detection—which was why she was astonished when five X-wings burst out of the planetary ring and headed straight for the TIE fighters.

"Evasive action!" she shouted, swinging her TIE around to avoid their main weapons range. The rebels had them outnumbered—no doubt by Piett's design. That imbalance would give one or more of the rebel ships a good chance to escape. She couldn't stand the unfairness of asking TIE pilots to risk their lives in an attempt to kill people the Empire wanted to keep alive.

How could she possibly delay a dogfight on the verge of happening this second?

Ciena adjusted her comms until she hit broadcast mode—a multifrequency signal that would supersede all others in the area, projecting her voice into every ship close enough to hear, including those X-wings. "Unidentified vessels," she said. "You are not authorized to fly in this sector. Please report your ship's identification codes and the system under which you are licensed or you will be taken into custody. Resist and you will be destroyed."

She could imagine Nash's consternation, but she hadn't violated protocol. Instead she had followed the procedure for unknown vessels, usually small-time smugglers or pleasure cruisers gone astray. If the rebels had the good sense to lie, the dogfight might be stalled for a minute or two, long enough for them to get away.

Except Nash was already bringing his TIE Interceptor up and around to cut off their most likely escape route, and her plan was ruined.

Damn, Ciena thought—before another voice came over the comms and turned her anger into horror.

Thane said, "This galaxy isn't big enough."

Maybe Ciena was right. Maybe the Force was bringing them together, over and over.

If so, Thane decided, the Force had a sick sense of humor.

He had no idea how Ciena would answer—whether she'd stick to official procedure or she'd speak to him as a human, the way he'd spoken to her. When the comm unit crackled, he tensed, but the familiar voice coming through wasn't Ciena's.

"Thane Kyrell?" Nash Windrider's incredulity came through loud and clear. "You're *alive*?"

"Hello, old friend." Thane refused to let himself be overwhelmed. Ciena was right there—in one of those TIE fighters soaring toward him—and Nash was there, too, and this was the last fight he ever wanted to be in. Kendy had to be beside herself, but unlike the rest of them, she had the good sense to keep her mouth shut.

But Ciena surely felt the same way. Nash would, too. Maybe this confusion would buy Corona Squadron the time they needed to get away.

Thane's viewfinder blurred with movement, and his eyes widened as he realized someone had just accelerated a TIE fighter to top speed.

"I thought you were dead," Nash said, each word lower and more ragged. "You would have been better off that way."

So much for the reunion.

One of the rebels gets to live.

Ciena seized on to that fact like a towline that could take her to safety. Saving Thane's life didn't violate her duty; it *was* her duty. One of the rebels had to make it out of there, and she intended to use everything she had to make sure he was the survivor.

But that meant she had to stop Nash, without his realizing it.

Nash had violated protocol by initiating battle without her order, but no one would reprimand him for targeting rebel ships at any time, in any way. Already the other two TIEs had accelerated to swoop in right on his tail. Ciena threw her own TIE into maximum speed and set her course.

If I come in from above, it will look like I'm triangulating our weapons. If I choose the right angle, though, I can get in Nash's way and stop his fire.

It didn't occur to Ciena to worry about Thane getting blasted before she had a chance to intervene. In a dogfight, superior piloting kept you alive—and nobody could ever outfly him. Nobody besides her . . .

The engine's roar filled the cockpit, even penetrating her thick black helmet. Ciena soared up high enough that the viewfinder showed her the X-wings and the debris of the planetary ring as so much glowing confetti on-screen—but as she dived down toward them, the shapes took form again. All the X-wings were now in full evasive action, but one of them moved with more agility, executing a perfect spin that threaded through the outer edge of the ring. She took a deep breath to steady herself. Her job was clear now that she knew which ship belonged to Thane.

But Nash had to know it, too.

Thane wove his way through the planetary ring, trusting in the asteroids to take a few of the blasts for him.

"Incoming from vector eight-one-two-eight—" Smikes sounded desperate. "Heavy fire!

A green blaster bolt shattered a rock so close to Thane's X-wing that some of the debris sprayed the cockpit; for one instant, he imagined it shattering, exposing him to the fatal vacuum of space. It held.

"Everyone move to preestablished hyperdrive coordinates!" the Contessa ordered.

Thane added, "Forget formations, get there however you can!" Formation flying sometimes provided protection—but in a situation like this, scattering would give them a chance to get at least a couple of people to safety.

Green blaster fire surrounded him, and he felt the telltale jolt that meant he'd been hit. Thane held his breath for the seconds it took to see the control panels holding steady—noncritical damage. The next time he probably wouldn't be as lucky.

"Rebel scum," Nash snarled. "I can't believe you'd ever stoop so low."

"I can't believe you're still with the Empire," Thane retorted. "They destroyed your planet, Nash! They killed your entire family! How can you—"

"Never speak of Alderaan to me!" By now Nash's fury had driven his voice halfway to a scream. *"Never!"*

On Thane's viewscreen he saw the other members of Corona Squadron locked in battle with two of the TIE fighters—but they had the Imperials well outnumbered because two of the TIEs were only coming after Thane. He must have been wrongly identified as the leader.

Which one of the green blurs on his screen was Ciena's ship? Would he kill her or see someone else do it in front of his eyes? Or maybe this was the day she would finally choose the Empire over him by taking his life.

Then a TIE fighter came down from above, so close Thane saw it through the cockpit as clearly as through his targeting device—flying between him and Nash.

The knowledge hit him so hard his chest hurt: Ciena was trying to save him.

"Get out of my way!" Nash shouted at Ciena.

"I don't take orders from you, *Lieutenant*." She fired in the general direction of Thane's ship but fired to miss.

On her screen she saw one of the TIE fighters vanish—another pilot lost for no reason—and then the quick blur that indicated at least two of the rebel ships had leaped into hyperspace. Then one of the X-wings vanished as well; the Empire had its first kill of the battle.

Thane would be heading directly to the coordinates where the first X-wings had gone into hyperspace. Ciena quickly shifted trajectory again, into a believable angle for attack but one that yet again would interfere with Nash's targeting. She was between them again, shielding Thane with her own ship.

Nash fired anyway.

He didn't hit her—but the bolts came close enough to set off every warning signal. The lights in her cockpit flashed red. Ciena swore.

Was Nash angry enough at Thane to kill him even if he had to go through Ciena first?

Thane saw the opportunity Ciena had given him and took it. At full power he sped toward the coordinates— saw the last of the other X-wings shudder into hyperspace just in front of him—and prepared for the jump to lightspeed.

He yearned to say something to Ciena before he

left. Anything. She needed to know that he realized what she had done for him, and what it meant.

But saying anything would only expose her to Nash and the other TIE pilot. Ciena had protected him; it was his turn to protect her by remaining silent.

Bolts raked his X-wing, and this time he'd taken damage—but not to life support or hyperdrive, so to hell with it. Thane set coordinates, put his hand on the control, and went for it.

The stars elongated into an infinite tunnel as he sped away, leaving Ciena behind.

Thane allowed himself a few moments of silence afterward before checking in with Corona Squadron. "Corona Four reporting in. How are we doing?"

"Confirmed, Corona Four," the Contessa answered, her voice heavy. "We lost Smikes."

Smikes—wary, pessimistic, and yet so courageous. Thane realized he had never made it clear how much he admired the man despite his curmudgeonly demeanor; now he would never have the chance.

"Hey," Yendor said quietly. "That was your Ciena back there, wasn't it?"

"Yeah."

"I saw what she did for you. So—I get why you went to Jelucan now."

Kendy added, "You were right, Thane. She's still Ciena."

It was the closest thing to an apology Thane would ever get for the way the others had shunned him, and it was more than he deserved.

Was Ciena in trouble now? Would they question her? Thane wondered if she would have to face the Empire's interrogators. The thought horrified him.

But if anyone was smart enough to come up with an explanation and save herself, it was Ciena. He had to believe in her.

Ciena took her TIE fighter in without exchanging one more word with Nash Windrider. No doubt he would be livid; he would report her to Piett immediately.

Thankfully, she could say she had been acting under orders, and Piett would never know the difference. It occurred to her, however, that Piett might not acknowledge the orders he'd given her. If the mission's objective had to remain completely secret, would she be sacrificed, too? Would the Empire execute a loyal officer for her loyalty if it furthered their ends?

Once Ciena would have believed that to be impossible. Not any longer.

She removed her helmet, took a deep breath, and

unlocked her hatch. Whatever would befall her next, she had no choice but to face it.

As she hopped down from the TIE, she saw Nash striding toward her, his eyes blazing with anger. Ciena found herself wishing for a blaster. Instead she stood her ground as Nash came up to her, looked her in the face, and gathered her in his arms.

"I can't believe he did that to you," Nash said. "Knowing you loved him, to leave you like that—to fake his death and put you through years of anguish— it's beneath contempt."

Ciena simply hugged Nash back as well as she could manage with both of them still wearing armor. She was grateful for the chance to hide her face against his chest.

"Forgive me for shouting at you. I realize now you must have been so shaken, so heartbroken—well, it would affect anyone's flying, even yours. You were even more eager to kill Thane than I was." Nash sighed as he pulled back far enough to look her in the face. The anger she'd seen before had melted into pity. "I should have let you do the honors. If I'd been thinking straight, I would have."

"I just can't believe it," Ciena said, which was both true and safe.

"That lowlife. We never really knew him at all, did we?" Nash straightened up. "Right, then. We'll have to report in. This won't go well."

It didn't. They were shouted at for some time about their failure to destroy all the rebel ships; Piett acknowledged Ciena's secret success with only a nod at the end, when nobody else was looking. Afterward, Ciena stripped off her armor, took a quick shower, and tried to calm her thoughts.

Thane could have died today. Nash would have killed him.

Shaken as she was to have encountered Thane in combat, Ciena was comforted by the knowledge that he'd gotten away safely. If they never met again, his last memory of her would be the moment she'd saved his life. As she stood there beneath the warm water, hands braced against the metal-tiled walls, she decided she could bear that.

But Nash? How could he have been so homicidally furious at Thane? She understood the sense of betrayal—she had felt it too, the day she'd realized Thane had joined the Rebel Alliance. Even when she had almost hated him, though, she had still loved him, too. Whereas Nash had mourned his friend for years, discovered he was alive, and instantly been ready to kill him.

That wasn't loyalty to the Empire. That was . . . fanaticism.

The engines shifted again, changing the slight vibration beneath her feet. They'd just come out of hyperspace. Ciena was chagrined to realize she'd been so caught up in her own thoughts that she hadn't even noticed when they went to hyperspace in the first place.

She toweled off and tugged on her off-shift jumpsuit so she could get a look at what was going on. A row of triangular windows lined the wall closest to the head, so Ciena could simply look outside for herself. No other ships had made the journey with them, it seemed. Why would they ever leave the Imperial convoy?

To make something ready for the Emperor's arrival. That was the obvious answer. But what? Ciena turned her head, studying the entire starfield, and saw that they were drawing near a planet, one orbited by a large moon so green and cloudy that she assumed it was rich with forest life. And yet something seemed to be orbiting that moon, something vast and dark—

Then she realized what she was looking at and gasped.

It can't be. They would never do that again.

But they had. Ciena couldn't deny what she saw—

—a second Death Star.

CHAPTER TWENTY-FOUR

CIENA'S HANDS HAD gone numb, but still she stood there, palms against the window, staring at the new Death Star.

Why would they ever build another one? It was only to stop the war before it began—and it failed—so why?

She knew the answer but could not yet accept it. Instead she stared at the massive hulk of the space station, which only seemed to grow larger as the *Executor* drew close. Ciena had often wondered how such a gargantuan structure could be built in the first place; even the enormous resources of the Empire had to be strained by the construction of something the size of a large moon. Now she could see the process for herself, because this Death Star had not yet been completed. Great sections remained unfinished, and she could stare into the guts of the thing, an ugly crosshatch of beams and struts surrounding deep, hollow darkness.

Her own words in a Valentia cantina echoed in her memory, taunting her: *The Emperor and the Moffs have to see, now, that destroying Alderaan did no good. It didn't stop the Rebellion. . . . The only reason to attack Alderaan was to prevent an even more devastating war. The war has begun anyway. It's too late to save the galaxy from that.*

No other reason could ever justify the destruction of an entire planet, or the deaths of billions of people. Only by restoring galactic peace could the Empire redeem those deaths.

But now more worlds would be destroyed for no reason—except to cause pain and fear.

Maybe they're doing this to finally end the war, Ciena thought. But the excuse was too feeble for her to believe even for an instant. If the Rebellion hadn't been cowed by the destruction of Alderaan, then the deaths of other planets wouldn't stop it, either. Instead, this would incite more people to join the rebel cause. This wouldn't end the war; it would intensify it beyond all imagining.

Whenever Ciena had a nightmare about Alderaan, she scoured away her doubts by remembering Jude. Her friend's loss had always helped Ciena balance the scales in her mind—to recall that massive death and destruction had been caused by both sides in the conflict. Today, however, she could only think that if Jude had seen the second Death Star, she would have recoiled from it.

She would never have wanted this done in her name. Never.

The cold had leached through to Ciena's bones. Finally, she pulled her aching hands back from the window, rubbing them in hopes of restoring blood flow. But no matter how hard she tried, she couldn't get warm again.

Once her shuttle from the *Executor* had docked on the Death Star, Ciena could see for herself how much had in fact been completed. From the outside, the enormous unfinished hemisphere dominated the view. Inside, however, they were anchored by a wholly functional tractor beam, disembarked onto a deck that was not only finished but polished, and walked into a space station as advanced as any other in the Imperial Starfleet. They had prepared well for the Emperor's arrival.

"So we're finally senior enough to get to see the Emperor himself." Berisse covered her mouth with her fingers, trying and failing to conceal a smile. "I don't know what I'm so excited about. We'll be crowded in with another few thousand officers. Probably we'll have a worse view than the back row at a podracing arena."

Nash had, as usual, fallen in step beside them. Ever since the dogfight in the Hudalla system, he had been more attentive to Ciena than ever. "Still, we'll be able to tell our grandchildren about the day we saw Palpatine for ourselves. And a big ceremony—well, it makes a welcome change, doesn't it? Just what you needed, Ciena. Something to cheer you up."

She'd been hearing variations on that ever since Hudalla. The irony was that she *did* have a broken heart—just not for the reasons he believed.

Yet that minor irritation hardly mattered next to Ciena's consternation. *How can they talk about the ceremony for the Emperor? How does any of that matter compared with the fact we're standing inside a Death Star?*

Then she checked herself. Yes, they were standing inside a Death Star, surrounded by hundreds of other officers—some stationed there, others from the advance vessels sent to ready an appropriate ceremony for the Emperor's arrival. Surely some of them shared her doubts, but others would not. Publicly voicing her opposition would send her straight to the brig. She could learn from her friends' self-control.

So Ciena remained quiet until the three of them miraculously wound up alone in a lift. Her command-track training had taught her that listening devices were rarely put in military lifts due to frequency changes, so talking there was likely safe. As soon as the doors slid shut, she said, "I can't believe they built another Death Star."

Berisse shrugged as she leaned against the wall, no longer military proper. "I can't believe they did it this soon. How long does it take to construct one of these? They must have started right after the Battle of Yavin. Good for them."

Ciena refused to believe she'd heard that right. ". . . good for them?"

"Well, we *had* to rebuild the Death Star. I mean, come on!" Berisse's frown revealed how confused she was by Ciena's reaction. "The single biggest and most powerful station ever constructed in galactic history, and it gets blown up by rebel scum? Re-creating the Death Star is the only way we could ever honor our people who died at Yavin. If we hadn't rebuilt it, then the terrorists would have won."

"You don't seem to agree, Ciena." Nash's tone was light, but she could see how intently he was looking at her. "What do you think?"

She realized she'd begun to sweat. "I think—I think that if we've built a Death Star, we plan to use it. That another world will die, just like Alderaan did."

Berisse scoffed. "No way. Once the station's complete and word gets out? Nobody will ever defy the

Emperor like that again. The Rebellion's going to melt away. Wait and see."

Even amidst Ciena's most painful doubts about Imperial tactics, she had believed that rule of law was always better than chaos—even when that law was harsh. But the future Berisse described was not rule of law. It was rule by fear, and therefore tyranny. Even the darkest atrocities of the Clone Wars did not compare with the destruction of an inhabited world.

And what did it mean that Ciena was afraid to say that out loud, even to her closest friends?

She tried to find the right words to make them understand. "When Alderaan was destroyed, we thought it would force the Rebellion to surrender. That we could prevent this war. But we've been at war for three years anyway." *And if someone as cynical as Thane can find rebel leaders to follow and admire, the Rebel Alliance won't vanish as easily as you think.* "Don't you see? Those tactics *didn't work.* If this station isn't used to protect the Empire's citizens from war, then how can we justify it?"

Nash stood up straighter, his eyes narrowing. When he answered her, his voice gave her chills. "Are you saying that Alderaan was destroyed in vain? *For nothing?*"

Ciena held up her hands. "Nash, please, I don't mean to—"

"Listen to me," he said. "Alderaan had to die for the

Empire's true power to be acknowledged. My home-world's end was also the end of the Imperial Senate, the end of the countless petty power struggles that had plagued Palpatine's early reign. Only then was the Empire's true strength revealed."

His gaze had become glazed, almost unfocused, like that of someone suffering from a fever. This was what his face must have looked like during the Hudalla dogfight.

Nash continued, "This war is only the aftermath of the conflicts that have racked the galaxy during the past century, the final useless gasp of those who would oppose us. Through sheer stupid luck, the rebels managed to destroy the first Death Star. By rebuilding the Death Star, and using it *as many times as necessary* to restore order, we prove that their luck only goes so far. We prove that we are the only galactic authority and always will be."

The lift doors slid open to the deck of the smaller docking bay that would soon welcome the Emperor. Countless officers filled the corridors, a crush that precluded any hope of speaking freely. Ciena felt vulnerable. Any of these people could and would expose her as a traitor—even her two best friends.

Then Nash's hands closed gently around her shoulders. "You're still not yourself," he said. "After learning how Thane lied to you, of course you're second-guessing who you can trust, maybe even what's real."

"That dogfight was one of the worst moments of my life," she said. At least she could say that with total honesty.

"Trust in your service. Trust in us. Above all, trust in the oath you took when we graduated from the academy. Your integrity defines you, Ciena. You won't go wrong if you only stay true." Nash smiled down at her in the way that usually made her think up an excuse to leave the room. The same crush she'd tried so hard to discourage had become her best shield against a charge of treason.

Berisse, meanwhile, had already moved on. "What are we waiting for? The Emperor's shuttle will be here soon. Let's get it together!"

During the next couple of hours of instructions and formations, Ciena stood separately from her friends; commanders had a marginally better position, though hundreds of captains, admirals, and top gunners still stood in front of her. Numbly, she did whatever was asked of her, shifting position as the organizers thought better of it. At least it was something to do. She tried to occupy her mind by observing the power play among the various members of the top brass, but even that didn't help. Seeing how petty their concerns were, and how often they betrayed fear of Lord Vader's anger, only reminded Ciena that the Imperial Starfleet she'd served was not the one she'd believed in all this time.

Finally, the hour came. Lord Vader strode out, black cape billowing behind him; from a distance, the white shuttlecraft looked like a star. As it came closer, Ciena could see the distinctive gray stripe on its nose, the marking that informed everyone this was truly the Emperor arriving.

To Ciena's surprise, Lord Vader bowed as figures began to descend from the shuttle. None of the other officers were required to bow. What could that mean? But the question was wiped from her mind as Emperor Palpatine came into view.

Palpatine's face appeared on countless holos every single day. Like anyone else in the Empire, she could have described him as well as she could members of her own family. Hair almost entirely gray but still thick, face betraying only the slightest lines of care and time, his posture straight, his eyes sharp. In other words, the face shown to the world had nothing to do with the reality. Ciena's eyes widened as she took in the face his heavy hood did not entirely conceal—the unnatural paleness of his skin, the inhuman folds and wrinkles.

He walked through the bay with his back hunched and without so much as a word or glance toward the hundreds of loyal officers assembled to greet him.

Don't be petty. So he's grown older. That's only natural! And surely the Emperor has other things on his mind than some silly ceremony—

The rationalizations didn't work. What shook Ciena wasn't merely the Emperor's appearance; it was the sense of almost depthless malice that radiated from him, so strongly she could have reeled. Even from a distance, Palpatine awakened in her a physical dread—primitive instincts telling her to escape or fight.

Only one other person had ever made her feel that way: Darth Vader. Ciena had always told herself that Vader was an aberration, unique in the Empire. So far as it went, that was true. But the most terrifying thing about him, the constant sense of malevolence and danger he inspired—that was shared by the most powerful person in the galaxy.

Is this who I've been serving all along?

This is a bad dream.

Didn't work. Thane could feel the iron bench beneath him, smell the grease-and-ozone scent of the repair bay. Every mundane detail made it clear he was wide awake.

This is a test. A drill. The Alliance leaders want to find out what we'd do when confronted with the worst-case scenario.

No way. They wouldn't risk pulling together the entire rebel armada for a mere drill.

But if it wasn't a nightmare and it wasn't a drill, it was the undeniable, horrible truth: the Empire had built a second Death Star.

Thane could think of words from three dozen worlds to describe how he felt, each epithet more obscene than the last. But he lacked the breath to speak any of them. He could only stare at the rotating holo in front of the X-wing squadrons as they received their briefing from General Madine.

"Exactly how are they going to take care of the shield generator?" Kendy asked. "They'll have dozens of troopers down on the forest moon of Endor, if not hundreds—"

"General Solo will take over from Major Lokmarcha, who was killed in action. Solo's team on the moon of Endor will handle the shield generator. Each person involved in this assault has enough to do on their own without worrying about someone else's job, Corona Five," Madine said sternly.

Thane whispered to Yendor, "Who the hell is General Solo?"

"You know. Han Solo! Captain of the *Millennium Falcon*?"

The ship name sounded vaguely familiar, but Thane couldn't quite place it.

Yendor's eyes widened with disbelief. "Come on! He's one of the guys who rescued Princess Leia from the first Death Star. You remember *that*, right?"

"I wasn't with the Rebellion then. I didn't join until right before Hoth."

"Oh. I guess Captain Solo got captured by a bounty hunter right after Hoth." Yendor's lekku drooped. "So you wouldn't know him—but, hey, he's one of the best."

"Indeed he is," interrupted General Madine, who had apparently overheard their entire conversation. Both Thane and Yendor faced forward and sat up straight. "General Solo will be joined on the forest moon strike team by Princess Leia Organa and Luke Skywalker. They'll have that shield down."

Luke Skywalker, again. Thane managed to keep from rolling his eyes. But Princess Leia he admired. If he could trust anyone, he could trust her.

General Madine continued, "Meanwhile, General Calrissian will be leading the starfighters diving into the core of the Death Star. The dispersal of the Imperial fleet gives us this unprecedented chance to strike. Due to the unfinished construction, the station's main reactor remains exposed and vulnerable. A strike team should be able to penetrate the Death Star and fire into that reactor, setting off a chain reaction that will destroy the station before it ever has a chance to become operational."

And who is this General Calrissian? Thane decided not to ask that question out loud. If the Rebel Alliance was happy turning over its two most critical missions *of all time* to a bunch of brand-new generals, okay, fine—

"Corona Squadron, your mission is to cover General Calrissian in the *Millennium Falcon* and the other starfighters in the Gold, Red, Green, and Gray Squadrons as they penetrate the Death Star," Madine continued. "The fewer TIE fighters they have to fight on their way in, the better their chances of a clean hit and a getaway for the entire fleet. This means you'll be dealing with TIE fire from both inside and outside the space station, as well as potential long-range fire from any larger ships the Empire can deploy."

At some point in the near future, Thane figured, he would completely freak out at the thought of going into battle against a Death Star. Right now, he could hardly comprehend the existence of the damned thing.

He had believed Ciena naive for arguing that the Empire would never again try to destroy another world. Only now did Thane realize that, on some level, he had believed it, too. The thought of another Alderaan was too much to wrap his mind around. No matter how long the odds against them, the Rebellion had to attack. From now on, this was not only the most important battle they had to fight—it was the only battle that would ever matter.

After the briefing he walked through the main hangar, which had become a frenzy of activity. Although many pilots were checking out their ships, others were making a point of hugging friends, shaking hands. Saying good-bye, just in case.

Thane stopped by the *Moa* first, where he shook Brill's paw and Methwat's long-fingered hand and for once hugged Lohgarra as tightly as she hugged him. But one member of the *Moa*'s crew turned out to be with Corona Squadron.

"I've needed a new astromech for a while," Yendor said as JJH2 was lowered into position aboard the X-wing. "You said this guy is the best."

JJH2 beeped inquisitively, and Thane smiled at the little droid despite himself. "Yeah, I said it and I meant it. Take care of each other out there, okay?"

As Yendor and JJH2 checked out systems together, Thane climbed into his ship. He'd already given his X-wing a thorough going-over after the Hudalla dogfight; he had nothing to do but sit in his cockpit and wait for the order to fly into combat against a Death Star—which sounded a lot like committing suicide.

The Rebel Alliance had managed to destroy the first Death Star, but they'd gotten lucky and they had to know it. A design flaw with an exhaust port? What were the odds? Thane shook his head as he imagined it. As a former Imperial officer, he knew very well how that kind of oversight would be punished. No engineer who had worked on the second Death Star would make a similar mistake. This station would be even stronger than the first.

For a moment he remembered being a brand-new graduate of the Royal Academy on Coruscant, flying toward his posting on the Death Star. When he had first seen the station, the sheer scale of it had awed him like nothing before. He still found it difficult to believe that the first Death Star had fallen, or that the second one ever could.

The old, cynical voice in his head whispered, *You know, you could cut out of here. All-volunteer military, remember?*

But Thane didn't listen to that voice much anymore. The other members of Corona Squadron and the crew of the *Moa* were as close as he had to a family now—maybe the closest he'd ever had. He might not share his comrades' wishful thinking, but he'd be damned if he'd abandon them on the eve of the most dangerous battle they'd ever faced.

And if the Empire won, condemning the galaxy to an eternity of its harsh, corrupt rule?

Thane decided he'd rather go down fighting.

It had been two days since Ciena had first seen the Death Star and the Emperor, and those two days had all but destroyed her.

Each horrifying realization struck her at a different moment, and no sooner had she thought she could bear one than another would undermine her completely. The Emperor's horrifying presence—the unjust conviction of her mother—Nash and Berisse's unquestioning acceptance of genocide as a military tactic—the many pilots who had died for no reason, their lives wasted by a command that didn't care—and Thane, even now at risk from the Empire every day of his life.

He was right about so many things, she thought dully as she went through the motions of her monthly physical. The medical droid's cold sensors allowed her to excuse her shuddering as a shiver. *I wish I could tell him that.*

Ciena still had not forgiven the Rebellion for Jude's

death. Nor did she believe it offered any hope of effective government. However, while she would never contemplate joining the rebels herself, she now understood how Thane could have done so.

"This isn't about whether or not we've kept faith with the Empire," Thane had said to her as he held her close in the Fortress. *"It's about whether the Empire has kept faith with us."*

An oath of loyalty remained binding even when the subject proved unworthy. It simply became more bitter.

Just as Ciena slipped back into her uniform, an alert began to echo through the ship. "All pilots to TIE fighters, immediately."

What was that about? Ciena didn't think the rebels could possibly know about the station yet, if the secret had been kept so effectively that even high-ranking officers on the *Executor* had not known. Probably it was a drill or some other display of firepower to show off for Palpatine. It made no difference; she wanted to be a part of it. More than anything else, she needed to fly.

By now Ciena's duties rarely required her to pilot anything smaller than a transport shuttle, and those only rarely. But she'd always kept her skills sharp, and she could volunteer for TIE duty at any point.

Immediately, she went to the ship's flight commander, who seemed strangely . . . smug. "I see,

Commander," he said, his thin smile snaking across his face. "Of course you want to be a part of this. Something to tell the grandchildren, hm?"

Yeah, one time I showed off for the loathsome, repellent Emperor who blew up entire planets. Ciena said only, "My next duty shift is six hours away, sir. I'm ready to serve now."

"Your courage will not go unrecognized, Commander Ree. Report to launching bay nine immediately."

As Ciena strapped on the black armor of a TIE pilot, she told herself it would all be okay soon, because she'd be flying. Flight remained her greatest joy and her only escape. Once she was aloft, soaring through space, she'd be free of all her crushing doubts. If only for those few minutes, she would be herself again.

In the melee of preparation, she caught a glimpse of Nash, who gave her a roguish smile. He still believed in her. But the pang of guilt had faded before Ciena had even climbed into her cockpit. Whatever else happened in the future, she intended to keep her distance from anyone she'd known before. Perhaps she could put in for some isolated backwater posting—the kind of job nobody wanted, something easy for her to get—and maybe a place where she could actually do some good.

Helmet: locked. Engines: full power. Ciena waited for her squadron's signal, then flew up and out of the docking bay. Hundreds of other fighters surrounded her, making precision flying necessary. Yet she found it soothing, even the vibration and roar within the cockpit. Takeoff always felt like casting off shackles and breaking free.

For a moment she thought of soaring over the Jelucani mountains in the old V-171, Thane behind her, the two of them flying as one. . . .

Then she shifted to wider sensors and gasped.

Ciena had known hundreds of TIE fighters were taking flight. What she had not guessed was that countless other Imperial craft were massed nearby, as well, including several Star Destroyers. It was beyond anything she'd expected, even greater than the attack force sent to Hoth.

Then the pieces came together.

We're expecting major action, and soon. That means the rebels are coming.

If the rebels are coming, they know about the Death Star and the Emperor. And if we have this tremendous a force waiting for them, we wanted *them to know.*

That's why Piett ordered me to make sure one of the X-wings got away. He needed someone to report the Emperor's movements to the Rebellion. We were setting a trap all along.

She'd always understood that on some level—why else let the rebels go free, if not to fill their heads with false intel? But she'd thought it no more than a feint to cover the Emperor's location. Yet the trap the Empire had laid must have been larger and more elaborate; she'd been only one tiny part of it. This wasn't any ordinary military action. This was the day the Empire planned to destroy the Rebellion for good.

Even as Ciena's hands tightened on the controls, her screen went crazy, spilling out so much data she could hardly take it all in. In the space surrounding the Death Star and Endor's moon, thousands of ships had materialized in an instant.

The Rebel Alliance had come, and the Empire was ready for them.

CHAPTER TWENTY-FIVE

"MAY THE FORCE BE WITH US."
Admiral Ackbar's voice crackled over the comm unit as the rebel armada headed toward the Death Star. Now that Thane saw it for himself, he had to believe—but he also saw how incomplete it still was. They weren't going up against a Death Star, just the shell of one. Thinking of it that way helped.

Okay, it didn't help that much. At the moment, however, Thane would take what he could get.

The shield generator should be down by now, he told himself as he checked his sensors. *We'll get the order to proceed any second now.*

The order didn't come.

And he wasn't getting any reading on the shield at all—up or down. Thane frowned as he tapped his controls. This would be a bad time to develop a systems failure.

Then General Calrissian's voice cut through sharply. "Break off the attack! The shield is still up!"

Thane swore under his breath. What had happened to the Endor team?

"Pull up!" Calrissian continued. "All craft pull up!"

As they curved away from the Death Star, Thane prepared to leap back into hyperspace for the humiliating but necessary escape. Then he heard Admiral Ackbar's voice again. "Take evasive action!"

Kendy spoke next. "Sector forty-seven—they're here."

Thane went cold as he saw what awaited them: it looked like half the Imperial fleet, including dozens of Star Destroyers.

The Rebel Alliance had just arrived at its own execution.

Ciena thought, *At least it will be quick.*

Her TIE fighter rushed forward with the rest to engage the rebel fleet. The incredible disparity in strength convinced her the Empire could win this battle within minutes. Even as she obeyed orders to target the medical frigate, however, she noticed the Star

Destroyers were making no move to join the combat. Why amass this much firepower and hold back?

Then she saw the Death Star's laser begin to glow green and had her answer.

She tensed, expecting Endor or its moon to explode. Instead, the laser hit one of the larger rebel cruisers. Instantly, the ship was obliterated.

If the station is fully operational, why bother sending us out to fight?

Once again, it was only theater. Only a show. TIE pilots would die by the dozens, if the hundreds, when not one of them was truly needed here. The Death Star could have eliminated the rebels on its own. But Palpatine wanted every admiral and general to witness this moment and believe their Emperor unstoppable.

We die for his glory, she thought bitterly. *Which means we die for nothing. Again.*

Flying into a battle with no hope of survival turned out to be the secret to kicking ass.

Thane's mind-set had kept him from losing his cool when they'd realized the shield generator was still operational, and when he'd seen how much of the Imperial Starfleet had been brought together for the express purpose of blasting the Rebel Alliance to atoms. He'd even been able to hold steady when the Death

Star destroyed the *Liberty*—the ship Corona Squadron had called home for months. Thane remembered the friendly Mon Calamari who had welcomed them; every single one had been killed in an instant.

Not that Thane's chances of survival were much better. The way he saw it, the Empire was going to kill him today no matter what he did. His only goal was to make the Imperials pay for it, with blood.

Over the speaker, General Calrissian ordered the smaller ships to get in close on the Star Destroyers—presumably because that would keep them safe from the Death Star. Thane could have laughed. *Like you were any safer next to a Star Destroyer.* Still, he was glad for the chance to see the damage he had caused.

"I'm going in close on the engines," the Contessa said over comms. "Who's with me?"

Thane braced himself. "Corona Four, right behind you."

"Corona Five, too. Let's do it!" That was Kendy, who sounded almost cheerful about the chance to wreak some mayhem.

Yendor didn't even answer out loud, but sensors showed him accelerating so fast he was going to get to the Destroyer before Thane did. Or at least he would have if Thane hadn't taken the engines all the way to maximum and dived straight toward the rear of the ship.

The mammoth shielding of a Star Destroyer could take intense levels of weapons fire without damage. The engines, however—you could get at those. They were too deeply encased within the impregnable ship to be destroyed, but even slowing the ship down or denying the crew full power would help in a battle.

Let's see how they like being stranded in space for a while. Thane grinned as he swooped around the back, the rest of Corona Squadron just behind him.

His old academy training returned; it was as if the schematics holos from Large Vessel Design glowed in front of him again, showing him the exact spots to hit. Thane zeroed in and fired, again and again. At that rate, he'd run his power down too far to jump into hyperspace for a retreat—but that didn't matter any longer. It looked like the entire Rebellion would die today; Thane only hoped to go out fighting.

He made his hits, but Kendy did even better. *She always was the best sharpshooter in the class,* he thought as he saw a small jet of sparks flare along the side of one Star Destroyer engine for the instant it took the vacuum of space to snuff it out.

A swarm of TIE fighters sliced through their

formation, so close Thane glimpsed a flash of one through the cockpit. He didn't flinch, just pressed his finger down on the firing button.

The Empire doesn't even give those pilots any shields. One hit and they blow. He fired twice and was rewarded with the spray of sparks and the blur of a TIE fighter spinning wildly out of control.

What next? Maybe he should dive for the main bridge, just smash his X-wing through it and take an Imperial admiral into death with him—

"The shield generator is down! Repeat, the shield generator is down!"

Thane had figured the Endor team for dead. *Damn,* he thought. *Those guys pulled it off!* He found himself imagining Princess Leia as the lone victor. Probably she'd blown that shield generator away with a grin on her face.

General Calrissian said to the fleet, "All fighters, follow me!"

"Let's go!" the Contessa shouted over the comms. Nothing frosty about her now—she was ready for blood. "Corona Squadron, let's head in."

"Corona Four, ready." He grinned as they regrouped into formation and headed straight for the enormous space station ahead. It looked and felt as if he was diving into a sea of black metal tiles. "Remember, everybody—this thing's so big you'll have to compensate for its gravitational pull!"

Thane banked sharply along the side of the Death Star, just under the gaping maw targeted by the *Millennium Falcon*'s attack. Beneath him he saw endless black metal, solid surface still broken by areas of construction; above, explosions flared and burst like fireworks on feast days back home.

Three TIE fighters appeared over the Death Star's horizon, and Thane didn't even bother with evasive action. He accelerated, targeted, and fired—and flew straight through the three fireballs left behind.

He didn't have to wonder whether Ciena was in any of those ships. She would've been smarter, fired first. She wouldn't have let them get away with going after a Star Destroyer's engines, either. No doubt she was safely on the bridge of one of those Destroyers, but Thane halfway wished she'd be the one to finish him off. Then at least they'd be bound together in some way at the end.

The Contessa reported, "We have entry! The *Millennium Falcon* strike team has entered the Death Star!"

It hit Thane then—they might actually win this thing.

"Why aren't you covering the engines?" Ciena shouted at the idiot TIE pilots who had let some idiot rebel damage the *Subjugator*. "Get back there! *Move!*"

The rebels were trapped and they knew it, but obviously they intended to kill as many Imperials as possible before they fell. Already space was littered with the debris of the enemy star cruisers targeted by the Death Star's laser. Ciena felt the same rush of futile anger at the waste of pilots' lives by callous commanders, but now her fury was directed at whatever rebel leader had dragged Thane back into this war.

But she was angriest with herself. Thane was only one of the rebels who would die because of a trap she had unwittingly helped set. Both she and Thane had been victims of the Emperor's malignant scheming and the terrible slaughter it had begun.

Ciena took her TIE Interceptor up over the main bridge area of the *Annihilator*, just in case some rebel pilot decided to fly directly into it and go out in a blaze of glory. The other TIEs stuck rigidly to established attack patterns, but her rank gave her the freedom and responsibility to judge the battle for herself and go wherever she was needed most. As she cleared the top of the Star Destroyer, she wheeled her ship around, checking sensors to establish which targets would come next—then stopped cold.

Their garrison on Endor's moon had failed. The shield generator had come down.

Her sensors showed the rebel fleet becoming aware

of their change in luck. Flight vectors instantly shifted, and the cloud of starfighters around her turned into darts headed straight for the most vulnerable part of the gaping, unfinished Death Star—the large shaft that led straight to the main reactor.

But what did they expect to accomplish? Yes, they could do some damage on their way in, but the maze of beams and cables would surely wreck any invading ships; even now Ciena saw TIE fighters closer to the space station zooming toward the same area to follow behind and finish the rebels off. It was all such a useless, meaningless waste.

She turned her attention to the next nearest Star Destroyer, her own *Executor*. It was only now beginning to engage the rebel ships directly; all the admirals had waited for the Death Star to strike first, another display of Palpatine's favoring theater over sound tactics.

Then she saw a damaged rebel starfighter spinning out of control, straight for the bridge deflector shields of the *Executor*. Cursing, she tried to get it in her target sights, but the starfighter was too distant and moving too fast—

An orange flare marked its impact, and in horror Ciena realized the extent of the damage. Neither that hit nor the earlier damage to the ship's engines could've crippled a Star Destroyer on its own, but the combination proved fatal. Jaw agape, she watched the *Executor* lose main power and begin to drift toward the nearest object with major gravitational pull—namely, the Death Star.

Even a Star Destroyer can't wreck the Death Star on its own, she reminded herself. *Stay on target.*

But the *Executor*'s destruction meant Berisse's death. . . .

Stay on target!

Ciena's breaths were coming so quick and hard that the inner visor of her black helmet had begun to fog slightly. She attempted to calm herself by focusing on the flight. If she thought of her attacks as piloting challenges—as an escape into the air—she could do this.

She set coordinates for a massive Mon Calamari star cruiser. If she could take out its bridge deflectors, she could even the score.

And I could fly into it just like that rebel starfighter did—but on purpose—to end this battle. Maybe I could even end the war.

That thought was . . . tempting.

Yet even as Ciena input her coordinates, the order came over comms. "All vessels, regroup at pre-battle coordinates. Regroup immediately."

"What the hell?" She couldn't understand why anyone would give such an order. The pre-battle coordinates stood too far away from the rebels and the Death Star to be effective. Her fingers flew over the sensors, widening her view so she could get an idea of what was going on.

And what she saw was the rebel fleet pulling away from the Death Star. Either they were retreating, or—

Ciena didn't finish that thought. Nothing mattered now but following orders. She had to empty herself out. *Refuse to think. Only react.*

As she swooped away from the *Annihilator*, she saw a couple of TIE fighters moving more slowly than the rest; they'd taken damage but could still fly. In training, TIE pilots were told that aiding fellow fliers was their lowest priority, a task only to be undertaken if nothing else needed to be done. Ciena decided to ignore the training. She took position behind them, covering them from any rebel fire as they headed toward the Imperial fleet and safety.

But as the moments went on, they fell farther behind. By now she'd realized the rebels were retreating in another direction; facing off had become less important than staying alive.

"Come on," she whispered to the limping TIEs ahead of her. They needed to go so much faster—

Thane's engine whined with strain as he pushed it to the limit. He and the rest of Corona Squadron had flown into the cloud of vessels following the *Millennium Falcon* away from the Death Star at top speed. If only they could get on the far side of Endor, to shield themselves from that thing—

Over comms he heard the Contessa call out, "Brace for impact!"

Here it comes. Despite the almost irresistible urge to look back, Thane refused to turn his head. If that thing blew, the light would be blinding. He'd be damned if the last thing he ever saw was the Death Star. Instead he gripped his controls and stared at the ships in front of him. The curved rear light of the *Millennium Falcon* arced just above the placid green surface of Endor's moon. *Did they save us? Have we saved them?*

"We made it!" Kendy called jubilantly. "We're out of the danger zone."

Made it? Thane had given his life up for lost. He couldn't wrap his mind around the words. *We made it?*

Then space itself lit up as if it were a sky. For the first instant Thane could only think it was beautiful. But the shock wave was coming.

The shock of the Death Star's explosion felt like crashing into solid stone. Ciena's TIE fighter spun out of control, all stabilizers gone. Desperately, she tried to aim for the nearest ship's docking bay—if she could land in one piece, she stood a chance.

The Death Star was gone. Had the Empire itself fallen with it? But there was no time to guess, even to think. Her sensors and the world beyond were both incomprehensible blurs. Nausea swept through her as she tumbled over and over toward the rectangle of light that represented her only safety.

The second impact was worse. Ciena knew her ship was skidding against solid metal, smashing into steel, and then the whole world vanished as pain cut her in two.

From the surface of Endor's moon, the wreck of the Death Star glowed like a golden supernova in the night sky. All around Thane, drums and pipes played victory songs; people laughed, drank engine-room jet juice, and embraced the friends they'd thought they would never see again. In the distance, by one of the bonfires, he could see Kendy dancing with someone who might have been General Calrissian. Yendor and Brill were doing a little patchwork on JJH2, who had come through with only a few scratches. Lohgarra seemed to be outdrinking an entire squadron. To judge by the hand gestures Methwat was making, he was telling Wedge Antilles about some tricky maneuver.

Thane sat at the very edge of the gathering, his back to a tree, mostly in the dark.

Many ships of the Imperial Starfleet had escaped the Battle of Endor—and many had not. The *Executor*, Lord Vader's own ship, had been destroyed. He knew now it was the Star Destroyer they'd seen crashing into the Death Star. *Ciena might not have been aboard,* he told himself—but she was a senior officer. She would have been needed. Ciena would never have run from a fight, so she'd probably been on the *Executor* at its fiery end.

If so, then the golden light slowly fading in the night sky was the only gravestone Ciena would ever have.

He was consoled only by knowing how Ciena would have reacted when she learned of the existence of a second Death Star. If anything ever had the power to break her loyalty and her steadfast oath, that would be it. When Thane imagined how she must have felt the moment she realized the Emperor planned to destroy yet more worlds—that the obliteration of Alderaan had not been to end a war but to make Imperial power absolute—she would have felt so deeply betrayed.

The Empire was never worthy of you, he thought.

Thane saw another spray of shooting stars, evidence of yet more battle debris burning as it entered the atmosphere. When they'd spotted shooting stars as children, Ciena had always said they should make a wish. He never had; he wasn't the type to believe in wishes.

Tonight, though, he did.

Thane didn't wish for Ciena to be alive—that was already determined, set, beyond anyone's reach or knowledge. Instead he wished for the New Republic to be at least half as righteous as the rebels claimed it would be. If he had helped destroy the Empire's power so it could be replaced with something better, Thane could believe the whole war had been worthwhile. Even if it had cost Ciena's life.

Ciena would have wished for that, too. Somehow that was the saddest part.

Ciena remembered virtually nothing of her removal from the wreckage of the TIE fighter—only vague impressions of the screech of torn metal and the horrible wash of light as they pulled off her helmet.

All she knew was the pain cleaving her in half.

At one point, as droids pushed her hover-stretcher toward the medical bay, Ciena strained to see her abdomen. One droid said, in a flat electronic voice, "It is inadvisable to visually inspect your wound at this time.

Psychological indications are that a patient would find it distressing."

Ciena looked down. A plate of metal jutted from her abdomen; it had shredded her flight suit and sunk in just under her rib cage, deep. The image was so gruesome as to be surreal. Dully she thought that no one could be injured like that and survive.

The surgical droids were working at full capacity, handling the injured in order of rank. Lower ranks had to wait. As Ciena lay there, panting through the delay for the painkiller injection to take effect, a figure appeared by her side, still half-garbed in TIE pilot armor.

"Ciena," Nash breathed. He took her hand; she was grateful for the gloves they wore, because it meant he couldn't actually touch her. "Hold on. You'll be in soon."

"Admirals—captains and generals—they go first." Her voice cracked on the words.

"Of course, but relatively few of them get seriously injured. You're one of the most gravely injured commanders, so you'll enter the operating bay any moment now."

A rush of dizziness swept through Ciena. Either the painkiller was taking effect, or her blood loss had taken her to the brink of death. She forced herself to look into Nash's eyes. "I need—my father—you'll tell my father—"

Nash shook his head as he cradled her hand against his chest. "No last words. Do you hear me? You're not going to give up."

But Ciena persisted. This was too important. "Tell Pappa—I love him and—and—I should have stood by the one—who stood by us."

Her father would know to find Thane and tell him, too. At least Thane would understand that she'd finally seen the truth of the Empire and that she'd been thinking of him at the end.

Nash said something to her in response, but she couldn't hear it. Dizziness washed over her again, stealing sound and light.

Maybe she would be reunited with Wynnet soon.

"Ciena?"

Why did someone want to talk to her? She didn't want to talk. All she wanted to do was sleep.

"Ciena, can you open your eyes? Please try."

She obeyed, blinking against the light. As her vision cleared, she saw Nash by her bedside—now in off-shift coveralls, with a small bandage on his forehead.

Circled around the foot of her bed were three medical droids, all of which beeped and hummed as they took readings.

"Good." Nash smiled the way people did when they were trying not to cry. "You're back with us."

"Why am I—" Ciena tried to prop herself up enough to see her midsection, but the movement sent terrible pain rippling through her. Breathing through her teeth, she sank back onto her medical bed.

Nash spoke in low, soothing tones, like a trainer calming a wounded animal. "You came through surgery, though they said it was a near thing. But they had to remove your liver. It was damaged beyond repair."

Most limbs or organs could be replaced by top-level robotics; the liver was one of the only exceptions, its functions too delicate to be easily replicated.

"For now they've hooked you to a life-support belt, rather like Lord Vader's suit, though you need only wear it around your midsection. You'll have to undergo intensive bacta therapy. It can take months to regrow a liver—the better part of a year—but it can be done." He tried to smile for her. "Leave it to you to find a way to take months of leave time without a reprimand."

Ciena swallowed, though her mouth and throat were too dry. "What's happening with the fleet?"

Nash's smile vanished in an instant. "The Death Star was destroyed. Emperor Palpatine, Lord Vader, and Moff Jerjerrod all perished—as did Berisse." He stumbled over the name of their friend. "The Rebellion is sending out mass communications claiming to be the new power in the galaxy. The Imperial Starfleet is regrouping to plan the next assault and name the next emperor."

"Another emperor?"

"You can imagine the power grabs we're seeing. Civil unrest across the galaxy, even on Coruscant. But the strongest will prevail, and we'll have the leader we need for these difficult times."

The most vicious and ruthless of the Moffs or admirals will take power. We won't have a better emperor who might be able to right our course. Instead we'll sink further into the mire.

"Don't cry," Nash said. "You're tired. I shouldn't exhaust you by forcing you to talk. Go back to sleep. You need your rest."

Ciena turned her head into the pillow instead of saying good-bye.

She didn't realize she'd slipped back into unconsciousness until she awoke again. To judge by the low lighting and lack of human personnel around, it was the medical bay's version of night. The life-support belt around her waist felt heavy and stiff, and the connector shunts jabbed into her flesh like needles in her belly; probably they would continue to hurt as long as she had to wear the thing. Ciena lifted one hand, and a droid rolled promptly to her side with some water.

After she'd sipped from the tube, she said, "When my armor was removed—I had a small pouch—a leather bracelet inside, braided—"

"The items were destroyed," the droid said. It was one of the models without eyes. "Nonregulation."

It's not against regulation to carry something in your pocket! she wanted to protest. But she remained silent. Only now did she realize her bracelet had been her lone, wordless defiance of the Empire—the one way in which she had refused to become entirely their creation. Now they had snatched that away from her. More than that, they had taken away Wynnet's window on the universe. Ciena lived her life for her sister no longer; Wynnet had fallen into darkness forever.

Ciena had no faith in the Empire, no loyalty, no friends, and not one possession to tie her to her homeworld. The galaxy was again slipping into chaos and anarchy. And she would never see Thane again. All she could do was lie there, helpless, as machines spent torturous months making her ready to serve again in a military force she now wanted no part of.

She closed her eyes and slipped into the strange space between imagination and dream. In her mind she took her TIE fighter in again, but this time she aimed for the deck. If she could slam into the deck hard enough, her ship would explode and she could stop worrying, stop hurting. She could just stop.

CHAPTER TWENTY-SIX

MEDICAL LEAVE demanded absolutely nothing of Imperial officers—primarily because officers who could not make quick recoveries were most often declared unfit for service. Rumors said the medical droids also treated those with severe injuries that involved long recovery times last, to better dedicate their resources to those who could serve the Empire again sooner.

Now Ciena was in the almost unique position of spending several months on medical leave, with no responsibilities. She was assigned to the space station Wrath mostly because it had room for a completely extraneous person. Nash had teased her about the golden opportunity to read holonovels or watch old spice-world dramas, but Ciena didn't want that much free time. It would only force her to think.

At least she got to undergo bacta therapy. They submerged her in the gooey stuff for at least a couple of hours every day, sometimes longer. Sedatives were always administered first, the better to ward off the severe claustrophobia that sometimes led bacta patients to panic and reinjure themselves. Ciena welcomed the moment the wretched life-support belt was taken off her body; she liked it even more when the needle slid into her arm, and the resulting darkness from the sedatives. Sometimes the stupor afterward lasted for hours.

During the brief periods when she was awake and cogent, however, she insisted on working.

Bridge duty was beyond her; piloting was impossible. So Ciena volunteered for one of the messiest, most complicated tasks facing the Imperial Starfleet in the wake of Endor—and one of the only jobs she didn't mind doing. Her mission was to confirm which Imperial officers were alive or dead, learn the definite locations of all survivors, and inform family members of the deaths.

(Supposedly, the death notices were her lowest priority. But Ciena spent far more time reaching out to those families than she ever did looking for a missing survivor who might have deserted. Through a little tricky record keeping and an excess of caution, she was able to avoid tracking down even one of those.)

In the wake of the Emperor's demise, the galaxy endured even greater chaos than Ciena had believed possible. Coruscant remained in turmoil; Grand Vizier Mas Amedda tried to keep the Empire together even as other forces threatened to tear it apart. Consolidating and confirming personnel information was hardly a top priority. So the Star Destroyers had only their own records to draw from, and even when that information was synthesized, the picture remained spotty at best.

To further complicate the situation, neither Ciena nor any other Imperial officer could be certain exactly which person they served. Declarations of a new emperor were so frequent as to be meaningless. No one figure seemed able to consolidate power. Already the propaganda holos spoke of "skirmishes" or "mutinies." The truth: would-be emperors forced Imperial soldiers to fight one another, spilling their blood in the service not of law and order but of one man's naked ambition. They seemed willing to tear the Empire to shreds rather than give up their own standing, Ciena thought with contempt. Already the Anoat sector had been cut off completely. What planets might fall next?

As for the rebels—they'd established their authority on worlds of their own. The only reports that emerged sounded so sunny Ciena believed they were propaganda, too, simply coming from the other side.

At least now there are entire systems safe for Thane, she sometimes thought. *He's no longer a hunted man.* Would he still be with the rebel armada? Ciena wasn't sure. It depended on whether he'd decided to trust this "New Republic" as much as he'd trusted the Rebellion.

Or whether he'd died in the Battle of Endor.

The rebels might have won the day, but they'd taken terrible losses, too. Ciena believed—illogically but unshakably—that she would have recognized Thane amid the melee. Didn't she know exactly how he flew? Wasn't that as unique to him as a fingerprint or a genetic code?

Even if that were so, it meant only that she hadn't killed Thane herself.

Any number of other TIE pilots could have killed him. Or he could have been flying too close to one of the star cruisers when the Death Star's laser struck. Maybe he had been among the pilots who flew into the station and smashed against the metal framework inside.

Don't think about that, she would tell herself as she sat at her portable data terminal, propped on a med-chaise. Lying down helped her bear the pincer grip of the life support belt doing the work of her still-healing liver.

You have to believe he's alive somewhere. If you can't have faith in any-thing else, you can still believe in Thane.

And yet sometimes Ciena felt that he must be dead. The galaxy could only feel that empty, meaningless, if he were no longer in it.

So she buried herself in her work, patiently untangling every bureaucratic knot, locating and rescuing marooned ships and garrisons, and helping families mourn their dead. In that small way she could uphold some measure of law and order amid the chaos; nothing else seemed worth doing. Her only comforts were the sedation of the bacta tank and sleep. Ciena could ignore everything else for days at a time.

Then weeks.

Then months.

Thane hadn't expected the Empire to collapse over-night. Some of the cockeyed optimists around him had woken up the morning after the Death Star's destruction talking about how they finally lived in a liberated galaxy, breathed free air, and other nonsense. He had patched up his X-wing and awaited the inevitable call to the next battle.

But he'd never expected to still be fighting a full-out war almost a year after the Battle of Endor.

"Incoming!" Yendor shouted through the comms.

Thane whipped his X-wing around to see another phalanx of TIE fighters zooming toward them over the crest of the cliffs on Naboo. These must have been the very last stragglers of the attack force that had descended on the planet the day before. Luckily, the New Republic's fleet had received a tip from defectors; when the Imperial ships came out of hyperspace, Thane's squadron and several dozen other starfighters had been waiting. Since then, he'd been finishing them off, one by one, just like he was doing right now. He fired even as his ship sliced through the air sideways, and he took grim satisfaction in watching three of the TIEs explode.

The others in Corona Squadron took care of the rest. The planet was clear now, or close to it. Kendy took a hit to her starboard wing but still managed to land her starfighter smoothly alongside the others on the broad pavilion outside the Theed Royal Palace. Kendy burst out of her cockpit swearing, which made the others laugh. "Come on," Thane called. "You've taken worse than that."

"Yeah, and I'm sick and tired of it!" She grabbed her tool kit and got to work.

The rest of them had a moment to breathe. Corona Squadron was different now; the Contessa had left, returning to her homeworld to stand for the presidency. (The others had all promised to show up for her inauguration if she won.) Yendor had taken over as Corona Leader, and two new pilots had joined them—one a rookie from Nea Dajanam, the other an exile from Coruscant. But Thane liked them both and felt good about how the team had come together. He leaned against the side of his ship, relishing the warmth of the sun on his face. Moments of peace like this came too rarely.

Naboo had been Palpatine's homeworld. As such, it had become a rallying point for Imperial sympathizers. Besides its symbolic importance, Naboo was a prosperous Mid Rim world, its economy and environment far healthier than those of most planets that had been under Imperial rule. As such, it was one of the most contested spots in the entire galaxy.

Three times now, the Empire had sent troops to invade; three times they'd been beaten back. Thane wondered how long it would take them to come back for number four.

"Hey," Yendor said as he helped JJH2 from his ship. "Some of us were going into Otoh Gunga tonight—if we don't get any more alerts, that is. Apparently there's this dessert they make there that takes at least four hominids to eat. They say it melts in your mouth and delivers you straight into a glorious sugar coma. You know you want a piece."

"No, thanks," Thane answered, but with a smile. His friends tried hard to look after him, but some things you had to go through on your own. "You guys have fun. I'll take night watch at the hangar."

Yendor shook his head, his long blue lekku swaying with the movement, but wandered off without further argument.

Jelucan had very specific mourning rituals. At least, the valley kindred did. Thane had learned about them from Ciena—and wasn't sure he remembered all the details correctly—but he was doing his best. (Jelucan remained under Imperial control, so Thane couldn't ask Paron Ree for advice or even give his condolences.) Thane wanted to weave and wear a bracelet so Ciena could see through his eyes, but she'd told him that honor was reserved for family. As dimly as he recalled the customary rituals for friends, they seemed elaborate enough and lasted for a full year after a person's death. He wore a cloth tied around his upper arm and would not remove it until the entire year was up. At the six-month mark, he'd prepared the customary meal of wine and bread to be left out at night for the spirits. He hoped it didn't have to be special bread, or some particular wine; he'd done the best he could with what he had. As Thane understood it, he didn't have to refrain from *all* leisure activity, but the ritual required him to spend several hours a week in meditation.

Okay, he wasn't exactly *good* at the meditation thing, but he tried.

Big symbolic gestures usually weren't Thane's style— but after Endor, he had needed to ground himself in some way and had no idea where to begin. In his desperation, he had sought Ciena in the rituals of her people. To his surprise he found the experience healing.

He mourned for everyone who had been lost: Smikes, Dak Ralter, the kindly Mon Calamari of the *Liberty*, countless other pilots he'd known . . . and for Jude Edivon and other cadets he'd known at the academy who had died on one of the Death Stars or in other battles. The Empire might have demanded that they sacrifice their souls, but at one point, the majority of those people had been no worse than any others. All that was good in them had been lost to the Empire and to the war; surely that was worth grieving for.

His meditations had led him to another unexpected place, a viewpoint he'd never expected to have—the New Republic truly had been worth the fight.

Sure, the transition had been uneven. With the war still ongoing, Mon Mothma, Princess Leia Organa,

Sondiv Sella, and other top officials could not establish total stability. Yet the provisional Galactic Senate contained only representatives chosen by the will of the people, and the first laws they'd passed had righted the worst wrongs of the Empire. Even the bickering on news holos about the merits of each proposal was wonderful, because it meant people were free to express their opinions without fear of Imperial reprisal. Resources weren't directed only toward the military; mass cleanups of polluted worlds had already begun, as had reparations for the species enslaved during Imperial rule. (Lohgarra said she was going to spend her share on new engines for the *Mighty Oak Apocalypse*.) However imperfectly, the course of the galaxy had turned toward justice and maybe, someday, peace.

Thane had never tried being an idealist before, but he thought he was starting to get the hang of it.

As he settled in for a long evening at the hangar, Kendy strolled over from her X-wing. He said, "Got it fixed?"

"Pretty much. I need a Louar clamp to finish up, but I can borrow one from Yendor tomorrow morning." She leaned against the wall, arms crossed in front of her. Her dark green hair flowed freely down her shoulders. "So. You're staying in tonight?"

"As usual."

"You're going to be here by yourself for *hours*."

"Yeah, I am. I'm going to sit on this comfortable chair with a good holonovel, underneath one of the most beautiful skies I've ever seen, on a world where the air's still clean and the birds still sing. Nobody's going to fire a blaster at me even once. After years of war, a peaceful night like that is my definition of a good time."

"Happy eightieth birthday, by the way."

"Come on." Thane had to grin. "You have to admit I have a point."

Kendy laughed. "I know. It's just—weird, you going all mystical and spiritual and stuff."

"I'm not." So many of the rituals had felt strange and false to him; yet Thane believed he'd gotten something out of the mere attempt. "This is just a thing I have to do."

"I get that. But will you answer one question for me?" Thane nodded, and she asked, "How long are you going to wear that?"

She pointed toward the strip of slate blue cloth still tied around his right upper arm. That was the Jelucani color of mourning—the shade of the sky in which they buried their dead.

"Once I've worn it for one year," Thane said, "I'll take it off."

"We're only a few weeks from the anniversary of the Battle of Endor. Is that when you'll finally be over Ciena's death?"

She hadn't understood anything. "No. It's the day I'll stop following mourning practices. But I'm not over Ciena's death. I never will be."

"That is . . . more melodramatic than I expected from you, Thane Kyrell."

He shrugged. "It's not melodrama. It's the truth." How could he get through to her? Slowly Thane said, "What we were to each other—when I lost Ciena, I lost a piece of myself. You don't get over that. You always feel the empty place where they used to be."

Ciena winced, holding her hand to her midsection. The medical droids had finally cleared her for active duty, but the pain lingered. Maybe it always would.

She straightened herself up and smoothed her jacket. When she'd put in her requisition order for new uniforms, she'd ordered them in the same size she'd always worn. Now, however, the clothes hung slightly big on her frame. She'd lost too much weight this past year. At least the cap fit.

According to her duty roster, her first task was to meet with Grand Moff Randd on the main bridge of the Wrath. Ciena could only assume that he would brief her on her new duties—though most commanders didn't receive their orders from anyone who ranked as high as Grand Moff.

Then again, those days all the old protocols had broken down. She could take nothing for granted.

Ciena walked to the bridge, waited until two minutes before her scheduled arrival, and then entered. Top officers liked it when you were early but not *too* early. The Wrath's bridge differed from that of a Star Destroyer; instead of data pits, more junior officers were located on long banks of stations that lined the vast octagonal room. No windows revealed Ponemah, the world that they orbited; after almost a year on the station, Ciena still knew nothing of that planet, not even what it looked like from space. The only view came from the enormous transparent dome overhead, which showed the endless field of stars. Yet a few elements remained familiar, such as the dull reddish glow of the lights at floor level, the mesh metal floors, and the sense of tension—even fear. She could take no comfort in any of that.

Grand Moff Randd stood at the far end of the bridge, his rank obvious from his rigid, imposing posture alone. He was pointing out battle plans to a few other officers, the images displayed on a two-dimensional screen that covered one of the shorter walls. Ciena expected to remain at attention behind him until such time as he was free to notice her—but as she came close, someone called out, "Commander Ciena Ree on the bridge, sir."

Randd turned—as did virtually everyone else in the room. Ciena's eyes widened as she saw Nash standing nearby, smiling almost like his old self. Why would he be here? Why had all these people stopped and risen to their feet?

"Well, Commander Ree." Randd smiled. "You return to active duty at last."

"Yes, sir." Ciena did not allow her expression to reveal any of the confusion she felt. Yet her heart pounded madly as she wondered if this were some sort of trap. Maybe they'd somehow guessed her lack of faith in the Empire and intended to make an example of her. . . .

"Hear this," Randd said to all those assembled in the room. "At the Battle of Endor, Ree fought bravely and very nearly sacrificed her own life in our effort to save the late Emperor Palpatine. During her long recovery, no one could have blamed her had she taken the rest she deserved. Instead, Ree took on the most difficult and complicated tasks that would help restore order to the Imperial Starfleet. While others schemed for their own gain, she shared information equally and without ever asking for special favors in return."

That wasn't anything heroic. That was the bare minimum required by duty. Had everyone else in the Imperial Starfleet completely abandoned their responsibilities to their fellow officers? Despite her disillusionment, Ciena couldn't help feeling contempt for those who had so callously shirked their responsibilities out of craven ambition or cowardice.

"In these times, few have proved themselves worthy of their rank. You have, Ree." Randd walked to the viewscreen as he added, "No doubt you expect me to inform you of your new assignment. Well, here she is."

On the viewscreen behind him, the battle schematics vanished and were replaced by the image of a Star Destroyer; an on-screen legend identified it as the *Inflictor*.

Randd said, "Herewith I present your first command, Captain Ree."

Applause broke out through the bridge, and Nash even cheered. She covered her mouth, too astonished to know how to react.

Ciena's first thought was the truest: *The Imperial Starfleet is in worse shape than I thought.*

Her service might have been exemplary, but even so, under normal circumstances an officer so young would never be considered for command of a Star Destroyer. Even if she'd been promoted to the rank of captain, she shouldn't have been given a ship like this. *The power plays and attempted coups have thinned the ranks. Everyone else with seniority has either defected to one of the splinter fleets or been eliminated.*

Deep within her, the piece of Ciena's soul that remembered her old love for the Empire wanted to take pride in this. *Captain before age twenty-five! Commander of a Star Destroyer!* These were honors she hadn't even dared to dream of back when she was an idealistic cadet.

Now, however, the promotion was only one more burden to bear.

"Sir," Ciena managed to say. "Thank you, sir."

Grand Moff Randd seemed pleased with his little show. No doubt he saw it as a demonstration to his underlings that anything was possible if they were only loyal and worked hard. She had once believed that herself. What a fool she'd been.

Numbly, she joined the procession down to the docking bay where she would board her new command.

Randd kept speaking the entire time. "Commander Brisney will be your ISB officer—ship systems are under the care of Commander Erisher—and as for your flight commander, I believe you already know Commander Windrider."

She turned to see Nash walking at her side, slightly behind, still beaming. Only now did she notice the changed rank on his insignia plaque; no doubt hers awaited on the bridge of the *Inflictor*.

"Congratulations, Ciena," he said. "I've hardly heard from you since I shipped out on the *Subjugator*."

"I'm sorry, I—"

"Don't be silly. I understand completely. Between the ordeal of your recovery and all the work you've done, I'm surprised you even found time to sleep." Nash showed no sign of jealousy or suspicion. Maybe he'd even gotten over his crush on her in the ten months they hadn't seen each other. In some ways, his guileless trust was harder to bear. "I only meant I look forward to seeing you regularly again."

"Every day," Ciena said, without expression.

After another brief ceremony on the *Inflictor*'s bridge, Ciena pinned her new insignia plaque to her uniform and went into the briefing room with Grand Moff Randd for a classified conference. As soon as they were seated, Randd's smile faded. Only the cool tactician remained.

"We're headed toward a major standoff with the rebels," he said. "We're committing a fair portion of the fleet, and if the damned Rebellion wants to stand a chance of keeping that sector, they'll have to do the same. This promises to be the largest battle since Endor." His long finger jabbed at the controls, and an image of a planet in brown, russet, and gold hovered above the holo-projector. "Here we have the desert world of Jakku—worthless on its own but soon to live forever in history as the place where the Empire defeated the Rebellion once and for all."

Maybe it would. Maybe they'd be sent limping away in defeat. Ciena didn't know or care. She only understood that despite her disillusionment with the Empire, she had to fight. The alternative would be to surrender to the rebels, and she could imagine how they dealt with captured enemies. And if she deserted her post as captain of a Star Destroyer, the Force alone knew what would become of her family—especially her mother, still enduring her forced-labor sentence in prison. Ciena had hardly had a chance to think of escape during her recovery, and now it was too late. There was no way out for her, not anymore.

Everything Ciena had worked for her whole life was a sham. Now she would continue this war only because she had no choice.

Jakku, she thought, looking at the world and imagining the battle that lay ahead. *Let it come.*

CHAPTER TWENTY-SEVEN

THANE DIDN'T LIKE the idea of going into battle without his X-wing. However, General Rieekan had insisted.

"We need people like you and Lieutenant Idele who have served on Imperial ships in the past," Rieekan said as Thane, Kendy, and other troops boarded a transport. "It's this simple—we need more vessels, and we need them faster than they can be built, especially while the Empire still holds most of the main construction facilities. The only way we're going to get those ships is by capturing them from the Empire."

Thane managed to respond to this politely, instead of with the scorn it deserved. "Sir, with all due respect, nobody has ever captured a Star Destroyer. And don't tell me it's because no one has ever tried. Yeah, way back in the day, we managed to take out a governor's destroyer over Mustafar, but since then, the Imperials have shored up their defenses against infiltrators. These days Star Destroyers are nearly invulnerable."

"Those crews aren't as die-hard as they used to be," Rieekan insisted. "We've had ships as large as attack cruisers switch allegiance in other battles, haven't we?"

"Those have thousands of crew members. Not *tens* of thousands."

"We only need enough sympathizers to help us shut systems down. Only former Imperial officers such as you and Idele can lead us to the most vulnerable areas."

Grudgingly, Thane took Rieekan's point. If they could get one of the auxiliary bridges, the engine room, and a couple of the gunneries under New Republic control, they could effectively paralyze a Star Destroyer. Actually claiming the ship would require intense intravessel combat, lasting days if not weeks—but it was possible.

A long shot. An *extremely* long shot. Yet possible.

"I feel so cooped up in here," Kendy grumbled as they took their places in the hold, harnessing themselves into slender seats that were more like those for a hoverbike than a space journey. "We can't even see the battle."

Thane found it incredibly strange, too—looking at the flat beige walls of the troop transport instead of the vastness of space, hearing not the hum of his engines or the screech of his guns but only the murmur of other nervous soldiers. "Maybe that's for the best," he said, though he didn't believe it. "We can focus on our plans for boarding."

Kendy leaned closer, glancing about her to make sure nobody overheard before she spoke. "Neither of us was ever posted to a Star Destroyer. I've only even *been* on one three times, and never for more than a day."

"We studied the schematics at the academy," he said as confidently as he could manage. "We both remember the most important information—especially about internal defenses. That's enough."

She sighed. "May the Force be with us."

Always the Force. Thane's year of meditation had not convinced him that there was any all-powerful Force at work behind galactic affairs. Still, let Kendy take her courage where she could find it.

Maybe he wouldn't have felt so uneasy if any element of the mission was familiar, but none of it was. Being without his X-wing was by far the worst; he'd have felt safer shooting down TIE fighters than running into the heart of a Star Destroyer. Yet smaller details rankled, too. Instead of his sturdy, full-cover helmet, he wore only a small one that fastened under his chin with an uncomfortable black strap. Instead of his orange flight suit, he wore a simple uniform of trousers, shirt, and vest that he associated more with days off than with battle. And around one arm was tied his grayish-blue mourning band.

Technically he should have taken it off four days ago, on the anniversary of the Battle of Endor. By then, however, Thane had known the Battle of Jakku was coming, and it had felt right to take it with him into the fray.

Once this battle is over, I'll take it off, he promised himself. *I'll burn it as the ritual commands, and I'll save the ashes until the day I return to Jelucan.*

In his mind's eye, he could already see himself entering the Fortress for the very last time. He would put the ashes there, with the old toys and the cast-off boots, and the pallet of blankets and furs where he and Ciena had made love. Then, at last, he could begin again.

"Which Destroyer is this?" Thane asked, wondering if it would be one he'd ever seen.

"The *Inflictor*," someone answered. He'd never heard of that one.

"At least they issued us blasters," Kendy muttered. "I'm even better with a blaster than I am with laser cannons."

"Then I'll stick by you," he said, and was rewarded with her smile.

"All hands," came the voice over the intercom, unnaturally calm. "Brace for impact."

Thane grabbed the straps of his harness. *Here we go.*

Whatever else Ciena Ree was, she was not a traitor. During the few short weeks she had served as captain of the *Inflictor*, she had done her duty to the very best of her ability. If she felt no loyalty to the Empire any longer, she understood her responsibility for the hundreds of thousands of lives under her command. So she had not given anything less than her best during the Battle of Jakku.

If other Imperial officers could have said the same, maybe they wouldn't be on the verge of annihilation.

"Status report!" Ciena called out as she walked closer to the data pits.

"Engine three is only at sixty-six percent capacity, Captain." The young ensign's face looked up at hers, his ruddy skin flushed with panic. "Engines one and five are still completely down. We only have full power on engines three and seven. Two, four, and six are each under thirty percent power."

Damn. If her repair crews could get engine two back up above 85 percent, they would still be able to jump into hyperspace and escape the battle. If they couldn't fix it—or if engine three took damage, too—the *Inflictor* was trapped. No option but retreat offered any chance of survival.

The main viewscreen displayed a disastrous panorama. Against the brownish-gold surface of Jakku were silhouetted hundreds of ships, both Imperial and rebel, from frigates and other Star Destroyers down to countless starfighters. Meanwhile, smaller screens on either side showed scenes of the ground battle, which was proving to be even more of a rout. Even as she watched, a walker took one hit too many, wobbled on its slender legs, then fell sideways so hard that sand exploded from the impact like a tidal wave. Everywhere Ciena looked, the rebels were attacking while the Empire tried in vain to defend itself. The advantage had been theirs from the beginning, to a point that made her wonder bitterly if the whole battle had been a trap. Maybe their plans for making a stand at Jakku had been betrayed by some admiral or Grand Moff whose power play had been thwarted.

"We need a change in strategy," she said, mostly to herself. Imperial battle tactics nearly always called for concerted, simultaneous effort by all ships engaged in combat, rigidly controlled by a central command.

When the Empire had possessed the advantage in strength and numbers, those tactics had made sense. Now Ciena thought they were clinging to the rules of a game that had ended more than a year ago.

The rebels had proved that smaller strike forces could be effective, even deadly. They often attacked on multiple fronts at once, segmenting their forces. That approach was riskier, but there above Jakku, it was getting results.

The *Inflictor* shuddered. Although the sensation was no more than a faint vibration beneath her chair, Ciena knew the damage was significant even before control screens lit up red.

"Explosive decompression aft starboard!" cried an ensign. "Losing atmosphere—"

"Seal off all affected decks!" With those words, Ciena knew, she had saved her ship—but condemned hundreds if not thousands to death by suffocation.

We can't keep fighting by the old rules. It's futile.

Ciena went to a viewscreen and pulled up a three-dimensional view of the battle, in miniature. If she could convince Grand Moff Randd to split up the fleet, to attack the rebel star cruisers from multiple directions, maybe even to send one of the twenty-gun raiders into the atmosphere to support the TIE fighters battling near the planet's surface—at the very least they'd shake the rebels up. They desperately needed any advantage they could claim.

Would Randd even listen to her? She might be captain of a Star Destroyer, but he was a Grand Moff, and he'd subtly made it clear that she owed her rise in rank entirely to him. . . .

Once again it struck her how absurd it was—how foolish, how wasteful, how *stupid*—that rank mattered more than ideas in the Imperial fleet. It angered her. It disgusted her. She hated the Empire she served, hated the values it stood for, hated the way everyone talked about Palpatine as though he were some virtuous martyr. She hated herself for having ever believed in it. Mostly she hated that it was all she had left.

But then she saw the other officers scrambling around her, trying so hard to fulfill their duty and to survive. Ciena owed it to them, at least, to do her best. If she had no other task worth the doing, she could simply try to get them home.

She began, "Open a channel to Grand Moff Ra—"

The entire ship trembled, hard enough to knock officers' caps from their heads and spill at least two analysts onto the floor. Ciena braced herself against the wall. "What was that?"

"Captain, we show another hull breach, port side, on decks RR through ZZ." The young officer's face betrayed her confusion. She looked up at Ciena, her skin tinted red by the light. "But sensors reveal no sign of vacuum."

Then the *Inflictor* shook with another impact. Another. A fourth. Each resulted in the same bizarre readings: gaps in the ship that had not resulted in vacuum. There could be only one explanation.

Ciena's gut dropped. Although she'd never been aboard a ship when this had happened, she had learned the signs in the academy and relived them sometimes in her nightmares. "We've been boarded."

Boarded. In the pitch of battle, that meant only one thing:

Her ship had to die.

"Get to the control center for engine three," Thane ordered through his comlink as he edged down a corridor already thick with smoke. "If we can take out their last fully functioning main engine, we have a chance."

Thane's job was simpler and far more critical. He had to disconnect the self-destruct systems as soon as possible. Not one Imperial officer would hesitate before ordering the mass suicide necessary to keep a Star Destroyer out of New Republic hands.

Ahead of him, along a perpendicular corridor, he saw blaster fire; the echoes of each shot ricocheted off his eardrums with painful intensity. Through the tinny ringing in his head, Thane could hear other reports coming in. Contrary to Rieekan's prediction, the crew of the *Inflictor* was putting up stiff resistance. The Imperial troops aboard this ship seemed to be more dedicated than most of the others. Just Thane's luck.

The blaster fire ahead cleared, and then Kendy's head appeared around the corner. "Cleared the way for you guys. Come on, let's go!"

Thane ran at the head of the platoon, hoping they could advance as far as the portside auxiliary bridge. If they could gain control of that, they'd be in a much better position to help the other New Republic soldiers throughout the ship.

But even as they charged into the next section, another wave of stormtroopers met them, blasters blazing. Thane flattened himself against the wall. The air smelled like ozone and smoke, and he saw no way out. *What do I do?*

They couldn't get to the self-destruct systems—not like this.

Which meant that, within minutes, the *Inflictor* would explode and kill them all.

Get through this, he told himself. *Go!*

"Captain Ree, you can't!" one of the junior ensigns protested. She couldn't have been more than seventeen. The Imperial fleet was stealing them from the remaining academies, even though they were still too young.

"I can and I must." Ciena took her seat as she mentally prepared herself for what she was going to do. More gently she added, "Don't be afraid, Ensign Perrin. We'll have time to get to the escape pods, and each of those is equipped with a homing device that will take it straight to the nearest Imperial vessel."

Perrin smiled shakily; around her, the other officers seemed to calm themselves, too. Why did regulations discourage speaking with any sense of moderation or compassion, when it sometimes did so much good?

At least the Empire's ruthlessness would help her after the battle. Once this was over—assuming they weren't all in a New Republic prison camp—Ciena would be called on to justify setting the self-destruct on a Star Destroyer, one of the most powerful and valuable ships in the Imperial Starfleet. She knew the game well enough to understand that any explanation she gave would be found inadequate. Before Endor, it would have resulted in a long, grueling prison sentence on Kessel; now, she would either be cashiered out of the service or executed on the spot. Ciena found she didn't care which.

"On my mark," Ciena said. "Prepare for self-destruct. Initiating in ten—nine—eight—"

The *Inflictor* shuddered again. Even loathing the Empire as she did, Ciena was too much a captain not to feel a pang at the wounds to her ship.

She finished, "Three—two—one. Initiate."

Ensign Perrin shoved down the lever that would set the self-destruct in motion. Ciena waited for the red lights, the siren, the automated announcement sending all crew to escape pods—her signal to seal the doors—but they never came. After the silence had lasted a moment too long, she raised herself from her chair to pull up ship schematics. Damage lights flashed in all the wrong places, in particular one area not far from the portside auxiliary bridge.

"They targeted the self-destruct systems," Ciena said, almost in disbelief. "They specifically took them offline."

Only a former Imperial officer would have known how to do that. In her head, she heard her father saying the words he'd told her once when she was only a child: *All traitors are damned.*

"Awaiting your orders, Captain," said a lieutenant standing in the data pits. She realized every person on the bridge—and probably throughout the ship—had no idea what to do next.

But she did.

The knowledge dawned inside her like the most beautiful day she'd ever seen. She could do her duty, fulfill her oath, and free herself from this madness forever.

Ciena returned to her chair and hit the switch that would project her voice to all stations and to every starfighter based aboard the *Inflictor*. "All hands, abandon ship. All starfighters, rendezvous with the next nearest Imperial vessel. All hands, abandon ship. You have ten minutes."

Around her, the rest of the officers stared. For the only time in her command, Ciena shouted at them. "What are you waiting for? Get to the escape pods! *Go!*"

As all of them dashed out, the comms crackled and buzzed. Ciena knew who it would be even before she heard the voice; only one person assigned to her ship would dare to question her now.

Nash yelled, *"Have you gone mad?"*

"Not sure what you mean, Commander Windrider."

"Don't you 'Commander Windrider' me, not now.

If the self-destruct were online, we'd have heard the automated signal. That tells me you're planning on destroying the ship by—some other means—"

Ciena sat back down in her black leather chair, as weary as if she hadn't slept in years. "Just say it."

". . . you're going to crash the *Inflictor* into the planet."

She began punching in the coordinates that would drive her straight into Jakku's surface. Already she could imagine the fire, the heat, the end.

Then she would have done her duty to the last and yet escaped all the ties that bound her to the Empire, forever.

"I have to keep the *Inflictor* out of rebel hands no matter what." Ciena tried to imagine she was talking to the boy she'd known at the academy, the boy who kept his hair long and braided back in Alderaanian fashion and whose impish sense of humor made them all laugh. "This is the only way, Nash."

"The hell it is. You can set the coordinates and get out of there."

"And leave the ship to the rebels? They'd take the bridge, change course, and fly off with their new Star Destroyer." She leaned her head back and stared up at the metal-tiled ceiling, so absurdly high overhead. Was the scale of the bridge meant to represent a kind of grandeur? Instead it only made the space feel empty and cold.

"Ciena, please." She could hear Nash's voice break, even over the distant roar of his TIE's engines. "At least tell me you'll try."

That was the last thing she wanted to do. Now that Ciena had found her way out, she felt only relief. The pain of merely existing day to day had become wholly clear to her only now that it had lifted, and she didn't have to bear it one hour more.

"I have to lock the doors now," she said. "Good-bye."

With that, she snapped off the comm connection to all TIE fighters. Never would she hear Nash's voice again.

As she went through the procedure for the bridge doors' security locks, Ciena thought of the other things she'd never again experience. Being with her parents. Flying a starfighter or, better yet, a V-171 she could take up above the clouds on Jelucan. Laughing at one of Berisse's dirty jokes. Trying to wake Jude up in the morning and hearing her usually logical friend whine into her pillow. Riding her muunyak along the mountain ridges. Piloting a speeder bike through Reitgen Hoops. Eating Mr. Nierre's snow-frosting cakes. Running on the Sky Loop while Coruscant glittered beneath her.

Being with Thane. Making love with him. Flying with him.

"Good-bye," she repeated softly, saying farewell to it all.

Thane froze in place the moment he heard the announcement. As the voice echoed through the corridors of the *Inflictor*, telling all hands to abandon ship, he tried to convince himself that it couldn't be her—

—but he could never mistake Ciena's voice.

"We just took out the self-destruct!" Kendy shouted. She didn't seem to have recognized the voice over the speakers. "How are they going to blow this thing?"

He knew what Ciena would do as surely as if he'd come up with the plan himself. "She's going to crash it." Quickly he grabbed the comm link that connected him to Rieekan. "We need to get everyone the hell out of here, now. If they can't reach our troop transports, they should go for the Imperial escape pods. Lights will mark the way."

Kendy, like everyone else on the blast-charred auxiliary bridge, began running for the pods even before Rieekan gave the orders Thane had suggested. Yet just as she cleared the final step down and got to the doors, she realized Thane wasn't following suit. "What are you doing? Didn't you hear? We've got less than ten minutes."

"I'll catch up," he lied. "Go." Kendy gave him a look, but she obeyed Rieekan's orders and ran to safety, leaving Thane alone.

Ciena was alive. She was alive, she was *there*, and he had to get to her before she killed them both.

Thane dashed for the farthest corner of the auxiliary bridge, where his dusty memories of Large Vessel Design told him he'd find a repair shaft. Sure enough, one of the metal mesh panels pulled away, revealing a plain, cold tunnel leading upward. He slammed his hand against the switch by the door, summoning the antigrav platform that could take him to any deck he wanted within moments.

When it appeared, he jumped on—then reeled as he grabbed for its safety handle. Thane had never actually ridden one of those things. They were more unstable than his classes had made them sound. A few more centimeters and he would have slipped from the platform and plummeted several kilometers to his death.

One deep breath and then he punched in the code that would take him to the deck where he could reach the main bridge.

As he flew upward at top speed, the gusts of air

yanked at his helmet until he pulled it off and let it fall. Thane tried to get a sense of how much time had elapsed. Three minutes? Four? By now the *Inflictor*'s engines didn't have to do any more work; Jakku's gravity would take care of the rest. Even now the planet was pulling the Star Destroyer down toward its doom.

Come on, he thought, gripping the safety handle even more tightly. *Come on!*

Finally he reached the right deck, kicked in the security plate there, and emerged into a corridor. After a moment's disorientation, he could have smacked himself for his idiocy; of course the main bridge wouldn't be so easily accessible. Thane ran for the doors, then skidded to a stop as they failed to open for him.

"Ciena!" he shouted, banging his fist against the metal. That was only to take out his frustration, because he knew she couldn't hear him through the blast doors to the main bridge. Not only were they too thick for sound to carry, but they also couldn't be destroyed by blasters or lasers, not even by a thermal detonator. She had sealed out every possible invader, including him.

But there were only so many ways for a captain to seal the blast doors.

Thane realized he knew which way Ciena would choose; he'd heard her explain, once. She would use the captain's-word method. Now the blast doors were permanently shut to anyone who didn't know the word or phrase she had chosen to lock herself in.

He leaned his forehead against the metal and put his hand to the manual entry panel. An automated voice said, "State the password."

Leaning down to the speaker, Thane whispered, "Look through my eyes."

CHAPTER TWENTY-EIGHT

CIENA BENT OVER the navigation station, one hand splayed across her aching abdomen, the other resting on the controls. The autonav system had repeatedly attempted to override her commands, but she'd finally managed to shut it down. Now all she had to do was wait.

She stepped back and sank into her chair. On the viewscreen ahead, the stars had been erased; nothing remained but the sandy surface of Jakku. With every second, the view of the world below became clearer. Ciena watched shadows expand into deserts and mountains. Sensors began to flare red, warning her of atmosphere breach. She ignored them.

At one point her vision blurred. When she lifted her hand to her face, her fingers came away wet. Ciena blinked quickly to clear her eyes. When her end came, she would not flinch. She wouldn't turn away. It was the last experience she would ever have, and she intended to be fully present for every single moment, even the pain.

To die with honor—no one could ask for more—

The bridge's blast doors slid open.

Ciena jumped to her feet. By instinct she reached for her blaster, but no Star Destroyer captain carried one on the bridge. How could anyone have gotten in?

Then she saw Thane.

The one person in the Rebellion—in the entire galaxy—*who could have guessed the right words to say,* Ciena thought in a daze, *and of course he's here.*

Maybe she was dreaming, or hallucinating. Her brain had conjured up an image of Thane so she wouldn't believe she had to die alone. He even wore a mourning band around one bicep, grieving like one of the kindred for a tragedy that had yet to come.

But then he breathed out in relief, a sound so subtle and yet familiar that it erased all doubt. This was real. This was happening.

"Ciena." Thane began toward her, then stopped when she took a step back. He paused and lifted his hands as if to show he held no weapon . . . but she could see the blaster strapped to his side. "It's okay. I'm going to get you out of here."

"I'm not leaving." The words seemed to come from a very great distance, as if she were hearing them instead of speaking them. "I'll stay with my ship."

"You know, we can have a long talk about honor and duty later. Right now, we need to get the hell off this thing before we're in full-on atmospheric entry."

Escape pods could handle planetary landings, but launching within the atmosphere was hazardous. Already the temperature readings outside the hull were climbing dramatically. Ciena felt her pulse quicken with fear—not for herself. "Thane, go to the nearest escape pod."

He lifted his chin, like the stubborn, prideful boy he'd been so long ago. "Not without you."

Anger flared in her. "You realize I ought to arrest you right now? Or shoot you?"

"We're kind of outside the regulations here already." Thane held out his hand to her, but she took another step away from him. Less than two meters separated them now. To either side of them, on the countless viewscreens and sensors, alarm lights flashed and scenes of battle and bloodshed flickered.

"You have to go! Don't you understand I'm trying to save your life?"

"I'm trying to save yours!" He had looked at her that pleadingly, that desperately, when he had first tried to talk her into deserting the Empire with him. For Thane, perhaps, nothing had changed in the five years since. She felt so much older. So much sadder. Hollowed out. But he kept standing there, his hand outstretched, believing he could rescue them both. "Come on, Ciena. We don't have much time."

Thane didn't see that there was no time left for her, none at all.

What have they done to her?

Ciena stood before him, so thin that she looked as if she could be crushed in a man's fist. Her uniform hung on her, and that combined with the frantically blinking warning lights going off all around them made the scene seem more like some ugly parody of an Imperial bridge than the real thing. What scared Thane most, though, was the blankness in her eyes. Nothing of Ciena's spirit shone through; he saw only anger and despair.

But his Ciena was still in there. He knew that only because she wanted to die rather than keep serving the Empire.

"Listen to me," Thane said, trying hard to sound calm even as the *Inflictor* shuddered with its first real brush with Jakku's atmosphere. The ride would only get rougher. "You don't owe the Empire a damned thing. They don't deserve your loyalty, and they definitely don't deserve your life."

"You don't even know what loyalty means."

"The hell I don't! Ciena, if I weren't loyal to you, would I be here?"

The ship shuddered again. Thane stumbled slightly to one side, and Ciena had to grab her chair to remain upright. She shouted, "Thane, you have to go! You have to get in an escape pod now!"

"I won't leave you here." He realized it could come to that—dying by Ciena's side, here, today, rather than escaping with his own life.

Thane wanted to survive. As much as he loved Ciena, he knew from the past year that he was capable of going on after her death, even healing and finding peace.

But he didn't want to live as the man who had left her behind to die.

He repeated, "I won't leave you."

"Please!" Ciena had begun to shake. "Please don't make me responsible for your death. All I ever asked, in all those battles, was not to be the one who killed you."

"I asked for it to be you. Because we're bound,

always, you and I—in life or in death. You know it as well as I do. That's why we have to get off this ship *together*."

Ciena remained silent for a long moment. The ship tilted to one side, artificial gravity warring with the real thing tugging them toward Jakku. On the viewscreen, the image of the planet's surface slowly swirled; the ship had begun spiraling down.

Then she took one step toward him, and another. Thane could have wept with relief. "Good. That's right. Come with me."

She stood before him at last. Their eyes met. And Ciena punched him in the gut, hard.

As Thane sprawled on the floor, Ciena grabbed his blaster from its holster. She stood above him and he stared at her, trying to catch the breath she'd knocked out of him. "Is that it?" he said. "You're going to shoot me?"

"Of course not," she said. "I'm going to stun you and drag you to an escape pod myself. But—before that— you know I'm only doing this to save you, don't—?"

Thane kicked her in the leg so firmly that she stumbled back more than a meter before falling on her back. The blaster skidded across the tilted floor, sliding far away from them both, and Ciena had to struggle to get back to her feet.

He was up, too, in fighting stance, blue eyes blazing. "You want to play this rough? Fine. We'll play rough."

One memory flashed in her mind, of how they'd met back when they were children—fighting for each other.

It looked like they were going to die the same way.

Ciena ran at him, and he couldn't dodge her well enough to keep her from tackling him. As she slammed his head back onto the mesh floor, she shouted, "Get your rebel ass off my bridge!"

Thane threw her off, pushing her sideways. Even as she rolled against the wall, he said, "I'm going to rescue you whether you like it or not."

Didn't he understand? Didn't he see? Why was he trying to steal her one chance to escape this hell and die with her honor? It was as if Thane had never known her at all.

She kicked savagely at him; the heel of her boot caught his jaw and sent him reeling. Ciena scrambled to her feet, which was when she caught a glimpse of the viewscreen—the image of Jakku was terrifyingly close, but it began to blur and blacken. The outside sensors were burning off from the heat of atmospheric entry.

The windows were now brilliant orange, cutting off their view as the ship was sealed in flame. The warring factions in the atmosphere and on the ground would be able to see the *Inflictor* gashing a streak of fire across the sky like a meteor.

Thane grabbed Ciena's leg and pulled her to the floor; the impact of her fall sent new pain stabbing into her gut wound. Even as Ciena gasped for breath, Thane seized the advantage, pinning both her wrists with his own. "Just come with me," he said, panting. "You have to come with me *now*."

She brought her leg up to knee him in the side and freed her hands. Ciena wanted to tell him to stop being an idiot, to run for a pod now, because it would be too late soon, if it wasn't already—but all she could say was, "Let me go."

Then she brought her fists together and swung them upward into his jaw. If she had to knock him out the hard way, so be it.

Even as pain splintered through his face, Thane saw the viewscreen blur and go black. They were out of time.

So he did something he would never, ever have believed he could do. He hit Ciena back.

But Ciena was a small woman, and he was a large

man. The same blow to the jaw that had made him stagger sideways laid her flat. Guilt lashed him, but he couldn't stop, not now—

She shoved herself upward; her shoulder hit his midsection under his ribs and stole his breath. As they both crashed into a control panel, he thought, *Anyone watching would think we're trying to kill each other, not save each other.*

Power began to blink off and on as more components caught fire on entry. He heard a deep, terrible groan— the massive metal framework of the Star Destroyer shifting as the heat hit the melting point. Through the few small windows he could see nothing of Jakku or the sky, only flame.

Ciena pushed him away from her just as the floor tilted again. Now they were both sprawling, unable to stay upright. Thane scrambled to get a handhold on one of the chairs, a strut, anything that would help him up—

—when he saw a flash of black metal sliding along the wall.

He threw himself at it. Even as he rolled, he heard Ciena's boots on the deck as she somehow got back on her feet. She ran toward him, the thumping of her steps faster, just as Thane got the blaster in his hands.

One flick of the thumb, set to stun and—now!

He glimpsed one second of horror on Ciena's face before the blue bolt hit her. She collapsed to the floor so heavily that for an instant Thane feared he'd accidentally set the blaster to kill. But when he crawled across the tilting floor to reach her, he saw her chest rise and fall.

"I'll ask forgiveness later," he whispered. On his knees, Thane managed to roll Ciena over and pull her body over his shoulders. He tasted blood as he staggered to his feet and headed for the nearest escape pod.

His breakneck ride through the service tunnels had refreshed Thane's memory of Large Vessel Design class, so he was pretty sure he knew where the pods were. What he didn't know was whether or not he could even get one to launch. If the metal clamps had melted in the heat of atmospheric entry, the escape pod would be useless except as a place to die.

And of course the fleeing Imperials and escaping New Republic soldiers might have launched all the pods already—

Go, go, go, go, go, he chanted inside his head as he stumble-ran through the corridors of the Star Destroyer. The first pod location he reached showed empty; that one had been shot into space long ago. But just as Thane felt panic clutching at his mind, he got to a second location and saw an escape pod still there, waiting.

He hit the control panel with his knee, and the doors spiraled open. It was one of the smaller pods, but two people would fit. Thane dumped Ciena inside; as he crawled through the entry tube to join her, the lights suddenly went out. He was in pitch blackness, save for the scarlet firelight from the small porthole in the escape pod, which flickered across Ciena's fallen body.

The power was gone. Would the doors close? Would the pod launch? If the explosive latches had melted instead of blowing, they were sunk.

Thane slammed his hand against the launch switch. He'd never seen anything more beautiful than the doors spiraling shut. As they locked, a terrible deep groan shuddered through the ship, like the dying roar of some massive beast.

Then the pod launched, shooting them away from the *Inflictor*.

The jolt knocked him against the pod's curved wall, and Ciena rolled to the side. Thane crawled down beside her so he could brace her body against his. The limited repulsorlifts and acceleration compensators in an escape pod meant they had a rough ride ahead; he wasn't sure the thing's landing capacities would even work that close to the ground. Through the tiny porthole, he saw only brief flashes of blue, then gold, then blue, then gold—sky and sand tumbling over and over. Impact could be only seconds away.

He curled around Ciena, buried his face in the curve of her neck, and held on for the crash.

The pod hit the ground with a severe jolt—then again—and again. It was skipping across the sand, Thane realized. He and Ciena were jostled against the wall, never hard enough to kill them but always hard enough to hurt. Finally, one impact stuck, slowing them down bit by bit as they tunneled through Jakku's desert and very gradually came to a stop.

Are we safe? I think we're—

The pod jarred forward, into the air, so hard that Thane first believed another explosive charge had been set off. But the deep roar he heard told him the truth. The *Inflictor* had just crashed into the planet, and their escape pod was being thrown forward along with a tsunami of dust and sand.

He wrapped his arms more tightly around Ciena as the pod tumbled over and over; the small window showed nothing but red-orange sand. What if they were buried? What if the already-battered pod could take no more and burst open? He didn't want them to smother down here, buried alive—

But slowly, the pod rolled to a stop again, this time apparently for good.

After a long second, Thane allowed himself to believe they'd survived the landing. But what if they were deep underground? Would his sensor beacon even be able to signal a New Republic rescue?

He switched on the sensor, waited a long moment— then saw the indicator turn green. Signal sending.

"We made it," he whispered to Ciena, who lay unconscious against his shoulder. Maybe in her sleep, her subconscious would hear him and subtly let her know everything was going to be all right.

A small line of blood marked a cut on her forehead. Thane untied the mourning band from his arm to use as a makeshift bandage, staring down at her in wonder.

Of all the ships in the galaxy, I boarded hers, he thought.

Maybe . . . maybe Ciena and Luke Skywalker and the other traditionalists were right about the Force. Maybe there was some power that bound the galaxy together and took you unfailingly to your fate. The Force must have guided him to her so he could save her life and they could go on together.

It felt like all the cynicism and anger of his old life had finally melted away. He lived under the authority of leaders who were fair and just; he had fought a noble war and was on the verge of winning; he served alongside people he both liked and respected. Ciena had been freed from the shackles binding her to the Empire, and from now on she had no limits. Neither of them did. How was it that a guy like him—without hope, without faith—had found his way here?

He leaned his forehead against hers. Despite the painful bruises swelling on his face and body, despite the blood still seeping into his mouth, despite the terrible shape Ciena was in and the stifling heat of the escape pod, he thought that might be the single most joyful moment of his life.

Thane heard sifting sounds above and lifted his face to see the escape pod doors shiver. Then they slid open, sending a small cascade of sand streaming down onto their feet and revealing a New Republic search team silhouetted against the bright sun.

"Am I glad to see you guys." He lifted Ciena in his arms. "Help me out, will you?"

"Sure thing, Corona Four." One member of the team leaned forward to pull Ciena through the opening to freedom; Thane crawled out just after and flopped down in the sand beside her.

The medic leaned down. "Do you need assistance?"

"I'd take care of her first," Thane said.

He expected the medic to begin examining Ciena's injuries. Instead all the other team members pulled their blasters as the leader kneeled down with a pair of magnetic binders for her wrists.

"What the . . . ?" The words died in Thane's mouth as he realized the New Republic soldiers were doing exactly what they were supposed to do. They were capturing a high-ranking Imperial officer who would have to be tried for her crimes.

He'd thought he was rescuing her, that the Force had miraculously intervened to protect them both. All Thane had done was deliver her to prison.

CHAPTER TWENTY-NINE

CIENA STOOD IN her cell, hands clasped in front of her. The energy field that separated her from the rest of the prison was almost perfectly transparent, tinting the world beyond slightly silver. She had not bothered looking out during most of her captivity—at times she'd been so depressed that she had lacked the will even to get out of her jailhouse bunk.

Today, however, she had a visitor.

She knew Thane by the heavy tread of his boots alone, or maybe that was only wishful thinking. Ciena had strained at every small noise outside the entire day, even though he hadn't been due until this hour.

But this time it *was* him.

Thane smiled when he saw her, though she could see the stricken look in his eyes. Did he feel guilty for caging her like a bird? *Good,* she thought. But probably he was more shaken by the sight of her standing there thin and plain in her prison dress, which was very nearly the light brown color of her skin.

"Autumn leaf," he said, more to himself than to her—then recovered himself. "Ciena. Thanks for finally agreeing to see me."

She simply nodded. There was no point in telling him that she'd relented after just one week, only to be told that he'd already shipped out on a mission. That had been a moment of weakness. Now she was finally ready to talk. "We have so much to say," she said. "It's hard to know where to begin."

"Tell me why you didn't allow me to visit before."

Ciena turned her head, unwilling to look him in the eyes as she said this. "I wish you had left me aboard the *Inflictor*."

"If you're waiting for me to apologize for saving your life, you'll be waiting awhile." After a brief silence, he added, "But I understand why you feel that way."

"Do you?"

"You wanted to do your duty and escape the Empire at the same time. Suicide was the only way to do that—to balance the scales. But you shouldn't measure yourself against the Empire. You're worth more than the rest of it put together."

Ciena glanced up at him then, touched despite herself. He looked even more handsome than he had in her daydreams. His hair had darkened slightly, more red than blond. Someone who had not seen him since his childhood might not recognize him now.

But she thought she would always know him, by his step or his flight or his eyes. Something about his eyes never changed.

"You do understand," she said quietly. "But I wish you'd respected my decision."

"You're glad to be alive, though, right?" Thane stepped closer to the barrier as he added, more hesitantly, "Aren't you?"

For a moment Ciena couldn't answer. Finally, she managed to say, "It's too early to tell."

He didn't seem to have a reply to that. She didn't blame him.

There were times she truly wished she had died rather than face this shame. At other moments, however, Ciena found herself enjoying the smallest pleasures of existence—the only ones available inside her cell. And then she felt she hadn't been ready to die just yet.

Looking at Thane now was one of those moments.

She said, "It's hard. Everything I worked for my

whole life has been destroyed. Everything I ever fought for is a lie."

"Not everything. In the end, you fought for me." His smile was crooked. "That's got to be worth something."

Her throat tightened against tears she refused to shed. "That's the only part still worth anything."

"Ciena—"

"It was the perfect trap. You know?" She had to clench her fist hard enough for her nails to dig into her palm; focusing on the pain kept her from breaking down completely. "I was so dedicated to honor that I became a war criminal."

"There's more than one kind of trap. For a second there I'd convinced myself that we'd fixed the whole galaxy, truth and justice had prevailed, so on and so forth—even started believing in the Force, of all things—" He laughed at his own folly. "So I had enough hope to take that impossible chance and come after you, but it turned out I saved you only for this. And now you're trapped here, where we can't even *touch*—"

"Stop. Please stop." Ciena hid her face from him; she could tell he'd turned slightly away.

For a few moments they both remained silent, struggling for control. Ciena had thought her own sorrow was too much to bear, but now she had to endure

Thane's, as well. It was too much for either of them— and yet they had no choice. When one was wounded, the other bled. He was a part of her, forever.

She managed to slow her breaths, regain her composure. By the time she lifted her head again, Thane had calmed himself, too. "So. Are you all right? They're treating you well?" He glanced around her small cell as if inspecting it.

She had to admit the truth. "Yes. They give me holonovels and simple games. I can claim up to seven hours of outdoor exercise a week—under supervision, of course—but the doctors agree I shouldn't do anything too strenuous until I've healed some more." Her hand stole across her abdomen, unconsciously shielding it.

He winced. "You know I would've been more careful with you if I'd realized how badly you'd been injured."

"Yes. I know." Though perhaps that would have been the death of them both, because it had taken that much force for him to overcome her. She felt strangely proud of that. "Anyway. I sleep a lot. The bunk here isn't much, but it's reasonably comfortable. I've been treated humanely by the Rebellion . . . the New Republic officers." She brushed a loose coil of hair away from her face, self-conscious about her next admission. "I had expected interrogation by torture. The Empire had taught me to think that was standard procedure—all any prisoner could expect. Instead I got medical treatment and information about my legal rights."

"Have you told them anything voluntarily?" Thane hastened to add, "I'm not pressuring you. I'm not here on behalf of the New Republic, and I never will be, all right? You never have to doubt whether they sent me in here to play you."

Ciena had harbored dark thoughts about that very scenario late at night as she lay in her bunk. But now she could honestly reply, "I believe you."

Visibly relieved, he continued, "I asked only because—you know, they'd cut you a break if you did."

As if that could ever persuade her. "My oath still holds, Thane. While I admit that I see the New Republic in a different light now, I'm not turning traitor. Nor do I accept their rule. From what I've heard, the war's still raging on, chaos has returned to the galaxy—"

"It's the normal disorder of planets trying to get their governments back together after years of—" Thane sighed. "Skip it. We both know each other's lines."

"There's no point anyway," she said. "They're not going to 'cut me a break,' no matter what I tell them. I'm a war criminal, remember? The New Republic will make me pay for my service to the Empire."

Maybe that was no less than she deserved.

Thane stared at her for a long moment; then, to her astonishment, he began to smile and shake his head. "You're going to get out of here pretty soon even if you don't talk. If you *did* share some intel, I bet you wouldn't even have to stand trial."

"What are you talking about?" Her appointed defender had shown her the list of charges against her; it spooled down several screen lengths and elaborated with great detail her service at the battles of Hoth, Endor, and Jakku. She could not deny that she was responsible for every single item on that list. "We both know I'm guilty. The New Republic will want to make an example of me. They'll need to prove that law and order prevail, precisely because it's a new law and a new order. The lines have been redrawn and I'm on the wrong side." At last she spoke her worst fear out loud: "I might be in this jail cell the rest of my life."

"We've had this argument before, too, you know." He leaned closer to the energy field. "My idealistic phase is over. I've remembered how the world really works. And the thing is, Ciena, things fall apart. Too many people had to work for the Empire for them *all* to be jailed. That's literally hundreds of billions of people, not even counting the troops who vanished with the rest of the Imperial Starfleet. You think the New Republic can punish every single one?"

"They'll free the clerks and the cleaners. Not a captain of a Star Destroyer."

But Thane was unconvinced. "You have useful talents. That's one of the things the New Republic is going to start looking for, sooner rather than later. Plus you have friends in high places—or I do, anyway, and I intend to have a long talk with every single one who could help you."

"I don't want you to ask for special treatment on my behalf," she protested.

"Too bad," he said. "Because the deck is always stacked, Ciena. All we can do is stack it in our favor."

Ciena remembered the first time they'd had this out. They'd been in a cantina in Valentia, the fates dividing them as never before, and they'd argued and pleaded until they'd finally broken down and made love. It felt like another lifetime—lying next to him, pulling him close—yet it felt like yesterday. She could never forget how she'd felt about Thane that day, and she never wanted to.

"So here we are again," she said with a rueful smile. "Debating order versus chaos."

"Maybe fate will finally settle the question for us. If you're right, then, yeah, you have some rough years ahead. But if I'm right—and the New Republic chooses freedom over vengeance—you'll be out of here in no time." Even through the silver shimmer of the energy field, she could see the tenderness in his eyes. "Either way, you know I'll be waiting for you, right?"

Ciena would have given anything to hold him then, even as she said, "You shouldn't."

"You would, if it were me inside that cell."

". . . yes. I would."

Slowly she raised her hand, flattening her palm against the edge of the energy field. Thane did the same. They mirrored each other, almost touching but forever apart.

"In the month since the Battle of Jakku, the Empire has attempted no further large-scale offensives. Sources report all Imperial vessels within the Core and Inner Rim staying within the boundaries defined by treaty." The woman in the news holo smiled as she continued, *"A few prominent members of the Provisional Senate have speculated that the New Republic's war with the remnants of the Empire has finally come to an end and that a final surrender may be imminent. However, in her address today, the chancellor warned that all planets should remain on high alert, and the New Republic Starfleet should be kept on a war footing for the foreseeable future. Here to discuss both sides of this issue are—"*

Nash snapped off the rebel propaganda from the

Hosnian system. He'd already learned all he needed to know—namely, that the so-called New Republic believed the Empire beaten. Fools.

Let them grow fat and lazy, he thought. *Let them congratulate themselves. Let them go slack.*

Commander Nash Windrider left his personal office and walked out into the main docking bay of his new ship, the attack cruiser *Garrote*. Every subordinate straightened at the sound of Nash's boots on the metal floor; not one of them turned away from his or her work to so much as glance in Nash's direction. Good. Already he'd managed to reestablish proper discipline.

For someone who had spent years assigned to a Star Destroyer, an attack cruiser posting might have seemed like a step down—but the Empire had so few Star Destroyers left. He was flight commander on a strategically important vessel, which was a step toward eventually receiving his own command. Nash took pride in readying the *Garrote* for the next stage of the war, the next assault.

The one the rebels wouldn't see coming.

He strode between the long lines of TIE fighters, all of which were being refitted with stronger weapons of new design. These would be able to punch through energy shields and starfighter hulls with a single blast, which meant the one advantage starfighters had over

TIEs—their shielding—would vanish. Changes like that could win the war.

Rather odious to think that Ved Foslo had invented these weapons. Nash had always assumed Ved's rise through the ranks was solely due to his father's interference, yet it turned out his former roommate had some aptitude after all. No doubt his adolescent arrogance had become completely insufferable in adulthood.

Nash sighed as he reminded himself that, of his two roommates at the academy, Ved Foslo was by far the least offensive.

To think that Thane Kyrell might have survived the war, might even be out there now smugly celebrating the Rebellion's temporary advantage—it sickened him. Why should Ciena have died while Thane lived?

But you couldn't look to the fates for justice. You had to take retribution into your own hands. The Empire had taught him that.

"Sir? Commander Windrider, sir?" Nash's assistant had begun to follow on his heels, as usual. "A question, if I may?"

"You may, Lieutenant Kyrell."

Dalven Kyrell stood before him, data tablet in his hands, visibly nervous. He had no idea of his brother's role in the Rebellion; Nash had elected to keep that truth from him and treat this Kyrell as an individual.

It seemed only fair. However, taken on his own merits, Dalven was weak and toadying, capable of no more than fulfilling the basic tasks he was given. Fortunately duty required no more of the flight commander's assistant. "I wanted to ask about the list of officers you nominated for top commendations."

Was Dalven going to ask why he wasn't on it? If he did, Nash intended to tell him. "What is your question?"

"You nominated Captain Ciena Ree for the Distinguished Medal of Imperial Honor. I think you meant the more common Medal of Honor—"

"I know precisely what I meant, Lieutenant Kyrell." Nash enjoyed speaking that surname with a slight sneer. "The Distinguished Medal of Imperial Honor is the highest medal we can bestow, and I can think of no one more deserving. To have remained aboard her ship when the autodestruct had failed—to personally crash it into the planet's surface to keep the vessel from enemy hands, at the cost of her own life—Captain Ciena Ree deserves to be remembered."

"Yes, sir," Dalven said weakly, but he continued, "I only meant—nominating someone for that honor is a big step, one others might comment upon as a sign of factionalism."

"Usually, yes. In this case, however, I have it on good authority that a number of captains, generals, and admirals intend to nominate her, as well. Even Grand Moff Randd may do so. The Empire endures its inner conflicts, but on this we all agree. The late Captain Ree died a hero."

"Absolutely," Dalven hastened to add. "Such a terrible way to die."

"Terrible? I would call it glorious. We all wish she were still with us, but that doesn't change the fact that there is no finer fate than to die for the Empire. I hope I shall get the chance myself someday."

"Of course, sir. Yes, sir." Dalven slunk away.

Thane had always said Dalven made fun of Ciena when they were children, mocking her poverty and her old-fashioned ways—as if everyone on Jelucan weren't a backwater bumpkin. Sometimes when Nash remembered that and thought of Dalven ridiculing a young, helpless Ciena, he wanted to find an appropriate suicide mission for the man.

But he could no longer assume Thane had been telling the truth. Apparently, Thane Kyrell was a master deceiver.

Nash walked toward the open mouth of the docking bay. Against his skin he felt the faint tingle of the energy shield that maintained atmospheric pressure—a sign he was standing too close. He remained near the edge anyway, the better to behold the sight before him.

Within the massive cloud of the Queluhan Nebula, hidden deep inside the glowing trails of ionized gas that confounded enemy sensors, waited the Imperial Starfleet. While the rebel pundits confidently predicted the Empire's disappearance and surrender—believed them divided against each other and helpless—they were instead rejoining forces and growing stronger than before.

In Nash's opinion, it had taken them too long to coalesce as a united front again; infighting had allowed the rebels to gain territory they could not have hoped to contest otherwise. Now, however, the Imperial Starfleet had reestablished a hierarchy of command. They had developed a long-term strategy. The old factionalism had been swept away, and at last they stood together, united again.

He liked to think Ciena Ree had something to do with that. Perhaps that was only sentiment, but there was no denying that her selfless act had inspired them all.

You reminded us what discipline truly means, Nash thought. *You reminded us that no price is too great to pay for victory.*

Before him, in the blue-and-violet glow of the nebula, he could see at least ten Star Destroyers and even more light cruisers. Each housed countless TIE fighters, to be manned largely by the new conscripts; training had to be faster and harsher these days, but the pilots were shaping up nicely. The Imperial Starfleet might not be as large as it had once been, but Nash thought they might emerge even stronger.

And this time, they would stop at nothing until the Rebellion had been permanently crushed. Thane and the others would pay for forcing Ciena to sacrifice her own life. They'd pay for everything.

Nash whispered, "You will be avenged—when the Empire rises again."

THE END

Read on for a sneak preview of
Leia: Princess of Alderaan by Claudia Gray.
Available September 2017.

CHAPTER ONE

THE DAY OF DEMAND had been announced months before. Guests had already arrived from worlds across the galaxy, and delicious aromas from the banquet being prepared wafted through the palace halls. The weather had failed to cooperate with the celebration plans—low dark clouds hung heavily over the city of Aldera, threatening a downpour—but even the threatening storm felt dramatic and grand, in a way.

It was the perfect setting for a princess to claim her right to the crown of Alderaan.

"Ow." Leia made a face. "That pulls."

"And it's going to keep pulling," promised WA-2V, Leia's personal attendant droid. Her bluish metal fingers swiftly wove one final braid in the complicated traditional style. "Today of all days, you must look your best."

"You say that every day." As a little girl, Leia had only ever wanted to tie her hair back in a tail. Her parents had said she was free to do as she liked. But 2V had held firm. Her programming demanded that she present the princess in grand style, and not even the princess herself could say otherwise.

"It's true every day," 2V insisted, coiling the braid in a loop and pinning it in place. "Standards are even higher for special occasions!"

Leia felt a small quiver in her belly, equal parts nerves and anticipation. This was the biggest day in her life since her first Name Day, when her parents had brought her into the throne room and declared her their daughter by adoption and by love—

She shook off the thought. That time all she had to do was be a baby in her mother's arms. This time, she'd have to stand up for herself.

Once the hairstyle was done, Leia gratefully slipped into the clothing she and 2V had compromised on: a simple white dress for her, bold silver jewelry for 2V. Just as she toed into her satiny slippers, the orchestral fanfare swelled from the throne room, echoing through the palace's corridors. It felt as though her parents were personally knocking on her door.

"One more thing!" 2V pleaded. She rolled to the cabinet on the small sphere she had for a base, then swerved back with a silver headband, which she neatly fitted into the braids so its pearl charm hung at the center of Leia's forehead. "Yes. *Yes*. That's it. You look absolutely stunning! I work miracles, I really do."

Leia shook her head in amusement. "Thanks a lot."

Oblivious, 2V shooed her charge toward the door. "Hurry! They're all waiting."

"It's not like they can start without me, TooVee." Still, Leia picked up the tail of her gown and hurried into the corridor. She didn't want to be late. The princes and princesses who had made their demands in ancient times had sometimes had to fight their way to the throne room. It was meant to be a moment of strength and command—in other words, not a moment to prove you couldn't even show up on time.

Alderaan's royal palace had been the work of more than a millennium. Their monarchy was one that dedicated itself to serving its people, so they'd never built high spires or commanding towers to dominate the landscape. Instead, new chambers were added every few decades, creating a sprawling labyrinth where modern data centers and holochambers existed side by side with ancient rooms hewn from stone. Leia knew each hallway, each door by heart; as a small child she'd reveled in exploring some of the most shadowy, out-of-the-way passages. Sometimes she thought she might've been the only person in centuries to have found every single room in the palace.

Fortunately, she knew the shortcut through the old armory, which got her to the antechamber of the throne room in plenty of time. The royal guards smiled when they saw her, and she grinned back as she straightened the cape of her gown. To the taller guard, she whispered, "How's the baby?"

"Sleeping through the night already," he replied. Leia mimed applause, and he ducked his head, almost bashfully.

Really she didn't know much about babies, except that parents were very proud of them even though they kept everybody up at night. But if the guard was happy to have a sleepy baby, then she was happy for him.

"We're lucky on Alderaan," her father had said as they sat by the library hearth. "We are loved by our people. We have their loyalty. That's because we love them and are loyal to them in turn. If we ever cease to appreciate those around us—from the highest lord to the humblest laborer—we'll lose that loyalty. We'll deserve to lose it."

Leia was jerked back into the moment by the rustling of the velvet curtain at the door. Swiftly, she went to the wall where the Rhindon Sword hung, grabbed it by the hilt, and took it in hand. She'd practiced with it a few times, but its weight surprised her every time.

Position: doorway center. Sword: both hands on the hilt, arms close to body, blade upright. Speech . . .

I remember the speech, she told herself. *I definitely remember it. I'm just blanking on it at the moment and it'll absolutely come back to me when I'm standing in front of hundreds of people—*

The curtain was tugged to the side. Brilliant light, tinted by vast panes of stained glass, fell on her. Two hundred guests turned as one, all of them standing on either side of a blue-and-gold carpet that traced a line directly through the room to the golden thrones where Breha and Bail Organa sat.

Leia marched forward, sword held high. A low rumble of thunder made her grateful for the candledroids projecting light through the windows; otherwise, the room would've been nearly pitch-black. She'd practiced this but didn't think she could do it with her eyes closed.

I don't know, it might've been easier if I couldn't see all the guests staring at me. Leia had spent her entire life appearing before crowds, but that day was the first time they would hear her voice.

Breha Organa wore a dress of bronze silk, her hair piled high atop her head in braids woven through with strings of beads. Next to her, Bail Organa wore the traditional long jacket of the viceroy. The crown itself had been brought back from the museum to sit atop a marble pillar, illuminated by a candledroid of its own. Her parents looked even more regal than usual—almost forbidding. Were they enjoying the charade?

Leia thought she was, or she would be if her parents had invited fewer people. Usually only a handful of off-worlders would be present, but this time her father had asked many of his diplomatic allies in the Imperial Senate—Tynnra Pamlo from Taris, Gall Trayvis of Osk-Trill, and both Winmey Lenz and Mon Mothma of Chandrila. Mon Mothma smiled wider as Leia passed her. Maybe she meant to be encouraging.

As long as she didn't think Leia looked *cute*. The Day of Demand wasn't about being an adorable little kid. It was about growing up.

When she reached the front of the throne room, only a few meters short of her parents, Breha called out the first line of the ceremony: "Who is this, who disturbs the queen in her seat of power?"

"It is I, Leia Organa, princess of Alderaan." Sure enough, the speech had come back on cue. "I come before you to hear you acknowledge that on this day it is known that I have reached my sixteenth year."

The "it is known" was an addition to the simplest form of the ritual, one used only when the eldest child of the king or queen was adopted. Leia had turned sixteen three or four days before; she didn't know her birthday for sure and didn't much care. She'd become a princess of Alderaan on her Name Day, and that was the anniversary they were marking.

"We acknowledge that you are of age," said Bail. Only the slight crinkling at the corners of his eyes betrayed the smile he was working to hide. "Why then do you come before us armed?"

"I come to demand my right to the crown." Leia knelt smoothly and held the sword overhead in one hand. Distant thunder rumbled, sending a small tremor through the floor. "On this day, you will acknowledge me as heir."

Breha's voice rang throughout the throne room. "The crown of Alderaan is not merely inherited. It must be earned. The heir must prove herself worthy in body, heart, and mind. Are you prepared to do so?"

"I am, my mother and queen." It was a relief to stand again and lower the heavy sword. "I have chosen three challenges. When I have undertaken these challenges and succeeded in them, you must invest me as crown princess of Alderaan."

"Reveal these challenges, and we will decide whether they are worthy," Bail said, as though he didn't already know each one. For a moment, she was tempted to make something up on the spot. *I'm going to learn to juggle and take to the stage as a feather-fire dancer. Aren't you proud?*

But she'd practiced her speech so many times that it poured forth almost automatically. "For my Challenge of the Body, I will study with a master pathfinder, learning to travel across any terrain and with no tools for navigation, until I am able to climb Appenza Peak." That mountain was visible from her bedroom window, spectacularly silhouetted against every sunset. "For my Challenge of the Mind, I will no longer merely assist my father in the Imperial Senate but will also represent our world in the Apprentice Legislature. And for my Challenge of the Heart, I will undertake missions of charity and mercy to planets in need, paying all costs from my share of the royal purse. Through these challenges, I will prove my right to the crown."

Breha inclined her head. "The challenges are worthy." She rose from her throne, and Leia stepped up on the dais and brought the sword back into position in front of her. Breha's hands wrapped around the sword hilt, their fingers overlapping for the instant before Leia let go. "May all those present bear witness! If my daughter fulfills these challenges, she shall be invested as crown princess, heir to the throne of Alderaan."

Applause and cheers filled the room. Leia curtsied to her parents, who were beaming so proudly that for a moment it felt as if everything had been put right. Like the ceremony really had made them *see* her again—

—until the guests crowded closer with congratulations and her parents turned away to greet them instead of congratulating their daughter.

Bail was in conversation with Mon Mothma and her fellow Chandrilan senator, Winmey Lenz. Breha had taken the hands of Senator Pamlo, clearly thanking her for her presence.

Already, Leia was forgotten.

"Leia, my dear girl!" Lord Mellowyn of Birren came to her, smiling beneath his bushy white mustache. They were cousins through intricacies of Elder House lineage nobody bothered tracing any longer. "You were wonderful."

"Thank you." She returned his smile as best she could.

It's true. I'm not imagining it. They don't pay attention to me anymore.

Did I do something wrong?

Or do they just not care?

She didn't think she'd made them angry. They hadn't turned from her in one moment of displeasure. Instead they had . . . ebbed away over the past six months.

Leia had never had very many friends her own age. As egalitarian as the Alderaanean monarchy was, there would always be a dividing line between those within the palace and those outside its walls. She'd gamboled around on the rolling grounds with some of the cooks' children, but for the most part, her companions had been her parents.

Bail and Breha Organa had waited a long time for a child. They had told her that many times, often as she went to sleep, as part of the story about when her father came home from a mysterious mission to surprise her mother with the baby girl in his arms. Leia would've known it even if they hadn't told her, though. No matter how many questions she asked, her parents never tired of looking up answers. When she had bad dreams in the wee hours of the night, they never left her to a human nurse or caretaker droid; one of them always came to her, sometimes both. Every time she entered a room where they were, they smiled. She felt as if she made them happy merely by existing.

Many children would've become hopelessly spoiled. But Leia always wanted to be helpful, especially to those she cared about, and she loved her parents more than she could imagine ever loving anybody else. So she tried to interest herself in everything they did. Breha planted Malastarean orchids; Leia planted orchids and